M000117729

the
LOST DIARIES
of
SUSANNA MOODIE

the
LOST DIARIES
of
SUSANNA MOODIE
a novel

CECILY ROSS

HARPER**AVENUE**

An imprint of HarperCollins Publishers Ltd

The Lost Diaries of Susanna Moodie
Copyright © 2017 by Cecily Ross.
All rights reserved.

Published by Harper Avenue, an imprint of HarperCollins Publishers Ltd

First edition

No part of this book may be used or reproduced in any manner whatsoever without the prior written permission of the publisher, except in the case of brief quotations embodied in reviews.

Excerpt from Margaret Atwood's *Selected Poems, 1966–1984* © 1990 Oxford University Press Canada. Reprinted by permission of the publisher.

HarperCollins books may be purchased for educational, business or sales promotional use through our Special Markets Department.

HarperCollins Publishers Ltd
2 Bloor Street East, 20th Floor
Toronto, Ontario, Canada
M4W 1A8

www.harpercollins.ca

Library and Archives Canada Cataloguing in Publication information is available upon request.

ISBN 978-1-44345-019-5

Printed and bound in the United States

LSC/H 9 8 7 6 5 4 3 2 1

For Basil

(you find only
the shape you already are
but what
if you have forgotten that
or discover you
have never known)

—MARGARET ATWOOD, *The Journals of Susanna Moodie*

Nothing in the world is single;
All things by a law divine
In one spirit meet and mingle.
Why not I with thine?—

—PERCY BYSSHE SHELLEY, "Love's Philosophy"

CONTENTS

PART ONE

1815–1819

GIRLHOOD

MARCH 2, 1815 (REYDON HALL, SUFFOLK)

So this is how it ends. Agnes, that scourge of the imagination and paragon of joylessness, discovered our manuscript this morning hidden at the bottom of the Indian chest and, after the most cursory examination, reprimanded Kate and me for "scribbling such trash" and carried it away, threatening to burn it. Kate immediately asked our eldest sister to intervene, but (as I knew she would) Eliza too expressed *horror* that we should waste our time with such trivialities, calling our nascent novel "a waste of good paper."

How many evenings have Kate and I spent huddled together in the attic amid the cobwebs and the dust, by the light of a sputtering candle, spinning this harmless fiction, this meagre escape from the dullness and damp? All winter long, the composition of a small tale of love and survival, of an Alpine boy and his loyal pet, has been our secret joy, a bright light in the endless darkness, a haven for spirits weighed down by the cold. How dare they?

When I protested, Agnes smiled a superior smile, said that our little project was "unsuitable" and announced that instead of occupying ourselves with such "juvenile nonsense," we are to gather in the library after supper for an impromptu reading of *Hamlet* (act 3, scene 1). Sarah, understandably, is to be Ophelia, and Jane will take the part of Gertrude; Eliza, the King *and* Polonius; while Kate and

3

I and the two boys, Sam and Tom, have been relegated to playing attendant lords who will start a scene or two and then be sent to bed, I imagine. Of course Agnes, that quintessence of dust, has reserved the lead for herself. Sarah threw herself into her character immediately, laying a limp hand upon her porcelain forehead and lamenting the lack of flowers for her hair this time of the year. Jane, her brow rearranging itself into the contours of a ploughed field, demanded to know how many costume changes would be required of her. And with that, *The Swiss Herd Boy* was doomed to oblivion.

But not by me. As much as I love Shakespeare, I had no intention of being distracted by Agnes's theatrical ambitions. I continued to object loudly to the injustice of my sisters' interference, saying that burning our manuscript was surely an even greater "waste of paper." Agnes looked down her impossibly straight nose at me and smiled. "You have a point, Susanna. Why consign to flames a pile of trash that will serve perfectly well as curling papers? I'll talk to Eliza. Now, hurry off. You have lines to memorize."

I threatened to go to Papa. "You cannot do this. I will tell," I protested as Agnes slid out of the room like Hamlet's ghost. I was about to run after her when Kate, who can't bear unpleasantness of any kind, placed a cajoling arm about my waist and, squeezing rather harder than was necessary, told me not to worry. "I'll get it back. You'll see."

How shall I ever achieve greatness when the stars, and all my sisters, are against me? Eliza's disapproval does not surprise me, but I had hoped Agnes might encourage our writing—Agnes who, when she is not bettering her mind reading Hobbes and Locke, has been known to compose the occasional poem in a style that Papa says is vaguely reminiscent of Mr. Dryden. But I now realize Agnes's dismissiveness toward our modest literary effort was entirely predictable.

Ever since Mama and Papa charged Eliza and her with authority over the rest of us, Agnes has become chief judge, jury and tormentor. Oh, how I wish the others would stand up to her occasionally so that I am not always the sole object of her condescension. But Kate, my supposed ally, appears entirely unconcerned about the whole affair. Curling papers indeed.

Sam, who watched the sordid scene without raising a single objection (but then he is still a child with little regard for the life of the mind), came to my room later. He has discovered a clutch of newly hatched starlings nesting in the elderberry at the back of the milk house and promised to take me to them after supper. "Perhaps you would sketch them for me, Susie," he said. He was trying to distract me and I humoured him, but I will not be thwarted. Our manuscript is gone, and since that avenue of expression is closed to me, I have decided to begin this journal, an outlet for my most secret thoughts and desires. I swear they will never find it.

MARCH 3, 1815

When Mama and Papa did arrive home from Norwich late yesterday, no mention was made of the confiscation of our manuscript for fear of dampening our father's obviously heightened spirits. We are all, but Mama in particular, keenly sensitive to his moods, as the world of business, of which (she is forever reminding us) we know nothing, is a place of such unpredictable flux that our dear father is constantly at the mercy of dastardly conspiracies and designs on his property, and it would be cruel to further burden him with our silly domestic concerns. Though he seldom complains, Papa is also subject to a dizzying array of physical afflictions, and now that Eliza and Agnes have assumed responsibility for educating the rest of us, tending to Papa has become our mother's life's work. Kate and I and the boys hardly see her, and when we do we are like those little starlings, chirruping madly until she seems relieved to be rid of us. Between them, Eliza, Agnes, Sarah and Jane Margaret form a kind of palace guard around our mother that we, "the little ones," dare not penetrate. I often hear them laughing together behind closed doors in the small parlour off Mama's bedroom. Sarah says Mama's nerves are fragile and we must not bother her with our childish concerns. But I am almost twelve, no longer a child and tired of being treated like one.

The reason for Papa's elevated mood at present seems to be his acquisition of a townhouse in Norwich, where he and Mama will live while he attends to business. The source of this newfound prosperity is a partnership he has entered into with a coach-maker of "impeccable reputation." Now that Papa has left his position as manager of the Greenland Docks in London to become an independent investor and a country squire, Mama says that "our position and our fortune are assured, because coaches, like coffins, will never fall out of fashion."

After coming in and removing his silk hat and riding boots, Papa ran up the stairs two at a time (his gout has apparently relinquished its grip) and returned moments later wearing a canvas overcoat and tweed breeches, a battered straw boater on his head.

"It is much too fair a day to be indoors," he said. "I am going fishing. We shall have trout for supper." And then he turned to my sister and uttered the words that were like a knife in my heart: "Catharine, bring your satchel; we will gather specimens for tomorrow's botany lesson on our walk. Agnes, Eliza, you will see to the little ones while we are gone . . ."

Little ones! I threw down my book and demanded to go with them. Sarah and Jane gasped at my impertinence. You would think

I was challenging the Almighty himself. Why are my sisters so meek and agreeable when our father has never raised a hand to any of us? Papa's face darkened, but then the cloud passed and he smiled and gave my hair a tug. As though I were an amusing pet.

"Now, now, Susie . . ." he began.

And smug, sweet-tempered Kate joined in. "Dear Susanna, don't be angry."

Eliza took me by the hand. "Susanna, we will have drawing lessons. Outdoors in the garden. The daphne is in bloom." I ignored her and turned my full wrath upon Kate. Kate, the perfect little botanist with her satchel of wilted weeds and notebooks full of Latin hieroglyphics.

"I hate you. I hate you," I said. Then, sweet-tempered Kate, my closest ally and friend, struck me in the face with her open hand, a blow so sharp it brought tears to my eyes. But the pain in my heart was even greater. Papa sent me to my room. How I detest my place in this litter of simpletons: the youngest girl, the runt.

MARCH 4, 1815

Katie has forgiven me (or was it I her?). No matter, we are closer than ever. No lessons again today. Mama heartily disapproves and has kept to her room all morning with one of her headaches. Papa ordered Lockwood to bring round the new barouche and the pair of greys. Surely Mama will want to be with us to show them off to the neighbours. Although we have lived at Reydon Hall for seven years, we are still considered newcomers, and our neighbours, the local gentry, regard us with a chilly reserve, as though waiting for some divine sign that we will do. The Stricklands are a respectable family, Agnes says, but our father and grandfather were engaged "in trade." (The disdain in Agnes's voice as she said this was acid enough to peel wallpaper.) We are not of noble lineage like old General Howard, the Earl of Suffolk, who lives in a vast stone mausoleum near Yoxford. (It is said he fought in the American War of Independence and that his wife is third cousin to the Queen.)

Nevertheless, the barouche is positively stunning, with brass side lamps and green velvet seats. It is pulled by a fine pair of dappled grey hackneys decked out in shining new harness. Even Lockwood is outfitted with proper coachman's livery complete with gold epaulettes and spurs. This marvellous equipage will convey us to the market in Bungay after lunch—all of us except Sam and Tom, who will remain at home with Nurse. At eight, Tom is still a baby, but poor Sam, who is ten and my favourite next to Katie, is being punished for ruining Mama's best hat box. I feel I am in part to blame, since yesterday's expedition was my idea. I thought how pleased Papa would be with our "specimens." Not the collection of wilted flowers and leaves that he and Kate spent all evening pressing into scrapbooks, but real living botany: a silky green frog, a warty toad and two perfectly darling baby ribbon snakes, all of which Sam and I gave up our tea time to procure. But it was Sam's idea to transfer them from the bucket to the blue hat box after we returned from the river. Mama found it where Sam had left it, on General Wolfe's desk in the library, and nearly passed out with fright when she opened it.

"You little chit," Father said when she reported my part in the affair. "If you're not careful, Boney will get you one day." (This childish threat means nothing now that I am grown. Indeed, I have decided that I am half in love with General Bonaparte.)

"No, he won't," I retorted, "because he's exiled at Elba."

For an instant, I thought my impertinence might land me in the nursery with poor Sam, but then I could see that Papa was more amused and proud than angry.

Oh, my most fervid imagination! How my heart pounds, my mind pitches and plunges like a sloop in a storm. While Agnes and Eliza helped Mama pick through bonnets and cooking pots at the Buttercross, Kate and I walked over the Broads beyond the village to see the ruined Bungay Castle. It is said to be more than seven hundred years old. And though it is in a sorry state, a collapsed mass of stone and charred rafters, the magnificent twin towers of the gatehouse still stand, rugged and fearless sentries defying the ravages of time and the elements. My sister and I clung to one another in the lee of the crumbling curtain wall while a fierce breeze buffeted the screaming gulls that hovered above the billowing marsh grasses. Shutting our eyes, we thought we could hear the battle cries of the approaching Roman hordes. (On the ride home, Eliza assured us it was likely just the sound of windmill sails on the slope behind us.) We returned to the village, tired and thrilled, and sat on the sun-warmed steps of St. Mary's, listening to the old men talking endlessly of war in France. Finally, noticing the four of us—Jane, Sarah, Katie and me—old Jonas, who they say lost his leg at the Gulf of Roses under Lord Collingwood, related a fearful tale, that of Black Shuck, the black dog of Bungay, a murderous creature that roams the countryside at night and whose flaming eyes portend certain death to all who encounter it. Kate thinks the story is perfect for a children's novel and says we must begin writing it at once. How could she suggest such a thing, knowing as she does my horror of the darkness and the mad mastiffs that lurk in the shadows? I shall not sleep tonight.

(And in any case, I reminded Kate, it would surely be seized by our duly appointed guardians.)

Now that I have begun, I am resolved to continue this journal no matter what obstacles I encounter. Only here, in these pages, am I free to reveal the real, true Susanna. To the world, if it notices me at all, I am just a girl, third youngest of eight children, one insignificant member of a large and boisterous household. Most days, I feel invisible, as though there were no me separate from them, as though my voice will never be heard above the din, and I am nothing more than one part of a many-headed monster that is slowly choking me to death. Oh, my dear diary, only here can I become someone. I swear upon these modest pages that I will be true to myself and to myself only! I shall endeavour to keep these writings secret, for they are emanations from my true heart and expressions of my darkest soul.

A few words, then, about the family prison that I inhabit, about the benevolent gaolers of my mind and spirit, the Stricklands of Reydon Hall. First, of course, is Papa. Thomas Strickland. How shall I describe him? A man of modest height and weight, with fine brown hair, a high forehead and even features, he would be unexceptional in appearance were it not for his eyes: wide-set and as brown as acorns, they are windows onto a soul that is intelligent, kind and fair. Of them all, it is Papa's favour I most seek and it is his quiet disapproval that compels me to rein in my temper, as much as his unspoken encouragement compels me to apply myself to my lessons (and secretly to these pages, for he has always urged us all to write). His new business takes him to Norwich for long periods, and the household grows restive when he is gone. When he returns, weariness and care are etched upon his open face like cracks in a dry stream bed, and his gout plagues him woefully, but after a few days among us, organizing our lessons and tramping through the woods and beyond, he becomes himself again.

Our mother, Elizabeth, was beautiful once. Her portrait over the fireplace in the library depicts a slender young woman with dark, mischievous eyes. The mischief is gone now, replaced by a vagueness I cannot penetrate. Sometimes, when I am sad, I stand in front of the woman in the painting and tell her things, and if I close my eyes, I can almost feel her hands holding mine, even though I know it is only the warmth of the fire. Our real mama is no longer slender and I would not call her beautiful, but her skin is still smooth, her hair glossy. In truth, I do not know her well. In matters of comportment and etiquette, she is firm and assured, but in matters of the heart, she is aloof and impatient. The education of the boys interests her greatly, and she and my older sisters share many secrets. (I have seen them whispering.) And Kate has Papa to herself most of the time. But me? I fear I am little more to Mama than a "noisy nuisance." Sometimes I think her primary concern is what the neighbours will think, as she talks of little else these days. And when she is not nursing Papa, she spends more and more time in her room and leaves most of the household matters to Eliza and Agnes. It is to them I turn for advice or even comfort when Papa is away.

Eliza, the eldest at twenty-one, has, with Mama's endorsement, appointed herself chief disciplinarian. She is bad-tempered and disapproves of nearly anything she cannot claim as her own idea. Her severity is matched only by her shyness, or perhaps one is the product of the other, I do not know. But sadly, these qualities are manifest in her person, which, like her character, is without adornment. Her strengths are a notable talent for drawing and a passion for rules and schedules.

Stronger and more confident than Eliza, Agnes (nineteen) is tall and solemn with thick, shining black hair that I envy dreadfully. She is certainly a handsome woman and the smartest of us all, according to Papa, but still without a jot of humour to soften her increasingly austere, though fine, figure. She adores the limelight and seems to expand in proportion to the attention she receives. She is competitive in all things. And I firmly believe that her efforts to prevent Katie and me from writing were motivated partly by her perception that we were trespassing on her territory. She can be domineering and careless of the feelings of others and lacks sympathy for the plight of those weaker than herself (Sam and Tom and me, for instance, and our constant banishment to the nursery). Nevertheless, I love both Agnes and Eliza dearly, though it is difficult, despite Mama's grand plans, to imagine them as anything but the severe spinsters they have already become.

Not so Sarah. At seventeen, she is nothing like the rest of us. Papa thinks that the stork that brought her to Reydon Hall must have been a little off course. Mama openly declares—to Sarah's obvious discomfort—that her third daughter, beautiful and serene, is the best hope for a brilliant match with a handsome (and prosperous) young squire, who is surely out there somewhere poised to bring fortune and enduring respectability to the "genteel nunnery," in Papa's words, that is Reydon Hall. (That, at least, is the dream.) Sarah is known as "the baker" for her cheerful competence in certain domestic occupations, tasks for which the rest of us display no talent whatsoever. Reading and literature bore her, and her application to her studies is woefully lacking, the pantry rather than the library being her chosen milieu.

Next is Jane, two years younger, a studious grey bird caught in that shifting territory between our older sisters and Katie and me and the boys. One day, Jane is the diligent taskmaster drilling us in botany and geometry; the next, she is a child screaming in delighted terror as we comb the attic for old Martin's ghost. We call her "the worrier" for her tendency to fret about everything. She is undemanding and gentle by nature, and I fear she is so overshadowed by the rest of us, her noisier siblings, that she spends much of her time by herself, reading or walking. Even when Jane is in the room, she makes herself so small that it is easy to overlook her altogether.

Then there is my beloved, gentle Catharine. At thirteen, she is a year and a half older than me and possessed of such a sunny disposition that when it is paired with my own stormy restlessness, we are as night is to day, as at odds as heaven and hell, and yet in our differences, we are like two sides of the same coin, forever conjoined in a single purpose. And though I often chafe at her relentless cheerfulness (as well as her status as Papa's obvious favourite), she is the light of my life.

As for the children, Sam and Tom, they are boisterous and charming but with characters as yet unformed, though Sam at ten shows signs of a shrewd, if manipulative, intelligence and a physical prowess I envy. He can outrun any of us without breaking a sweat.

MARCH 6, 1815

Napoleon Bonaparte has escaped and is marching to Paris! Papa gave us the news on his return from Norwich at suppertime. I could not contain myself and whooped loudly for joy. "My prince is on his way!" I shouted, jumping up from the table. I thought Mama was going to faint. "Mr. Strickland, this is too much. These seditious outbursts must stop. Do something, please." And so I am confined to my room again.

Never mind, I have started a new poem: a ballad to heroic love. I shall call it "To the Fleeing Emperor."

More news: Sam and Tom are to attend school in Norwich beginning in the fall. They will live at the new house there with Mama and Papa on weekdays while the rest of us remain here at Reydon in the care of the servants. Papa, who has always insisted that a good education is as essential for girls as it is for boys, was almost apologetic when he gave us the news. Oh, how I should love to go to a real school. I was tempted to beg Papa, but once again Kate dissuaded me. ("I know your behaviour might suggest otherwise, but you're a *girl*, Susanna. Accept it.") Then she pointed out how blessed we are to have at our disposal an extensive collection of reading material inherited from Sir Isaac Newton. (Papa's first wife was a grandniece to the great mathematician.) And she's right. The hundreds of volumes include important works of philosophy, history, mathematics and science, which have been invaluable to our collective education. But I still think it isn't fair. Papa has promised Agnes that she and Eliza may accompany them to Norwich from time to time to avail themselves of the libraries and booksellers there. As for the rest of us, our schooling will continue under the supervision of the two eldest, a haphazard affair at best. Not like real school. If only I had been born a boy, then I should read history and geography and great literature and never again be bothered with needlework and drawing. When I expressed these sentiments to Sam, he scrunched his face into something resembling a cabbage and dared me to race him to the river and back. I shall miss him, though, and little Tom too. Much as I love dearest Katie, sometimes her goodness is too much to bear.

APRIL 10, 1815

This morning, after breakfast, I returned to my room and spent more than an hour sitting in the alcove under the gable watching the mist drift over the river like shreds of linen. Rooks called from the green willows; black-and-white cows ambled along the far bank. I wanted to capture the beauty of this familiar scene somehow, but the words would not arrange themselves in my head; and the strange and lovely feeling was gone before I could grasp it, like a stone thrown into a pond, leaving only ripples of melancholy and then nothing. I spent the whole of our French lesson sitting there pondering the elusiveness of my imagination and was not missed until lunchtime.

Mama says we are to hold a ball here at Reydon Hall. She says it is time Eliza, Agnes and Sarah were introduced to society. Eliza is mortified and insists she has no interest in coming out—or marrying—ever. I suspect it is too late for her anyway. Agnes pretends to be above it all, but I think she is secretly pleased. Only Sarah allowed her excitement at the prospect to show. Poor Jane, forgotten again.

MAY 7, 1815

Tomorrow, we travel to Norwich by coach for our final dress fittings. Mama says Kate and I are too young to take part in the dancing but that we shall nevertheless have new gowns of cream-coloured muslin, mine with blue satin ribbon at the bodice, my sister's pale green, and both with matching reticules. Eliza's and Agnes's dresses will be trimmed with gold and silver braid. Of course Mama has her matrimonial hopes pinned on the beautiful and saintly Sarah, but Papa says she is far too young to marry and that providing six daughters with dowries will surely land him in the poorhouse. He seems to view the prospect of the imminent ball with bemused contempt.

"A young woman today would be better off pursuing an education than a husband," I overheard him telling poor bewildered Vicar Sexsmith, following last Sunday's service. Since only eldest sons can inherit property, the necessarily few eligible bachelors are hopelessly outnumbered by the hordes of desperate spinsters preening and parading themselves in the faint hope of making a suitable match. (At least that's the way he made it sound, as though we are a pack of beribboned hounds pursuing a single golden fox.) Mama sighs when he harangues her on the subject and continues with her Debrett's.

"Do you think," she muses, "that we should have the dancing in the long drawing room or, if it is a warm night, in the conservatory with doors open onto the garden?"

In any case, the only young men invited other than the new curate, Mr. Headford, who has nothing to recommend him save a fearful stutter and a conspicuous squint, are the magistrate Mr. Beauchamp's two sons, whose acquaintance we have never made, but whose pallid visages I have often observed peering from the windows of their father's offices in Bungay, where they serve as junior clerks. And then there is Robert Kent, heir, Papa says, to a London distillery fortune. His family settled into the stately hall at Fornham St. Genevieve only a fortnight ago. Not gentry exactly, sighed Mama, but then . . .

Agnes has agreed to accompany us to Norwich today, but only grudgingly. Like Papa, she now considers the entire project folly. She is influenced, she says, by her recent discovery in the library of a book written by a woman, Mary Wollstonecraft, who, says Jane, wears blue stockings. Odd. It is called *A Vindication of the Rights of Woman* and Agnes has begun reading it aloud to us by candle-light after Mama and Papa have retired. I think the book has made a strong impression on her, as she goes on and on about independence and equality between the sexes. In spite of her demonstrated opposition to the literary arts, she spends an inordinate amount of time in her room composing dramas and poems, which she is only too happy to perform for our education and entertainment.

The dance will take place on the eve of the summer solstice.

Robert Kent has accepted our invitation to the ball and will be accompanied by his two cousins (male or female—he did not specify). Mama immediately ordered new crystal from Staffordshire and table linens from Ireland. Her customary lassitude has vanished. Instead, her blue eyes sparkle like the sea and roses seem to bloom on her smooth, pale cheeks.

"Your extravagance will be the death of me, Mrs. Strickland," said Papa, but his protests are muted by his obvious pleasure in our mother's renewed vigour.

"You will see, the expense is a double necessity," she responded. "It is high time the older girls had proper trousseaux; their clothes are in a shameful state. If they are to have suitors, they must have the appropriate accoutrements."

The whirl of activity as Mama and Lockwood ready the old house for the merciless scrutiny of society has infected us all—from Molly, the scullery maid, to young Tom—with unparalleled joie de vivre. Even Eliza is positively giddy, though she takes great pains to hide it. This morning, Katie and I observed her humming to herself as she settled down to her needlework.

All this talk of suitors and trousseaux! Yes, I am eager for the dance and very curious to glimpse Robert Kent and his cousins, but I swear upon these pages that I will never marry. I dream of writing great books, of fame and fortune and independence—not for me the strictures of parlours and nurseries and bedchambers. When I told Kate of my resolve on our walk this afternoon, she smiled patiently and said she longs to fall in love and that marriage must be a woman's greatest adventure. I was quick to remind Kate of Agnes's devotion to Miss Wollstonecraft's notion that marriage as it exists is little better than slavery for women, and that, ideally, relations between the sexes should be based on "a higher friendship" between equals. I do not see any evidence of this in the marriage of my own parents, who, when they are not squabbling like children, seem to tolerate one another with amused condescension.

JUNE 20, 1815

Napoleon has been defeated in a fierce battle at the town of Waterloo in Belgium. Papa says we shall see if the war is well and truly over this time (a war that began in the year of my birth!), and if it is, he declared, the world is poised on the brink of a new era—whether better or worse, he would not say. I did not mention that my ardour for Bonaparte lives on though his fate seems doubtful. I cannot risk courting Papa's or Mama's disapproval with the great festivities so close at hand.

Kate and I will be allowed to remain downstairs until one hour after the dancing has begun, and then we must join Sam and Tom in the nursery. No amount of cajoling has moved Mama in this; she refuses to weaken and I fear that continued petitioning will only harden her resolve.

Much consideration has been given to how the dancing will commence. Agnes insists that convention decrees that Mama, as mistress of Reydon, must have the first dance with Mr. Kent. Though he's not of high rank, his substantial fortune makes him easily the most desirable match in attendance. Mama, for her part, says that the honour of the first dance belongs to the eldest daughter, but Eliza must not dominate the young man's attention. "Perhaps a minuet and one or two reels, my dear, and then you must present Mr. Kent to your sister Sarah."

Hearing this, Sarah blushed fetchingly and smiled the enigmatic smile that is often upon her lips these days as she contemplates her almost certain destiny as doyenne of Fornham Manor. We were in

Mama's chambers, supervising Georgia, the housemaid, as she set out our ensembles—the gloves and reticules, the petticoats and caps—in readiness for tomorrow evening. Eliza's face reddened with shame or anger, or both, at Mama's words. Perhaps if my eldest sister smiled from time to time, she might have suitors too.

Agnes sniffed and resumed her scribbling. Then Jane, with a vehemence that shocked us all into silence, spoke up. "Perhaps Sarah's God-given gifts of a fair complexion, flaxen hair and a talent for baking will win her a husband one day, but I, for one, do not consider them accomplishments. I shall be in the library if you want me." And with that, she strode out of the room.

JUNE 22, 1815

Robert Kent is a troll! He and his absurd retinue (two gleaming coaches, each drawn by four chestnuts and attended by six footmen clad in scarlet livery adorned with enough gold braid to hang an earl) arrived promptly at 8:00 p.m. Mr. Kent occupied the lead coach, while his two cousins, Mr. Cecil Dalton and Miss Charlotte Dalton, were in the second with a lady's maid. Two grooms on bay mares rode behind. Their approach, heralded by the crunch of scores of hooves on gravel and a drawn-out series of trumpet blasts, could be heard long before the parade reached the Hall. We all, including the servants (even Cook and Molly left the pheasants unattended in the ovens), gathered on the portico to witness the spectacle. Mama tried to shoo us inside as Mr. Kent's entourage pulled into the driveway, but to no avail; we were frozen stiff with astonishment, none of us having ever encountered such lavish ostentation.

"A thoroughly tasteless display," Mama said this morning, "for someone whose antecedents were likely pirates and rum-runners." (I heard Papa murmur, "Or dockworkers like me.") I fear that Mama, who claims a tenuous ancestral connection with Catharine Parr, one of Henry VIII's unfortunate wives (indeed, my dear sister Kate is her namesake), sometimes loses sight of Papa's humbler beginnings.

In any case, Mr. Kent is very rich indeed, but his lack of breeding, to say nothing of his short stature, bowed legs, balding pate and high-pitched voice, was a grave disappointment to us all, particularly Sarah. After acknowledging his arrival, loudly announced by one of his footmen, Eliza presented herself with an adequate, if somewhat awkward, curtsey and ushered her companion into the conservatory, where the couple began the first quadrille accompanied by Mrs. Sexsmith, the vicar's wife, who had been commissioned to play the piano, and a Scottish boy from Southwold, who has attained legendary status on the violin.

Katie and I, being forbidden to take part, positioned ourselves halfway up the staircase, from whence we enjoyed an uninterrupted view of our dear sisters' initiation into local society. The conservatory, lit with hundreds of candles, and these in turn reflected in the dusk-darkened windows, glittered like the sea on a moonlit night. The nearly forty guests formed two lines and began walking about in pairs, each man holding his partner's hand high while the ladies grasped their skirts with the other. The men and women, old, young, stout and thin, circled one another, engaging in brief conversation, before passing on to the next partner and beginning the same sedate walkabout again. The scene was nothing like the "dance" I had conjured in my imagination—an abandoned tumble of whirling slippers and glinting spurs. This was more like a leisurely stroll on the common than the ecstatic celebration I had anticipated.

"Poor Eliza," whispered Katie. "How wretched she looks."

"No more than usual, surely?" I responded, and immediately regretted my unkindness as Eliza did indeed appear miserable.

Conversation has never been easy for my eldest sister, and what the quadrille lacks in athletic demands, it makes up for in social necessities. Eliza stared fixedly at her feet as she passed from one man to the next, some trying gallantly but vainly to elicit a few brief words from her as she trudged along with all the grace of a lame cart horse. Mama's fears that her awkward eldest daughter might commandeer all Mr. Kent's attentions proved unfounded. He gave Eliza no more than a cursory nod as they were reunited at the end of the first round before mincing off, his chinless jaw thrust forward like a turtle's, in search of more genial feminine company. He quickly spotted the lovely Sarah and was headed to where she and Agnes and the Hardwick sisters, Catherine and Elizabeth, stood in a small circle by the potted palms, fanning themselves. But alas, the unfortunate Mr. Kent was a moment too late.

"Oh, Katie, look." I pressed my forehead into the space between the banister rails. "I believe Mr. Dalton is asking Sarah to dance."

Cecil Dalton, unlike his illustrious cousin, boasted the suave good looks of a young squire. He was a little shorter than my sister, perhaps, but possessed of a full head of fair hair, broad shoulders, straight legs and unblemished cheeks.

I grabbed Katie's hand and squeezed it rather harder than I meant to. "Do you think Mr. Dalton may be heir to a distillery fortune too?"

Katie winced and delivered one of her withering (and I must say wearying) sermons. "My dear Susie," she began, "it matters not the size of a man's purse so long as his character is unsullied and he is kind and forbearing in all his—"

"Shhh. Oh no. Mama . . ." We watched as our mother, overseeing the unfolding drama from her position on the dais by the door to the library, glided through the mingling guests with the intention of intercepting Mr. Dalton and diverting him from Sarah so that she might be open to the full attentions of Mr. Kent. But Mama was too late and could only watch in dismay as Sarah and Mr. Dalton turned toward whatever destiny had in store for them. I must say, they looked like a prince and princess, and I found my heart beating like an African drum as I watched them cross the floor together. Mama, in an attempt to salvage the lost opportunity, grasped the hand of Agnes, the daughter nearest her (Jane had scurried away like a little mouse at our mother's approach), and placed it on Mr. Kent's forearm before giving both young people an encouraging squeeze and retreating with a forced yet determined smile to our father's side.

Agnes bowed her head dutifully and led poor bewildered Mr. Kent into the fray. Despite his ungainly bearing, he proved a graceful dancer, and to my utter astonishment, it seemed that our hours of practice every afternoon in the drawing room before tea (throughout which Agnes grumbled and stomped like an angry hen) had paid off. She conducted herself so admirably that Mr. Kent soon shed his air of distraction and gave himself over wholly to the dance. Mrs. Sexsmith and the boy stepped up the tempo somewhat and launched into a lively reel. Before long, the hall was charged with excitement. The last thing I observed before Agnes, who had managed to extricate herself from Mr. Kent's charms, came to shepherd Kate and me to bed was that the handsome Mr. Dalton was no longer dancing with our promising sister Sarah, but had taken up with the equally beguiling Elizabeth Hardwick. Mama, half hidden by the potted ferns at the window, glowered.

OCTOBER 11, 1818

Three years have passed, and despite the best of intentions my commitment to these pages has suffered grievous setbacks. Those days when I revelled with what now seems like childish delight in the harmless drama and carefree diversions of family life are gone. The interruption can be blamed in part on Eliza, who confiscated and destroyed more than a year's worth of musings, but also on the fateful circumstances that have so cruelly and suddenly deprived us of our beloved Papa. In the aftermath of his passing, words seemed useless, almost an affront before the tidal wave of loss that assailed us all. But now, tentatively and in the hopes that my writing might provide some small consolation, I begin again.

Katie, Jane and I visited dear Papa's grave this afternoon in order to ready the small plot for oncoming winter, only to find the yellow rose we planted early in the summer has bloomed anew with a determination and brilliance that should have made my heart glad. "Surely it is a sign of better times to come," said Kate, clutching my hand in hers.

"A comforting thought," I replied, though mine were filled with darkness.

Papa is buried in the churchyard at St. Margaret's, and one or two of us have managed the short walk from Reydon Hall to pay our respects nearly every day since his passing last spring. How dearly we miss him! He will remain in our hearts forever, and his demise has plunged all of us into an orgy of sadness. This little pilgrimage to his grave constitutes one of the few outings we have to look forward to in these dark days. Ever since the failure of Papa's affairs in Norwich—of which Katie and I knew nothing at the time, and which surely contributed to his untimely death—our household has declined both in substance and in spirit. The earth had barely settled on Papa's grave when Mama gathered us all together in the small parlour and laid out the gravity of our situation. She told us Papa's capital was gone, seized by the bank when a loan he guaranteed for his business partner was not repaid. All that was left is this draughty old house and a small pension from Mama's late father, barely enough, she reported in a tight voice, to sustain one person, let alone a family of eight children. Her face, as she delivered this news, showed no emotion. Eliza and Agnes did not react, just nodded solemnly like a pair of twin crows in black crape. They had known for some time, of course. But it was news to the rest of us, who were so preoccupied with our sorrow and the unimaginable prospect of a life deprived of the spiritual nourishment of our beloved *père* that we had given no consideration as to how we were to come by the basic necessities of life now that he was gone. Up until his passing, my life was an idyll of sunshine and carefree days. How I took for granted those simple pleasures and childish joys, and how ashamed I was at that moment of my angry outbursts, my selfish disregard for the sacrifices made by my dear mother and father so that we, their children, could idle away our days, oblivious to the precariousness of all we held dear.

The air in the parlour seemed to shiver after Mama spoke. It was Jane who broke the silence. "But what are we to do?" Sarah, seated by the window, wept softly. I watched through the glass as the sun passed briefly behind the locust tree in the garden, causing it to blaze defiantly and give off a yellow light so thrilling that, for a moment, the tree's brilliance lit up the room and our hearts. I glanced at Kate and, by the radiance in her face, I knew she too felt the presence of our father in this brief, bright explosion. Mama blinked and bowed her head, then raised her chin and fixed her gaze on the étagère in the corner. The light in the room dimmed again.

"We shall do as your father would have wished. We shall persevere." Then she closed her eyes against her tears and whispered the words he had so often uttered: "God helps those who help themselves."

And so we have no choice but to carry on. Though I am afraid (Kate's unquestioning faith in Providence notwithstanding) that no matter how frugal and diligent we are, it will take more than the good Lord's intercession to compensate for the nearly empty larder and the imminent onset of an English winter.

Today is my fifteenth birthday. Only Kate remembered, presenting me with a simple sketch of the scalloped gables of our beloved Reydon Hall. Underneath were the lines "May the home of your childhood live on in your dreams / Wherever you wander, whatever your schemes." I thought it very accomplished, but my sister blushed when I tore off the tissue paper. "I have no talent for drawing," she said, "but I wanted you to have something. I'm not much of a poet either, I'm afraid."

"It's beautiful, Katie. I shall treasure it always." I kissed her on the cheek, touched to the point of tears. Her gesture means more to me than silver and gold. I tell myself that riches are merely the physical trappings of rank and that true social status is more than an accumulation of goods. I consider Mama's hand-wringing futile and unnecessary, because appearances are only the outward manifestations of respectability. As Susanna Strickland, youngest daughter of a distinguished and erudite, now sadly missed, gentleman, as a member of a family of exquisite sensibility and excellent education, I know where I stand in the natural order of things, and though my cuffs are frayed and my bonnet out of fashion, I can hold my head high, proud of the Strickland name and certain of our innate superiority.

I delivered a version of this speech to Agnes, who raised one jet-black eyebrow and shook her head. "I hope you're right, Susanna, but rank and respectability will not pay the taxes or purchase coal."

I hesitate to mention it, but my bleeding has begun, accompanied by excruciating pains in my lower abdomen and an overall feeling of dullness and nausea. When I told Kate, she turned quite pink and agreed that the situation is unfortunate but inevitable, and that at least the release of excess blood will make me less emotional. Excess blood? Surely there must be more to it than that. It seems inconceivable that God would allow such a disgusting and inconvenient state of affairs to exist for such a flimsy reason. Why endow women with too much blood in the first place? I know Eve caused a lot of trouble, but must all women atone for it for all time? There is no one to ask. I am beginning to realize that one of the most difficult things about growing up is learning acceptance.

It seems our first Christmas without Papa will be a meagre affair. The Daltons have kindly contributed a goose (though Mama is under the impression that the unfortunate bird wandered into the stable yard one day in answer to her prayers). We dare not tell her the truth; her pride is the only pillar supporting her as she watches her hard-won status crumble day by day. We are fattening the bird with table scraps and bowls of milk, which means watery, lumpy porridge for our own breakfast. The cats gather longingly to watch Her Grace the goose slurp the victuals that at one time would have been theirs to enjoy. Sarah says we shall be glad of the sacrifice when we slice into the golden roasted reward in a few weeks. I am ashamed to admit I can think of little else. Meat of any kind in our reduced circumstances is a treasure more valuable than all the pretty ribbons I once delighted in.

Who will dispatch the goose is another matter, not just because we have made such a pet of it, but also because the beheading has always fallen to one of the tenant farmers and they are gone since these past two months to take up positions at the cotton mills in Lancashire. Hungry as I am for crackling fat and moist goose flesh, I have no appetite for butchery. We will have to roast it ourselves as well since Cook and Lockwood were let go amid much wailing and anguished tears, though I rather think they were not truly sorry to leave such an unruly household. Fortunately, Sarah is confident she can produce the promised feast with the help of Georgia, who continues as housemaid, and Molly, the scullery maid, though Mama worries constantly about how she will pay them. The stables are empty too, but for a few chickens we keep for eggs, and, of course, Her Grace. Father's fine carriage horses are sold and the carriage with them. The donkey cart remains, though no donkey. We are reduced to borrowing the Daltons' ass for our infrequent excursions to Bungay, or to taking the public coach to Norwich (a mode of transport Mama adamantly insists is beneath her), where we still maintain a house so that the boys can continue to attend school there. Eliza is constantly grumbling about the expense and complaining that while we subsist on the turnips and onions that we have grown with our own toil, our young brothers enjoy fine cheeses and roasted meats daily for their lunch. (Surely she exaggerates.) Meanwhile, our education, once so important to dear Papa, languishes and, because we are girls, has become our own affair.

Mama seldom leaves her room, though how she can bear the cold is a mystery. Most of the second floor and the large reception rooms on the ground floor are closed off to save precious coal. We restrict our daily activities to the kitchen and scullery, and when the dampness and chill make it unbearable, we light a small fire in the library, which gives little heat and barely enough light to read by.

Nevertheless, reading has become our primary diversion during these dreary months, with Eliza and Agnes away during the week in Norwich, where they have been keeping house for the boys. On the weekdays, Katie, Jane, Sarah and I are kept busy with the endless mending and the preparation of a steady supply of dark bread and potage, bread and potage, bread and potage . . . until I think I might happily sell my soul (or at least my last quill) for a bit of cheese! Mama accepts the bland diet without complaint. Her central concern is with keeping up appearances and maintaining some semblance of our tenuous social standing—that and deciding what else can be sold to help finance our ongoing descent into genteel penury. General Wolfe's desk is next, I fear. She laments, too, about the state of our wardrobes, which are not only threadbare but sadly out of fashion.

When I am not in the kitchen playing a common drudge or scribbling in these pages, I plunder the library looking for literary entertainment I may have overlooked. I confess that though I am surely better for having read Locke and Descartes, and Miss Wollstonecraft is indeed an inspiration to the fair sex, I find that the novels of Jane Austen thrill me more than any philosophical treatise ever has. Mama does not consider them appropriate for young women of our class, and Agnes claims to prefer the rigours of historical argument to the "fevered imaginings of an aging spinster." (She seems oblivious to the hypocrisy contained in such a statement.) The other day, I happened upon a dog-eared copy of *Clarissa* tucked away on an upper shelf behind the Gibbons. I was barely two chapters on before Agnes seized it and made off to her room, where she remained into the night and for much of the next day. I have not seen it since.

Katie and I are obliged to wait until the ghouls have left for Norwich and Mama is taking her afternoon nap so that we can read aloud to one another from the forbidden texts. Our most recent passion is *Northanger Abbey*. Its observations on the institution of marriage have provided my sister and me with hours of fierce discussion on the predicament of being born female. When I came across Miss Austen's comparison of marriage and dancing, the sad truth of it made me laugh out loud: "You will allow that in both," she wrote, "man has the advantage of choice, woman only the power of refusal."

Like nearly everything in the relations between men and women, it does not seem fair.

The goose was superb. Sam, the eldest male and now head of our diminished household, carved the bird with great perseverance. Then we paid heartfelt tribute to Her Grace before consuming every last morsel. Strangely, I felt nary a twinge of remorse as I devoured my share, my empathy for the poor creature having been thoroughly exhausted four days ago when Jane and Kate (the boys not yet home from Norwich) were compelled to carry out the necessary execution. Shall I describe the ghastly business here?

By mid-morning of December 22, the event had been postponed long enough. We huddled together in the cold drizzle and watched Her Grace slurp her last supper of bread crusts and milk, reaching out her sleek neck and throwing her head back to utter the greedy exclamations of a practised glutton.

"How disgusting she is," I remarked in a small voice, Sam's hatchet hanging by my side.

"Yes," Jane agreed, hoping, like me, to harden her heart against the inevitable. "She is a vile creature. Her little eyes, her fat grey body, those ridiculous orange feet."

At that moment, the goose spread her wings and ran, or rather waddled quickly, across the stable yard toward us, hissing angrily. She stopped at our feet, retracted her neck and, with a shrug of her feathers and a disdainful honk, turned and marched back to her trough. At that point, my nerve deserted me.

"There, Katie. You do it, then," I said, shrinking from the attack. "I cannot kill a living thing, stupid or not. I think I would rather have mashed turnips for our Christmas supper than harm a single feather."

"For heaven's sake," Katie began, grabbing the hatchet from my limp grasp. "How would you survive in the wilderness? We have to eat."

There is a toughness to my sister's character that is easily overlooked; underneath the sweetness beats the heart of a bloodthirsty butcher. She coaxed Grace into an empty stall, and while Jane used her body to pin the squirming, squawking bird to the ground, Katie removed its head with two swift and mighty hatchet blows. Believing the carnage was over, I opened my eyes, which had been tightly shut during the ordeal, and released the air from my lungs. Jane relinquished her hold on the bird's warm body. (She later said she could see its heart still beating wildly in its breast, though it was dead as it could be—or so we thought.)

Then, to our horror, some spectral force propelled the headless carcass from its deathbed and out through the stable door into the muddy yard, where it flapped in frantic circles before staggering blindly up the path toward the house with Jane and Kate in squealing pursuit. The spectacle, though ghoulish in the extreme, is indelibly etched in my imagination, and once we recovered from the shock, Sarah and I were so overcome with hilarity that we could barely stand.

And yet, despite the comedy, the event has made me consider the mysteries of life—where it begins, where it ends. If that goose had a soul, when did it depart its poor murdered body and where did it go? Indeed, what is life? Is it merely a beating heart and blood flowing through our veins, or is there some other life force apart from the flesh? These thoughts kept me awake for much of the long night, though they had no impact on my enjoyment of Her Grace when she later appeared, crackling brown on a platter, decorated with sprigs of holly and sweetened with the last of Cook's crabapple jelly.

Still, it was, being our first Christmas without Papa, a bittersweet affair. We exchanged modest gifts of needlework and pressed flowers. There were knitted socks for the boys, and after supper, Agnes and I read our poems aloud. It pains me to admit that hers are rather good.

DECEMBER 27, 1818

We had a visitor to Reydon Hall today, an event that lamentably occurs with less and less frequency as our circumstances decline. Lacking the basic necessities to properly entertain guests (the silver tea service and the pianoforte sold), we seldom do, the result being that we in turn receive fewer and fewer invitations. I, for one, do not care and question the value of friendships that depend more upon social conventions and appearances than on ordinary human kindness. But Mama talks constantly about our standing in the neighbourhood, and I fear she keenly misses the male companionship that our father, with his friendships and business relations, bestowed on our otherwise cloistered existence. Therefore, you can imagine her excitement (and discomfort) when Mr. Harral came to call.

A light snow had been falling since early morning, melting as it reached the ground but clinging prettily to the copper beeches lining the drive, when Jane and I, sitting by the kitchen window, she intent upon the sock she was mending and me composing a poem in my head, heard the faint laughter of harness bells, and the veil of snow parted to reveal a handsome black horse pulling a two-wheeled chaise. It was as though Father Christmas had appeared, late—but better that than never.

Mr. Thomas Harral, editor of *The Suffolk Herald* and an old friend of Papa's, who shared his passion for fly-fishing and love of reading, often came to visit in happier times. He sometimes brought his children, Anna Laura and Francis, to play with us while he accompanied our father to the river to spend the arc of a bright June morning casting for speckled trout. Later, over an early dinner (of sweet fried fish), our table would come alive with discussions of politics, scientific ideas and literature. Imagine the joy, then, with which we greeted his surprise visit!

Sam and Tom helped Mr. Harral settle his horse in the stable, even managing to offer it a few dusty oats, while Agnes fetched the key to the rosewood tea caddy and Sarah put the kettle on. Kate and I laid a hasty fire in the library, where Mama, amid much clucking and curtseying, showed Mr. Harral to the best chair by the hearth. Wearing a silk cravat and moleskin breeches, he struck a fine figure, and I was suddenly painfully aware of the meanness of our surroundings, the dampness, the mouse droppings in the corners and the sour smell of boiled cabbage. Mr. Harral was too well bred to appear to notice. Instead, he expressed interest in our writing projects, particularly turning his attentions to Kate, the former darling of those fishing expeditions.

"I have written a book," she announced, casting aside all pretense at modesty.

A book? I thought. *What book?*

Our mother raised her eyebrows and murmured, "Now, dear . . ."

"A book?" said Mr. Harral, leaning forward in his chair and holding out his hand. A smile played on his lips. "What kind of book?"

Kate placed her fingers in his outstretched palm and blushed a pretty shade of pink. If I had not known Mr. Harral to be a gentleman (and a married one at that), I might have thought he was flirting with my sister, who, despite her slender bearing, is no longer a child.

"A novel. For children. About a Highland piper who is blind. He befriends a crippled collie, and together—"

Her words were like a slap in the face: a blind boy, a wounded dog, Alpine changed to Highland. She was describing *our* book. Our book. Curling papers no longer. I jumped up from where I was seated on the sofa. "Kate," I began.

Sarah pinched my wrist and hissed. Kate smiled at me and placed her finger to her lips. She returned her attention to Mr. Harral.

"Together, they overcome all manner of—"

Mr. Harral interrupted her with what appeared to be genuine interest. "Well, I should very much like to see this book of yours, my dear."

Our book. When had she intended to tell me about this? I sat down again, hands gripping the edge of my seat to stop from shaking. Kate skipped out of the room to fetch her manuscript, and Eliza and Agnes exchanged dark glances. They too knew nothing of our sister's project.

Mama, oblivious to the tension in the room, offered Mr. Harral more tea. "My, what nonsense girls get up to these days. And to think we have all these edifying volumes at our disposal." She lifted her eyes and gazed at the shelves rising to the ceiling. "Novels!" she snorted.

"I have been writing too." It was Agnes. We all turned to look at her. "Poetry," she said, her chin raised, shoulders high. "In fact, one of my poems has been accepted for publication in the *Norfolk News*."

"Really, Agnes?" said Mama. "How wonderful. I do love a rousing poem. You should have told us."

Mr. Harral turned his attentions to Agnes.

"Well, well, a published authoress in the family. And what is your poem about, my dear?"

"I have called it 'Death of a Monarch,'" Agnes continued. "It is a tribute to poor Queen Charlotte."

Agnes too? Taking time off from her historical studies to write doggerel? At least the work was her own. But Katie? Claiming credit for our work, hers and mine, the collaboration I had thought destroyed years ago? I could hardly breathe.

At last, Kate returned and placed a stack of foolscap in Mr. Harral's hands. She was clearly excited. "When the boy falls to the bottom of a deep crevasse, the little three-legged dog runs all the way to . . ." She blushed again. "Well, you'll see if you read it."

Yes, it was the same story that I assumed had been sacrificed to the interests of perfectly turned ringlets. The Swiss herd boy transformed into a sightless Scot, the loyal marmot into a sheepdog? The story that I thought had been ours together I now found my sister had been working on all this time without telling me. I was aghast at her perfidy, her betrayal.

We waited in silence while Mr. Harral perused the pages, slowly at first, and then more quickly, nodding and making faint grunts, whether of satisfaction or dismay I could not tell. Agnes's literary triumph, to her obvious chagrin, was apparently forgotten. At last, Mr. Harral looked up from his reading and, removing his spectacles, turned his attention to Mama.

"Mrs. Strickland, I hope you will allow me to take these pages with me on my next visit to London. I do believe they have some merit."

"Mr. Harral, they are the scribblings of a child, the, the . . ." —Mama's hands were shaking as she wrung her handkerchief—"the product of an idle imagination. Surely . . ."

"Believe me, madam, times and tastes change, and there is a growing appetite in the city for fictions such as these. I have a friend in the publishing business, and he has told me he is on the lookout for talented writers, many of them women such as your daughters, whose stories he can put into print."

"But to what end?" cried Mama.

"To be blunt, Mrs. Strickland, to a financial end. Educated, well-off people are hungry for such entertainments and they will pay for them."

"Are you suggesting my Katie will receive money for this . . . this silly recreation?"

"I am. And it is one of the reasons for my visit today." He looked around the room. "Please forgive me for my directness, but it is clear that since the passing of my dear friend and your loving husband, Thomas, your finances have been"—he paused and cleared his throat—"have been strained. Your girls, as lovely and accomplished as they are, have little hope of marrying without dowries. I doubt their departed father would disagree with me when I say they would not be ill-advised in making use of their natural talents so that you, Mrs. Strickland, can have some hope of maintaining your cherished home in something approaching a livable condition."

Containing my rage as best I could, I concentrated on Mr. Harral's speech and on Mama's reaction. Despite the dearth of heat emanating from the hearth, her face turned crimson at his words. She stood and began rearranging the tea tray and, without looking at him, said finally, "Well, Mr. Harral, as always your perspective is most illuminating. I hadn't quite thought our situation as dire as you seem to imagine. But perhaps you are right. Perhaps I should consider encouraging young Kate here—and Agnes too, it seems—to put at risk her most precious asset, her respectability, for the sake of a few shillings."

"My dear Elizabeth, I am not suggesting sending them out on the streets to fend for themselves. I only meant that times are changing and we must change with them. At least allow me to show Catharine's story to my publisher friend . . ."

"Please, Mama, please," said Kate.

Agnes joined in. "Mama, what harm is there?"

And when the others (even I joined the chorus) cried out in support of the idea, Mama gave her reluctant assent. Mr. Harral shook her hand warmly, and I showed him to the door.

"Are you a writer too?" he asked as I handed him his greatcoat.

"Well, yes, I . . ."

"Keep it up, then. There may be a future in it," he said before I could finish, and he was out the door and away.

After he left, I hurried upstairs to find Kate, who had repaired to her room, apparently to gloat in private.

"You, you," I sputtered. "How could you?"

She calmly reminded me that she had told me she would deal with Eliza and Agnes. "And that's what I did, Susanna. I quietly persuaded them to return the manuscript, saying I could read it aloud to the little boys at bedtime. They relented and forgot about it, as I knew they would. As you can tell, I have made many changes to the story since then."

"But you didn't tell me. You hid it away all this time and didn't say a word. It was my idea, the fruit of my imagination. Who are you? Who would do such a thing?" In a torrent of rage, I began ripping the quilts and pillows off her bed and hurling them on the floor, calling her a cheat and a traitor. She did nothing to stop me. But she called me "wild" and "unpredictable" and said I must control my temper and curb my tendency to look for drama and perfidy at every juncture.

"You have taken the collaboration of our two imaginations," I sobbed, "and made it into something unrecognizable, without even asking me. How could you?"

"Susie, *The Highland Piper* became my creation long ago." She looked at me kindly. "If you are going to be a writer, then you must write. Thinking about it is not enough."

I had nothing to say to that. I left her room and went to sulk in the cold and comfortless library. I am calmer now, but her betrayal still rankles. Not so much over the appropriation of our story, because what she said is true: I do spend more time dreaming than actually putting pen to paper. What really hurts is that, in my mind, Kate and I are soulmates; my thoughts are hers, her triumphs partly mine. And so to know there is a part of her she does not share with me, a part that is about her and not us, is difficult to accept.

Later, at lunch, Katie was as serene and gentle as a summer's day, betraying nothing to the others of our disagreement. In her mind, the matter is closed, while I continue to suffer silently. How good she is. She has the uncanny faculty for forgetting past sorrows and dwelling on the present. We are so unalike, it is a wonder we ever agree on anything. While I rail at the injustice I see at every turn, she seems to accept her fate with an equanimity I cannot fathom. Beside her, I feel like a wild Suffolk girl, my heart bursting alternately with anger and passion. There are times when I cannot bear her imperturbable patience, and yet I wonder what I should be without it.

JANUARY 1, 1819

A new year. With Kate's example in mind, I have resolved to apply myself to composing the poetry that is roiling inside me like a storm at sea. Agnes has brought to my attention the verses of Sir Walter Scott, whom she says she is trying to emulate in her own writings. I intend to outdo her; she has grown unbearably smug now that her work is to be published. Still, I envy her diligence (she is at her desk from after breakfast until noon every day without fail), and her glossy dark brown hair. How I detest my mouse-coloured frizz.

I have just finished the most remarkable novel, a tale of horror and hubris. It is called *Frankenstein*. How it made its way into the library at Reydon Hall, I shall never know, but it fell into my hands quite by accident as I was retrieving a cloak from Eliza's room and it fell from the pocket. The book is fearfully dog-eared, proof it has been making the rounds with my elder sisters for some time, though likely withheld from Katie and me for fear of disturbing our young and fertile minds. The author is called Anonymous, which only deepens the story's strange aura. How I should like to meet him someday.

Spring has come to Reydon Hall. Daffodils cluster among the trees and along the drive, yellow explosions in the sunshine. Today is the first truly balmy day after a month of rain and fog. Katie works steadily on more children's tales. I am applying myself diligently to one of my own, the subject of which I will keep to myself for now . . . for obvious reasons.

Kate and I have become friends with Mr. Harral's daughter, Anna Laura. Of course, we often played childish games with her and her brother, Francis, when Papa was alive, but I had not seen them in at least two years. What a pleasure it has been to reconnect with this fine young woman and her very handsome sibling now that Mr. Harral has taken such a kind interest in our affairs. He lost little time in inviting Kate and me to spend an afternoon at the family's home near Southwold. While not grand, the Harral house is filled with books and paintings and has an intimacy which I'm afraid our beloved Reydon with its cavernous rooms and labyrinth of corridors will never achieve. Anna Laura was shy at first. She and her brother are reserved and polite, perhaps as a consequence of their father's restrained and erudite bearing (he is nothing like Papa despite their shared interests), or it could be the household's subdued energy has something to do with the presence of the second Mrs. Harral, the first having died of consumption around the time of our own father's death.

"Papa says she is still getting used to us," Anna Laura remarked after her stepmother came upon the four of us playing a game of jackstraws in the drawing room during our visit.

"Anna Laura, dear, would you mind lowering your voices," Mrs. Harral said without acknowledging my sister and me, though we had not yet been introduced. "I have a most fearful headache." She pinched the bridge of her nose between a thumb and index finger, then craned her neck to see what we were doing. "Really, Francis? Children's games? Surely you have better things to do?" And she was gone.

Francis scooped up the scattering of coloured sticks from the carpet and began sliding them into their wooden box. "How can she get used to us when nothing we do is right?" He was pale with anger. "I'm going for a walk."

Kate put a hand on his arm. "Let me go with you, Francis. I should love to see the garden."

After they left, Anna Laura's earlier reticence disappeared. "Please excuse my brother. Our new mother, is very hard on him. Papa says she loves him, loves both of us, that she only wants the best for us. I understand. It must be difficult to be a mother to someone else's children. But it's hard for us too; she is so often out of temper."

She jumped to her feet, pulling me with her. "Come on. I'll show you the stables. We have new kittens, only a week old."

Since then, whenever we visit, Mrs. Harral continues to act as though we do not exist. Eliza says she is older than Mr. Harral and that she was obliged to marry "beneath her" because of her age, despite having a modest income. How my sister discovers these things, I do not know, only that she and Agnes return from Norwich each week with many such stories. I do not care if Mrs. Harral holds us in contempt. What can she do to us? Her husband's encouragement and influence are the important things.

Katie's Highland piper story is to be published. Imagine our amazement when Mr. Harral appeared at our door and called my sister to him. Without a word, he pressed five golden guineas into the palm of her hand (which she promptly dropped on the floor, so great was her surprise, where they scattered like laughter and sent us all scurrying to retrieve them). Mr. Harral says his publisher friend was delighted to pay such a sum for the work. The book shall be called *The Blind Highland Piper and Other Tales,* and will be published in the fall. I am, of course, filled with envy, but also overcome with happiness for my sister's success. We celebrated with a bottle of claret at dinner; even Mama was flushed with excitement, and with her blessing, we have decided to spend a portion of the money (the rest will be set aside for repairs to the east wing roof and next winter's coal) on a trip to London at the kind invitation of Papa's cousin Mrs. Rebecca Leverton of Bedford Square in Bloomsbury. I cannot wait to make her acquaintance. Mama, in an unguarded moment (the claret, I imagine), treated us to a detailed description of our wealthy cousin, married to the prominent architect Thomas Leverton, who built, among many other things, a splendid triumphal arch in Yorkshire, commemorating the American victory in the War of Independence. Eliza, Agnes, Kate and I will make the journey and stay for a fortnight.

Of course I am delighted with my sister's success, but I cannot deny that something ugly slithered inside me at the news. It distresses me that I sometimes harbour flashes of ill will toward my sisters, particularly Agnes and Kate. I cannot reconcile my love for them with the cold fingers of jealousy that grip my throat when I consider their successes. There is something wild in it, some part of me I cannot tame, a place where love and reason do not reach.

PART TWO
1827–1830
LITERARY LIFE

---------◆---------

JUNE 14, 1827 (REYDON HALL)

Despite the fine weather, Anna Laura and I spent the afternoon indoors revising our poems, mine a bucolic tribute to the strenuous labours of the men and women who toil daily in the fields and meadows of Suffolk. I have called it "The Reaper." Anna Laura is composing a sonnet in praise of friendship: a celebration, she says, of our ever-deepening connection. When we emerged from the library at tea time, we were dizzy with exhilaration. I have great hopes of finding a publisher for these, my most cherished works, even though my children's stories and rustic sketches are most in demand. Indeed, my first book, the *Spartacus* novel for children, has sold so well that I am besieged with requests. (Well, perhaps that is an exaggeration, though Newman, the publisher, has asked for more of the same.)

I do not think the thrill of seeing my words in print will ever pale. Five years ago, when I unwrapped that novel and held it in my hands, felt the weight of it, the texture of the paper between my fingers, and read the fine, orderly type, it was like an affirmation of my own existence, the birth of something real. Since then, I am blessed to have seen my writing published again and again, and the novelty never wears off. But it is my poems I love best, and wherein I believe my rendezvous with destiny lies. Perhaps cousin Rebecca will see fit to subsidize my work as she has so generously done for

Agnes's two poetry volumes. Indeed, my elder sister spends much of her time in London these days, staying with cousin Rebecca at Bedford Square, which is within walking distance of the British Museum. That great institution provides Agnes with a trove of ideas for historical plots and themes. She has become quite the society belle, spending what little she earns on hats and dresses. Indeed, I believe she will soon join Eliza (an editor now at the *Court Journal*) and take up permanent residence in London.

Kate, whose success with children's stories continues, thinks that Agnes's increasing immersion in London society has made her distant and superior, but I think our ambitious and handsome sister is well on her way to literary greatness. I am determined to follow in her footsteps, and I intend to visit the metropolis again as soon as I can manage the fare to London. If I cannot stay with cousin Rebecca, I will presume upon the hospitality of our cousin Thomas Cheesman (the other "Coz"), whose house on Newman Street is, in Eliza's opinion, "an unfit venue for respectable young women." I told her that I am certain Cheesman's relations with his housekeeper are entirely, as he claims, above board. He is harmless, a good-natured eccentric, a painter who, though he lives in a state of perpetual chaos, is nevertheless immersed in the world of arts and letters to which I aspire. Kate can continue to piddle away her time here in the country turning out children's stories if she wishes, but I do think the engine of publishing resides in the city.

JUNE 15, 1827

It seems that the clear, pure air and rural quiet are not the only attractions Reydon holds for Kate. When Anna Laura and I emerged from our work this afternoon, we surprised my sister and Mr. Francis Harral engaged in an obvious tête-à-tête. They were sitting together on the small wrought-iron bench under the plane tree outside the conservatory. Anna Laura's brother appeared to be rescuing a tendril of Kate's hair that had escaped from her pins. It was a tender moment—the dappled light, the tentative angle of her chin, his attitude of rapt devotion—and I made an immediate mental note of the tableau as future material. Anna Laura, realizing we were about to intrude on their privacy, tried to pull me back through the French doors, but the couple were all at once aware of our presence and came apart in a little dance of embarrassed confusion. A pretty scene, indeed.

I am delighted, really, that my dearest friend's brother is courting my favourite sister. Although I have little desire to assume the marital yoke myself, wedlock has long been my sister's cherished ambition. Kate and Francis: I wish them well. It promises to be a perfectly appropriate conjunction of our two families. Mr. Harral has proved a valuable mentor to me and my sisters. He has generously published our poetry in his newspapers, The Suffolk Chronicle and The Bury Gazette, and Agnes in particular has benefited hugely from his vast knowledge of history and the arts.

Perhaps Anna Laura will accompany me when I next go up to London—although her cough has returned, and Mrs. Harral is rather strict about her stepdaughter's comings and goings. Still, I am dying to show her Westminster Abbey, where cousin Rebecca took me on my last visit. A Gothic miracle.

Agnes, Kate and I have been asked to dine with the Harrals this evening as Mr. Harral says he has an important announcement.

JUNE 16, 1827

The Harrals are moving to London. Mr. Harral is to become editor of a new magazine called La Belle Assemblée, which he described to us over an excellent dinner of roast lamb as a "fashionable journal devoted to literature and the royal court." This is sad news for Suffolk society but a tremendous opportunity for Mr. Harral. He pushed his chair back and stood, glass of wine in hand, and made a modest little speech, trying, without success, to conceal his immense satisfaction at the appointment. Mrs. Harral was not at the table. Anna Laura says her stepmother prefers to take most of her meals in her room, claiming the excitement affects her nerves. But I am certain she cannot bear the presence of my sisters and me. Mr. Harral appears not to notice. He has promised there will be ample opportunity for all of us to publish our poems and stories within his magazine's pages. He particularly singled out Agnes as a potential contributor because of her social connections and her growing interest in the aristocracy.

I am beginning to feel as though my life, my real life, has finally begun.

We returned home to find Mama sitting up and reading aloud to Jane and Sarah. At long last: a letter from Tom. We have heard nothing from our little brother in nearly six months, not since his ship, the *Helena*, became becalmed off Gibraltar en route to the Azores. Mama has been frantic with worry, but thank God, all is well. He was only fifteen when he left to join the Merchant Marine. It is hard to believe that the baby of the family is now a man of twenty. Of Sam and his adventures in the wilds of Upper Canada, there is much news in the monthly letters he sends, extolling the wonders of pioneer life. In the two years since he sailed for the New World, my former comrade in mischief has married and become a widower in a tragically short space of time. And while we are saddened to realize we will never meet poor Emma, his late wife, the widowed Sam is now father to a little son, Mama's first grandchild. I wonder if we shall ever meet him, or see either of our brothers again.

I have been keeping company with a certain Mr. William Mingay, whom I met at Cheesman's, where I have been staying since a week ago Tuesday. The visit with my cousin has been an adventure, I must say. Dressed in his signature uniform of paint-splattered smock and felt chapeau, he presides over a perpetual clutter of books and musical instruments and half-finished paintings with a restless and infectious glee. At his cramped rooms, an atmosphere of benign frivolity prevails, and the premises are frequented by all manner of literary rakes and artists. It is here that I encountered the aforementioned William, a rather handsome poet possessed of an admittedly impetuous nature. Within minutes of being introduced (and under the influence of a generous bowl of claret), he was speaking to me of his undying love.

And so, we have been walking out together. As with all men, I have learned not to take too seriously his fine speeches, but William does have a particular energy and charm that appeals to my vanity. I am not immune to such encomiums coming from so fair a person, and so I am inclined to bask in the light of his admiration while there is still something about me to admire. And as my financial circumstances allow me little hope of marriage, surely a harmless flirtation should be permitted.

Yesterday, we strolled around Bloomsbury for most of the afternoon. We were hardly unchaperoned, as it seemed all of London was out enjoying the fine summer day. The shaded benches of Bedford Square were occupied almost exclusively by young lovers such as ourselves taking advantage of whatever modicum of privacy such a public garden could afford. Romance, like the buzzing of bees in the buddleia blooms, was in the air, and though I was fully aware that I was toying with a young man's affections (and he with mine), I'm sure we were both carried away by the beauty of the day and our surroundings. Oh, how lovely to be young and admired!

Next week, I move to cousin Rebecca's to join Kate and Agnes, who are coming up to London from Reydon Hall.

AUGUST 1, 1827 (BEDFORD SQUARE, LONDON)

I know what this is about. This morning, when I took cousin Rebecca her daily breakfast of warm milk and toast, she at first feigned sleep though it was well past nine o'clock. When she finally roused herself, instead of engaging me as she usually does in a lively discussion of the previous evening's events (one of her *sparkling* Bedford Square literary soirees), she merely reached a limp hand from beneath the counterpane and dismissed me with a flutter of her fingers.

It is quite apparent that my cousin does not approve of my acquaintance with Mr. Mingay of Claremont Square, the young poet who has expressed an interest in both my person and my poetry. I have been expecting this. Yesterday, when I returned from my walk with William, my sister Agnes drew me aside and, in a stern and parental tone, said that I had "been seen exchanging intimacies" (a little hand holding, a chaste kiss—nothing more, I assure you) with a young man of questionable repute, and that she had reported the matter to our cousin, who then took to her bed in the middle of the afternoon. That evening at the soiree (which I have just described as "sparkling," though "flat" is perhaps more to the point), one or two of the gentlemen guests paid me more attention than I am sure was necessary, and emboldened by my afternoon adventure and irritated by my sister's spinsterish disapproval, I allowed myself to be charmed, and though truly I am almost sick of their flattery, the laughter and blushing that ensued enlivened the evening considerably.

Despite the luxurious accommodations at Bedford Square, I am beginning to miss the less constrained atmosphere at Cheesman's. Here, a pinched air of propriety governs even the most banal daily events. When we visit, my sisters and I are expected to dress for lunch and dinner, a hardship for penniless country girls like ourselves that the wealthy Mrs. Leverton nevertheless insists upon. Cousin Rebecca is constantly coaching us in matters of comportment and etiquette, and while Kate and Agnes accept her attentions with good grace, I chafe at what I consider to be useless affectations. But in an effort to remain in my cousin's good graces, I deliver a breakfast of hot milk and toast to her rooms each morning I am here. While I greatly enjoyed provoking Agnes, I do regret that I am likely the cause of the coolness with which Rebecca bid me good night, and of this morning's rejection.

Two of my poems and a brief sketch of rural life will appear in the February 1828 issue of *La Belle Assemblée*, my first appearance in Mr. Harral's august publication. I am very excited. Although my meagre earnings will never make me wealthy, when they are combined with my sisters' efforts, we have at least been able to provide some relief to Mama's situation, surely all we can ask.

AUGUST 2, 1827

Today when I delivered my cousin's breakfast, she was ready for me, sitting up amid a cloud of pillows and reading a prayer book. (Although she is a faithful churchgoer, I had not been aware until then that her literary tastes ran in that direction.) When I entered the room and placed the tray on a low table, she put down her book, looked up at me over her spectacles and, sighing with weary condescension, asked me to sit on the edge of the bed.

"My dear Susanna," she began, "it pains me to have to say this, but your behaviour has caused much consternation in this household."

At this, I tried to protest, but she placed her hand gently over my mouth to stop my words. "I have not finished. You must hear me out." She pulled herself up and leaned forward slightly. "You know perfectly well it is not proper for a young woman of your background to draw attention to herself in this way. Those men—"

"But, cousin, they merely wished to discuss my poems and stories. You do not think for a moment I would encourage improper advances." (I was being somewhat disingenuous here, for I had felt their eyes upon me almost as keenly as I had felt William's caresses earlier in the day.)

"Susanna, do not toy with me this way. I am only too aware of your passionate nature. And while I appreciate and indeed celebrate your spirit, you must not misinterpret my sympathy for permission to misbehave. A woman in your situation has nothing but her good name to recommend her. Do not squander your most important asset. Beauty and intelligence are nothing without virtue. Indeed, beauty soon fades and a show of intelligence is not the prerogative of the fairer sex. I agree it is unjust, but there it is. I have consulted with Agnes, and we have agreed that you will return to Reydon Hall and remain in Suffolk until your infatuation with this young man has cooled, and the recent spectacle—"

"Spectacle!" I cried. "But I did nothing more than laugh and accept their—"

"Hush!" She raised her hand. "Until the recent spectacle in my drawing room has receded from memory."

With that, I was dismissed. I wish I could have told her that I am not a fool, nor was I born yesterday. I do not take Mr. Mingay's protestations of eternal passion seriously (though I rather hope his admiration for my poetry is genuine).

I do miss London, but my rural exile has not been unproductive. I have devoted myself to writing more poems and sketches for *La Belle Assemblée*. I will also have stories in the *Suffolk Chronicle* and a London annual called *The New Monthly*. They are by no means my best work, being overburdened with the sentiment and effusions of valour and romance that are so much in demand these days. Still, they should, God willing, yield a few shillings so Mama can replace her bonnet, which is so tattered and torn that she refuses to leave the house for fear the neighbours will mistake her for a common farmer's wife.

Agnes continues to curry Rebecca's favour, rather shamelessly in my opinion, and has been invited to stay for another fortnight. Mama received a letter yesterday from Agnes saying that our dear cousin has offered to finance the publication of another volume of poetry, *Worcester Field*. She (Agnes) boasted of meeting her hero, Sir Walter Scott, at a recent literary evening. She marched right up to him and introduced herself, and he, the great man, shook hands with her and complimented her on her poems! How bold she is. I should never attain such confidence in a million years.

My current project is a children's novel, *The School Boy's Friendship*, a cautionary tale about a boy who unwittingly associates with criminals. I hope that, like *Spartacus*, it will rival Kate's successes in the realm of books for children. Mr. Harral has read my nearly finished draft and pronounced it eminently publishable, though he expressed some reservations about the "dark" nature of the subject matter. It's true. I do have a fascination for the malevolence that is within us all. Katie finds my interest in such matters "disturbing" and has urged me to "look for goodness and light and to celebrate all God's miracles" lest I be dragged into the slough of despond by my oppressive imaginings.

Mr. Harral continues to inspire and encourage my sisters and me in our literary ambitions. I admit, though, that I find him rather conservative, a stalwart Anglican and fervent supporter of King George, especially regarding the Catholic question. ("We must keep the papists out of Parliament at all costs," I overheard him declare to Agnes once.) I do value his opinions and admire the strength of his convictions. But would it be sacrilege to suggest that surely one church is no better than another? I have been reading John Bunyan and I find I am in sympathy with his spiritual turmoil and his struggle to find a simpler way to worship God than through the hierarchical traditions of the Anglican Church. These matters occupy my mind rather more than I would ever have thought possible mere months ago.

Nevertheless, I realize how fortunate we are (in particular Agnes) to enjoy Mr. Harral's enthusiastic mentorship. Kate has just returned from a visit to London, where she reports she spent a "pleasant afternoon" with Francis Harral. They are not betrothed, but Anna Laura has written from London to say she is certain their union is imminent. When I suggested as much to Agnes this afternoon, she raised her dark eyebrows and muttered, "We shall see."

As for my own romantic inclinations, Mr. Mingay is completely forgotten. I was nevertheless amused to learn from Eliza that he is reported to have eloped with the daughter of a prominent bishop, and the couple has taken lodgings in Bath. I have assured both her and Agnes that I was never in danger of succumbing to such a fate.

APRIL 5, 1828 (BEDFORD SQUARE)

Francis Harral and my sister Kate are to be married. Kate is keeping her elation in check as it may be some time before the marriage can take place. Francis has plans to become a doctor first, and a medical education is lengthy and expensive. To no one's surprise, Mrs. Harral is not in favour of the match. However, her husband, Kate says, continues to overrule his wife's objections. "He says it matters not that we are penniless. The Stricklands are well-established members of the Church and the community. He has given Francis and me his blessing."

What a joy to see dear Anna Laura again. We met today for the first time since our parting last winter, and how changed she is from the pale, sad thing who waved to me then from the departing carriage. I do believe London life suits her. Her skin glows with well-being, and her person—well, country girl that I am, I never knew she possessed such style. I fussed over her hat with such enthusiasm that she took me straight to her milliner, a tiny shop with a brightly painted front window, tucked away on a narrow street near her family's new home, and ordered one just like it for me in pale blue; hers is green. We spent the rest of the afternoon walking around Bloomsbury in the sunshine, and Anna Laura chattered on about "the literary life." She is most keen to introduce me to a Scottish poet called Pringle.

APRIL 6, 1828

I have met the most fascinating individual, and after just one evening spent in his company, I am as a child wandering in the woods who, thinking she has been on the true path, finds instead that she has lost her way and yet stumbles blindly on. Oh, my restless imagination. Oh, my crass and craven soul! To think that I once wasted selfish hours agonizing over the state of my dress and the opinions of frivolous young men when there are such injustices in the world!

Mr. Thomas Pringle of Finsbury and Hampstead Heath is a poet after my own heart, a Scot who recently worked as a newspaper editor in Cape Town, South Africa, from whence he was compelled to leave before his outspoken views on that country's shameful treatment of its indigenous people, the poor oppressed Negroes, landed him in jail or worse. Here in London, he is secretary of the Anti-Slavery Society, a group I have resolved to join. At dinner last night at the spacious new townhouse in Claremont Square where Mr. Pringle and his wife, Margaret, reside, the table—which included Agnes, Kate and Francis, Anna Laura and me—sat rapt as our host condemned with quiet passion and restrained anger the terrible institution as it is practised in the American colonies and the Indies. His singular mission is to draw attention to the inhumanity of the traffic in human flesh, which, although illegal these past twenty years, continues anyway and will go on until governments such as our own ban slavery in our colonies once and for all. For the Pringles, this cause is more than mere rhetoric. Indeed, they have taken into their household a former slave from the island of Antigua called Mary Prince. I was so overcome with emotion that I asked Mr. Pringle if I might meet the woman whom they call "Black Mary," and without hesitation, she was summoned from the kitchen. Wearing a simple navy dress with white collar and cuffs, the middle-aged woman answered my questions about her impressions of England with quiet dignity. After she left, Mr. Pringle turned to me and suggested that perhaps the next time I come up to London, I might hear more of Mary Prince's story.

"I should like that," I replied.

(*La Belle Assemblée* has accepted two more of my stories, "The Little Quaker" and "I Will Be My Own Master"!)

APRIL 23, 1828

I have dined twice this week with the Pringles at their country house in Hampstead. With no children of their own, they have embraced me as a surrogate daughter, and I admit the attentions of dear "Papa"

Pringle fill a void in me that has gaped since the death of my own dear father. Agnes disapproves of many of Mr. Pringle's views, which she describes as "going against much that we hold dear," and of the fact that he is a Methodist. But I find his denunciations of "Tory smugness" refreshing. No doubt, it helps that he praises my poems extravagantly. Even so, Papa (I shall call him that from now on) applies a razor-sharp attention to the smallest detail and is teaching me to rid my work of cliché and lazy diction.

"Every word must matter," he says, "and in poetry, as in life, convention is your enemy." He is also very well connected and full of advice on how to approach publishers. As well, he asked me last night if I would undertake to transcribe Mary Prince's story of her life as a slave, with the intention of shaping the woman's own words into a narrative for publication. I have agreed.

JUNE 12, 1828 (REYDON HALL)

The calibre of Reverend Rouse-Birch's sermons continues to deteriorate alarmingly, and attendance at St. Margaret's on Sunday has gone down, it seems to me, in direct proportion to the growing inanity of his weekly message. Only a handful of the still hopeful continue to attend services in search of Christian solace, where little is to be found. Empty pews provide silent censure and are testimony to the shameful neglect of our once-vibrant Anglican parish. May God forgive me for casting aspersions on one of his servants, but at this morning's service, not only was the Reverend R-B (a nephew of the baronet of Langham, in whose possession our precious church lies) a quarter of an hour late for the nine o'clock mass, his person bore unmistakable evidence of the previous evening's post-hunt celebrations. In addition to his sour breath and a cassock so hastily donned that one corner remained tucked into his riding boot, the good reverend assaulted us with a sermon on the delights of "huntin' and fishin'" with nary a single allusion to the peril to which the souls of his parishioners are subject without spiritual comfort. I fear I cannot tolerate the situation much longer. I have made my dissatisfaction known to a recent acquaintance, the Reverend Andrew Ritchie. An old friend of Papa Pringle's, Mr. Ritchie urges me to consider the Congregational church in Wrentham, where he is pastor to a group of simple farmers and their families seeking spiritual solace in an environment free from cant and hierarchical dogma. Mr. Ritchie has been dropping by Reydon Hall every week, and we have enjoyed many enlightening conversations concerning the nature of faith. I am certain his views on the abuses of the Anglican Church would cause my staunch and proper sister Agnes to turn as purple as the English thistle. How I should like to witness that.

Kate has sold her *Sketchbook of a Young Naturalist* for the tidy sum of twelve pounds! Meanwhile, she has said nothing to me, but I have the feeling her romance with Francis Harral may be cooling.

JUNE 17, 1828 (CLAREMONT SQUARE, FINSBURY, LONDON)

June in London! Was there ever such wanton beauty in the midst of all the noise and confusion? Everywhere is a profusion of pale pinks and deep purples. Peonies bow extravagantly before the breezes; carpets of forget-me-nots spread out under the cherry trees; hydrangeas bloom with all the fury of a snowstorm. I have spent the past week with Papa and Mrs. Pringle at their house in Finsbury. It has been an unparalleled privilege to associate there with such literary and artistic lions as are too numerous to mention. These men of letters are effusive in their admiration of my modest literary efforts (a few poems and sketches here and there), so much so that I am tempted to doubt their sincerity. But like Papa Pringle, they offer only praise and encouragement. It is difficult not to swell with pride at such attentions, to feel the twin creatures, hubris and ambition, rising inside me, burgeoning monsters that care for nothing but personal glory and the approval of others. At such times, I am ashamed of my vanity, of my insatiable thirst for recognition, a force that gives no thought to the well-being of my fellow man, but is only an aggrandizement of my selfish desire for attention. I have sworn henceforth to withdraw myself from all attempts at notoriety and to employ my God-given gifts, such as they are, in the service of Him and those whose unfortunate circumstances do not allow them to speak for themselves.

Fame is a dream! The praise of man as brief
As morning dew upon the folded leaf;
The summer sun exhales the sparkling tear,
And leaves no trace of its existence here—
That world I once admired I now would flee,
And to win heaven would court obscurity.

Much to the consternation of my family, I have taken to calling myself a "nonconformist." Agnes says I am like "a madwoman and a fanatic." She said she believes I am acting out of sheer perversity and that my "spiritual crisis" is an insincere attempt to make myself the centre of attention and to create a scandal for its own sake. I do not care what she thinks.

My historical romance, "Voyage of the Sirens," is to appear in *The Keepsake*. These anthologies are expensive entertainments but not exactly high art. Still, I am ashamed to say a frisson of excitement, as automatic as a dog slavering at the sight of food, ran through me at the news. And then there is the money. How am I to reconcile the necessity of earning a living with my desire to do good? Oh, "Frailty, thy name is woman."

I spend my days as though in a dream, or more accurately, a nightmare, from which I cannot awaken. And though the terrors are not visited upon my own person, still I feel I am living through them. Each afternoon, I sit in Papa Pringle's commodious drawing room, listening to Mary Prince tell her story so that I may record it for posterity. It is a tale of unimaginable savagery. In a quiet, uninflected voice devoid of self-pity or acrimony, Black Mary relates for me and Margaret Pringle the horror of her life as a slave on the island of Antigua. Her dignified and restrained manner belies the cruelties she has endured in her four decades on this earth.

In silence, I take down her words without flourish or romance. I am merely the conduit for her simple, oppressive story. And as I write, the rain gathers on the windowpanes and runs down in rivulets that are like the combined tears of all the victims of this brutal and inhuman institution.

Mary is a gentle, unassuming creature, and I have become quite attached to her in the short time we have been together, perhaps due to the extraordinary intensity and intimacy of this literary venture. This afternoon, after describing the floggings that were a routine occurrence on the sugar plantation where she toiled, she slowly turned her back to us and, unbuttoning her chemise, let it drop to her waist. Margaret could not contain her emotion on beholding the tangle of raised welts woven onto Mary's black skin like a nest of vipers. The three of us embraced, Margaret and I weeping, not just for Mary Prince, but for the damned souls of those who would inflict such cruelty. Mary's eyes were dry. "I have no more tears," she said, retying her bodice.

I have received a proposal of marriage. Against all odds, I know, but there it is. His name is Fitzwilliam Asker, second son of Sir William Asker of Norwich, and he was recently appointed vicar of Ipswich and St. Edmundsbury.

We have known one another since childhood, he and his family occupying the pew immediately behind ours at St. Margaret's every Sunday. Can it be that the habit of gazing at the back of my head week after week so permeated his boyish imagination that when the time came to take a wife, his thoughts turned automatically to me? I had hoped there was more to it than that, but I cannot imagine why else Fitzwilliam Asker has singled me out as marriage material, since there has never been the slightest spark of recognition between us. I remember a shy boy leaning against the churchyard wall while my sisters and I held hands and danced around the bronze angel in the cemetery. If we asked him to join us, he would bury his face in his hands and run away. Since then, nothing, until he began calling on me this past July, every Saturday afternoon at 2:00 p.m. sharp.

Today, Fitzwilliam and I walked out across the lower meadow toward the river, enveloped in a weighty silence born of a mutual reluctance to broach the subject on both our minds. In the upper pasture, Ned Tilford and his family were stoking the second cut of hay, and the sounds of the boys and girls calling to one another, their scythes flashing in the cricket-filled air, reminded me of the simple virtues—hard work, piety, a joy in nature—that I so long to live by. (I resolved at that moment to visit the farmer and his family at their cottage soon so that I might become more familiar with their unassuming way of life.)

A flock of rooks surged above us like a scattering of seed, like a living cloud, blackening the air, and then they were gone. Finally, Fitzwilliam removed his hat and held it at his waist with both hands.

"Miss Strickland . . . Susanna . . . you know, I think, the purpose of my visits," he began. I nodded but did not speak. This was the moment I had been waiting for all my life, and now that it had arrived, I could not reconcile the feeling of satisfaction that flashed behind my eyes like a shooting star with the dead weight of the stone in my belly. He went on, his voice quivering, belying his outward composure, and a rush of tenderness for the boy he once was wavered inside me, then fled.

"We have been acquainted these many years," he said, "but it is only in recent months that I have come to admire . . ." Here he stumbled slightly. We had entered the woods by then, and the path was beset by a warren of exposed tree roots. Regaining his balance, Fitzwilliam continued: "I have come to recognize in you such qualities as would complement my situation . . ."

I was determined not to assist him in what was becoming a proposal of exceeding clumsiness. I had imagined professions of undying love, instead of what sounded like an offer of employment between strangers.

"As you know, I have obtained a sinecure at Ipswich and St. Edmundsbury and intend to divide my time between the two when I am not detained by family business in Norwich. Both parishes come with a plausible manse and are in need of a mistress . . . I do hope you will consider—"

"Mr. Asker," I could contain myself no longer, "is this a proposal of marriage?"

He stopped and turned to face me. "Why, yes. I suppose it is," he said, a hint of surprise in his voice, as if he had just realized his own intentions.

Right then, I was aware, despite my frequent protestations to the contrary, of how often I had dreamed of a moment something like this. We all do, don't we? Imagine the day our prince arrives? But standing there, confronted with the possibility of fulfilling my proper destiny as a woman, I felt the stone in my stomach grow heavier. Not so much at the idea of marriage, but at the prospect of this one in particular. Although I find his face and stature presentable, even fair, there is something in Mr. Asker's manner, a querulousness, a limpness in bearing that would surely be insupportable over time. Not wanting, however, to immediately discard perhaps the only such offer I may ever receive, I feigned delighted surprise and promised Mr. Asker he will have my answer within a week.

His suit is, at least superficially, entirely desirable—good family, respectable occupation, satisfactory appearance. But though I am moved by his attentions, the prospect of a shared future is difficult to contemplate. And yet I fear I have been leading him on, as I have done nothing to discourage Mr. Asker, though not much to encourage him either. It is as though I am trying to keep all doors open. But that is cruel and ridiculous. Why is it so difficult to know my own heart? Anna Laura said it best in her letter: "You cannot have it both ways, Susanna. Marry him or don't, but do not keep the poor man hanging on."

I think my friend has grown impatient with my dithering. How I wish she and I could be together. How tedious she must find my correspondence, filled as it has been with all this verbal hand-wringing. There she is, weakened by illness again, and yet I go on and on about myself. If I could face her, share my confusion, I know my dear friend would come to understand and support me. I have been tempted to take Kate into my confidence. She, like all my sisters and Mama (though I have said nothing to any of them on the subject) is clearly delighted with the possibility of my becoming Mrs. Asker, and I have been unable to bring myself to douse their expectations. Indeed, I have been carried away on the magic carpet of their unspoken though obvious excitement. Their certainty that I will accept my "young man" and drop my misguided flirtation with religious heresy is palpable. How little they know about me.

I finally decided to confide in Kate this evening during our walk (after swearing her to secrecy), and she almost exploded with happiness. "I knew it. Imagine you, Susie, a vicar's wife. How splendid. Have you told Mama?"

I sat down in the grass at the river's edge and, removing my shoes, told her I did not think I would accept him.

"Susie . . . you don't mean it. Of course you must marry." She paused and plucked a blade of tough river grass, sliding it carefully between her fingers. "Does this have anything to do with your new ideas?"

"Perhaps. Probably. I don't know." I slid my bare feet into the cool, slow-moving water. Effusions of sweet pea ruffled the opposite bank. "I have often said I would never marry, but it isn't that. Or the fact that he's a stalwart Anglican, while I . . ." I let the sentence dwindle. The sound of cowbells came to us on the breeze. "I think it's the awful predictability of a life with Fitzwilliam Asker. I want to be surprised. Is that too much to ask? When I meet him, the man I am to marry, if I ever do, I want to be carried away by my feelings." I took her hand. "Like you and Francis. When it happens, I will know."

And now I must write Mr. Asker.

JANUARY 6, 1829

My scalp is still tingling. Robert Childs, the noted phrenologist, has examined my skull and pronounced me "a creature of extremes, a child of impulse and the slave of feeling." If he only knew. Every second Monday evening, a group of us gathers at my new friend Reverend Andrew Ritchie's comfortable, if modest, home in Wrentham to discuss politics, literature and advances in scientific thought. This week's meeting turned into an experimental clinic after our special guest, Mr. Childs, asked one of us to volunteer for an examination so that he could demonstrate his technique. I, of course, jumped to his side immediately. Running his fingers through my tangled curls, he probed each nob and bump on my skull with painstaking intensity, making copious notes, while the others—our hosts, and Kate and Sarah, who had agreed to accompany me only because morbid curiosity outweighed their reluctance to set foot in the house of a "dissenter"— looked on in silence. At first, I was embarrassed at the intimacy of his touch in such a public venue, but Mr. Childs's manner was so detached, my head might as well have been a potato he was probing, and I relaxed into a kind of trance as he did his work. This new science of the brain holds much promise for the understanding of human nature.

"You are a creature of rare sensibilities, Miss Strickland," he said before offering his diagnosis. "I foresee a life of great extremes ahead of you. But you would be well advised to rein in your vanity." With two fingers of his right hand, he pressed firmly at a spot just behind and above my left ear. "This protrusion here—number ten—is the seat of self-esteem. It could prove your undoing."

"Uncanny," exclaimed Reverend Ritchie, who, now that he is my spiritual mentor, has advised me that I must cultivate patience and humility. Mr. Childs bowed slightly and rolled his protuberant eyes back into his head. He is a strange, intense fellow with tufts of black hair springing from his skull, giving him the look of a mad scientist. He offered to repeat his performance on my sister Sarah, but she turned pale at the idea and shrank into her chair.

"I'm sure the dissection of one Strickland is enough for the evening," she demurred. Mr. Childs bowed again with exaggerated courtesy.

"How," asked Mr. Ritchie, "did you come upon this knowledge, Robert? Where does one go to study the human skull?"

"Aha. When you are next in London, you must visit my skullery and I will show you my collection of human specimens and diagrams of my scientific research."

He issued this invitation with a twisted grin, rubbing his hands together in a most unsettling manner. Apparently, the distinguished Professor Childs obtains his experimental material through connections he has at Bedlam and other houses of misery. The thought sent a shiver of disgust and fascination through me. Despite his obvious eccentricities, I fully intend to take advantage of his hospitality when I am next in London. (Agnes derides my enthusiasm for what she calls "the unproven fantasies of a fanatic.")

All during our long, cold trip home from Wrentham, a feeling of wonder lingered in my brain. The rain ceased soon after we set out, and an infinity of stars embroidered the night sky, giving some guidance to poor mouse-coloured Mrs. Dushfoot as she trudged homeward with her shivering passengers. We took turns leading the ass and huddling together in the little cart, our way lit by the silvery puddles underfoot. As we lurched homeward at a pace that would have given the proverbial tortoise pause, I wrapped my cloak tighter, feeling feverish with thoughts of the evening's entertainment, and I found myself captive to the mysterious, uncertain night. A chill, not of cold but as if from beyond the grave, went through me. And as I gazed up at the bottomless night sky, a vision unbidden penetrated my mind—a vision of my dear brother Sam out there somewhere amid the dark, impenetrable forests and the wild, rapid rivers of Canada. I distinctly felt something, some incorporeal being, tugging at my collar, causing the back of my neck to prickle. Then it was gone. So stark and real was this premonition that I gripped Kate's arm cruelly, causing her to cry out.

"Do you believe in Sympathies?" I whispered loudly.

"Of course not." She shrugged out of my grasp. "Don't be a goose."

"No, please, I mean it. Sam, our little brother Sam, is thinking of us now, out there in the vast wilderness. I can feel—"

"Susanna, stop this. I will not stand for it another minute. You are frightening me."

"Oh, I do believe it." I threw my arms around her and leaned my head against her breast. "I believe there is a secret intelligence that unites us through our thoughts with absent loved ones and friends. Can't you feel it? Shhh."

Perhaps to humour me, Kate paused for a few seconds as if to listen. Sarah, who was leading the donkey, giggled nervously, then clucked loudly, urging the animal on. I thought I would swoon, so profound was my joy at the aura enveloping me on that starry night. My sisters were not persuaded. Sarah snorted.

"Susanna, either your imagination has taken possession of your senses or you have a fever. It's time we put you to bed with a hot toddy.

"Get on, you lazy ass!" She gave Mrs. Dushfoot a brisk swat on the behind just as the reassuring chimneys of Reydon Hall came into view above the trees.

I passed a long night of vivid dreams and awoke this morning with a burning throat and Katie's cool hand upon my forehead.

"Be still, Susie. You are on fire. Rest."

But I cannot. Still in the fog of heightened perception, I have penned these lines:

Say didst thou never feel within thy soul
That strange mysterious link which doth unite
The thoughts and sympathies of absent friends
Bringing them back though distant to the view
All fresh with the realities of life?
Oceans may flow between us but the soul

Bound in this viewless chain can traverse space
And hold communion with a kindred spirit
E'en in the cold dark chambers of the tomb.

Another stimulating evening at Mr. Ritchie's. The discussion was lively indeed, as our host held forth most convincingly on the subject of religious freedom and the virtues of the Congregationalist Church. The reverend objects strenuously to our having to pay taxes that solely support the Anglican Church when free-thinking dioceses such as his own modest, nonconformist chapel must go begging. I have attended services there the past two Sundays and have been impressed with the quiet dignity and simplicity of worship.

Agnes tells me I have turned into a pious bore. Katie refuses to discuss religious matters with me. She (and the others) steadfastly adheres to the tedious and pretentious rituals at St. Margaret's, while I walk the three miles to Wrentham to spend the Sabbath among common folk for whom I am developing a growing affection. There is something pure about singing hymns without the ponderous moaning of an organ or the distraction of hymnals. The sight of the young men in their homespun—their faces ruddy, their feet bare and dirty with the grime of honest labour, singing with the lusty enthusiasm of true disciples—sends tingles through the very centre of my being.

At lunch today, Agnes scolded me for giving up my Sunday school class at St. M's, but truly, I have always loathed ramming the catechism into the spoiled, overfed little dunces of the neighbourhood. It is certainly not my calling. She is apparently so concerned with my spiritual well-being that she came to my room again this afternoon to plead her case for the Church of England. At first, her tone was patient, cajoling, but when I pulled the counterpane over my head, she lost her temper.

"For heaven's sake, Susanna, give up this dalliance with, with the devil. What about your reputation?" (Speaking of pious bores . . .) "Consider us, your family. You are the talk of the neighbourhood. And what's more, you look like a common strumpet lately. It's one thing to consort with the rabble, but must you resemble them as well? For the love of whatever God it is you are worshipping these days, do something about your hair and dress. You would be well advised to spend less time on prayers and more on grooming."

And become a preening, self-satisfied society matron like you? I wanted to say. "Fine clothes and curls are nothing to me!" I retorted. "They are the stuff of vanity and self-indulgence. I can assure you, Sister, our dear Lord is unimpressed with such matters."

It seems everyone is against me. Mr. Harral has rejected my story "The Curate's Daughter," saying it is too "didactic." And when I showed it to Papa Pringle, he concurred gently, saying it is not my best work, although he, like Reverend Ritchie, supports and encourages my wish to find a better path to true goodness and redemption.

(How cruel of Agnes to say such things about my hair. She knows these impossible locks are my nemesis. She can take her crowning glory and stuff it in her bonnet for all I care!)

JANUARY 30, 1829

Smith and Elder have accepted my *Enthusiasm* poems. I think this is the most important work I have ever done, a tribute to the simple faith of the unlearned and those of low estate. When I showed the poems to Agnes, she said if they are published, she will have nothing more to do with me. I do not care, for they express what is in my heart, the true way to God.

Harp of the soul, by genius swept, awake!
Inspire my strains, and aid me to portray
The base and joyless vanities which man
Madly prefers to everlasting bliss!
—Enthusiasm, and Other Poems

Yesterday, on a moonless, starless, rain-filled night, I attended the chapel at Wrentham, and after a beautiful service and touching sermon, as I quietly prayed at the back of the chapel, my heart humbled by the enormity of what I was about to undertake, Reverend Ritchie walked down the aisle to where I sat and placed his hand lightly upon my bowed head.

"Come, child, and be received by our Lord Jesus Christ so that you may find everlasting peace."

There were tears in my eyes as I turned my face up to his, and I felt a release deep inside me such as I have never before known, as though my free will had been taken from me and placed in the hands of a gentle and forgiving God.

"Yes, Father," I whispered, and I rose and followed him to the vestry, where he left me alone while he read to the congregation my reasons for dissent from the church of my birth, and then proposed me as a member. As I listened, there was no joy in my heart, for I understood too well how this decision would alienate me from my old friends and family. All that is left to me is a deep conviction that our Saviour would surely bless this simpler form of worship, and the knowledge that I am following my conscience. With unusual tenderness, the reverend gave me his arm and led me to stand before the congregation as their clear voices rose in a torrent of song, "My Shepherd Will

Supply My Need," welcoming me into their midst. So great was the storm of emotion in my heart that I covered my face with my hands and wept, whether with joy or sadness I cannot say. Perhaps both. (*No more a stranger, nor a guest, but like a child at home.*)

And thus I have severed forever my ties with England's church. I regret the shock this has been to Mama and my sisters, but it is beyond my control; it is the will of God. Agnes's only response has been an icy and unbending silence. Poor Katie is distraught at the rupture and has pleaded with both of us not to let these matters of conscience come between us. Sometimes I fear my sweet sister's naïveté is boundless.

APRIL 23, 1829

Kate woke me this morning, bearing an astringent message from Agnes. I was barely awake when she knocked, and she let herself in before I could raise my head from the pillow. Wringing her small hands and leaning against the door jamb, she began in a voice quivering with distress.

"I am to tell you," she said, "that until you abandon this preposterous campaign to discredit the Strickland name, you will henceforth take all your meals here, alone in your room . . ."

"I beg your pardon?" I said.

She nodded and her face started to crumple. "It's Agnes, Susie. She is apoplectic over your conversion. They all are. But Agnes . . ." She threw up her hands and sat down heavily on the side of my bed. "Why, Susie? Why are you doing this? I can't bear it. Mama says she is ashamed to set foot in St. Margaret's. She will not leave her room. Agnes calls it heresy—"

"Heresy? Don't be ridiculous. Is this really necessary? Sarah declared herself a Quaker more than a year ago, and none of you so much as caught your breath. My beliefs are my own affair. Why do Mama and Agnes care so much? Why do you?"

"I don't. You know I don't. But I cannot bear such animosity between my sisters. I feel crushed under the weight of it. And as for Sarah, her beliefs are her own affair. No one takes any notice. But you, Susanna, you know perfectly well you are a celebrated authoress now. What you do and say matters to people." She clasped her hands together as if in prayer.

"Katie," I said, "sometimes I think Agnes will do anything to silence me. I believe she considers herself the only poetess in this family, that she is jealous of my successes."

Kate covered her face with her hands. "And when your *Enthusiasm* poems appear, what then? I think Agnes will explode."

"That would be one solution," I observed, and threw back the bedclothes.

"The Harrals too are most distressed at your conversion," she continued in a small voice. "Mr. Harral says he fears for your sanity. And, Susie, you must be aware that this has only given Mrs. Harral more ammunition in her campaign against me. I fear they may withdraw their consent altogether."

I had not considered this. Indeed, the entire affair has caused far more gnashing of teeth than I ever expected. But I have taken a stand and I cannot back down now. Can I? Oh dear. Is it my pride or my principles that I am defending?

"I'm sure it will not come to that, Katie," I said. "Now, please leave me alone."

Later, I met Agnes in the front hall as she was preparing to leave for London. She brushed by me with no acknowledgement at all. It's going to be a long, cold spring.

I am staying with Cheesman, the only relative who will have me since my descent into certain damnation. I am *persona non grata* at cousin Rebecca's, and Eliza and Agnes continue to have nothing to do with me. Mama sighs and sputters when I am around. Thank heavens Kate, Sarah and Jane are not so judgmental. And if it were not for Papa Pringle, whose support has been unconditional, I am sure I should not have been able to cling to my convictions this long.

Anna Laura has remained loyal despite her father's disapproval. She has grave reservations about the direction my beliefs have taken, but after long discussions, she says she can see they are the result of a great deal of soul-searching on my part. I appreciate her patience and understanding, and at the risk of giving her false hope, I have assured her not to despair, that I may yet return to my senses. And so we have agreed not to discuss the matter further. A relief. Rebellion can be so tiring. She visits me here when she feels strong enough, and if it isn't raining, we walk around Bloomsbury and talk and talk. Like me, Anna Laura does not think she will marry, though for different reasons.

"I doubt I will live long enough," she said the last time we met. The words caught me by surprise and I could see she regretted them immediately. Her obvious fragility and the polite but persistent coughing are things we do not speak of. I worry terribly about her health, but she always dismisses my concern. This admission of weakness was unlike her. I tried to make a joke.

"Now that would be taking the easy way out," I said.

"Perhaps you're right." She laughed. "I should miss you, though."

"And I you." An uncomfortable silence ensued. We passed an old man in Bedford Park selling roasted chestnuts from a cart. I bought a bag and we found a bench and sat down, scorching our fingers as we tried to peel them.

"Promise me something?"

"Anything," I said.

"Promise me that whichever of us goes first will come back, will appear somehow from the other side."

These words unloosed a flutter in my throat like a sparrow trapped in a chimney. "I promise," I said.

"And I too."

MAY 13, 1830 (REYDON HALL)

My darling Anna Laura is with the angels. Why is it that the most resilient natures are so often the most fragile in body? As though God endows the frailest people with a compensating spiritual strength. Despite our rupture over my nonconformist beliefs, I have written her father to express my condolences. She was the light of his life. Both Kate and I are bereft and have been doing our best to console one another. With the coming of warmer weather, Anna Laura had seemed so much better, but then, unaccountably, her cough worsened and she was gone within three days.

She was the dearest of friends to us both. It seems impossible that she was here, in all her freshness and laughter, and now there is nothing except the sense of her in the breezes that lift the curtains of my bedroom window, in every flower that blooms. Her very absence is like a living thing.

The funeral was last week. Kate and I travelled up from Reydon. She was not invited to sit with the family, and so we remained discreetly at the back of the chapel. It was the first time I have attended an Anglican service in more than a year, and the familiar music and ritual touched me in places I had forgotten about. I deeply regret the awkwardness between me and the Harrals, and the ways in which my behaviour may be contributing to my sister's woes. Kate's engagement to Francis shows no sign of culmination. They have been betrothed for two years and have yet to set a date. The subject is a sensitive one, but I decided that after we returned to Reydon Hall, I would raise it anyway.

In the end, Kate brought it up. We were climbing the hill overlooking the orchard, now a sea of apple blossoms, a sight as matrimonial as nature has ever provided. We stood contemplating the perfection of the morning, and Kate took my hand in hers.

"I know he loves me, Susie, and I am certain the impediments to our happiness—"

"I fear I am one of them."

"Yes." She smiled and walked on ahead of me. "Having a heretic for a sister has not exactly endeared me to Mrs. Harral. But I have come to believe nothing about me pleases her. You are a small part of it. I know we will sort it out in due course. Let's not cloud this beautiful morning with any further speculation."

And so I let the matter drop. But my actions have caused so much woe that I cannot tell if God is testing my new faith or condemning it. He cannot be on both sides at once.

One good thing: Agnes asked if I would consider collaborating with her on a literary project. Of course I accepted. Not a word was said about our differences. We are to compose a collection of eight poems, four each, in celebration of England and the monarchy. It is to be called *Patriotic Songs*, and our lyrics will be set to music and published by J. Green of Soho. With Agnes's growing notoriety as a writer and my own modest successes, we have high hopes the project will prove lucrative. I am certain Kate had a hand in this unexpected reconciliation. How else to explain Agnes's change of heart? The forgiving spirit of Anna Laura lives on though she is gone.

PART THREE
1830–1832
LOVE AND MARRIAGE

How quickly things change! Yesterday, I was resigned to the prospect of lifelong spinsterhood, the gradual but inevitable slide into the shrill and severe domain of the unmarried middle-aged woman. And today, in my twenty-seventh year, I find myself the object of one man's ardent courtship. Today, I am like a girl again, blushing and foolish, my heart so stirred that I can scarcely eat or sleep or concentrate. All morning, I have been preening and battling my wretched tangled curls, trying to tame them into some semblance of order. I have changed from one to the other of my only two decent, albeit threadbare, afternoon dresses so many times that I have torn the best one and now must settle on the pale green muslin, so hopelessly out of fashion that I blush with shame. Yesterday, I could not have cared a whistle for the state of my wardrobe. Yesterday, I would have sneered at any of my sisters for displaying such vanity. Today, I am the perfect example of feminine frivolity. Can this be happening?

John Wedderburn Dunbar Moodie. How to begin? He is six years older than I am. And short, shorter than me by a scant few inches. Sturdy—no, muscular; strong from a decade spent wrestling sustenance from the arid soils of his South African farm. (Already, I know all this about him, and that he fought against Bonaparte and was grievously wounded. His left wrist bears the scar.)

Chestnut brown hair. A weathered complexion and dancing blue eyes. A ready smile, infectious laugh. A Scot of ancient, distinguished lineage. A writer and lover of books and ideas. An excellent flautist. Ebullient, voluble, charming where I am reticent and intense. He called on the Pringles without notice yesterday afternoon. Mr. Moodie and Papa P. knew one another well in South Africa and worked together diligently to curb the evils of the slave trade. My patron had no idea Mr. Moodie was in London and received his unexpected visitor joyfully. We had just sat down to tea.

"Moodie! My most excellent and dear friend," exclaimed Papa, leaping from his chair as the maid ushered the ruddy-faced stranger into our midst. After a hasty introduction, Papa clapped his comrade on the back and bade him join us—Margaret and me and Mary Prince, who has begun taking tea with us at Papa's insistence. Her status in the household is somewhere between servant and poor relation, and whereas it would be unthinkable to extend such liberties to a common housemaid, there is something so noble in the former slave's bearing that she seems to belong to a class all her own. In any case, I am becoming accustomed to this breach of convention, but I thought I detected a brief ripple of surprise cross Mr. Moodie's brow as he realized he was to sit down with a Negro. Papa Pringle seemed oblivious.

"My dear Moodie. What on earth brings you back to civilization? Why, only this morning I was thinking of you, picturing you outrunning elephants on foot and chasing thieving Bantus across the veldt."

Mr. Moodie laughed heartily. "Why yes, sir, I am so worn out from wrestling lions with my bare hands and fording crocodile-choked rivers that I felt sorely in need of a rest, so here I am returned to your tame and gentle city environs, to take tea and biscuits in the company of beautiful ladies." He raised his teacup and, to my astonishment and discomfiture, fixed his sapphire eyes directly on my own, holding my gaze in a most direct and brazen manner until I could only lower mine and pray that my blush was not as noticeable as it felt.

It seems Mr. Moodie is in London to locate a publisher for a book he is writing about his African adventures. Later, while the maid and Mary Prince were clearing the tea things and Mr. and Mrs. Pringle were occupied in the front parlour, I stood by the French doors, looking out onto the bustle of Claremont Square, at the comings and goings of people and carriages, both fashionable and rudimentary, a veritable hive of activity, of business and civility, playing out under a benevolent late-afternoon sun. I was reflecting on how good it was to be alive and part of all this, and I did not notice Mr. Moodie approaching until he stood close behind me.

"It is a fine sight indeed," he said softly.

And when I turned quickly, I found he was looking not out the window, but rather directly into my eyes again. I felt myself colour.

"Walk out onto the terrace with me," he said without preamble. "It is such a glorious day, it seems a shame to remain indoors."

We let ourselves out and stood holding the railing in silence while a warm breeze tousled the peonies in the garden below and street hawkers called out to passersby. Standing closer than was necessary or even acceptable, Mr. Moodie spoke quietly and urgently.

"Miss Strickland, forgive my forwardness, but I am a man of action, and I must declare without hesitation that finding you here, a guest in the home of my great friend Mr. Pringle, seems to have more to do with fate than mere accident. I beg you to indulge my forthrightness, but I should like to see you again soon. Tomorrow, if it can be arranged."

I, who am seldom at a loss for words, found myself as tongue-tied as a two-year-old. When I had recovered my composure, I replied,

"Mr. Moodie, I should like that very much." And so we arranged to take a stroll on Hampstead Heath this very afternoon.

And now the aftermath. Oh, what a tempest of confusion, joy and ecstasy courses through my veins as I contemplate my excursion with dearest Moodie. (Dare I, dare I call him that so soon? Is this madness?) And yet in the centre of my being, there burns a hot flame which hours of prayer and two glasses of wine have done nothing to extinguish.

The situation is almost laughable: a man I met only yesterday declaring his undying love for me. Me! The world-weary woman of letters, whose purpose is set upon a life of ideas and virtue and good works, is ready all at once to throw everything away and vanish into the wilderness of the heart. Laughable! And laugh we did. Indeed, we did. Strolling up the Sandy Road toward Parliament Hill, the gorse and hawthorn in glorious full bloom, with Moodie taking my hand and I, unresisting, trotting by his side like an adoring puppy, he prattled non-stop about his farm in the Cape Colony. A miserable, barren outpost if there ever was one, though my Moodie described the isolation and the hard-scrabble existence with such enthusiasm and good humour at his own expense that whatever trials he has encountered seem as nothing to him now.

"But oh, Susanna, when you see the sun rise over the veldt on a winter morning, the sky as wide as the universe, pulsating rose and orange above the banyan trees, it makes a few blisters and a diet of millet and sorghum seem as manna from heaven." And with that, he ran ahead of me, leaving the path to collapse in a heap in the long grass, feigning the attitude of an exhausted farmer overcome with fatigue and exertion.

"Mr. Moodie, are you all right?" I exclaimed, whereupon he exploded in laughter and pulled me to the ground beside him, reaching out to pluck a handful of forget-me-nots and cowslips, which he placed in my hands with such charming mock ceremony that I fell into a fit of giggling. Before us, in the distance, we could see the dome of St. Paul's, and all around us, the Heath buzzed with the inevitability of summer and the promise of love. Sitting up and leaning on one arm, Moodie pulled me to him and kissed me on the mouth, and I responded with an ardour such as I had no idea I possessed. I tremble just thinking about it. So powerful was the current running through me that I jumped to my feet at once.

"Oh, Susanna," Moodie groaned as he stood too, and I fell into his arms once more.

On the walk back to the Pringles', we were as familiar as though we had known one another for years, not mere hours. Moodie regaled me with hair-raising tales of running away to join the army at sixteen, of engaging Boney's troops in Holland, of the foggy magic of his boyhood on the island of Hoy in the Orkneys. For an entire afternoon, I thought nothing of myself and the constraints of my pinched existence, aware only of his voice and the rhythm of my beating heart.

Ye are wither'd, sweet buds! But love's hand can portray,
On memory's tablets, each delicate hue,
And recall to my bosom the long happy day,
When he gathered ye, fresh sprinkled over with dew.
Ah, never did garland so lovely appear,
For his warm lip had breath'd on each beautiful flower,
And the pearl on each leaf was less bright than the tear,
That gleamed in his eyes, in that rapturous hour.

I have called it "Lines on a Bunch of Withered Flowers Gathered on Hampstead Heath."

JUNE 10, 1830

Indeed, yes, John Dunbar Moodie is courting me. Courting me with such enthusiasm that I wonder if in his romantic delirium, he is making me up, conjuring a goddess when it is only me, the same skinny, thin-lipped, dark-haired spinster who looks back at me from the glass each day, the once proud authoress, now reduced to a blushing, stammering idiot in the face of my suitor's fine words. A note arrived this morning in his assured, unhesitating hand: "My whole soul is absorbed in one sweet dream of you—you must be mine . . ." and "let me press you to my heart and I will live upon those dear lips . . ." Dear Lord, my hand shakes and my face burns. It is laughable. Me! And yet he has awakened in me a longing over which reason has no sway.

I cannot wait for Kate to meet him. I wonder what she will think.

JUNE 12, 1830

We dined this evening at the Pringles', and I cannot remember a time that Papa and Margaret's dining room reverberated with such gaiety and energy. Moodie's vivid tales of hunting elephants and leopards and snakes had all of us so rapt that the roast beef grew cold on our plates and the trifle was forgotten. How brave he is, how drawn to the thrill of danger. Listening to his stories there in a cocoon of candle-light and conviviality, I shivered at the thought of what I know in truth must have been more ordeal than adventure. Moodie has spoken to me in quieter moments of the loneliness of his African years, when his nearest English neighbour was more than twenty-five miles distant and, he said, "I lived without human contact, and my very ideas became confused for want of intellectual companionship."

Still—excited by his memories, perhaps—he talked tonight of returning someday and held my eyes with his across the table in a manner so filled with portent that I looked away in confusion.

After supper, Moodie played Scottish airs on his flute and I struggled to accompany him at the pianoforte, while Papa and the girls executed admirably credible renditions of Highland dances. We were still flushed with happy exertion when our guest got up to leave. While Moodie went to retrieve my wrap, Papa took me aside and, placing a fatherly hand on the small of my back, leaned down to kiss my cheek. "You are a woman of no small talent, Susanna," he whispered. "Do not let yourself be distracted by vanity and convention."

His face was grave and kindly, but his words took me by surprise. I was about to ask what he meant when Moodie returned, laughing and exuberant. He wrapped my shawl about my shoulders and shook hands with our host before we tripped out into the lamp-lit streets so that we could say goodbye properly before I returned and went to bed.

JUNE 22, 1830

John Moodie has asked me to marry him and, throwing caution and prudence to the four winds, I have accepted. Next week, we will travel to Reydon so he can ask Mama for permission—a touching formality, I'm sure. I can hardly imagine her delight and surprise when she learns her youngest daughter will be the first to wed. The only cloud, and it is a small one, a passing shadow, was Kate's muted reaction to the news. When my sisters Eliza, Agnes and Kate met my intended last week at a luncheon arranged by cousin Rebecca, I could tell they were charmed, as everyone is, by his energy and affability, especially Agnes. Moodie paid her particular attention, knowing as he does of our previous antagonisms. She told me later he reminds her of our dear father, "a man of purpose, good humour and genuine principles. And a committed Presbyterian, Susanna, which is important, don't you think?"

But Kate—the sister my beloved knows is dearest to my heart—was not as easily won over. I can only assume she sees Moodie as a rival to my affection for her. She shook his hand and then, rather pointedly, I thought, and without preamble, began asking about his writing: What was the book he was working on? Who was his publisher? Did he think there is much interest in Africa? Her cross-examination went beyond mere interest and contained a vein of wariness that was unlike my usually trusting sister. To his credit, Moodie took her questions at face value, and in the end, Kate too was disarmed by his candour and seriousness, the latter a side of him I admit I have not often seen. Afterwards, she said she found him to be "courteous and well-intentioned. He will make a fine husband, Susie."

Perhaps it was too much to expect her joy would match my own, but as I saw Kate struggling to put on a brave face, I knew that my good fortune had compounded her own growing disappointment.

"Katie, I know how this must make you feel. I wish, at least . . . I think Francis . . ." I struggled not to sound condescending.

"Don't, Susanna. Your gain is not my loss. But sometimes it is hard to be around such happiness. I am trying."

"I only want you to love each other as I love both of you." As I said this, I knew it was untrue. Moodie's love is the last thing I want to share with anyone.

She gave me a look of sad exasperation. "In time, I know Mr. Moodie will be like a brother to me. But he will be *your* husband. You must tend to that."

JULY 3, 1830 (REYDON HALL)

Mama has given her consent (how old-fashioned those words sound), but not without reservation, it seems—a development I had not anticipated. I was certain her relief at being divested of one of her gaggle of chicks would know no bounds. Instead, this solemn occasion was solemn indeed.

Katie and I waited in the garden after Moodie let himself into the drawing room to make his intentions known. The afternoon was grey, the air humid and still, and we sat on the stone bench under the shelter of the magnolia tree in case it should rain. But nothing as fickle as the weather could squelch my excitement.

"Oh, Katie, I so wish Papa was with us. He would have loved John Moodie. I know he would have."

My sister smiled. She really has been trying. She slipped her arm through mine and leaned into me. "I am so happy for you, Susie. Love has made you more beautiful than ever."

"Don't be a silly," I returned. "Love has made me into a simpleton. I can scarcely think a coherent thought, and other than a few overwrought love poems, I have not put pen to paper in weeks."

She squeezed me harder and said nothing, but I could hear in the lightness of her laughter a peal of sadness.

"Where do you think you and Mr. Moodie will be wed?" she asked.

"Oh," I said, pulling my feet up onto the bench and hugging my knees through my skirt. "Yes. That."

It was a good question. I am embarrassed to admit that my non-conformist fervour has given way lately to passions of a different sort. After all the trouble my conversion has caused her, Kate has almost as much invested in it as I do. I can hardly contemplate my own fickleness. Moodie, though not deeply religious, is deeply, deeply connected to the church. He treats my flirtation with "the dissenters" as just that, a youthful aberration, and seems to take it for granted I will tire of it soon enough. I have not disabused him of this. Can I really be so shallow?

"We haven't made plans," I replied, "but I am certain it will be an

Anglican ceremony. It is what he wants, as well as what the law warrants." I kept my eyes straight ahead as I said these words, not wanting to see Katie's expression.

But in her generous way, she merely gave me a warm hug and murmured, "Welcome back to the fold, my darling. Mama and the others will be so relieved." She paused. "It appears you have become a convert to John Dunbar Moodie."

Just then, Moodie burst out through the scullery door, tripping and nearly falling over a basket of freshly dug carrots. "There you are, my darling." He pulled me to my feet and kissed me firmly on the mouth. His handsome face was flushed with excitement, and I noticed with absurd delight that his vest buttons were unaligned like a little boy's. My fond heart lurched happily. "My dearest soon-to-be Mrs. Moodie." He grinned at Katie and hugged her too. "Your mama would like to speak to you. Go now." He pushed me lightly. "Go."

Mama remained seated when I entered, her back half turned toward me, her gaze fixed on the empty hearth.

"Well, Mama?" I finally inquired into the lengthening silence.

"My dear, I am very happy for you. I am sure Mr. Moodie will make a fine husband. He is a gentleman of good family and high moral character."

"Thank you, Mama," I replied without fanfare for I could tell by her tone and the set of her mouth, her lips rolled in like a clamshell, that there was a caveat to her good wishes.

"You understand I would do nothing to stand in the way of your happiness," she continued, turning to face me, "but I must ask, how on earth will you live?"

I sighed and fairly flopped into the chair opposite her. "I know, Mama, I know. He is not a wealthy man, but—"

"To put it mildly. I have questioned him closely on this matter, and Mr. Moodie may be rich in charm and character, but his military pension provides him with an income far too confined to support a wife."

"I have my writing. Just this week, I placed another poem in *La Belle Assemblée* . . ."

"Susanna, really, my dear."

"All right, I know it's not much. But Mr. Moodie still has his farm in South Africa, and we are considering returning there as soon as he can raise the capital." As I uttered these words, I knew they were a lie. Moodie and I have never discussed the possibility. Africa? The very idea fills me with horror.

"Don't be absurd, Susanna. Africa? A young woman of your background? It's out of the question."

"Mama—"

"And what do you mean 'raise the capital'? How?" she asked.

"In a few weeks, Mr. Moodie intends to visit Scotland to petition his relatives. His uncle has extensive land holdings. And there is an elderly aunt of whom he is very fond; he is hopeful one of them will support our venture."

Mama smiled a little sadly and took my hands in hers. "Then I'm sure you will find a way, Susanna. I will not oppose you. You have always been the most determined of all my children, and Moodie is a good man. But not Africa. Please. Now go and tend to your poems; you have a trousseau to save for."

I had expected her to be proud of me, the first of her daughters to marry, but there was little sign of that, just her usual preoccupation with money and appearances. The old vagueness returned and she dismissed me as though she had already lost interest in the whole affair. But she is right: we don't have a plan. We talk about everything, my fiancé and me—books, music, politics, ideas—but other than ill-formed literary schemes and Moodie's faint hope of some kind of inheritance, we have no idea how we shall live. On love? I left the meeting feeling more subdued than I have since this romantic adventure began.

AUGUST 19, 1830

A letter from my soldier! To think, just days ago his ship sailed past Southwold and my dear Moodie peered into the fog and imagined me walking alone on the beach.

"Kind heaven give me only your love; I ask no more from this world to make me happy!"

My intended has left for the Highlands with high hopes that his pleas for family support will be fruitful. But I fear that as the youngest of four sons whose ancestral home was sold years ago to pay off debts, he'll find his optimism may not be enough. Before his departure, he set about singing the praises of life on the African veldt. I knew this would come up eventually. When I immediately objected, we came close to quarrelling, and not wanting to send him away with a stain between us, I promised to consider his proposition. But in my heart, I cannot imagine leaving my beloved England for what by all accounts is a hot, dusty outpost overrun with snakes and tigers . . . and slaves. My spirit rebels at the prospect. As much as I pine for my dearie's return, I am filled with melancholy at the thought of ever leaving the comfort of the walls and gardens, meadows and streams I have known since childhood. And yet, the life of poverty facing us on English soil—a half-pay military officer and his scribbling wife—is a comfortless alternative.

Another revolution in France! It is fifteen years since Napoleon Bonaparte went into exile and the Bourbons were reinstated. And now this. They say the streets of Paris are running with blood, King Charles has fled the country and he is hiding here in England, in a castle somewhere in Devon. The situation fills me with fears that Moodie's regiment may be called up again.

I must try not to worry. These golden days at Reydon, with Mama tending her roses, and Agnes and Jane composing odes to imaginary heroines, are for me a welcome hiatus from the blue-stocking strivings of London and all it stands for. A life of wifely domesticity holds more appeal than I would ever have imagined. Is it possible that my true vocation lies in service, not to a stern and ascetic God, but to my lifelong and only husband? And what of my writing?

Speaking of which: I have sent prospectuses of *Enthusiasm, and Other Poems* to Papa Pringle to distribute among the London literati. My hopes for an enthusiastic critical reception and a craven desire that sales may yield enough income to purchase wedding clothes are at odds with the poems' humble genesis. Am I a failed idealist or nothing more than a rank hypocrite?

SEPTEMBER 10, 1830

The Reverend Ritchie called this morning, walking all the way from Wrentham. It was such a fine late-summer day that after he took a glass of cider and some bread and butter with Sarah and me (Mama and Agnes declined to join us), I offered to accompany him partway home. I was eager to have Mr. Ritchie alone to try to explain my truancy from the Congregationalist flock (it is less than a year since my conversion and yet I have not seen him or any of my new friends in nearly two months). But before I could raise the matter, he launched into a sermon about the weakness of the flesh and the higher spiritual calling to which I had so passionately committed such a short time ago.

"Miss Strickland, you cannot imagine how much we miss you," he concluded, his battered bowler clutched to his bosom. "Marriage is a desirable state, but there are other ways to serve the Lord."

With that, he laid a heavy hand on my bowed head until I thought he would push me to my knees. Stepping back from his ministrations, I curtseyed quickly and dutifully promised to attend services this Sunday. I left him at a bend in the road, just at the spot where the plain red church with its rows of watchful windows comes into view. Its simple presence shamed me, and as I turned toward home, I was filled with confusion and guilt. In my bewilderment, I left the road and took a shortcut across the meadow, only to find the fields thick with sharp grasses and burrs, so that my skirt and stockings are nearly ruined.

A letter from Moodie was waiting for me at home and it seems there is hope. His uncle, Sir Alex Dunbar, has welcomed his grand-nephew and urges us to move to Orkney to be near him. I am suffering my fiancé's absence keenly and am so hungry for his return that I sometimes think I should be happy with John Moodie anywhere, whether under the burning suns of Africa or building a nest among the eagles of my hero's native land. Later, I lay on my bed, trying to imagine the swirling storms on the craggy isle of Hoy, and to picture us together amid the rocks and windy seas. But try as I might, the vision would not hold.

OCTOBER 3, 1830

The History of Mary Prince is to appear as a pamphlet early in the new year. Of course, my name will not be attached, as it is to be Mary's story, told in her own words, an authenticity I tried very hard to achieve. Although the small publication is not officially sanctioned by the Anti-Slavery Society, Papa Pringle has great hopes for its salutary effect upon the good citizens of England in advancing the

Abolitionist cause, and for whatever the profits from its sales can do to provide for Mary and her family. I confess I cannot help but feel proud of this small anonymous endeavour. With *Enthusiasm*, on the other hand, I am less than enthused, possibly because my enthusiasm for the nonconformists has waned somewhat since its writing. My mother and sisters will be appalled, I know, when my poems appear in print. Still, though my religious fervour has cooled, my heart yet goes out to the low-born, unlearned congregation at Wrentham, where, true to my word, I attended services last Sunday and was welcomed with a warmth and sincerity that surely I do not deserve.

NOVEMBER 30, 1830

It is almost six weeks since I injured my foot climbing down from the stile leading to the north pasture. The lower step gave way as I put my weight on it. It has been five years since Sam left for the wilds of Canada, and without his stout heart and strong back, the fences, like everything else here at Reydon, are in a chronic state of disrepair. A twisted ankle has kept me confined to this couch for so long now that I fear Dr. Lay is mistaken and that I did, in fact, break some bones after all. In any case, two bottles of medicine and as many boxes of pills have done nothing to change my situation except to render my purse lighter by a pound. Poor Moodie may be forced to marry me in my chemise.

How I long to be in London again. Still, even as I chafe at my forced inactivity, it has given me ample opportunity to write. My sonnet ("The Boudoir") has been accepted by Mr. Ackermann's literary annual, the *Forget-Me-Not*, and I have completed a tale based on Moodie's African adventures ("The Vanquished Lion"), which I shall also submit to Ackermann. At present, I am working on a story about a man whose miserliness estranges him from his son.

Opposition here in Suffolk to the Duke of Wellington's heavy-handed pressure for reform has led to riots in Bungay and Yoxford. I am much concerned about the King's failure to attend the Mayor's Day Procession for fear of violent disturbance. I do wish he would take a bold step and stand up to his unruly opponents. History is taking place and here I languish with a broken foot!

December 6, 1830

Today, my twenty-seventh birthday has passed without comment. No good wishes from my beloved or my family. Sometimes I wonder if I even exist.

December 15, 1830

Oh, how dreary and dark the days are. As I grow thinner and sadder, Moodie writes home of his perilous adventures at sea, a long letter describing a near shipwreck in the Pentland Firth, aboard a sailing dinghy with his young cousin Angus: "My darling Susie, a storm so savage beset our small craft that I prayed for deliverance and am convinced that only divine intervention and my love for you spared us from certain death upon the rocky shores of Hoy."

Perhaps I am affected by this endless fog, but I wonder why, if his devotion to me is so strong, he continues to take such risks. His obvious delight in these adventures puzzles and disturbs me . . .

And in a postscript, my dearest adds (almost cheerfully, I think): "Poor Uncle Alex is in even more desperate financial straits than we are. I rather suspect he had hoped to lure us here in order that we might support *him* in his dotage. Grand fellow, though." At least I can now relinquish the prospect of spending the rest of my days clinging to some bleak, rocky brae overlooking a distant Scottish firth.

Now that my foot is nearly healed, I intend to accept the Pringles' kind invitation to visit them in the new year.

JANUARY 15, 1831 (CLAREMONT SQUARE)

Agnes and I spent the morning at Montagu House, deep in research for the *Patriotic Songs* poetry project. In the afternoon, we met with the composer Edward Cruse at his townhouse in Bloomsbury to discuss setting our words to music for the pianoforte. He was most complimentary and happily obliged when we asked him to play something for us—a choral rendition of the Apostles' Creed he is working on.

This evening, we attended a reception at the home of Edward Lytton (MP). About my age and an established novelist (under the pen name Bulwer-Lytton), he was not at all what I expected. Seated on a high stool in the centre of the large drawing room, wearing a dark purple waistcoat and what I am certain was a wig, he fanned himself ostentatiously with a silk scarf (though the room was quite cold), all the while receiving his guests as though he were an incarnation of the dauphin.

"They say the ladies find him irresistible, though I don't understand it," Margaret Pringle whispered in my ear. And indeed, five or six tittering belles were lined up, waiting for a chance to exchange a few words with our host, who seemed bored beyond redemption at the attention. The historian Thomas Carlyle was also in attendance, but he was such a crabbed-looking creature that I did not care to make his acquaintance. They say he is writing a history of the revolution in France and that he believes a similar situation may be imminent in England because of our treatment of the poor here. "When Paris sneezes," he was heard to remark, "the whole of Europe catches cold." It is turning out to be a very chilly winter indeed.

Tomorrow, we are invited to a soiree at the home of the painter John Martin. Cheesman says such invitations are highly coveted.

Despite the frivolity of such gatherings in these troubled times, I relish the chance to mingle with like-minded souls. The companionship of other writers ignites in me a small spark of legitimacy, a sense of community, of belonging, of being my own mistress. I wonder what Moodie would think if he could see me like this, surrounded by the young men of London, the object of their compliments and fine speeches, their tributes to my "genius." Genius!

I wonder.

I am dizzy with work and parties and growing more in love with London every day.

Moodie seems so very far away. And the idea of marriage, something like a dream. How I miss him. Five long months he has been gone, much longer than the few weeks we spent together last summer before he left. I close my eyes and try to summon his image, but it will not come, and though I struggle to banish it, a tiny bud of resentment—that he is not here, and that marriage and motherhood will surely take me away from all this—swells inside me and would flourish and bloom if I let it. Am I doing the right thing?

JANUARY 25, 1831

It is over. Though it breaks my heart, I have written Mr. Moodie to break off our engagement, which I see now was too hasty. I do regret having raised his hopes this way and imagine he will hate me forever, but call me a flirt or a jilt or whatever you please, I don't care. I have come to realize that the whole business has been a terrible mistake. I cannot marry a soldier or leave England.

It was Papa Pringle who put the final nail in the coffin. Perhaps he noticed my silence at dinner yesterday. I had received a letter from Moodie that afternoon, and reading it filled me with despair. (His Orkney adventures continue; he longs for me, dreams of nothing else; his aunt is as penniless as all his other relatives, but no matter, we shall live on love, on crocodile meat and dates. I do not know . . .) We had finished our meal, and as I rose to leave and go to my room, I saw Papa give Margaret a meaningful nod.

"Susanna, I should like a word with you in the library for a moment." He took my elbow and guided me to a chair by the fire, then pulled up another and sat facing me, his eyes burning into mine.

"My dear," he began. "I cannot keep silent any longer. Despite my regard for our mutual friend, Dunbar Moodie, I can't stand by and see you throw your life away like this."

I looked at him in disbelief; it was the shock of hearing the silent rumblings in my own head given voice.

"I beg your pardon," I stammered. "I don't understand. Throw my life away?" Surely nothing could be as welcome to him as my betrothal to one of his oldest friends.

"I'm so sorry," he began again. "I don't mean to cause you pain or to cast aspersions on Dunbar's character. He is a good fellow, honest and well-intentioned, but the life he is offering you is no life for a woman of your talents." When I started to respond, he silenced me. "Hear me out, I pray." And taking my hands in his, he continued. "As you know, Margaret and I lived for seven years in the Cape Colony. You have listened many times to our tales of despair and disillusionment at the treatment of the Negroes there, of the way our own government has condoned slavery and of its treatment of the Boers. We did our best to push for change during that time, but in doing so, we risked not only social rejection but also violence to our persons, as well as the possibility of prison. We returned to England because it became evident that our voices and efforts carry far more weight here than they ever could in Africa. You are one of us now. Why would you even consider going to live in a country that engages in the terrible practices of which poor Mary Pringle is a sad victim? And then there is the isolation, the want of anything resembling culture, the dust and heat . . ." He straightened and placed a weary hand over his eyes as though trying to wipe away the memories before continuing.

"But we have no plans to live in South Africa," I said, confused that he would assume this was the case.

"Susanna, that is indeed Mr. Moodie's intention. He returned to London last year not just to secure a publisher, but also to find a wife to share his pioneer experience. He may not have pushed the issue, but I can assure you he will. I beg you to reconsider and reject Moodie's suit; I feel certain you will thrive in the world of letters here." Then his expression changed; his eyes crinkled with excitement. "We are at the dawn of a new age of information; I feel certain of it. And with my connections and support, you cannot help but prosper."

I heard him out and then could no longer hold back my tears. In a rush, I told him of my indecision, of our dwindling prospects, of my fear that love would not be enough to sustain us, and of my growing suspicion I am unsuited for marriage, and certainly for Africa. I returned to my room in a tempest of confusion. Outside, a light snow was falling, and through this pale curtain, I gazed for a long time at the serried townhouses across the square, the ordered facades, the unbroken lines of windows and doors, their severity softened only by swirls of wrought iron. Somehow I was calmed and reassured by the sight and I made my decision.

I have found temporary lodgings at Middleton Square in Finsbury, just steps from the Pringles. And so my life as an independent woman of letters begins in earnest. For the next three months, I will board with the William Joneses, friends of Thomas Harral's (with whom I am once again on speaking terms). I have a pretty back drawing room to write in that opens onto the garden. From my desk, I can see the magnificent new St. Mark's church with its splendid stone tower. Spring is in the air! And soon the squares and gardens outside my door will explode with daffodils and cherry blossoms. (All this for only twelve pounds, ten shillings for the quarter.)

I imagine Moodie will have my letter by now. The memory of him is fading like a bolt of silk left out in the sun. A sad, shimmering remnant of passion. Surely I am doing the right thing.

La Belle Assemblée has decided to publish my poem "The Old Ash Tree." Why now (Mr. Harral has had it for two years), I cannot imagine. Perhaps they are desperate. Nevertheless, it is one of my favourites, though Katie called it "apocalyptic" when I showed it to her.

"Why is your imagination drawn to such violence and destruction?" she asked me. "A poem about an ash tree destroyed by a storm? It would never occur to me."

Thou beautiful Ash! Thou art lowly laid,
And my eyes shall hail no more
From afar thy cool and refreshing shade,
When the toilsome journey's o'er.
The winged and the wandering tribes of air
A home 'mid thy foliage found,
But the graceful boughs, all broken and bare,
The wild winds are scattering round.

I don't know the answer, but it's true: the furies of nature, of passionate love and untimely death—these are my preoccupations. I am as thrilled by adventures of the mind as Moodie is drawn to adventures in the flesh. (Still no word from my former love.) Kate thinks I have been hasty. She is much too polite to say anything (and in any case, I do not want to hear it), but I can read it in her face. I think the rupture of my relations with Moodie has made her wonder why she persists in the belief that Francis Harral will defy his stepmother and marry her someday.

FEBRUARY 13, 1831

I have met the most compelling and tragic figure in the person of Mrs. Mary Shelley, whose wondrous and terrible novel *Frankenstein* I read years ago when I was a girl. I remember the story made a deep impression upon me at the time: the image of the brutish monster, at once hideous and pathetic, and his chastened creator, who strayed beyond the frontiers of reason into realms he could not fathom. For many months, my nights were riven by visions of the soulless creature, monster of the north, doomed to endlessly wander the vast, frozen wasteland of human ingenuity gone wrong; a creature arousing sympathy and horror in equal measure.

All these forgotten sensations came rolling back to me at Bulwer-Lytton's grand conversazione on Monday night. Almost as soon as I arrived, our host swooped down and, taking my elbow, propelled me across the drawing room into a circle of men—Allan Cunningham, Hobart Caunter, Daniell the painter, Whister the musician, and I cannot recall who else—who surrounded a diminutive, unprepossessing-looking woman of early middle age.

"Mrs. Percy Shelley," Mr. Bulwer-Lytton roared, "I should like to present Miss Susanna Strickland, a woman—nay, a literary lioness after your own heart."

I blushed to the bottom of my being at these words and had no alternative but to make a respectful curtsey. And as I was doing so, the realization that I was speaking to the noted authoress finally took hold.

"Mrs. Shelley," I stammered as the gentlemen looked on, "what a great—"

"Never mind that." She grasped my hand firmly as though it were a lifeline thrown from a sinking ship. "How kind of you to come. I am delighted to see you." She tilted her black bonnet back and up to face the circle of gentlemen, who were frozen in mid-sentence by my inadvertent intrusion. "You will pardon us, won't you?" she said, her apology smooth as butter on her tongue. "Miss Strickland and I have much to catch up on." And with that, she led me quickly into a narrow passageway opening onto a back stairway and pulled me down beside her on a small settee placed there as though in anticipation of a moment such as this.

"Ah," she exclaimed, tugging at her gloves and hat so that even in the dim light I could clearly see her pale, delicate face, no longer pretty, the years and the trials with which we are only too familiar having put paid to whatever beauty she may have once possessed. Instead, her deep-set hazel eyes, long, narrow nose and thin lips gave her a look of sad intelligence. Dressed entirely in black, though her husband, the great poet, has been dead for nearly ten years, she exuded a careworn dignity and an air of weary insouciance.

"I do apologize. You must think me mad, but I could not bear another moment of the hot air billowing from that collection of buffoons."

Her dark eyebrows rose and she tilted her head slightly as though beckoning me to affirm her opinion of our fellow guests. I laughed and nodded happily for her words expressed what I had only a few moments earlier been thinking myself.

"I am honoured to meet you, Mrs. Shelley . . ." I began gushing once more, but she stopped me with a raised hand.

"Mr. Lytton says you are a writer? What are you writing, then?" She was fanning herself with one hand, and I could see small beads of perspiration gathering on her forehead.

"Are you ill, Mrs. Shelley? Let me get you something to drink."

But she shook her head and smiled.

"Go on. Tell me about your work. It is so reassuring to meet another woman engaged in such a merciless occupation."

Nervous and star-struck, I began babbling on about *my* successes, my sketches and stories and most of all my poems, while she, Mary Shelley, listened quietly. And perhaps I flatter myself, but her interest seemed genuine. When I finally drew breath, she said, "I should like to see them sometime."

"Really? You can't imagine how—"

"Then we shall meet again soon and you will bring a few of your poems with you." She took my hands in hers and squeezed them warmly. "There are so few women at these affairs; I am in need of a like-minded friend if I am to return to society."

And with that, we rose and rejoined the party.

FEBRUARY 15, 1831

Mrs. Shelley has invited me for tea tomorrow at four!

I have learned from Papa Pringle that the usually reclusive authoress has been making appearances at literary salons of late to bring attention to the publication of a new edition of *Frankenstein*. He said that, as far as he knows, she lives in north London and seldom ventures into society, preferring to live quietly with her son—the only one of her four children to survive infancy. I am ashamed to admit that I have not read any of her other novels, none of which captured the public's imagination as thoroughly as her first. (To think she was a girl of eighteen when she wrote it!) For the most part, she devotes herself to promoting her late husband's writing, and it is said she is putting together a "collected works" for publication. Interest in the life and poetry of Percy Shelley has assumed cult-like proportions in London, and according to Papa P., Mrs. Shelley is under pressure from her publishers to advance her own interests and those of her late husband by being more visible in literary circles.

I am beyond excited at the prospect of seeing her again tomorrow. How fortuitous that as I commit myself to a career in letters, I should meet someone whose example stands as a shining star, lighting the way to the realization of my own ambitions. When I consider her poise and self-assurance, her tragic dignity as she basks in the admiration of her peers, I am filled with an emotion that is akin to awe.

Enough. Inspiring as they are, such thoughts are only keeping me from my work. Lately, I spend long hours, pen in hand, attempting to unstop my sluggish imagination and write something that does not end up in the wastebasket no sooner than it is on the page. Perhaps it is the dampness. I long to throw a few extra coals on the fire, an unwise extravagance given my current circumstances. If I cannot generate an amusing sketch as promised for *The Athenaeum*, I am doomed to freeze to death.

FEBRUARY 16, 1831

I have left three of my *Enthusiasm* poems with Mrs. Shelley. I feel they are my best work, even if the emotion that gave birth to them is somewhat diminished. She received them without comment and placed them on the desk she was sitting at, evidently hard at work, when the maid let me in. Her small house, a cottage really, is exceedingly modest though decorated with surprising exuberance given the owner's understated presence.

There were books everywhere, of course, but also mementoes from the years she and her husband spent in Paris and Venice and Geneva: paintings of soaring alps under impossibly blue skies, of narrow city streets shining in the rain; carpets woven in the Orient and carried by camel and riverboat to Swiss merchants; a length of fuchsia silk framing a deep-set window; a bowl of lemons (brought to her by her old friend Leigh Hunt, just returned from Greece). But most touching of all was the small portrait of her angelic son William, who was only a year old when he was taken by malaria in 1819.

"We called him little Willmouse," she said, taking down the painting from the wall beside her and passing it to me. (I don't know if I will ever have children of my own, but the loss of a babe such as this would finish me completely.)

Despite the colourful accoutrements, my general impression of Mrs. Shelley's parlour was one of genteel poverty, with which I am only too familiar. The upholstery was threadbare, the wood floors worn, and the unmistakable odour of mould and mouse droppings hung in the air. How chilling to think the widow of one of the most successful poets of his generation (and herself a noted author) should be forced to live in such a poor state. It was enough to make my own lofty ambitions sag a little.

While we waited for tea, she talked quietly about the weather and her hopes for her son Percy, who goes away to school next fall. I must have been shivering; I had given the maid my coat when I arrived, and my best dress was no match for the draught coming in through the front window. Mrs. Shelley noticed my discomfort immediately.

"Here," she insisted, "take my shawl. I have a cupboard full of them." She stood and placed it, a garment of the finest merino wool in a soft shade of lavender, upon my shoulders. "Now, Miss Strickland," she said as she pulled a dark blue scarf from the back of the settee and drew it tightly to her, "I must hear all about your life. You are new to London, I think? And how do you find it here? It is very brave of you to strike out on your own. I have found out myself how hostile the world can be to unmarried women such as ourselves. But then, marriage is not for everyone . . ." She widened her eyes and hesitated as though waiting for me to finish her thought, which I did, not wanting her to think that my spinsterhood was an unavoidable condition.

"Indeed it is not," I proclaimed. "As a matter of fact, in the interests of pursuing my writing, I have recently broken off an engagement that was dear to my heart."

"Really? You would rather endure poverty alone than in the company of a good husband?" Her laugh as she said this was small and hard. Then she shrugged and smiled lightly. "I assume your former intended had little to offer in the way of property or security."

"As much as a half-pensioned soldier can offer," I said. "It is less than the small amount I manage to wring from my writing." Though I hardly knew her, I found myself wanting to unburden myself to this woman, who had borne so much in her life. I wanted her to affirm the decision that I am beginning to realize weighs heavily on my heart. "He would have us live on his farm in southern Africa," I continued as Mrs. Shelley poured the tea. "But it is a prospect that truly I cannot bear to contemplate."

"Miss . . . Susanna—may I call you that? And you must call me Mary." She settled back in her chair and stirred her tea slowly, gazing into its porcelain depths as though they held the secret to all the vagaries of the heart. "After the loss of my sweet babes, my heart grew so insensible that I thought nothing would ever penetrate the carapace of suffering that encased it. And indeed, the news of my dear Percy's sudden death was like one more wave pounding a rocky shore. I could not absorb it. I was immune to pain, beyond suffering, alive and sensible in fact but not in essence. At the time, I did not have the stores of emotion necessary to mourn his loss. The years passed and the ghosts of my children continued to linger, as they still do, spectral memories, my constant companions, while my absent husband's spirit hung in limbo, a non-existence to which I had banished him."

She paused to sip her tea. "You know," she said, a smile touching her lips, "Percy would recoil at what I have become—the keeper of his flame, the faithful wife even in death, the loyal servant of his memory and his art. He believed in free love. We all did. I was brought up in a household where monogamy and conventional marriage were seen as a form of slavery. And we lived by those covenants." She paused. "You know of my parents' work, I assume?"

I assured her immediately of my reverence for A *Vindication of the Rights of Woman* and of my familiarity with Mr. Godwin's ideas, although I said nothing of my thoughts on the notion of anarchism as a moral good. Mrs. Shelley nodded and continued.

"There were other women for Percy, many of them, and for me" —she hesitated—"lovers, yes . . . and close friendships. But I did not know then what I came to realize in the years after his death: that Percy was my only husband, my true love, not just in the eyes of society but according to whatever divine law exists."

Then she did the most remarkable thing. Bending to open a lower drawer in her desk, she took out a small grey silk bag and loosened the drawstring that kept it closed. Shaking it lightly, she released its contents onto the palm of her hand. I leaned forward to behold what looked like a dried and shrivelled piece of leather about the size of a large walnut. I raised my inquiring eyes to hers.

"Percy's heart," she said, cradling the dreadful item in both hands now.

I tried to recover myself. "Oh, I see." I sat back in my chair.

"I keep it as a reminder that the body is nothing." She looked down at the very, very prosaic item she was holding. "Nothing more than this. It is the soul that prevails. The soul, the poetry—these are where the heart truly lies. His spirit is with me always and will live on. But this"—she slipped the desiccated souvenir back into the bag and put it away—"this is merely matter. Ugly and temporal. Nothing."

She appraised me with narrowed eyes. "You are shocked," she observed. And I admit I was. Of course, I had known of the radical individualism practised by Percy Shelley and Lord Byron and others, but hearing such an admission on the lips of someone as outwardly respectable as Mary Shelley was another matter altogether. A self-confessed adulterer, other men, and women too? Her husband's heart in a drawer, and now my newest friend?

"Oh no, it is not my place to judge . . ." I could feel the colour rushing to my cheeks.

"Of course it is, a country girl from a good Anglican family. But never mind. I have given all that up. Our experiments caused us nothing but pain." She straightened her shoulders and threw out her tiny chin. "I have come to believe that a woman's greatest gift to society is her role in the family. Without the compassion and affections that are natural to the gentler sex, there is little hope for the world. I believe it is a woman's duty to nurture those values within the context of marriage, and by doing so, triumph over the violent and destructive tendencies of men. Only then will they be free to express the sympathy and generosity of their better natures."

A provocative afternoon. But my new mentor's conflicting messages baffle me still. How can she be so unconventional in some ways and so conservative in others? I am beginning to see it is possible to hold two contradictory passions in your heart at once.

Papa Pringle is now cautioning me against associating too closely with Mrs. Shelley (or "the notorious Mary Shelley" as he referred to her on our walk this morning). And this after the previous week's admonition that I seek out the society of other writers as a way of honing my craft and, above all, making connections in the literary world.

"Mrs. Shelley has indeed achieved a degree of success in publishing seldom granted to the gentler sex," he said as we made our way along Islington High Street, "but it is due less to talent than to her association with her poet husband." Here, he lowered his voice in consideration, I suppose, of the delicate morals of the ragged boys begging outside the Angel Coach House as we passed by. Papa tossed one of them a sixpence and walked on. "Shelley's reputation as an adulterer and insolvent, I daresay, outstrips his artistic renown."

At this, I felt a shimmer of irritation. "Surely, Papa, you will not deny that Percy Bysshe Shelley is one of the great poets of our age?"

"Of course not, my dear. But the mantle of greatness carries with it a responsibility to conduct oneself in a manner befitting a public personage." It was a brisk, bright morning, and the round, red tip of Papa's generous nose glistened as with drops of dew. "And then there is the notoriety of Mrs. Shelley's parents."

"But have you read *Frankenstein*?" I protested. "Did you not think it a work of disturbing and uncanny prescience?"

He flipped his fingers in the air as though brushing away a fly. "Oh yes, years ago. A horror story. A tale for children. Not to be taken seriously. Now promise me, my dear, that you will let the acquaintance drop. It will do you no good in the long run. You have a great deal of work to do, and while I sympathize with much of the reformist fever sweeping England these days, one must still choose one's acquaintances with care. There is an overzealousness in the air."

Just then, as though to lend weight to Papa Pringle's measured opining, a strange figure in a long black cloak and red tricorn galloped past us on a milk-white horse. In his wake, a procession of blacking boys in scarlet cockades, carrying long poles wound with red streamers, surged through the streets, crying, "Hunt forever," and "Radical reform," until our ears would gladly have shut themselves against their teeth-jarring chants. We learned from fellow bystanders it was the radical farmer MP Henry Hunt arriving in London to take his seat in Parliament. Judging by the spectacle we witnessed, Hunt will add more than a little liveliness to the business of government.

"An unprincipled demagogue," sniffed Papa as Hunt and his motley parade passed before us. We watched them gather and mill about at the tollgate, unable to muster the money to pay. It was, I must say, more circus than serious protest. I was surprised, however, at Papa's distaste for the spectacle, as I believe he shares Mr. Hunt's opinions on the matter of universal suffrage and the need for parliamentary reform.

"I thought you were in favour of his ideas," I said, "his views on the excesses of power and wealth that perpetuate slavery and other ills." My confusion was genuine.

"Susanna, my dear, reform is always desirable, but it must come from within. Change can be effected only by men of education and moderation. Otherwise, the rabble rules, and misery and bloodshed are the only outcomes. Look at France. Look at what that nation's capitulation to passion over prudence has led to. Your new friend Mary Shelley is not a reformer; she is a radical, her zeal no doubt tempered by age and misfortune, but a radical nevertheless."

Anger flared inside me like a scarlet banner. I halted and turned to face him right there in the street.

"You have counselled me against marriage and convention, and now you are warning me of the dangers of living outside those conventions. Forgive me if I do not see another way. Are you telling me all my choices are bad ones?"

He placed a consoling arm about my shoulders. His manner was gentle, patient, as though reasoning with a child. "Shhh. Of course not, my dear. There will be other paths. Be patient and you will find them."

I stepped away from his embrace and faced him again. "I think you are being hypocritical. Mrs. Shelley has offered to help me. She is a friend when I badly need one. Would you deny me this?" I didn't wait for his answer but hurried home on my own so that he would not see my tears. Other paths? For the life of me, I cannot fathom what they might be.

FEBRUARY 20, 1831

Is it not a strange coincidence that Mary Shelley's dear husband died these many years ago in a sailing accident? And that my own misplaced Moodie also risks his life for the dubious thrill of exploring the savage seas of his native land? Since my conversation with Mrs. . . . with Mary, I have given more thought to the nature of a woman's obligations to society. Surely, my mentor's conviction that keeping watch over the temple of the heart should be the female vocation is the very idea I am trying to outrun. What of my writing? If Mary

Shelley has put her husband's memory before her own ambitions, who am I to aspire to such independence? But how can I be mistress of my own destiny when I am a servant to others?

And yet sometimes I fear I have as much hope of succeeding in the world of men as does a grub in a chicken coop. My heart is torn like a sail in a tempest. Moodie is very much on my mind.

Mr. Harral has accepted "The Vanquished Lion" but passed on my long poem "Arminius." Two weeks in the making and nothing to show for it.

MARCH 1, 1831

Moodie has returned, though we have not met. I dread our reunion and yet can think of nothing else. Kate informs me he is lingering in Bungay for a day or two and then plans to come up to London. She saw him briefly just yesterday and reports his heart is broken by my rejection.

"I never thought I would ever see the most cheerful man on earth in such a state," was her rather cruel (to me at least) assessment of my former betrothed's condition. I must harden my resolve.

Despite Papa's cautions, or perhaps in reaction to them, I have invited Mary to dine with me here at my rooms tomorrow. I hope she will not mind the modesty of my circumstances. The more I come to know her, the more I am attracted to her quiet resilience and the glimmer of a spirit undiminished by the accumulating years. They say that when a woman loses her youth, she becomes invisible, but Mary Shelley is living proof of the durable beauty bestowed by the intelligence and forbearance of the "weaker" sex. I know of no man her equal.

I have ordered a pork pie (two shillings, six pence—a rare extravagance!). And I shall open the claret, a gift from Mr. Harral last fall.

Do I dare ask about my poems? My heart recoils at the possibility of discouragement.

What a fool I have been. How naive of me to think a woman of Mrs. Shelley's worldliness would seek out someone of my limited accomplishment for intellectual kinship alone! I fear that all along her purpose has been to lure me into an intimacy whose true nature I dare not reveal here . . . though where else should I unburden myself? I do fear her purpose in regards to me is Sapphic in nature. Oh, dear Papa, I should have listened instead of almost letting myself be drawn into what surely might have been a mire of immorality such as I can scarcely imagine. As soon as she left yesterday in a whorl of black lace, I threw myself on my knees and begged our dear Lord to forgive my weakness and to give me strength to calm my spirit, which I fear is sorely shaken.

It began with such benign intimations: a mild late winter's night, the air as still as lake water. The blue-grey sequined sky outside my windows seemed to promise a rare intimacy, an encounter of mythic proportions. And in truth, I was breathless with anticipation of my guest's arrival. Yes, I admit it. I have been infatuated by her gentle demeanour, her air of lingering sadness, her attentiveness to my struggles. How privileged I felt to be able to bask in another's under-standing of what it means to love and lose, to stand alone as a writer and a woman in a world of men. But not this! No, surely not. I am overcome by feelings I cannot name or even acknowledge.

Mrs. Shelley, Mary, arrived at the appointed hour, stepping down from the cab, her small feet visible for an instant under the skirts she held lightly, and then she seemed to float across the garden to the back-door entry to my small rooms. I watched her approach, through the quartered windowpanes, which had the odd effect of reproducing her image so it appeared that four slender widows were making their way over the wet stones. And I wondered then, as I do now, whether her immense (to me at least) presence was by this illusion quartered or quadrupled.

I showed her in and she seemed flushed, her usual composure perforated by a new animation. We sat in two chairs placed close to the small burner and talked of mundane things: her son and his struggles with his studies, the beauty of the night, the difficulty of living a writer's life. At times, her eyes met and held mine with such intensity that I had to look away or I feared I might burst into flames. The air felt electric, shot through with unseen energy, as though she were sending me an unspoken message. (And I too dense to decipher it.)

We ate the pie by candlelight, which cast shadows on her face, deepening her already deep-set eyes and highlighting the angular bones of her cheeks. She seemed spectral and mysterious in a way I had not previously noticed. Perhaps it was the wine, but I felt mesmerized by her voice and the warmth of the room, by the slow pulsing of my own heart. So hypnotized was I that now I struggle to recall what was said between us. I just remember her taking my hand between her small palms as I reached for the decanter to refill her glass. Her hands were strangely cold, and though the gesture surprised me, I did not flinch.

"I know how impulsive this will seem, but I have a proposition." She turned my hand so that it lay lightly upon her upturned palm, and with a forefinger, she traced the blue veins on the back of my hand slowly and softly. The sensation made me feel faint, and a flood of heat poured through me. If I had been standing, my knees surely would have buckled. But I did not pull away. "What if we two were to join forces?" she said, not looking up. "I have the house; my son will be going away in a few weeks. You could have his room for less, I'm sure, than you pay here."

She risked a glance to gauge my reaction. I could hardly breathe. I was speechless, both flattered and frightened.

"I have read your poems," she continued, now squeezing my hand with surprising vigour. "They are full of passion. I could help you harness that emotion, teach you to shape and control it." Her tone was earnest, pleading. "You have the most luminous eyes, Susanna." Embarrassed, I withdrew my hand. "Never mind. I am making you uncomfortable. I don't mean to. It's just that I find myself unexpectedly drawn to you . . . No, it's all right. Please let me finish. I long for the comfort of a close friendship such as I know is developing between us. I promise I would never push you beyond an intimacy you do not desire. But I feel in my heart that there is something possible between us, something durable and fine."

These last sentences came out in a torrent, and I fear I sat there stunned, not meeting her eyes, my hands now clasped tightly in my lap, the full import of what she was suggesting slowly dawning on me. And I cannot explain it, but something came over me, an ice-cold breeze, and the spreading warmth in my abdomen turned to nausea.

"I think you had better go," I said, my voice catching in my throat. "I am not what you think," I added weakly, and with that, I stood, shaking. Mrs. Shelley found her shawl and bonnet and left without a word.

I have resolved to banish Tuesday's events from my mind. Already, it is as if I dreamed the entire encounter—the flickering candles, the shadows, the night sounds, and Mrs. Shelley, her hazel eyes shining, the hushed timbre of her voice, the pressure of her fingers . . . Enough. It is over. She is right. I am a country girl, a good Anglican girl, bound by convention. Her proposition is something I could never condone.

Moodie has written to say he is coming up to London tomorrow, that he must see me. I will hear what he has to say.

MARCH 5, 1831

He sat in the very chair she sat in beside the fire while sleeting rain tapped an irregular yet persistent rhythm on the windowpane. I could just glimpse, over his shoulder, the hansom cabs in a line under the bare chestnut trees surrounding the square, the horses' heads down, their rumps turned into the weather. His hair was damp and tousled, his face mottled red, and his breath issued in quick gasps as though he had sprinted here through the blackened streets. But his voice was strong and urgent. At the sight of him, I felt a mighty surge, like the tide rushing in, coming home, as though my mind, which has rejected him, and my body, which longs for his touch, were in complete opposition to one another. How can this be? He reached for me and, without intending to, I fell into his embrace.

"I beg you, my dearest, my only Susanna. Please, please tell me what has altered your heart. I cannot contemplate a life without you. What have I done? What has happened to pull you back from the brink?"

It was an apt allusion, because, indeed, the idea of marriage has made me feel as though I were standing on a precipice, lured irresistibly, inevitably into a life of companionship, yes, love, perhaps, but also the drudgery of domesticity, the deadening necessities of marriage and motherhood.

"It isn't you, nothing you've done," I said. I could not look into his face, could not bear to see his eyes bright and burning as I knew they were. Bright and burning with love for me. "I was afraid," I stammered and covered my face with my hands.

"Of what? Dear, dear Susie. Afraid? Oh no, no. I would never put you in harm's way. I would give my life to keep you safe. I want nothing more than to look after you."

I stepped away from him and reached for the poker, stirring the coals, urging a little more heat from the hearth. How could I tell him the truth? That I rejected him so that I might keep myself? That for a brief, exhilarating time, I chose Susanna Strickland. Right then, I could feel her slipping away again as I was drawn inexorably back into the circle of his love—pulled, yes, by the magnet of my own desire, dormant all these long, lonely months and now like a fire rekindled. And so I told him I was afraid of Africa. I told him of my need to write. But I did not tell him how unnerved I was by my brush with unconvention, how filled I am with self-doubt. And he, tears bathing his ruddy face, promised, "I only wish to love you, to keep you near me forever." And so I relented and allowed Mr. Moodie to take me in his arms again, to reassure me with promises of tenderness and safety. As the fire came to life in the grate, I whispered, "Yes, yes, I will be your wife."

MARCH 7, 1831

I have reiterated to Moodie my terror of South Africa and its wildlife, of the prowling lions and stampeding elephants. Now that we are firmly reunited, he has reverted to his usual bonhomie. He was openly amused and teased me mercilessly about what he assures me are groundless fears, the stuff of childhood stories, of bogeymen and demons. So tickled is he by such timidity in his betrothed that whenever the opportunity arises, he conceals himself in doorways or behind trees on our daily walks on the Heath and leaps out to surprise me, roaring like the lord of the jungle himself. I can feel my natural irritation rising on these occasions, but Moodie's high-spiritedness is impossible to resist and I am growing accustomed to his silliness. He makes me laugh despite myself and allows me to see things in a brighter light than that cast by my tendency toward brooding pessimism.

I did, however, extract a promise from him that he abandon forever his plans for our return to his African farm. He agreed at first with his usual playfulness, going down on one knee and taking my hand in a demonstration of subservience. "I swear, my own true love, never again to utter the words 'veldt' or 'kaffir' in your presence. No more tales of derring-do or purple sunsets on the savannah," he insisted. "Africa is as dead to me as you are alive."

I brushed him off with the hauteur of a Zulu princess, but later, as he walked me home after supper at cousin Rebecca's and his mood turned serious for a moment, I pushed my case once more, reminding him of our mutual abhorrence of slavery.

"How can you contemplate living in a place that not only condones but fosters an evil we are pledged to eradicate?" I pleaded. "You know of my work with Mary Prince. But perhaps in your heart you aspire to own a few Negroes . . ."

This was cruel of me, and Moodie immediately protested. But he also swore he would never raise the matter again.

"And I intend to continue writing after we are married," I said.

"Of course, Susanna. I would not have it any other way. We will be a pair of writers. I have my stories of Africa and the war, and if these do not provide for us, there will be your amusing sketches and rhymes."

I let it go at that, reassured I have made the right decision. We are a good match: His cheerful temperament acts as an antidote to my darker moods; my natural skepticism has an ameliorating effect on his somewhat excessive spirits. (Optimism cannot always be justified.)

We share a love of reading and music, and a strong sense of our place in society, as well as compassion for those less fortunate than ourselves. As well, I have only to consider the situations of my sisters—Eliza in her cramped London room, toiling without respite as editoress of *The Court Journal*; Agnes, who struggles to keep up appearances she cannot afford since her elevation to the status of society poetess; and poor Jane, earning what she can with her stories, trapped at crumbling Reydon Hall with Sarah and the increasingly irascible Mama—to realize that marriage to a good man is a far better fate than what awaits all of them. To think that a short time ago, I aspired to "glorious" independence that I now see as a consequence of spinsterhood. My sisters are all, I fear, too old to be saved by marriage. (Except Sarah. With her gentleness and beauty, there is still hope.) But I fear most for my dearest Katie, whose marital prospects continue to dwindle. We dined together at cousin Rebecca's last week after she came to London to meet again with her fiancé.

"I am doing everything I can to raise Francis's spirits," she said, explaining that the senior Mr. Harral faces serious financial difficulties—a consequence, Kate claims, of his wife's extravagance. The situation has only added fuel to Mrs. Harral's dissatisfaction with her stepson's engagement. "I think she is determined Francis must marry someone of means if the family is to maintain its position." Kate paused, her sad face staring down into her soup. "The poor man is torn between duty and devotion." There were tears in her eyes.

It saddens me to think that while my prospects have taken a turn for the better, hers are bleak indeed.

APRIL 4, 1831

It is done. I am, for better or worse, Mrs. John Moodie. I love my husband with all my heart, but there was a moment during the mercifully brief (Anglican) ceremony at St. Pancras in Camden when I thought I might turn and flee. Only Papa's strong arm leading me down the aisle and my dear Kate's hand gripping mine as we stood at the altar gave me the will to go on. But I pronounced the fatal "obey" with every intention to keep it. Now it is over, I feel calm and determined.

Moodie looked more terrified than joyful, no doubt sensing that I was poised to bolt. Once the final vows were uttered, his complexion lost its purple hue (I fear he had been holding his breath for the duration) and he clasped me to his bosom in an embrace that, had she been there, would surely have rendered Mama speechless. It was, of course, too much to think she might travel all the way to London. I take consolation in the fact that Mary Prince, wearing a new dress for the occasion, rode with the Pringles and me to the church and took her place in a rear pew. Cousin Cheesman entertained our small party at his Newman Street rooms, raising a toast to our long life and happiness amid the usual chaos and clutter. And so . . .

I write these few words as I wait for my husband to return to our rooms with something for our wedding supper, though I can scarcely consider the prospect of food, so great is my anticipation for what must follow. These stirrings are nothing like those I felt in the presence of Mrs. Shelley, which seemed to come from a place of strangeness and shadow. My longings for John Moodie are as robust and exhilarating as the beginning of spring. Perhaps the wild Suffolk girl is a little frightened of her own passionate nature.

APRIL 16, 1831

The last fortnight has passed in a blur, but reality must of necessity insert itself into our unashamed bliss if we are to eat, let alone pay our rent. And yet whenever I raise the matter of our soon-to-be

desperate circumstances, Moodie tries to distract me with affection-
ate teasing that inevitably results in an entire afternoon once again
passing with pen and paper left untouched.

At last, this evening, as we lay in the fading light amid a tumble
of linens and the remains of a hasty supper of bread and cheese, I
once again reminded him of the seriousness of our situation.

"Ah, but I do believe I could live on love!" was Moodie's response.
"What more is there to life than this." He giggled, tugging on the
lacing of my camisole.

I slapped his hand away. "Please, Moodie, stop it." These were the
first harsh words between us since our marriage, and though I was
only teasing, his angelic face collapsed like an underbaked cake. He
looked so downcast that I relented and pulled him to me once again.

In the midst of our happiness, Kate's world has collapsed.
Mrs. Harral, in an act of unprecedented cruelty, placed a mock wedding announcement in *The Spectator* this week, heralding the upcom-
ing marriage of "Mr. Frankly Harried and Miss Katydid Stickmouse
[sic]." Embellished with lurid illustrations of grimacing cupids, fauns
and angels wrestling with one another in a tangle of wilted flowers,
the advertisement shows a tall, handsome bridegroom with his back
turned to his intended bride, a stout farm girl carrying a chicken under
her arm and pleading for his attention. We are all stunned at the
effrontery. Surely the woman has lost her mind. Kate met with Francis
for the last time yesterday and offered to release him from his bond, a
gesture he accepted, she said, "with an expression of relief on his face
that made me wonder why I have held on to this dream for so long."
He immediately left for Dorset to take up an apprenticeship to a phar-
macist, his dreams of becoming a doctor apparently abandoned.

My only consolation is that my sister is not so crushed in spirit
that she has been unable to rouse a vivacious fury at the authoress of

her fate. "I abhor and detest her," she sobbed as I held her slender and shuddering frame in my arms. She raised her reddened eyes to mine and they shone with a hatred I did not think she was capable of. "Malicious bitch," she said.

MAY 2, 1831

Kate continues to mourn the rupture of her engagement to Francis Harral, but now that the initial shock has softened, she will not hear any criticism of her former fiancé, coming instantly to his defence if I dare cast aspersions on his character, and mewing meekly about her own shortcomings. Oh, how I would relish seeing fickle Francis and his stepmother tarred and feathered and run out of town. I am still in a rage! I offered to intercede with Harral senior on her behalf, but Katie will not hear of it. I do think anger is the best medicine in situations such as these. But dear Kate has spent whatever reserves she may have had and is fading before our eyes, barely able to eat, let alone write. Even Moodie, whom she has come to adore, has been unable to elicit much more than a wan smile. She remains at Bedford Square under the watchful and generous care of cousin Rebecca, who has proposed that Kate accompany her on an extended tour of Bath and Oxford and a visit to her country house in Hertfordshire. I hope a few months away from this wretched situation will ease my sister's distress. Seeing her like this makes me appreciate my good fortune in marrying a man as constant as my Moodie.

Agnes and I continue our work on *Patriotic Songs*; we are nearly finished. I am still flattered, and frankly astonished, that she asked me to collaborate. My most arrogant sister has never before encouraged my work in any way; indeed, her dismissive attitude toward my verses has been a source of some resentment on my part. These days, however, she is positively effusive in her encouragement. I can only surmise that my dear husband has charmed her out of her hair shirt. She giggles and preens like a schoolgirl whenever they meet.

Moodie is in particularly good spirits; his youthful soldier reminiscence, *A Narrative of the Campaign of 1814 in Holland,* is published to quiet but enthusiastic acclaim. Rather than basking in the glow of what is likely to be a short-lived and muted notoriety, he is now putting the finishing touches to an account of his adventures in South Africa, from which, if it takes anywhere as long to see publication as his first book, we are unlikely to enjoy much in the way of proceeds for decades. At the risk of seeming excessively mercenary, I do wish he would tackle shorter projects of a more lucrative nature.

My *History of Mary Prince* is published at last, and I am proud to report that it is to be laid before the Houses of Parliament. Of course, my name does not appear. I only hope it has some effect on the abolition in our great dominions of such gross injustice and awful criminality.

JUNE 22, 1831 (SOUTHWOLD, SUFFOLK)

How my world has changed. Instead of looking out at the tiled rooftops and blackened chimneys of Finsbury, my gaze this morning falls upon the blowing grasses and rolling grey seas of the Suffolk coast. We have let a small cottage, three rooms and a back kitchen, set in the lee of a treeless knoll, which is our only protection from the fierce breezes blowing in from the North Sea. It is owned by the Kitsons, a crusty old mariner and his wife, who live next door. Mrs. Kitson has been friendly to the point of intrusiveness, but I believe she is kind. The money we save by moving away from London has allowed me to hire a girl to help with the domestic duties that are my not-altogether-unwelcome fate. Hannah comes to our small household from Reydon Hall and is highly recommended by Mama, who claims she is "energetic and reliable." I hope so, but I detect an air of resentment beneath her respectful silences. Moodie says I am imagining things and that Hannah is not yet accustomed to our much smaller household. Our tiny house is within walking distance of Reydon Hall, and Jane and Agnes often visit. Even Mama, who seldom leaves her room, has deigned to inspect our little mansion. I find that a strange lassitude envelops me these days, and I seem to have lost the will to write. I fear my blue stockings have turned so pale that they will soon be quite white. Oh, what has become of me? Tamed by love, I suppose. And impending motherhood. We have told no one, but by this time next year, God willing, Moodie, and I will be three.

He too is beguiled by the rhythms of rural life, and we spend our days reading aloud to one another and walking along the shingle, listening to the mutter of waves upon the shore. In the evenings, I knit small things for our babe with a clumsy and uncharacteristic determination. Moodie plays the flute and makes me laugh. I long to share these peaceful days with dear Katie, whose letters contain a forced cheerfulness that I know masks the beating of a broken heart. But for her sadness, my persistent nausea and our continuing penury, I should be perfectly happy.

JULY 17, 1831

I knew it would happen eventually. My dear husband's unquenchable thirst for adventure has been rekindled, this time by the appearance of one Robert Reid. He is my little brother Sam's Canadian father-in-law, the widowed Sam having married again to Mr. Reid's daughter Mary last year. Mr. Reid has recently returned to England from Canada, where, to hear him tell it, he and his family of ten children live like wealthy English squires, spending their days tending orchards and planting flower gardens. I exaggerate, but only slightly.

Moodie had the "good fortune" to run into Mr. Reid at the Crown Tavern in Southwold, where my husband spends many afternoons (mornings, he is at his desk) gathering "news" and sharing opinions with the local grandees, while I lie abed with only a basin and a wet cloth for company, thankful, really, to have our little place to myself in my present state. Have I ever endured such misery? (I am certain Agnes suspects my condition but is too delicate to mention it.)

In any case, the two of them (Moodie and Reid) returned in the full flush of good "spirits" just in time for the supper I had not prepared. Nevertheless, we made do with yesterday's soup and some stale bread and beer.

Mr. Reid was full of enthusiasm for the wonders of the New World. "Why, with a little hard work, a man will soon find independence and even wealth on the other side of the water," he said, his mutton chops quivering with excitement. "What future is there for you here, my good man?" He pounded the table with a weathered fist while Moodie's red face shone like the moon over the North Sea. "This country is doomed," Reid said. "The price of wheat is lower than a groom's britches on his wedding night." (At this, he paused to nod at me and apologize for his colourful language. "Beg pardon, ma'am. I've been too long in the backwoods and my manners are a touch rough.")

"Look around you," he went on. "Tenant farmers can't make their rent; they're being tossed out of their cottages. The poorhouses are bursting at the seams." He raised his voice. "It's a revolution, an industrial revolution. I hear tell that in the coal mines, children as young as ten or eleven work eighteen-hour days pulling loads of coal that would break a horse's back. Demon coal is robbing millions of their livelihood, fuelling machines that do the work once done by honest men and women. Why, anyone with the necessary means and a modicum of good sense is leaving." He sank back in his chair as though the very idea exhausted him, and then, most inappropriately, winked a bleary eye in my direction.

"And then there's Canada," he almost whispered, "with its congenial climate, its fertile soil . . . Why, my land north of Peterborough—where your own brother, Mrs. Moodie, young Sam, has settled—why, that land yields forty bushels to the acre in a good year. Yes, Canada. It's close to mighty waterways and only a short voyage from these verdant shores . . . and best of all"—here, he leapt to his feet, the whisper escalating to a roar—"there is no bloody taxation!"

After he left, Moodie took up the emigration banner, waving it high. His blue eyes flashed like sunlight on a wild sea and the hair on his head fairly stood on end as he paced about our small parlour, waving his arms like a demented preacher.

"Nothing. There is nothing for us here," he exclaimed. "What, my dearest," he said, bending down until his nose was only inches from my face, "what is to become of us? And what of our child?" He reached out to place a hand on my belly. "How will we feed another mouth? There is no hope for us here." His face was ruddy with drink, and I knew that to argue would only pour oil on the flames.

I looked around our little cottage, at the fire burning in the hearth, at the pictures on the walls and at the modest but comfortable furnishings. I thought of the blowing broads spreading away to the shore and the path winding from our door all the way to my childhood home. I pressed my lips together and went back to my needlework. I said nothing, but I would rather live upon brown bread and milk in this English cottage than occupy a palace on the other side of the sea.

The terrible heat of the last few days oppresses my spirit almost as much as it enlivens Moodie's. The sea heaves soundlessly, not a ripple mars its surface, and a brackish odour hangs in the air. If only Moodie would cease trying to cheer me up and leave me to my misery, leave me to wallow in the torpor that afflicts me like a bloated whale.

Foolishly, I had thought the matter forgotten. But no. This very morning, Moodie rose from his breakfast and announced he must hurry to meet Tom Wales (a black-eyed rascal if I ever knew one) to attend a public meeting in Norwich. When pressed, he admitted its subject was that land of milk and honey, Canada. Later, as I was reading in the front room by the open door to catch the full benefits of the sea breeze, Mrs. Kitson, our landlady, sailed into the room, billowing black satin and lace. Her seafaring husband followed in her wake.

"So," she said with no preamble whatever, "you will soon be leaving us for the colonies." She delivered this news not as a question but as a reliable statement of fact.

"Whatever are you talking about?" I replied.

"Oh, come now, Mrs. Moodie," said Mrs. Kitson, her gaze falling on Hannah, whose generous backside was visible through the scullery doorway as she laboured over a sink full of linens. "The walls, as they say, have ears."

"Hannah," I called out, "if you don't soon get that wash on the line, the sun will be well on its way to China."

After the girl had left the cottage, I turned to the captain and Mrs. Kitson. "I'm afraid, Mrs. Kitson, that you have been misinformed. We have no intention of going anywhere."

At this, the captain banged his cane on the wooden floor and removed his pipe from his mouth while his wife looked on, arms folded across her chest and head held high.

"My dear, we happen to know that good Mr. Moodie and that young hothead Tom Wales are this very hour in the thrall of some lying land-shark preaching about the wonders of colonial life."

Although I owed the meddlesome couple no explanation, I held my anger and calmly assured them that while the matter has come up between us, we have no plans to emigrate.

"And a good thing," roared Captain Kitson, "for I have come to tell you I know from experience that the wilds of Canada are no place for the likes of you and Mr. Moodie. I don't mean to insult you when I say that a fine settler's wife you would make, you who is always taking to your bed with one complaint or another, and when you're up, spending all your time reading and writing. I have visited the colonies many times during the American War, and I assure you that sort of business won't wash in a rough country like Canada. Think of the bairn." (I hadn't begun to show and yet they knew about even this.) "Better stay here, where you've a nice cottage furnished by your own hand, lovely views of the sea from these front windows, an oven, a pump and a coal bin all under one roof . . ."

I was on the verge of reminding him that the oven smoked badly and, anyway, the matter was none of their business, but instead I thanked them politely and showed them the door.

Sure enough, Moodie returned from his outing determined once again to break down my resistance. I am not sure if I have married a gullible fool or a relentless goad. Both, it seems. All day long, it was Cattermole this and Cattermole that. William Cattermole, a land agent with the same Canada Company that my brother Sam worked for when he first arrived in the colonies, lives in Bungay, and it was he who delivered the lecture in Norwich extolling the Edenic pleasures awaiting one in the New World.

Moodie spent the morning fairly pleading with me to "see common sense," and the afternoon demolishing my objections one by one. "My dearest sweet girl, your fears are without foundation. The land is blessed, the climate fair; think how your own brother has prospered while we languish here, destined to be paupers, our children doomed to certain penury. What are you afraid of? There are no snakes, no lions or elephants in Canada, just wide-open spaces, free land, ours for the taking. And if civilization beckons, there is York, a brief carriage ride from our backwoods estate. Mr. Cattermole says it is equal to any provincial town in Britain. Where is your spirit of adventure, Susanna?"

Adventure. Is he mad? How can he be taken in like this? I finally turned on him as he followed me along the path to Reydon Hall, where I was going to meet Agnes. "Moodie, can you not see through Mr. Cattermole's fine talk? He receives a commission for every fool he ensnares with his promises of heaven on earth. Do you really want to count yourself among them?"

Moodie's lust for adventure has taken possession of his good sense. Is he to be fair game for every huckster who crosses his path?

AUGUST 5, 1831

Oh dear, I had hoped Agnes would prove an ally in the stalemate that has arisen between my husband and me. But no, when I unburdened myself, asking her to intervene on my behalf, she refused.

"Susanna, I cannot come between a man and his wife. You must settle this yourselves; that is what the good Lord intended when he blessed your union. He will give you the strength and wisdom to sort out all things. Now go home and . . ."

And so on and so on and so forth until I thought I might leap upon her and scratch her pious eyes out. Instead, I stamped my foot like the petulant child I am so often reduced to in her presence and demanded to know her opinion on the matter of emigration.

On this she had a great deal to impart, not much of it to my liking. She reiterated Moodie's argument that we have no hope of social advancement here. When I pointed out that surely she herself is in a similar situation, she countered that on the contrary, her writing has provided her with an entree into court society that is ("no disrespect intended") surely beyond *my* expectations (my "undeniable talents notwithstanding") now that I am to be burdened with the responsibilities of domesticity. She went on to enumerate Moodie's admirable qualities, including a "natural joie de vivre" which would surely sour and atrophy without the challenges and adventures a new world would most certainly provide.

"Do you want the strangulation of a vibrant spirit such as your husband's on your conscience? It is your wifely duty to follow where he leads, to support him in all his endeavours, to be his helpmeet and closest companion."

When did my independent-minded sister turn into such a mouthpiece for dull convention? But now that my anger is cooling, I can't deny the common sense of much of what she had to say. Moodie, as a half-pay officer, is eligible for a land grant in Upper Canada, surely an opportunity not to be wasted, as Agnes observed. She told me her favourite brother-in-law once complained to her he was in danger of "Suffolkating" here in the Southwold countryside that is so dear to my heart.

Then she informed me we are about to become the beneficiaries of a small (after being divided between eight of us) legacy from our father's sister Jane, whose passing, I'm sorry to say, I knew nothing of.

"It is not much," said Agnes, "but enough to pay for your passage and perhaps sustain you until you find your footing in the New

World. Look how Sam has prospered. I urge you to spend it wisely, Susanna. Don't squander it on a way of life you cannot afford."

Such condescension. "Wifely duty" indeed. What of *my* "vibrant spirit"? I had hoped for her support, but now I think she would like to be rid of me, and the competition for literary distinction I surely represent. I have written Kate, whose good judgment and concern for my well-being I know I can count on.

"All right, I will think about it." That was all I said, but those seven little words set in motion a series of events that has acquired the momentum of a team of horses heading for the stable. I capitulated only because Kate too has counselled me to follow Moodie's wishes. She says I am the "most fortunate of us all" to be bathed in the radiance of love and marriage. "Of course, Agnes is jealous," she wrote. "I think she is half in love with Mr. Moodie. And why not? He is a fine man, and I do believe you two stand as good a chance for domestic happiness as any two persons I know."

She went on to say that I must not be ruled by my natural tendency to anticipate demons and doom lurking around every corner, chiding me for my familiar pessimism. "It cannot be as bad as all that in Canada," she offered. "Thousands are embarking for those shores every day. Are they all dupes and fools? And judging by Sam's accounts, it is a land of opportunity. Trust your good husband's judgment, Susanna. Though I hate the thought of losing you, I hate even more the danger to your future happiness if you persist in this line of thinking."

Moodie is a whirlwind of activity, making preparations for what now, despite my still-considerable reservation, seems inevitable. And now that he assumes my acquiescence, my dearest husband is happier than I have yet seen him, frantically writing letters to every notable personage either of us has ever encountered, in an effort to, as he puts it, "smooth our way into colonial society." He is quite convinced that a word or two in the right ear will land him a sine-cure of some kind—postmaster or customs officer or something of that nature, a position with a salary to supplement our farm income and his pension. It is hard not to be carried away by his enthusiasm, and I try not to give voice to my negative thoughts, but I sometimes think his optimism has taken his better judgment hostage. I remind myself we are embarking on a life in the Canadian wilderness, not a holiday in the Cotswolds.

Despite (or perhaps because of) this, we have never been happier, and as long as I muzzle my uncertainty, our days are as light-hearted as the strains of Moodie's flute and as passionate as his ardent affec-tion. I have written to Kate to tell her of our congealing plans, and my sister has quit cousin Rebecca's company and is returning to Reydon so that we may spend as much time as possible together in the months to come. "I cannot believe we will soon be parting," she wrote back, "perhaps for years and possibly for life."

Can this really be happening?

DECEMBER 1, 1831

We fell upon one another as soon as we met, weeping like little chil-dren. How long has it been—four months? five?—since I last held my dear sister's hand and walked beside these marshlands by this changeable sea? It is impossible to imagine a lifetime without her. I could see her trying to hold back, to smile through her tears and shore up my doubts with encouragement.

"Oh, Susie, it will be wonderful. I will miss you unbearably, yes, but I envy you too. To think, a whole new world, a whole new life. I have come to believe travel is good for the soul. Why, these last few

129

months away with cousin Rebecca have altered me in ways I can hardly express. Exposure to new vistas transforms one, oddly making one even more one's self. I assure you, I am a changed person since I saw you last." Her eyes shone and I admit she looked radiant, her cheeks fatter and pinker than when she left. Time and travel have done their good work, and I believe she has shaken her attachment to Francis Harral for good.

We stopped to rest (swollen feet, swollen everything these days!) on the small bench Moodie fashioned last summer, as though he foresaw the relief it would give me now. Rough-hewn from the remains of a tall pine blown down in a spring typhoon, it faces the sea. How many warm evenings have my love and I sat on that very bench, watching the gulls career against a cloudless sky or an approaching storm race across the bay? It takes my breath away to realize I may never again feel those consoling summer breezes against my skin. Today, as my sister and I wrapped our cloaks tightly against the cold drizzle blowing in from the sea, I told her of our plans.

"We will leave as soon after my confinement as is possible, in May or June, we hope. Mr. Cattermole says it is best to arrive in time to build a small house and clear a few acres before winter sets in. Tom Wales—you remember him? Young and a bit wild, but Moodie says he's a good sort. Tom sailed this fall and has promised to stake out a choice lot for us on the Otonabee River, close to Sam." My voice deserted me then, and I prayed Katie would not notice my tears. I held her hand in both of mine and tried to laugh. "Otonabee. It sounds so strange."

"Otonabee," she repeated, and we sat for a moment in silence, not daring to look at one another while the rain wet our faces. There will be plenty of time for tears.

We have a house guest, one of Moodie's fellow officers and country-men, Thomas Traill. He will remain with us for a week before going on to London to attend to unspecified business matters. My dearest is beside himself, delighted at this reunion with someone with whom he can reminisce about their common Orkney roots and share sol-dierly escapades, stories that I am ashamed to say I am sick to death of hearing.

While I find Mr. Traill a dignified and well-mannered guest, it is difficult to see what besides the aforementioned he and my husband have in common. Tall, skeletal and serious, he seldom speaks except in one-word assents to Moodie's vivacious chatter. Mostly he nods in a sage manner, or removes his pipe to allow a half smile to enliven his long face, or knits his considerable brow in sympathy with the ongoing discourse. They are like day and night. On his first evening with us, while Moodie was bedding Pegasus (yes, we have acquired a mule and cart, though I was compelled to dip into Aunt Jane's legacy to pay for it) down for the night, Mr. Traill stood and, taking a candle from the dining table, used it to peruse our modest but steadily growing library with great interest. "Ah, Voltaire, Rousseau," he said. "*Vous êtes très au courant, n'est pas?*"

"Not really," I replied. "They are a little beyond me, I fear. Mr. Moodie is the true scholar in our household," I said with perhaps exaggerated modesty. "If my French were better. You speak fluently?"

"I do," Traill said without airs.

"And Greek and Latin too, I imagine?"

He nodded and pulled our copy of the *Inferno* from the shelf. "Italian and Spanish as well, I'm afraid." He arched his tangled eye-brows in an expression of amused embarrassment and replaced the book. "Perhaps while I am your guest, I can make myself useful by giving you lessons. We can read passages of Montaigne together and then discuss *en français*. I understand the French language is widely spoken in the colonies."

"I should like that," I said just as Moodie returned.

"*Assez tôt*," my husband said, shaking the rain from his hat and coat and tossing them on the stairs. "Lessons, yes, soon enough. But if this infernal rain lets up, we shall go shooting tomorrow, my friend. It will be grouse for my lady's supper or I'm a parson's ass."

I reminded Moodie that tomorrow we dine at Reydon Hall, where our guest (a widower!) will have the dubious pleasure of meeting five of my all-too-available sisters. In his laconic way, I do believe Mr. Traill is looking forward to it.

Despite his rather austere bearing, I like Mr. Traill. I only wish Moodie would cease his endless talk of emigrating. I fear our poor guest will doze off if he hears another sermon about mighty rivers and inland seas.

JANUARY 31, 1832

I believe Mr. Traill is wooing my sister Kate! It is an odd match, I must say, considering Katie's irrepressible optimism and Traill's dour outlook on the world. "I am not disposed to be sanguine about anything," I overheard him telling Moodie the other day as my husband regaled his friend with predictions of the wealth that surely awaits us in the New World. (Perhaps this is why I have a soft spot for Mr. Traill; he is a pessimist after my own heart.) But as their friendship certainly attests, opposites attract. I only hope dear Katie is well and truly over her recent disappointment and not looking for comfort in the arms of another.

Mama and Agnes are appalled. Like Moodie, Mr. Traill is from a distinguished, though bankrupt, Scottish family. But he is more than a decade older than Kate, and he has two young sons, now living with his late wife's family, while he has moved to London in hopes of improving his fortunes. (Moodie confided to me that his friend is burdened with debts.) I fear marrying a penniless country girl will do little to improve his circumstances. Still, Kate is radiant, and after so much recent sadness, I celebrate that.

I do not know how much longer I can endure my pregnancy. It is against nature to be this large and awkward. Only a few more weeks, surely. Moodie teases me unmercifully as I waddle from room to room, saying I resemble a giant pumpkin and speculating that if I grow any larger, we will be forced to vacate our small cottage. Despite my discomfort, I cannot help but be amused by his teasing, and laughter is better than tears. We are convinced it will be a boy, whom we will call Thomas after dear Papa. Apparently, my husband has hopes our son will be a musician, as he spends his evenings serenading my great belly with the sounds of his flute. Such nonsense.

Mr. Traill is a frequent guest. The courtship continues, often by the fire in our own front parlour, while Moodie and I retire to the kitchen hearth to allow the couple a modicum of privacy. When they are not whispering together, they are both full of questions about Canada, and Moodie is only too happy to spread out his pamphlets and hold forth on the innumerable benefits of emigration.

To pass the time (which seems to drag unbearably), I have begun collecting the clothing I shall need for our new life: flannel petticoats, a pair of sturdy boots, knitted stockings. And just this morning, Mrs. Kitson came by and presented me with two warm cloaks she says no longer fit her. She also brought a pile of swaddling cloths she has kept, she confessed, since losing her own dear little ones many years ago. I had not known until then of her sorrow and I received her gift gratefully, ruing the uncharitable opinions I had previously held of her and the captain. Even meddling busybodies have their hardships to bear.

I have only the dear Lord to thank for the fact that I am sitting here on this bright spring morning with all its newness cradling our dear little daughter in my arms. That we both live and breathe is truly a miracle. I could not call myself a writer if I did not attempt to put into words some of what I endured to bring this sweet babe into the world.

My waters broke on Sunday evening a fortnight since. Moodie and I were reading by the last light of a dwindling candle, and I remember thinking, *Another day done and still we wait.* As I pulled myself to my feet, silently lamenting the fact that I would have to venture out into the wet and cold to visit the privy or I would surely not last the night, an involuntary cascade of warm fluids ran down my legs and I knew my time had come. With surprising calm, for I was aflame with excitement and dread, I told Moodie he must fetch the midwife and send word to Reydon Hall that the birth was imminent.

Ha! Imminent? It was to be another two days and a half, until one thirty in the morning of February 14, that my agony continued, the last seven hours beating all that I had ever imagined of mortal suffering. Thank heavens for my dear Katie, who remained at my side for the duration, never once succumbing to the panic that threatened to overwhelm me, even when the midwives (for Bessie Brown soon required the assistance of her sister-in-law Molly) openly despaired of this baby ever being be born alive. There was talk of sending for the doctor, and through my delirium, I wondered how we would ever pay him. Then, as another battering ram of pain came over me, I reflected I was unlikely to be around to care. Many times during my lengthy ordeal, I thought I would surely die, and in my great distress, I am ashamed to admit I heartily cursed the dear man whose attentions had brought me to this nadir.

And now it is as if I dreamed the whole event. But I will never forget those merciless waves of pain rising in a crescendo of agony and then subsiding like the ebbing tides, only to return again and again and again. And on the edges of my awareness, the whispering women in their dab caps and smocks, the smoke from the neglected fire, the sounds of children outside, on their way to school, people going about their everyday lives while time stood still in the realms of my exhaustion. Until, with one final Herculean effort, I pushed my daughter out into the cold, cold night.

Before they would let me hold her, they took her away to make her ready, as though it would not do for me to see my own infant in the bloody, dishevelled aftermath of her birth. As though we must put the primal mess of it behind us, out of mind—the temporary loss of reason, the glimpse of the savage within—and proceed, eyes forward, into the future, as though we had some control over that. I could hear the midwives clucking over her as they cleaned and weighed her, a bustle of handmaidens laughing softly. I strained to sit up. I wanted to see what they were doing; I wanted to see her.

At last they brought her, swaddled in a soft blanket, the dark hairs on her head still wet, smelling of soap, her face scrunched and blotchy. They placed her at my side, against my bare chest, and she nuzzled my breast like a kitten. We recognized one another at once, and a great spreading joy like melted chocolate flowed through me. "Hello," I said.

Now, in the lap of calm reflection, I am amazed that my own mother brought forth eight of us in such a manner and never once during the past nine months did she ever so much as hint at what I, the first of her daughters to bear a child of her own, was heading for. I have asked her since and even petitioned my older sisters for their memories of what surely must have been events that rocked the old Hall. But like Macbeth's witches, to a one they smiled their mysterious smiles, cooed at their precious new niece and grand-daughter and declined to speak of it. Am I, with this account, break-ing an age-old code of silence? If so, I vow here and now to shatter it.

Moodie was banished for the entirety of my labour and spent his time among his friends at the Crown, where he was kindly provided with a bed and sustenance. Oblivious to my trials, he passed the time drinking, telling stories and taking bets as to the sex of our unborn child.

We will christen her Catherine Mary Josephine, dear little Kate. Our daughter continues to thrive and is a perfect angel in every way. Mrs. Kitson says she has never met so contented a baby. Even Agnes is charmed.

APRIL 16, 1832

I am sworn to secrecy, but I fear I may explode if I do not tell some-one soon: Kate and Mr. Traill are betrothed. There it is. My sister will defy our mother's obvious disapproval and link herself to a man she has known less than three months. As wonderful as this news is to me (I have seen them together and there is real affection between them, of that I am certain), it was Kate's next announcement that catapulted me from the chair I was sitting in as though I had been shot from a cannon.

I should have guessed. How else to explain their patient interest (and what I had assumed was merely polite curiosity) as evening after evening, Moodie went over in minute detail the plans for our New World adventure? How else to account for the looks of rapture on my sister's face, the intensity of Mr. Traill's concentration as my husband spread out his maps and pamphlets and assaulted them with his enthusiasm for emigration. Apparently, insolvency is a powerful motivator, powerful enough to persuade a cultured linguist and philo-sopher to abandon civilization and try his lot in the wilderness. Of

Kate's resilience I have no doubt, but Mr. Traill does seem an unlikely pioneer. Moodie cannot see it and dismisses my skepticism.

"Once an Orkney man, always an Orkney man," he said. "Beneath my friend's stooped shoulders beats a heart steeped in the churning seas and buffeting winds of our homeland. He is tougher than he seems, Susie. You will see, my dear."

I truly doubt it. Nevertheless, I was overjoyed when Kate told me. Her eagerness is like a flock of tiny birds borne aloft on a summer breeze. Already, I can feel it infecting my spirit.

Mama will be inconsolable.

APRIL 28, 1832

I have relented under pressure from Moodie and Mama and arranged for Hannah to join our party, even though in the months she has been with our household, I have been less than impressed. Nothing specific—she carries out her duties competently—but there is something, a whiff of resentment in the way she clears the table, a habit of looking past me when she speaks, her brisk way with little Katie. Moodie says I am imagining things and we should count ourselves fortunate to have obtained the services of one so young and yet so experienced. Mama too, whose household Hannah served for several months before joining ours, is to my mind unaccountably enamoured of the girl. But they are not with her all day long. This morning, as I was nursing little Kate, I was suddenly thirsty and asked Hannah, who was in the kitchen, to bring me a glass of water.

"There's water in the jug by the bookshelf, ma'am," she called back in a tone that seemed to me verging on insolence.

"If I could reach the bookshelf from here," I replied, "I would gladly fetch it for myself, but as you can see . . ." By this time, she had appeared, leaning against the doorway, wiping her hands with a cloth.

"Yes, ma'am," she said, and without another word strode over to the water pitcher, poured a glass and set it by my side.

When I try to describe incidents like this to Moodie, he laughs and tells me I have too little to occupy my mind and that the boredom of the nursery has turned me into a grumpy Gertie.

"The thing is impossible, Susie. You cannot do without a maid."

In any case, while she has agreed to the arrangement, Hannah has shown little enthusiasm for the prospect of emigration (on that point, at least, we agree). But her current circumstances leave her no recourse. It seems she has been seduced by one of the farmhands at Reydon Hall, and although she now finds herself in a position where marriage is a matter of necessity, the young man has refused to have anything to do with her. Moodie, in his inimitable way, sees this situation as an advantage.

"Children are a blessing in the wilderness," he said. "And if we raise the young one well, it may grow into a well-trained servant someday."

Exhaustion blankets me like a thick fog and I do not have the strength to fight him on this or any other of the myriad preparations I seem to have abdicated all responsibility for.

I sometimes think a kind of madness has overtaken us all.

MAY 13, 1832

Today, my sister Kate was joined in holy matrimony to Thomas Traill in a small ceremony at St. Margaret's. Agnes and I were bridesmaids. Moodie gave the bride away. Mama was in attendance but only at the insistence of Agnes, who could see that all attempts to dissuade Kate from going through with the union had been exhausted and it was time to accept the inevitable.

"The heart will have what the heart wants," is how my elder sister put it to me on the eve of the wedding, "though why Kate wants this man is a mystery to me."

It seems that everyone but Moodie and me is outraged at the idea of Katie marrying Mr. Traill. Sitting beside Mama in church, I could hear her grinding her teeth in anger, and once the deed was done, she bade Sarah take her back to Reydon Hall without even acknowledging the happy couple. Agnes thinks Mama will never get over it.

As she and Sarah walked past where I was waiting outside the church, knee-deep in a tangle of fading daffodils and bright green grasses, beside a garden of tilting headstones, Mama stopped to grip my wrist. "Your sister deserves better. Look after her, Susanna."

MAY 15, 1832

Kate and Mr. Traill departed from these peaceful shores this afternoon, headed for Scotland and thereafter to his birthplace at the island of Sanday. He will introduce his new wife to his family there before continuing on to Glasgow by coach and the voyage out. My sisters and Kate made their impossible goodbyes while Traill waited, leaning on the bow of the rowboat hired to take the newlyweds to the steamer Leith-bound that was waiting offshore. Then Kate and I stood on the broad scimitar of pebbled sand at Southwold, holding one another for a long time while the gulls swooped above us, their sad cries carried out to sea by the wind. We all watched in silence until the steamer was a bobbing dot on the waves and they were gone.

Moodie and I are to leave as soon as he returns from his business in London. We intend to depart directly from Leith, sailing north around the top of Scotland and on to the New World, where, God willing, my beloved sister and I will be reunited with our brother Sam and begin our new lives together in the wilds of Douro. But oh, what oceans of unknown lie before us until then.

This morning, I paid a last visit to my childhood, my beloved Reydon Hall. Agnes, Jane and Sarah were there, and of course, Mama. Eliza, I fear, I will never lay eyes on again, as she is, as always, detained in London by her work. We shared a simple and bittersweet lunch, and then my sisters left me alone with Mama, who made a most shocking and unsettling request. I shall never know if they all were party to it, but it has shaken me so completely that I feel as though I am embarking on a voyage to living perdition.

She was sitting in her chair by the fire with her tiny granddaughter on her lap. And I was thinking how diminished she seems in so many ways, not just physically but spiritually too. How her brittle, uncompromising pride, her insistence on keeping up appearances, has gentled now, making her less formidable, yes, but emptier, as though she has given up, defeated by all the years of trying to hold together this crumbling house and her ever-dispersing family. I was thinking as I watched her cover my child's tiny hands with kisses how hard she has been to love, and now how sad it is that perhaps through this new child there was a chance for Mama and me to finally understand one another, a chance that is about to be swept away like dry leaves before a storm. I was about to say it, that I loved her and the thought of leaving forever was ripping me apart, when she looked up, her lined face alight with its old force.

"Susanna, I beg you, leave little Katie here with me."

My earnest unspoken thoughts faded like a dissonant echo. I could not believe my ears. "My baby? Here? You can't be serious . . ."

"Oh, but I am. I am, Susanna. Here she will be loved and cared for, surrounded by family—"

"Mama, you are asking me to abandon my child? Isn't it enough I am leaving my home, perhaps forever, and now you wish me to leave a slice of my heart, a portion of my very self, behind as well?"

The baby, who had been chewing strenuously on an arthritic knuckle, seemed to pause at the sound of desperation in her mother's voice. I quickly pulled her into my arms and she began to whimper and tug at my bonnet string. Mama rearranged her skirt, pulled a handkerchief from her purse and began rolling the finely stitched hem between her fingers.

"It is the child's welfare I am thinking of. You must consider the advantages of—"

"Of what? Of being deprived of both her parents? What are the advantages of that?"

"Of a proper education, of society and culture . . ."

"Mama? Consider what you are proposing. Please."

She turned her face and looked out the window. I followed her gaze and I do not know if her mind was registering the extravagance of the yellow briar rose climbing the garden wall. It is said to be more than a hundred years old, the oldest of its kind in the parish. And it struck me right then as I held my babe to my breast that its thorny beauty would likely outlive us all, that it would bloom year after year without reservation or prejudice whether we stayed or sailed. The reflection made me feel as tiny as a grain of sand. Mama looked again at me, her eyes faded and blue, and the sadness there moved me nearly to tears.

"I cannot bear to lose you both," she whispered.

I placed Katie once more in her arms and let myself out into the garden for a last look. Standing in the deep shade of the chestnut trees, I could almost hear my long-lost brother, little Sam, entreating me to hurry, to catch him if I could, as he vaulted the stile, dodging the sheaves of newly cut hay on his way down to the river. I thought how cruel that I should be leaving dear England just as the colours and sounds and smells of my girlhood are at their most striking, that the gorgeous exuberance of an English spring should be in my memory forever enveloped in a bittersweet haze.

MAY 21, 1832

High winds and driving rain have prevented our departure for the past two days as attempts to row out to the *City of Edinburgh* have proved impossible in the billowing seas. Moodie says we must leave tomorrow no matter what the weather, or we are in danger of missing our connection at Leith with the ship on which we have booked passage to Canada. So violent were the waves pounding our Suffolk shores yesterday that I thought our party would surely drown before my husband at last relented in response to my pleas and ordered the boatman to return to the beach. Even in the midst of my terror, I marvelled at Moodie's courage as he stood in the rowboat's bow, drenched to the skin, clearly exhilarated at this chance to pit himself against the wild and indifferent seas, as though by sheer force of will he could conquer what God had wrought.

As Hannah and I cowered with the infant in the stern, I thought of Lord Byron's lines: "and should I leave behind / The inviolate island of the sage and free, / And seek me out a home by a remoter sea."

Now, safe in my own rooms, at least for the moment, I cannot help but wonder how, if we were nearly defeated by the waves pounding this "inviolate island," we will fare on the arduous voyage that lies ahead?

Until tomorrow.

JUNE 15, 1832 (LEITH, EDINBURGH)

It has been nearly a month since our arrival in this carnival seaport where everyone seems to be on their way to or from somewhere else, and the crooked, cobbled streets are a babel of tongues from around the world. I have never seen the likes of it—the harbour crowded with brigs and schooners, the stone quays and warehouses piled high with Norwegian barley and timber, furs from Quebec, Dutch clocks, Russian wheat, and wines from Portugal and Spain. The native Scots are as warm and romantic as Moodie has always described them, and I have spent many hours trying to capture the cadences and rhythms of their speech on paper. Edinburgh is surely a city of romance and poetry. The day Moodie and I climbed Arthur's Seat, the hulking rock that presides over the city like a sleeping dragon, and looked out over the steeples and turrets of this ancient metropolis, I almost wished that our journey might begin and end here in this exalted and civilized place.

But with these endless and unforeseen delays, the dread that dogs me like a mangy cur has returned. We did indeed miss our connection, and our passage sailed without us two days before our arrival here. I suggested to Moodie that we might travel by coach to Glasgow and find a ship there, thus sparing us the necessity of sailing around the stormy northern tip of Scotland, but my husband rejected the notion, saying the forty miles of road to the west coast is a pothole-strewn track. Perhaps, but I believe his true motive is a hope of gazing one last time upon the red sandstone cliffs and rocky outcroppings of his Orkney home as our ship sails past. In this, I cannot fault him.

Still, not many ships anchored here travel that route, and so our choices have been limited. If Moodie has his way, we are to leave the day after tomorrow aboard *The Flora*, bound for Quebec. But when he took me this morning to the docks for a last-minute inspection of the vessel, I was appalled at its filthy condition and the fearful appearance of the captain, a one-eyed, lame wretch whose vigorous and constant cursing turned the air black and blue. Aboard this floating prison, we are meant to share a vermin-ridden cabin with fourteen other unfortunate souls of dubious origin. I insisted Moodie cancel our booking at once.

"Susanna," he said, "stop this. You will do as I say. We have no choice but to proceed as planned. *The Flora* may well be the last ship to sail this season." His tone made my jaw ache with anger, but I said nothing. I am resolved, however, to find another ship to deliver us to our uncertain future. Surely it is not my wifely duty to agree to the unthinkable.

JUNE 16, 1832

We have booked passage aboard *The Anne* on July 1; it will be the last ship to leave this port for Canada this year. I saw the notice nailed to a gatepost yesterday on one of my rambles about the city and ran back to the Black Bull, where I found Moodie in earnest conversation with some of his new friends. We immediately located the ship, and I was relieved beyond measure to find it a floating paradise compared to the ark of pestilence to which my husband had previously condemned us. Moodie has deemed her a small but worthy vessel. A ninety-two-ton, single-masted brig, she is captained by a dour but well-spoken Scot called George Rodgers and has a crew of seven and an energetic terrier named Oscar. Our small party will be the only cabin passengers sharing a spartan but clean outer room with an adjoining berth for me and little Kate. Another seventy-two cheap fares will travel below decks in steerage. Weather permitting, the voyage will take about six weeks to reach Montreal, and I admit that now it is settled, I cannot believe how eager I am to be off.

PART FOUR
1832
–
1833
THE NEW WORLD

---◆---

August 11, 1832 (Grand Banks, Newfoundland)

For ten days now, our ship has floundered and flapped like a dead whale adrift in seas that heave and roll and heave and roll, enveloped in a fog so thick, it makes it difficult to breathe. Suspended here between the briny depths and the invisible sky, we inhabit a kind of purgatory, silent and windless, with the creak and groaning of timbers, the flap of sails constant and yet not loud enough to drown the moans and cries that emanate day and night from steerage. Whenever I think my own misery is too much to bear, I try to consider the plight of the seventy-two wretched souls below, crowded into a space not more than sixty feet long and ten feet wide. Men and women and children, all their belongings sharing the fetid hold with the rats and the stinking bilge for seven weeks now. It is a miracle none has died and disease is not rampant. I fear, however, that whatever empathy I may once have mustered for the lower classes has deserted me entirely. The smell, even here above deck—a nauseating miasma of rotting food and unwashed bodies, of vomit and excrement—fills me instead with waves of revulsion for their sorry lot.

Captain Rodgers says we are becalmed on the Grand Banks of Newfoundland, and that if the fog would only clear, we might even catch a glimpse of land by now. He says there is no telling how long these doldrums will last. So near and yet so far. Land. Occasionally, an iceberg emerges from the fog, brooding and magnificent, but of land we have seen nothing since leaving Scotland.

The steerage passengers are starving, the provisions they brought with them long gone or spoiled. We are all of us in more or less the same boat. The captain is rationing what little fresh water remains, as well as the ship's store of hard biscuits and a few sacks of oatmeal. We are obliged to consume copious quantities of ale (which, absurdly, adds an edge of merriment while its effects last, making the tedium slightly easier to bear) or the strong, bitter tea brewed by the crew. Until these last endless days, I have been spared the seasickness that has plagued so many, but finally, these roiling, roiling seas have prevailed and turned me inside out with a wretched nausea. I am unable even to nurse my little Kate, who must subsist on the spoonfuls of thin gruel I manage to coax into her tiny mouth. Hannah, perhaps infected by the prospect of egalitarianism that awaits us at our destination, has abandoned her nursemaid duties, claiming her "condition" prevents her from carrying on. And yet she seems well enough to engage in the most shameful flirtation with our supposedly Calvinist captain. With little to do as *The Anne* bobs like a cork in the ocean, the pair spend many hours in the "privacy" of his berth while Moodie and I pretend not to notice, since we have learned that confrontation of any kind is to be avoided in such close quarters.

My husband is not bothered by the deplorable conditions; indeed, he seems to relish hardship. He says he views these trials as a challenge to his ingenuity. It is the boredom, the excruciating monotony of life at sea that afflicts him most. And so he spends his days shooting at seabirds or trolling for codfish that the crew say can grow to more than ten feet in length. What he would do if he were to hook such a leviathan, I do not know, but so far luck has eluded him.

This morning, Moodie proposed that he and a tall fellow called

MacDonald take one of the lifeboats on a little fishing excursion. Captain Rodgers, to his credit, forbade it, saying the unpredictable winds could come up at any time, and if that happened in their absence, *The Anne* would be compelled to sail on without them. I placed a fond, firm hand on my husband's arm and silently thanked the captain for his prudence and authority.

Playing the part of the submissive, forbearing wife is a role that continues to prickle like a burr in my stocking. Even when I know better, I am expected to smile and submit. It is not in my nature.

SEPTEMBER 11, 1832 (COBOURG, UPPER CANADA)

We disembarked at Cobourg's ramshackle jetty two days ago, just as darkness was falling over the town. I must say Cobourg is not much improved by daylight—what little I have seen of it, that is— but at least we are all fed and somewhat rested. The window of this hotel room, which is ours only until tomorrow, looks onto the unpainted side wall of a smithy, and we have been serenaded since before dawn by the steady clang of iron on iron and the intermittent exhalations of a very large bellows. Nevertheless, now that I have the luxury of four walls and a table to write on that does not pitch and roll like a wild horse, I am determined to chronicle the rest of our journey into the dark heart of this incomprehensible land while the memory is still fresh. Tomorrow, we move to the Steamboat Hotel, which Moodie assures me has a pretty view of the town's crescent-shaped harbour, where three schooners and our own *William* are moored. My husband has been waxing enthusiastically all morning about our prospects, until I fear I was compelled to ask him to leave me to my writing. But as soon as he left, I was over-come by an uncontrollable fit of weeping and longings for home that I could hardly suppress. I know he is trying to cheer me up, but

I cannot fathom his optimism and I find it has the opposite effect on my own spirit.

Our first sight of Canada came in the early hours of the morning on the second-to-last day of August, after we had been at sea for more than eight weeks. It was not, however, the joyous occasion I had anticipated, as the high cliffs of the Gaspé, when they finally emerged from the thick fog, seemed as unreal as an obscure dream, without the reassuring solidity I had imagined for so long. Percé Rock was little more than a shadow lurking on the horizon. The place is called Cape Rosier, and we sat at anchor there for a day or so while a party went ashore to take on fresh water and, thanks be to heaven, some milk for the baby, as well as a store of potatoes and coarse bread, which the captain distributed among the steerage passengers, who received their rations quietly and gratefully. When we finally pulled anchor and began our voyage down into the mouth of the St. Lawrence, I felt as though we were being swallowed whole by a great and terrifying unknown.

Two days later, we arrived at Grosse Isle, Quebec. From a distance, in the early morning, the island looked like a slice of paradise. Moodie pulled me from my berth just as the sun was rising out of the endless blue expanse behind us. It cast a rose-and-yellow light on the wide, misty river and the still far-off but unmistakable shorelines before us.

We pushed through the throng of steerage passengers already gathered on deck and found a place at the portside rail, from where we could see Grosse Isle, one of an archipelago of green and rocky outposts that would be our first landfall after so many weeks at sea. With one arm wrapped tightly around my waist to shield me and our daughter from the jostling crowd, which, like us, fairly vibrated with excitement at the sight of our new land, Moodie stabbed at the clear morning air with his free hand.

"Will ye look at that, my darling girl," he said in an awed whisper.

"A sight for sore eyes, shore an' it is." (After so many months in the company of his fellow Scots, my husband's brogue had become as thick as the porridge he loves.)

There, floating in the calm waters before us, lay a low expanse of green rocks edged with white sand beaches and dotted with black-roofed cottages. So placid and idyllic did the place appear that it occurred to me we might have been approaching the dear, dear shores so recently left behind. Whether it was from sadness or antic-ipation or simply weakness brought on by so long at sea, I felt a cramp of longing rising in my throat and tears burned my eyes.

The Anne anchored into a quiet bay a mile or so off shore, and the chaotic process of disembarkation began—men, women and children crowding one another for places in the two boats that would ferry them to dry land. As cabin passengers, Moodie and I were not required to go ashore, but all those in steerage were instructed to leave the ship to be inspected for signs of cholera and other diseases before being allowed back on board. As well, every article of bedding and clothing had to be taken ashore and washed thoroughly. Captain Rodgers told us that anyone showing signs of illness would be placed in quarantine (that's what the tidy cottages—actually rude sheds, I soon learned,—were for) and left there until they either recovered or died.

When I remarked upon the pleasant aspect of our destination, the captain laughed. "Many things look well at a distance," he said in what might have been one of the longest speeches I had yet heard him deliver, "which are bad enough when near. Isle of Death is what I'd call it."

Despite this dire summation, I could hardly wait to set foot on terra firma, and the closer we came, the more I was overcome by an almost maddened craving for a slice of freshly baked brown bread and English butter. Imagine my distress when our captain refused me permission to leave the ship, saying Grosse Isle "was no place for a lady." Instead, Hannah was sent ashore with our laundry, and a gleeful Moodie and Captain Rodgers joined the last boatload to see about obtaining more badly needed supplies.

"Bread and butter," I called pitifully from the top deck as I watched them pull away in the ship's crowded dinghy.

They returned a few hours later, empty-handed (the supply ship would not arrive from Quebec until the next day) but with the welcome news that the captain had relented and I would be allowed off the filthy prison after all, perhaps the following day.

I soon came to see why the captain had been so reluctant to allow me to go ashore. If the watery doldrums we had endured a fortnight ago constituted purgatory, then the scenes of debauchery and misery I witnessed on the swarming island could be described as hell on earth. While the captain pulled rhythmically at the oars, his back to the approaching land, Moodie and I sat in the stern with little Kate in my arms and Oscar the terrier bouncing at our feet. From a distance, the thousands of persons scurrying here and there over the rocks and sand appeared as busy and diligent as worker bees, laying their blankets and cloaks to dry on the sun-warmed stones, scrubbing shirts and breeches in the kettles provided or in the natural indentations of the rocky shore. Children cavorted in the mid-afternoon sun, with the gulls screaming and flapping overhead.

The idyllic scene began to disintegrate the closer we came. The first thing that assailed us when we were within hailing distance of the island was a chorus of curses and complaints, raucous laughter and ear-shattering screams, the noise carrying across the water as clearly as though we were sitting in the midst of the writhing mass of humanity before us. It seemed that each hideous syllable was hurled like a jagged rock in our direction. Oscar's persistent barking could barely be heard above the din. Finally, I gave Kate to my husband to hold and placed both hands over my ears in rebellion against the onslaught of curses. Rodgers continued rowing with uninterrupted intention, a broad smile cracking his leathery face.

"So, Mrs. Moodie, welcome to Canada."

I looked at Moodie in amazement, and not wanting to appear squeamish in front of the captain, I suppose, he cocked his head to one side in a gesture of helplessness.

"It's the Irish, Susanna." He pointed to a ship just visible around a point of land to our right. "They arrived yesterday, three hundred and fifty wretched souls added to the thousand or so sick and dying already abandoned here."

A few moments later, our little boat scraped ashore and Rodgers jumped out and pulled it onto the granite shelf. Moodie gave me his hand, and with great awareness of the symbolic import of the occasion, I placed one foot upon the unforgiving surface of my future.

And then, as quickly as I could, I drew it back with a cry of surprise. Because that rock was as hot as molten lead. How the shoeless throngs milling all around us could bear it I do not know. Moodie urged me on and we skipped as quickly as we could over the undulating shield, through the half-naked savages who, in their animal delirium, paid no attention to our respectable little party. As much as I could, I kept my eyes fixed on the ground, not just to avoid the scenes of pandemonium, but also because, in places, the rocks were slick with excrement and vomit. There was a real danger of falling and, despite Moodie's steadying arm, being trampled in the melee. Delighted to be on land, Oscar wove through the crowds in delirious circles while the screaming children chased him with sticks. Half-naked women, their skirts rolled to their waists, bosoms bared to the world, fought over scraps of clothing and tattered blankets. Men lay about drunkenly in the afternoon heat, cradling bottles of brandy and rum. To my great disgust, I was obliged to witness a filthy youth *in flagrante delicto* with a woman who by all appearances was completely insensible. I could see that even Moodie was disturbed by the atmosphere of anarchy and misrule that surrounded us, and when a tall, ragged man wearing only a tattered greatcoat leapt into our path, brandishing a shillelagh, my husband pushed him roughly and sent the demonic fellow sprawling face-first to the ground.

Captain Rodgers, no longer amused by my intense discomfort, hurried us through the crowd toward a wooded area on the other side of the small bay, giving the quarantine sheds a wide berth. Even at a distance, I could see they were little more than cattle pens, and we could clearly hear, over the general din along the shore, the cries and moans of the poor wretches housed there. And every breath of the intermittent breeze carried with it a smell so foul, it paralyzed the senses. At long last, Rodgers ushered us into a sheltered glade beside a stream, and there we rested, surrounded by an Eden of evergreens and flowering shrubs, while he left to attend to his business. I was numb with the shock of it all, and I lay down on a soft bed of pine needles with my head on Moodie's lap while Katie slept.

"My poor Susie," he crooned, stroking my forehead as he had so often done on the endless, unendurable voyage. "It will be better. You will see."

I was too tired to protest, only glad in that moment to be alone with my husband and child. The comfort of his hands upon me seemed as encompassing as the vast and cloudless sky. As I lay there, the very earth beneath me seemed to rock and sway as though we were still at sea, and I slid into a light, untroubled sleep. Then, as the sun began to slip below a great ridge of trees to the west, Captain Rodgers and

Oscar returned to escort us back through the gauntlet of unruly immigrants that lay between us and the relative comfort of *The Anne*.

That evening, sitting on the deck of the nearly empty vessel, after a supper of beef and onions and potatoes—and yes, bread and butter—I was troubled by the intensity of my reactions to all I had witnessed that day. I have lived in proximity to the lower classes all my life: the hard-working Suffolk farmhands, the merchants and tradespeople in the towns and villages, the maids and cooks and stable hands of Reydon Hall. They had their place and I had mine. That was the order of things, an order as immutable as night following day, as roses blooming in summer. But I realized that I had never really been among them, other than during my flirtation with Reverend Ritchie and his simple church. And even that turned out to be an idealistic dream, a work of my imagination. What I saw that day at Grosse Isle, for the first time, gave those people a face and a voice. And I did not like what I saw and heard: the naked hostility in their eyes as we tiptoed onto the rocks, onto the unyielding footing that was as much theirs as ours.

"It's the Irish," my husband repeated. "Rascals and drunkards all of them." But I know better. It has nothing to do with where they are from. It's where they are going that matters, and they know it. The cheap fares aboard *The Anne*, honest and hard-working Scots who all during the filthy, claustrophobic voyage deferred to their betters and knew their place, changed once they set foot on land. On that fetid rock that day, the invisible bonds that had always held everything in place were ripped away. I knew there was no going back, and I was afraid.

Our next stop was Quebec, where most of our fellow travellers disembarked on their way to a better life. Moodie insisted on going ashore too despite the cholera that was rampant in the city as, hour after hour, the bells tolled each death from the dreadful disease. But this time, I chose the safety and quiet of the ship over the open sewers and general chaos that, judging by the vessels of every description crowding into the harbour, must have awaited in the busy lower town. In any case, the view from the deck was superb. *The Anne* was anchored at the foot of sheer cliffs of black rock rising up to the stone fortifications of the citadel, its walls standing like stern sentinels guarding the river and surrounding wilderness. Across the wide, swirling waters, the vast purple forests of the south shore spread out toward infinity under a cloud-dappled sky. For the first time, I felt a stirring of something like gratitude or even awe at the majesty of the untamed place called Canada.

The following day, with Moodie no worse for his adventures, a steamer escorted *The Anne* upriver to Montreal, and there we said good-bye to the little brig that had been our only home all summer long.

Of Montreal, what is there to say? Dirty, disordered, with open sewers, thoroughfares ankle-deep in mud and the disgusting effluvia of the wretched hordes of speculators, soldiers and sailors crawling all over the city. Coffins stacked six deep outside the cemetery gates, ragged urchins, starving dogs, half-naked women begging for coins. On our first night there, we elected to remain on board the ship, but when one of the crew came down with cholera, we took up residence at Goodenough's Hotel, a tolerable oasis in that pestilential place. Thankfully, it was just one sleepless night before we boarded a stagecoach to Lachine. The rest of the journey is a blur, five days of dusty, bone-shattering roads, then two more by steamboat to some other unknown place—Cornwall? At Prescott, we boarded another steamboat, the *William IV*, bound for Cobourg and Toronto. At Brockville, we took on a party of ladies, which after days spent travelling in mostly masculine company, I greatly welcomed. The weather turned cold and stormy and a fearful gale assailed our little vessel, so that when I ventured on deck as we passed the famed Thousand Islands,

I was soon forced back to my berth by the driving rain. The monotony of the voyage—and an entire night's sleep—was finally broken by the antics of a fellow passenger, an Irish rascal who struck up a raucous, incomprehensible tirade outside our cabin door. When one of the lady passengers appeared and bestowed upon him several well-aimed kicks, it only accelerated his bombast.

"Ladies, I'm at yer service; I only wish I could get a dispensation from the Pope, and I'd marry yeas all." Despite our immense fatigue, the unruly immigrant's antics provided comic theatre worthy of Mr. Congreve, and Moodie and I were overcome with a mirth that verged on hysteria. We held each other close and laughed until our tears and exhaustion and the silent swells of the turbulent Ontario finally rocked us back to sleep. The following day, our *William IV*, plying the grey waters of the north shore, at last brought us to Cobourg (gateway to the backwoods). The scale of this vast land is already beyond my comprehension.

The weather soon turned, and it was barely dark on a thick and humid night when our small party made its way on foot through the lurid streets and noisy throngs of ragged, cursing immigrants, until we arrived at a small hotel only to be greeted by the news that the inn was completely full. After Moodie departed in search of other accommodation, I settled my weary bones against some sacks of corn piled in a corner of the main-floor tavern and dispatched a sullen Hannah to the kitchen to find bread and milk for my poor hungry babe. Katie's exhausted cries had finally ceased, perhaps in despair at the futility of competing with the cacophony of carousing Canadians who milled about the airless room. In spite of my dishevelled state after all our travels, two drinkers stared blatantly in my direction with looks that could in no way be interpreted as mere curiosity, and I blushed with shame as well as fear for my person. As I contemplated the prospect of spending the night in such circumstances, I suddenly thought I glimpsed a familiar face. I looked again, but he was gone. And as I struggled to place those darting black eyes, I feared I had been seized by some kind of madness. How likely was it that I would meet someone I knew in this unholy backwater? Then, sure enough, there he was again, this time grinning like a madman, a young man of medium height and build, with hair to his shoulders and a thick, unruly beard. Despite the heat, he was wearing a tattered coat that appeared to be made of animal skins pieced together in a most haphazard manner. By his expression, it was clear he recognized me too, but still I could not place him. And then it came to me. Those eyes! Of course, I would know anywhere Moodie's old Suffolk friend Tom Wales, who had sailed for these far shores six months before us.

So overjoyed was I to encounter a familiar face in this ghastly place that I burst into tears, and handing little Katie to Hannah (the maid's incessant whimpering ceased momentarily at my shriek of joy), I fell into Tom's arms as though he were the Saviour himself. He reeked of sweat and woodsmoke and tobacco, and something else that I later learned was bear grease, which he had smeared on his face and hands to keep the mosquitos at bay. Despite all this, I have never been as happy to see anyone in all my life. And the poor man (whose litany of woes I will elaborate upon later) did indeed prove to be our saviour.

"You shall have my room," said Tom. "I insist. It isn't much, but you shall have a bed at least, and some privacy. I will sleep in the parlour, wrapped in a blanket Indian-style. Don't worry, I am quite used to worse than that," he said, silencing my admittedly weak protests.

By the time Moodie returned, I had accepted Tom's offer and fallen into a deep and tormented sleep.

And so, here we are.

Tom Wales continues to make himself useful, and although he is not much of a comfort, he is kind and full of concern. To think that I disparaged him when he was part of our old life and now I find him the gentlest of souls. My husband, however, has taken an inexplicable dislike to his old friend. When Tom came by our room at the Steamboat this morning with a bowl of strong, bitter tea for me and some milk for the babe, I noticed he was shivering so violently that he resembled a man possessed by some terrible demon. His forehead shone with fever, and I immediately expressed concern and cleared a place for him on the disordered bed so that he could sit down.

"It is this blasted ague," he said through clenched teeth. "I have been afflicted since I arrived in the bush last spring." He glared at us with wild eyes, rocking back and forth and hugging himself in an effort to control the shaking. "Of course, our good friend Cattermole failed to mention the mosquitoes when he sang the praises of this earthly paradise. Or the blackflies, the impassable roads, the endless, impenetrable forests and swamps, the cheating land dealers, an interminable diet of potatoes and pork fat . . ."

Moodie, who must have been as alarmed as I was by this outburst, put a hand on Tom's shoulder. "Now, Tom, get a hold of yourself. It can't be that bad." Poor Tom did not answer; he buried his face in his hands and began to weep in great wrenching sobs that made his shoulders heave. Moodie looked at me and said, as though Tom were not sitting there before us, "Susanna, the poor man is obviously not in his right mind. He is ill or drunk, or both. You mustn't take notice." Moodie took him by the shoulders. "Tom. Stop this. Look, you're frightening Mrs. Moodie out of her wits."

But Tom would not be silenced. He continued weeping and moaning. "All this, and now, with winter coming, it can only get

159

worse. Six months in the bush and I am a broken man, financially, physically, spiritually. As soon as I can raise the money, mark my words, I intend to make the next passage home."

I did not know how to respond to such misery, but my heart was filled with horror and apprehension at what we had undertaken. Tom fixed his frantic, yellowed eyes on mine and took a long draught of his tea, which seemed to still his quaking body momentarily. At length, the spell passed, leaving him pale and shaken, but he did not recant. After he had left, I was rigid with dread. Moodie tried to make light of it. He chattered merrily about the good burghers of Cobourg and the many civilized conveniences available in the town (among them, an academy for boys and girls, a weekly newspaper and an Anglican church).

"Poor Tom," said Moodie. "He never was the most reliable fellow. Drink can do terrible things to a man." And then he tried to distract me with the amusing fact that black bears can frequently be seen strolling the streets and avenues of fair Cobourg. I shuddered and hugged my poor mewling Katie closer.

My spirits lifted when my husband presented me with a creased and tattered letter from Catharine, which she had left behind for us at the hotel desk. To think she and Mr. Traill passed a night in Cobourg a month ago before being swallowed by the backwoods on their way to Peterborough to reconnoitre with our brother Sam. How bereft I am that we missed them! How thankful to know they are alive and well. Poor Kate wrote that she fell ill soon after arriving in Montreal, and though she relates her ordeal with characteristic understatement, her symptoms sound very much like the cholera that is rampant there. She wrote that she is fully recovered, but that she and Mr. Traill decided not to linger in Cobourg for fear of some other illness befalling them, and so, having no idea of our where-abouts, they hastened onward to their final destination.

My dear sister's impressions thus far of this new land diverge greatly from my own, I fear. Where she saw neat white cottages and well-kept orchards hugging the shores of the Ontario, I saw only the dark shadow of the vast forests rising like storm clouds behind the meagre human settlement. Where she noted meadows of familiar flowers—goldenrod, valerian, viper's bugloss—I was preoccupied with the coarse bread, bitter tea and grey waters we encountered en route to this muddy outpost. We seem to agree on one aspect, however, and that is the unremitting rudeness of our fellow settlers, especially the Yankees and the Irish, who are everywhere. In both our experiences, these low-born rustics show little respect for their betters, and in particular I have been disturbed by the widespread practice of allowing servants to sit at table with their employers. After seeing for myself the anarchy that results when civility and order are abandoned, I am determined there will be no such New World innovations when my own household is established.

Still, Kate's fresh and good-humoured account of her experiences has provided a welcome anodyne to Tom Wales's dire predictions of the years of back-breaking labour we face if we are ever to succeed as farmers in the bush. Moodie has dismissed Tom's tales of woe as the product of a wild imagination and a weak constitution.

"I endured ten years on the South African veldt," he boasted. "This will be as nothing to that, I promise you." Moodie's efforts to discredit Tom seem rooted in his desire to reassure me that we have landed in paradise—not, as I am beginning to fear, the fourth circle of hell.

My husband spends his days downstairs in the smoky tavern, buying drinks for all and sundry, who are, as far as I can see, a disreputable collection of promoters and pioneers. When I question him, he says he is trying to get the lay of the land before deciding on our next move.

"There are good farms to be found in these parts, Susanna, at reasonable prices. We could make a nice profit if we are smart."

Tomorrow, while he meets with his new friends, I intend to venture into the town to see for myself if Cobourg bears any resemblance to what Mr. Cattermole described in his lectures as "a handsome and thriving place" with every "convenience anyone could desire." As I write this in our new and barely respectable accommodations, the breeze toying with the soiled lace curtains carries the distinctive odour of fermenting grain (Cobourg boasts two distilleries) and the sounds of a lively brawl taking place on the boardwalk outside.

SEPTEMBER 16, 1832

Although my tour of Cobourg revealed little in the way of civility, I returned from our walk this morning convinced that the town's scant resources represent a far more desirable situation than the hardships that surely await us in the backwoods. Tom Wales, despite his fever, insisted on accompanying me on my foray, saying that even in daylight, the streets and avenues of this rough-and-ready place are not safe for a lady to venture out alone.

Once we left behind the teeming harbour area with its taverns and Yankee boisterousness, a quieter atmosphere prevailed. But most of the hundred and fifty or so houses here are little more than wooden shacks. The few residents we encountered exuded an air of desperate respectability, their once-fine clothing stained and mended to a sad state of disrepair. Our first stop was the office of the *Cobourg Star*, where, upon presenting myself to the editor, Mr. Chatterton, I was pleased to learn that he had already made my husband's acquaintance, and that my brother Sam has sent him some of my poems and stories. He also has more than a passing acquaintance with many of the London literati I have left behind forever. Oh, how lovely it was to share a few moments of intelligent discourse. Eager to promote his adopted home, Mr. Chatterton apprised us of the fact that Cobourg boasts a printing office, a music school and a book society. When I questioned him further as to the latter, he admitted that the only books currently available here are the novels of Sir Walter Scott and a few editions of Lord Byron's poetry, which society members have been rereading and discussing diligently, as it takes up to two years for bestsellers to arrive from England.

"But we are confident a shipment of new reading material will certainly arrive before winter sets in," Mr. Chatterton predicted with a native optimism that seems to infect so many Canadians. "I hear that the novels of Miss Austen are meeting with much enthusiasm," he said. "Have you, by any chance, encountered her work?" I assured him I had and, indeed, that I had brought with me to Canada, along with my Shakespeare, Tennyson and other precious texts, two of Austen's novels, also Bulwer-Lytton's *Paul Clifford* and a new edition of Mary Shelley's *Frankenstein*, which is signed by the authoress herself, and which I assured him I would be happy to share with him once my husband and I are settled. Chatterton urged me to submit more of my writing for publication in his newspaper, an opportunity that I will avail myself of as soon as possible. The prospect of publication in this modest enterprise almost makes up for Cobourg's otherwise utter lack of civilized amenities, and I am eager to take up my pen once again.

Next, we lingered outside the much-vaunted church—little more than a chapel, really—prettily constructed of rough boards painted white with an absurdly handsome tipped spire that gleamed optimistically in the September sunshine. The sight of it immediately gave me hope. When I suggested we enter, Tom demurred, citing his rough appearance and a complete lack of faith, the result, he says, of his conviction that he has already endured a living hell. It being a Sunday, I knelt briefly in the back, ignoring as best I could the curious stares of my fellow worshippers, and listened as the Reverend Mr. McAuley delivered his sermon in an accent as plummy as any that ever reverberated through the cloisters of my beloved Suffolk. And sitting there on that splintered pew, I closed my eyes and prayed for the strength and patience to meet and overcome whatever lies ahead.

When Moodie returned to our rooms this afternoon, I described my day and began beseeching him to consider postponing our departure for the backwoods. As much as I long to be reunited with my sister and brother, I believe that Cobourg, for all its limitations, is a better situation for us at present.

"Please, Moodie, you must see by now that it will take us years to clear even the small amount of land necessary to sustain ourselves. I have little Kate to care for, and I fear Hannah will never agree to accompany us into the bush when she could easily find a more comfortable position in the town." I placed the flat of my hands against his shirt and began stroking his chest as though he were an excitable horse. "And anyway, it is fall already, too late to begin a homestead now."

I was trying to maintain my dignity, but I was prepared to beg if necessary. To my surprise, I looked up to see he was nodding his head in agreement.

"Susie, I have been thinking the very same thing. I feel certain we are better off spending some of our capital and buying cleared land here, even if it means forgoing our free land farther north, at least temporarily. I have been introduced to a land agent called Charles Clark, and he assures me there are working farms to be had at very good prices." Moodie's voice was rising as his excitement grew, and I had to hush him for fear of waking little Kate. "Mr. Clark is eager to welcome settlers such as ourselves to the area. There is an element of Yankee riff-raff, he says, unruly squatters on some of his properties, whom he would dearly love to be rid of. He assures me that if we are patient, our money will be well invested."

He sat on the edge of the bed, grinning, and began taking his boots off. "What of that, my little chick? Married to a gentleman farmer after all. Are you surprised?"

Surprised and relieved in equal measure. I fell into his arms and, pulling him down beside me, tried to demonstrate the full extent of my gratitude, which I admit has been wanting these last few terrible weeks. Tomorrow, Moodie and Mr. Clark will investigate several suitable properties.

In the meantime, I will take Mr. Chatterton at his word and send over some of my previously published poems for publication in his rustic little newspaper. It is no *La Belle Assemblée*—that is certain. But as my dear absent sister Kate would say, "We must make do."

SEPTEMBER 19, 1832

Moodie has purchased a farm! A farm, yes, two hundred acres of cleared land, a barn and a house in Hamilton Township. It is about eight miles west of here and four miles north of the fancifully named village of Port Hope. I struggle to keep my imagination in check, knowing full well that the term "house" in this wild country is open to interpretation. Still, I can hardly quell visions of rolling green meadows and at least a few of the meagre comforts of home. Oh, how I long to leave this filthy, crawling community of low-bred Yankees for more peaceful pastures and perhaps the more congenial society of respectable landowners.

Moodie was cagey at first but finally confessed he paid three hundred pounds, nearly all our capital, for the farm (which he has christened Melsetter after his Orkney birthplace). He assures me it is a very good price, given the rapid influx of settlers and the resulting high demand for property in the region. So great is my relief in knowing we will not be proceeding into the bush that I did not protest. But three hundred pounds!

To celebrate, I gathered together a picnic of cold sausage, brown bread, apples and beer (again throwing frugality to the four winds), and Moodie and I, carrying little Katie, walked along Cobourg's sandy beach out to the edge of the marshlands beyond the town. It was a beautiful day, warm as summer under a hazy blue sky, so warm that I sorely regretted the heavy woollens that are the extent of my Canadian wardrobe. As we walked along and the seething hive of coarse humanity receded behind us, for the first time since leaving England I felt something like contentment. We sat on a great tree trunk that had washed ashore and looked out at the shimmering waters of the Ontario, a lake so vast it might as well be the great ocean. The sound of gulls crying as they balanced themselves on the wind above the harbour triggered memories of home. Everything else, though—the tall grasses and low-growing flowers that I could not name, the texture of the sand, the crouching rocky shoreline, even the weight of the air I breathed—was as strange to me as a foreign tongue. My husband, who has seen far more of the world than I, seemed not to notice and rattled on excitedly about our new farm. He is full of plans for a fall planting so that we may have wheat to harvest come spring. I cannot imagine how this will come about, as we have neither seed nor equipment, let alone the capital necessary to acquire either. I kept silent, however, and listened happily while Katie crawled about on the stony beach, examining every pebble and clamshell with grave intensity. It came to me all at once that to my little daughter, these will always be the sights and sensations of home, as sustaining to her as the meadows and rivers of Suffolk are to me.

My reverie was interrupted by loud honking sounds in the distant sky. Moodie and I watched as strings of long-necked wild geese, thousands of them, wove their way toward us over the water, finally landing near the shore in a cascade of flailing spray and noisy greetings. We laughed out loud at the spectacle and Katie burst into a babyish imitation of their raucous cries. A few of the handsome birds with their black-and-white plumage waddled ashore, oblivious to our presence, and haggled noisily over the crusts of bread I tossed them.

"The locals call them Canadian geese," said Moodie, waving his arms to see them scatter. "I'm told they make a tasty stew, and if you're very nimble, it's possible to catch one with your bare hands."

He grabbed me by the waist and twirled me in a gleeful dance, round and round on the stony beach, his head thrown back in joyous laughter.

"You see, my darling girl. I told you it would all be wonderful. I told you, didn't I?"

Thanks to my brother Sam, "Lines Written amidst the Ruins of a Church on the Coast of Suffolk," one of my favourite *Enthusiasm* poems, appeared in the *Star* today. Seeing the glorious lines, upon which I lavished such craft and emotion, published in this rough-and-tumble rag is, I confess, a little like handing my first-born over to the devil. But Chatterton has asked for more and is even promising payment! I have also sent him samples of Moodie's work, including a sketch called "The Elephant Hunt."

SEPTEMBER 20, 1832

Moodie returned from his daily dealings yesterday to report that the house we have purchased is still occupied by the previous owner, a Mr. Joe Harris, and his wife and eight children, who are refusing to leave. It seems the unfortunate Harrises are bankrupt, and so Mr. Clark repossessed their farm and sold it to Moodie. However, Mr. Clark neglected to inform my dear husband that while his three hundred pounds has purchased title to the property, occupancy is another matter. Are we to remain homeless, with what little cash we have left going to cover food and lodging in this den of filth, the Steamboat Hotel?

Tom Wales, who is to stay with us on our farm until his fortunes improve, laughed so hard when he heard this news that I feared he would become hysterical. I did not share his amusement. Indeed, it was all I could do not to burst into tears of rage. But Moodie dismissed my anger.

"Susie, Mr. Clark warned us we must be patient. This is a very fine farm at a very low price. You have to expect a few inconveniences . . ."

"A few inconveniences! Mr. Clark is using you to finance his efforts to evict a nest of Yankee vermin. You must go back to him at once. Where are we to live, Moodie?"

Then, as carefully as he could in the face of my anger, Moodie explained that Mr. Clark had arranged for us to rent a small house on an adjacent farm (also owned by him) for four dollars a month. He exhorted me to have some sympathy for the poor Harrises. It seems old Joe Harris's wife is with child and not fit to travel until after the snow falls and roads north into the bush are negotiable by horse and sled. Later, after Moodie had left to make arrangements for our move, Tom told me he has met Clark's sort before, and that he and others like him are getting rich preying on the misfortunes and naïveté of settlers such as ourselves.

When I pressed Moodie last night for more details on the "small house" we are to inhabit, he assured me the business with the Harrises was a minor misunderstanding and that the matter is sure to be sorted out within a few weeks. I have a bad feeling about this. How is it that we have purchased a proper home only to find it occupied by someone else? But when I questioned him again, my husband cheerily dismissed my concerns and, stroking my neck and shoulders, reminded me that he had promised to make things right and that is what he would do. But it is clear to me that he is not going to let anything, neither my fears nor Clark's dubious integrity, puncture the bubble of his certainty. Perhaps his unassailable mood had something to do with the wine, a musty half bottle of port that the owner of the Steamboat Hotel had presented to his soon-to-depart guest that afternoon. Perhaps it was because our discussion took place in the glow of ebbing passion. (It was a fumbling operation, given the close quarters we share here with Hannah and the babe. Our muffled gropings did not wake them; however, I fear we were less than cautious in other ways. An increase in our numbers at this time would be an unwelcome consequence.) Finally, as I lay in my husband's arms, trying to keep a lid on my festering doubts, he conceded that Mr. Clark is, indeed, always on the lookout for an opportunity. Moodie claims, however, that a bond of true friendship has grown between them during their short acquaintance.

"For all his rough ways, Mr. Clark is a good sort, and I feel we share a certain way of seeing the world, one that is not hamstrung by reticence or negativity," he said. "I like his spirit and his head for business; they are akin to my own. Indeed, we have talked about investment opportunities we might collaborate on. Why would he hoodwink us now when our continued good relations can only prove mutually beneficial in the long term?"

Because he is a land-grabbing scoundrel, I wanted to say, but to avoid a quarrel, I once again kept quiet.

In any case, although Moodie has not seen the place, Mr. Clark has assured him that with a little ingenuity and forbearance, we will be quite comfortable in our temporary quarters.

Ingenuity and forbearance will be about as useless as thimbles in a flood. One week after our moving in, our living conditions in this unspeakable hovel are barely suitable for livestock, never mind a respectable family. This is not a cabin; it is a cattle shed, a pigsty. And despite our ongoing efforts to make it livable, I cannot see how we are to continue in this intolerable situation.

Hannah's incessant whining is the least of it. The silly girl has not stopped weeping since we left the Steamboat Hotel last Saturday (though I confess I have not been much better). On that day, while Moodie, our new servant, James, and Tom Wales stayed back to finish loading the two ox carts containing our belongings, Hannah and I went on ahead by wagon and hired driver. I was reluctant to leave without my husband, but he assured me he would be right behind us, indeed it was likely he and his load would soon overtake us.

The farther we bumped and rattled into the countryside on what began as a fair though breezy day, the more boisterous Hannah's complaints became. She grumbled about everything from the gathering rain clouds to the towering trees until I was compelled to give her a firm slap on the back of her head. With that, her moaning stopped, though a noisy snivelling continued, making me wonder if she was leaving a young man behind in Cobourg. Fair young women are at a premium in these parts, though one would think Hannah's advanced condition makes her an unlikely romantic prospect.

Fortunately, little Kate slept for most of the hour it took to reach our inauspicious destination. Despite the appalling state of the "road" (little more than a footpath), the glowering skies and the steadily falling rain, this was my first foray into the inner regions of Canada, and I was curious to compare it with my dearly missed homeland. It does not stand up well. Nothing prepared me for the rough texture of the landscape, the darkened ploughed fields lined not with tidy hedge-rows, but with fences fashioned from piles of rocks and split rails, some of these arranged in ugly zigzag patterns. Blackened piles of stumps and brush smouldered in the dampness. The few houses we passed were built of logs, and all, whatever their size, had the same hastily assembled appearance. I saw not a single flower or decoration, or any exception to the unrelieved utilitarian pioneer spirit. It was a dreary, brutish scene. A few residents (our new neighbours, I suppose) stopped their toil to watch us pass, but they did not wave, nor did their impassive stares betray the slightest curiosity.

As we proceeded north and west, the land rose steadily until, looking back, we could see the great lake behind us, and before us the unending forest, a riot now of orange and scarlet and gold, which, I admit, outdoes any arboreal display I have witnessed in my entire life. At least nature remains undaunted by the prospect of what is to come. At the crest of a high hill, bare except for a low canopy of rose-coloured sumac trees, the carriage stopped to let poor old Dobbin, his sides huffing like a living bellows, catch his breath. A small herd of deer burst out of the bushes and froze in our path for only an instant, but long enough for their leader to hold my gaze with its velvet-brown eyes, before dashing off, a blizzard of white tails flying down the steep slope. Our driver, who thus far had rationed his commentary to the occasional monosyllabic grunt, raised one arm and pointed to a low structure in a small clearing, studded with stumps and surrounded by thick, dark forest.

"That be your new home," he said, then chuckled to himself as he slapped the reins on the horse's rump and proceeded down the hill. (It seems obvious he was fully aware, as I imagine the entire town is by now, of the swindle Mr. Clark has committed against us. Moodie is surely a laughing stock.) When our carriage pulled up beside a ramshackle shanty with a sagging roof, no door and one small, broken window, I insisted to the driver that there must be some mistake. Hannah had resumed her sobbing, the baby was crying with hunger, and a cold rain was falling. Numb with horror, I watched as a pair of brown-and-white cows ambled out through the open doorway of the cabin to welcome us.

"I can tell you were raised in the old country," the driver said as he unloaded our bags and, after shoving the curious beasts aside, kicked our belongings in through the gaping entry. "Ye have much to learn, I'll tell youse that." He spat an extravagant missile of brown juices in the direction of the carriage and smiled through his matted beard, making no move to help us down into the mud. "I imagine ye'll know a good deal more before winter is done. Now git out with youse."

"You can't just leave us like this," I pleaded. "My husband will be along in a moment. Please." And despite myself, I too began to cry. What a sorry spectacle we were, Hannah and I, sitting there in the cold rain, clinging to one another and weeping like babies.

"Git. Come on, now, git out," the driver repeated and began prodding Hannah with the butt of his whip. I'm ashamed to admit that my servant was the first to dismount. I followed with Kate in my arms, looking round the small clearing, terrified lest the cows with their ferocious horns should return and trample or gore us to death. The fury of the weather gave us no choice but to enter, and as our eyes adjusted to the dimness, I could hear a rustling in the back corner. Then two pairs of eyes, glowing like silver coins, emerged from the dark. They belonged to two smaller cattle that charged our way, almost knocking me down as they fled out into the yard. I began screaming so hard that Hannah had to take me by the shoulders and sit me down on an overturned trough, the only piece of furniture in the room.

An hour later, the men arrived to find us pale and speechless, perched there, shivering in the wind and rain that was gusting in through the open doorway, the broken window and the countless cracks in the walls.

"Where have you been?" I cried, but Moodie ignored me and surveyed the interior of the shed without comment. "Did you know about this? Did you?" I ran at him, fists flying, and he caught me by the wrists and held me at arm's length. Through my tears, I could see that even he was unprepared for the scene confronting us. "We cannot live here," I pleaded.

"We have no choice," he said through clenched teeth. And then, as though he had just spotted a handful of magic beans, he cried, "Aha!" and, bending down, pulled the missing front door from a pile of debris and animal droppings. "Come on, James, give me a hand and we'll have this back on its hinges in no time."

I have worn myself out begging my husband and the good Lord to deliver us from this situation, but neither of them is listening. Tom Wales applied himself to the cleanup and unloading of our belongings without a word. But I sensed behind his silence a grim satisfaction that his predictions are proving all too true. The tension between him and Moodie is palpable. My husband continues to assure me that we will be here for only a few weeks, and then there will be snow and the Harrises will surely leave. Snow. On top of everything else, snow.

From the tiny, cracked pane of glass at the back of our hovel, I can look across a cleared field and see the house we have paid good money for and by rights should be occupying this very moment. At least Mr. Clark has arranged for us to store our trunks and furniture in the barn. Our barn. But as a bitter wind blows in through the walls and the musty odour of aged cow dung mingles with the smoke leaking from the crumbling chimney, I can't help imagining the high ceilings and clear windows of our Melsetter homestead, a four-poster bed with a feather ticking, a fireplace and proper washtub, a privy (not a bucket, but a privy!), and I am filled with molten fury. But the Harrises, who have not even acknowledged our arrival, except to send over their rooster, which marched off with two of our laying hens one afternoon last week, continue to live in a style they have no reasonable claim to. Moodie has twice paid Old Joe a visit, and both times has met with overt hostility and demands that he "clear out before I let the dogs loose on youse."

I cannot endure it.

Today, after four days of unrelenting rain that virtually cascaded through the patched roof, creating large puddles on the earthen floor and rendering the fireplace nearly useless, the weather has cleared enough that I am able to sit outside in the wan sunshine, on this overturned bucket, and jot a few lines. Moodie has disappeared into the woods with his new musket, determined to bring down a goose or even a squirrel if all else fails.

"We shall have fresh meat for supper, my darling," he said, chucking me under the chin and hurrying away from the wrath he knows I can barely contain. He has not looked me in the eye since we arrived in this place. But I have kept my temper in check and applied myself to the tasks at hand, only letting my anger show once on our second day, when Moodie suggested Hannah join us at the make-shift table for a hasty supper of hard biscuits, pork fat and cabbage.

"Moodie . . ." I said, giving him a look that could not be mis-construed.

"Damn it, Susanna, the poor girl . . . I mean, there is barely room to turn around in here. Where would you have her take her meals?"

"Hannah," I said, ignoring this, "you will wait until we have finished, and after you have cleared the table, you and James may sit down and eat your supper while we prepare for bed."

This brought on a renewed onslaught of tears, but she did as she was told.

"Moodie," I hissed in his ear later, after the candles had been snuffed and we lay in the rough bed he had constructed for us, "just because we are reduced to living like animals does not mean we should forget who we are and from whence we came. I will not let our current circumstances lower the standards of behaviour I hold dear. If we let propriety slip, then we will soon lose our way altogether." I would have continued in this manner except that by the sound of his breathing, I could tell he had fallen asleep. I lay there seething in the darkness, clinging to this one idea as though it were a life raft in the swift current that has swept away the world I have always known, and that is my determination that this uncompromising country will not get the better of me easily, or change the person I am. I know my place, and in my household, the maid will always know hers. If I am doomed to live in a cowshed, then I will be the Duchess of Cowsheds.

OCTOBER 8, 1832

While Moodie and James carry on their farming activities during the day (the land, unlike the house, is at our disposal), sometimes travelling to Port Hope to spend what little of our capital remains on livestock and ploughs (and a new bake kettle for Hannah), and poor Tom lies shivering with the fever that comes and goes in unpredictable waves, I have been entertaining a parade of curious neighbours. I must say they are as varied a slice of humanity as God ever assembled in one place. One of them, a plain-spoken woman called Betty Fye, dropped by on what was obviously a reconnaissance mission, bearing a basket of apples. She planted herself in the centre of our shed, by now dressed up to resemble a rustic drawing room, and placing her hands on her broad hips, she looked around and snorted loudly, making no effort to hide her scorn.

"Clark again. Right bastard," she said as though to herself. Then, fixing her knowing eyes on me, she handed over the apples, saying, "You'll be needin' more firewood, I'm sure. I'll send my Albert over with a load if you'll part with one of them silver candlesticks. Can't think why a body'd need more 'n one." I saw her point immediately and agreed to the bargain. Mrs. Fye leaned down, gave little Kate a pat on the head and was gone. And so began a kind of rough barter system that allows me to lend or trade such prized possessions as lice combs, towels, a looking glass, assorted pots, even our new plough, in return for such necessities as milk and soap and starter for the rudimentary bread Hannah is learning to bake.

Much of this trade also involves our resident squatter, Old Joe Harris, whose initial hostility has been dropped in favour of an aggressive familiarity. He and his children—seven daughters and one son—seem to think they are entitled to visit whenever they like in order to paw through my personal possessions, looking for goodies they might "borrow." The utter lack of respect in this uncouth land for privacy, property and one's betters is astonishing. That Yankee weasel himself dropped by one afternoon and, as though we were the best of friends, sat in our only chair and began telling me the story of how he came to find himself squatting on the farm, now ours, that he inherited from his father.

"It was that bastard Mr. Clark what brought about our ruin," said Old Joe. "Two years of failed crops, and there he was, knocking on our door, a proper angel of mercy, with enough cash to set us back on track again, to get us through a winter when the young 'uns might have starved had we not taken the loan. And then, when I could not repay him, that foul usurer"—here he spat energetically on the dirt floor—"forced me to bankrupt and practically stole the land my pa bequeathed me. Now," he closed his eyes and curled his upper lip, "he's sold the farm that's rightfully mine to you, you waistcoated, tea-sipping fools with your servants and silk petticoats, for twice what he paid me fer it. Ah yes, Mr. Charles Clark, the settler's best friend . . ." He leaned back in the rocker so far that I feared he would tip over. "Well, don't say I didn't warn youse. But mark my words, that vulture is circling, just biding his time until he can swoop down and pick your old-country carcasses clean."

I couldn't muster a response. The Harrises, with their low ways, have obviously been ill-used by Mr. Clark. Will we be next? Or will Moodie's claim to a friendship with the land agent spare us a similar fate? I offered my guest a cup of rum (surely what he had come for) and asked him as politely as possible when he thought he and his family might be moving out of our house.

He knocked back the liquor, grimaced briefly and laughed. "When hell freezes over, missy. When hell freezes over." *Which should happen in a few short weeks,* I thought.

"That house is ours, Mr. Harris. We paid good money for it."

"Bah. That house was built by my own father. I won't be goin' nowhere if I can help it. You folks'd be better off goin' back to where you come from." He slammed the mug on the table and walked out, leaving me half convinced he is right.

Poor Tom Wales's health continues to deteriorate and his appearance is fearful. He is as gaunt as a ghost; his feverish dark eyes, the whites as yellow as yolks, dominate a face obscured by a tirade of greasy hair and whiskers. Even little Kate, whom Tom adores, screams at the very sight of him. Now that he is determined to leave, his mood is sanguine, though he complains constantly about our diet, which, I admit, is an unending ritual of salted pork, bannock and the occasional cabbage or turnip, like those Old Joe contributed yesterday, in return for the cup of rum. But Tom's most irritating habit is his tendency to regale us aloud with his dietary fantasies, daydreams that mainly concern freshly baked white bread slathered in butter. I was finally compelled this morning to cut short his gastronomic musings.

"We are all suffering the same deprivations, Tom," I said. "And Hannah is doing her best with limited resources, so I would appreciate it if you could refrain from deepening our collective misery with your constant reminiscing about luxuries that are beyond our ability to provide."

His innocent face under all that hair crumpled at my reprimand, and he turned his face to the wall and resumed shivering so violently that his whole bed closet shook. Before falling into a restless slumber, he observed that his wishes would soon be granted as he would be leaving for England aboard the *William IV* in a matter of days. And so Moodie and I are contemplating a diminished household. I confess I am looking forward to having some space to breathe and a civilized degree of privacy. Still, I shall miss poor Tom.

A pewter sheen of frost covered the ground this morning, and as the sun rose, whispers of mist floated up from the creek bed and disappeared among the trees.

OCTOBER 10, 1832

Hannah is gone. She pleaded to be allowed to accompany James today when he drove Tom Wales to Cobourg and the awaiting *William IV*, and I relented after giving her instructions (and the funds necessary) to purchase quills and paper (which I am sorely in need of). When she failed to meet James at the Steamboat Hotel for the return trip, he decided that "she'd likely taken up with a finer household than yourn and Mr. Moodie's."

The hint of mockery in this observation did not go unnoticed and made me wonder if James is contemplating a similar move. I must say I am not particularly surprised by Hannah's delinquency—her advanced pregnancy apparently no obstacle to her bettering her situation—or sorry to see the back of her. Her natural truculence has only worsened since we came to Canada. But dear God, what am I to do now? How am I to steal the time to keep up my correspondence and to attend to my poetry? Letters from home and the prospect of publication are the only things that brighten my days. I have nearly finished a thirty-stanza verse called "Autumn," which expresses through the beauty of a dying summer the melancholy in my own heart.

Moodie has said he will assist me with the household chores until a replacement for Hannah can be found. But with the fall planting to attend to, the idea of him pitching in with the laundry and the cooking as well is absurd. I considered hiring one of the Harris girls, but their slatternly demeanour makes me wonder if laundry is even within the realm of their experience. I am ashamed to say a part of me is in sympathy with their apathy, which, in my desperation, seems a kind of freedom. Indeed, I almost envy the possibility of giving up all thoughts of keeping up appearances. However, after taking a brief stroll around the perimeter of our farm in the brisk fall air, and then resting for a spell on a large, flat boulder to watch our plucky little creek bubble happily on its way, oblivious to all earthly cares, my spirits rallied, and I returned to my husband and child and whatever lies ahead.

OCTOBER 14, 1832

Thank God. Moodie returned last night from Port Hope with a packet of letters from home and new servant girl, a young Scottish lass called Isobel. She seems very young, but the sound of her misty

Highland burr as she goes about her chores is as nourishing to my spirit as a bowl of porridge (and a welcome contrast to her predecessor's blunt Yorkshire banter). For the first time in four days, we will sit down to a proper meal: leavened bread from the bake kettle, which the new girl has some experience with, and roasted quail! When Moodie returned from the woods this morning with a brace of birds, I was at a loss as to what to do with them. Then Isobel, in her quiet, competent way, set upon dipping them one by one in boiling water, a process that rendered the feathers as loose as leaves in autumn. We sat in the clearing, the four of us, and plucked the grey-brown plumage until the ground and our clothing were littered with feathers, and for a short time, I was distracted from my woes by that comical sight.

In the end, we were obliged to share our bounty. And the thought of wasting those delicacies on such an unscrupulous intruder still makes my teeth ache. Just as Isobel was readying the bake kettle for the anticipated feast, Mr. Clark rode up to our door, and Moodie, with his usual bonhomie, invited him to dinner. It was the first time I had laid eyes on the author of our misfortunes. Thin and narrow-shouldered, with a sallow complexion, he was nothing like the dashing figure I had imagined from Moodie's enthusiastic stories, though he did seem tolerably well mannered.

"Mrs. Moodie, my pleasure," he said, taking my hand and pressing it to his lips. "Now that your husband and I are doing business together, I do hope that you and I shall have a chance to become better acquainted."

Bel and I managed to set a respectable table, using, for the first time, the silver flatware I had brought from home. As we pulled apart the crisp-skinned, pink-fleshed quail, Mr. Clark ran his greasy fingers through his lank hair, picked up his glass of beer and raised it in a toast.

"To our mutual prosperity," he said.

"Prosperity?" I could not keep quiet. "We are living in a shed and you talk about prosperity?"

Clark picked up a tiny drumstick with his thumb and forefinger and nibbled daintily. He shook his head and a look of great sorrow came over his face. "Ah, Mrs. Moodie, I agree, it is unfortunate. But temporary, I assure you—a temporary setback. I predict that before long, you will be the envy of every woman in the township." He leaned closer. "And if I may say so, you are certainly the most handsome."

If Moodie heard this, he gave no sign.

Mr. Clark clapped my husband on the shoulder and spread a slab of lard on the heel of his bread. "It's all part of the plan, eh, Moodie?" He raised his glass. "Here's to the greater good."

After he had gone, I quizzed my husband and learned to my dismay that he and Clark have banded together to "clean up" Hamilton Township by repossessing farms from indigent locals such as Joe Harris and his ilk, and selling the land to respectable English settlers such as ourselves. Since we have no funds to invest, Clark has agreed to let Moodie in on the scheme on the strength of his signature alone. We stand to make a fortune, Moodie claims. I heard him out, and not wanting an altercation, I took my shawl and fled the claustrophobia of these four walls, hoping that a little fresh air and a few moments staring up at the great big sky would once again silence the roaring in my head. When I returned, Moodie had fallen asleep in his chair.

OCTOBER 24, 1832

The *Cobourg Star* published my "Autumn" poem this week, as well as the first part of Moodie's sketch "The Elephant Hunt." Part two is to appear next week. Judging by my husband's bragging, you would think he had made the pages of *The Spectator*. Each evening, instead of performing his usual flute serenade, the author reads his memoir aloud to our small household, a captive but increasingly unwilling audience. Only Katie's enthusiasm has endured in the face of such nightly repetition. The rest of us long for the return of a few Scottish airs. I am delighted, of course, at my dearest's success and the fact that Mr. Chatterton has asked for more. Meanwhile, the editor kindly described my poem as "full of feeling and sensibility."

On seeing my words in print again, I briefly entertained a fantasy that I might aspire to a life of letters here in Canada. But the sight of a skiff of snow on the fallen leaves this morning and my frozen fingers as I hold this quill quickly destroyed my illusions.

Now that the weather has turned cold, the close quarters are affecting us all, and tempers have been running short. Indeed, The Weather is all anyone talks about. In the absence of culture or any kind of intelligent social discourse, weather is the only thing that happens here. And everything seems to depend upon it. The old-timers are predicting an early, harsh winter. And so we wait. The glories of autumn have given way to a muted stasis. The days darken and the nights grow longer. And yet a remorseless beauty prevails. A stand of beech and maples on the far side of the marsh seems to rise out of a mist of blood-red dogwood, the trees like dark skeletons limned against a sullen sky. And the constant chatter of the little creek outside the door continues to console me, a reminder that all things come and go in an unending process, and this too will pass.

DECEMBER 5, 1832

The snow began yesterday, falling thick and furiously throughout the afternoon and evening. Fierce, howling winds pummelled the shed all night long, the snow coming in through the cracks, forming thin white drifts across the cabin floor. By morning, a veneer of frost coated the four inside walls and ice crusted the water buckets. The single window was transformed into a jewelled kaleidoscope through which the brilliant morning sunshine glinted in wild fluorescence. Our first blizzard has spent its fury, but we woke up to find ourselves entombed, the front door blocked nearly to the eaves by snow. While Moodie and James began digging us out, Bel and I huddled by the rejuvenated hearth with little Kate and marvelled at the spectacle slowly revealing itself outside.

A blinding whiteness, a million sequins spread out under a sky as blue as heaven. The creek, a silver-and-ebony ribbon struggling gamely through cliffs of ice, each rock shellacked and shining in the sunlight. The monumental spruce shivering, their blue-black boughs weighed down by snowy pillows that explode in slow motion with each breath of air, letting loose a veil of whiteness. And silent. And still. As still as a painting.

The woollen skirts and capes that only a few weeks ago rebelled against the heat are no match for this cold, and we are obliged to wrap ourselves in blankets before venturing outdoors. Bel and I wear gloves at all times; I have snipped the fingertips off one pair so that I can hold a needle and this pen in my numb fingers. Our boots, though they spend all their spare time by the fire, never really dry out, and so every trip to the woodpile or the new privy is an ordeal. Poor Katie, bundled in multiple layers of bunting, creeps around the damp dirt floors as best she can. She is as filthy as any London beggar, but it is much too cold to bathe her. I think back to the oppressive chill of Reydon Hall's rambling decrepitude in winter, but nothing, nothing compares with this.

Moodie and James have not returned from checking on the livestock. Though the barn is only a few hundred yards from our door,

I cannot imagine how they made it through snow that in places is waist-deep. Now the morning's quiet brilliance has turned sullen, and a fitful wind blows curtains of white that block out the sky. The longed-for winter season is here. And with it, some hope that once this storm has passed, Old Joe and his family will move on.

DECEMBER 20, 1832

Still the Harrises refuse to leave. And Moodie tells me we have no recourse, that we shall likely be forced to spend the winter in this place. I am ashamed to say I broke down completely, and in full view of everyone. I wept and exhorted God to deliver us from this purgatory. It was a pitiful display of weakness and a stain upon the resilient English spirit I have always taken pride in. This journal has been a solace, a private place where I can express my terrible longings for the life I have left behind. I pray it helps to give me the strength to endure.

The snow lies everywhere, deep and silent and foreboding. The only respite from days and nights imprisoned in our dank and smoke-filled hovel are a short, well-trodden path from our front door to the woodpile and another in the direction of the barn, paths that are obliterated daily by a dogged wind. There is no escaping the cold, no relief except sporadic sessions in front of the fire before I return to my chores with stiffened limbs and a heavy heart. The tips of my fingers are bloodless and white, as numb as my nerves are livid. Moodie and Bel are not as bothered by the freezing temperatures and carry on with almost cheerful resignation. Their stoicism shames me all the more. But James, like me, seems weighed down by the harsh weather and the low, brutish light. Katie seems oblivious, creeping around the cabin, happily exploring the only world she has ever known and (the thought is like a knife in my heart) may ever know.

The idea that in a few months, likely next June by my calculations, our dear girl may, God willing, be joined by another little one should be a source of great joy. Instead, I am beset by doubts about bringing another child into this coarse, cold country. It is as though childhood does not exist here. The young offspring of our neighbours are as dull-eyed as aged mules, worn out already by an inadequate diet, a lack of any kind of discipline and the want of a proper education. They are as wary and wily as hardened criminals, and whatever innocence they are born with turns as sour as spoilt milk almost before they can talk. Old Joe's eight children are a slovenly, listless lot, and yet their desperation touches something in me. Just a week ago—hearing that the eldest, Phoebe, a girl of about fifteen or sixteen, was ill—I put aside my ill will and went by the house to see if I might help. To my dismay, I found the girl feverish and shivering in a heap of old blankets, attended to by two old women trying to persuade the patient to swallow a bowl of raw eggs, and plastering her thin chest with reeking poultices of mustard and chicken fat, treatments intended to "drive out the poisons." I pleaded with Mrs. Joe to call a doctor, but she refused, saying her daughter is prone to these fevers and would be as good as new by morning. Last thing I heard, the girl is still ailing and her condition has become one more reason the family cannot leave the premises. I am determined not to let the Harrises' hostility erode my civility. Perhaps if they get to know me, if I reach out to them as a neighbour and a friend, I can appeal to their better natures and persuade them to leave. It is what Kate would advise, I am sure.

Moodie is ecstatic at the thought of enlarging our family and is certain this time I will surely bear him a son.

A letter from Kate. It has taken three months to find me by a route so circuitous, I cannot begin to describe it. Mail from England takes less time to get here. My sister has written to say that she and Mr. Traill have been living at the Douro home of their generous neighbours, the Stewarts, until their own house, eleven miles farther north, is built.

"My hostess, Frances Stewart, emigrated ten years ago," Kate says. "She is generous and cultivated and has become my dear, dear friend. I cannot tell you what I have learned about pioneer life from this remarkable woman." Kate claims she is now an accomplished baker, botanist and anthropologist, having amassed a large collection of Indian artifacts and all manner of plant specimens. From the sounds of it, my sister and her new friend spend their days playing the piano and pressing weeds between the pages of Ruskin and Hobbes.

Meanwhile, my brother Sam has secured for the Traills a land grant adjoining his own farm on the shores of Lake Katchewanooka. While the women amuse themselves with arrowheads and bits of pottery, my brother is familiarizing Thomas Traill with the intricacies of axes, ploughs and scythes.

"You cannot imagine what a comfort it is to have found such civility in so remote a place," wrote Kate. "We have landed in an oasis of Englishness far removed from the Yankee squalor of Hamilton Township, your descriptions of which have made me laugh until I cried.

"Happy Christmas, dearest Susanna, to you, Mr. Moodie and dear little Kate."

Her letter filled me with hope that I too might find a friend, someone like her benefactress, Mrs. Stewart, schooled in the ways of a settler's existence and yet familiar with the values I continue to cherish, though I admit none of them has prepared me for this life. I know nothing about even the most basic domestic duties— baking bread, wielding an axe, dispatching a chicken, planting peas. Yesterday, Moodie plunked a muslin-wrapped parcel on the table and, hands on his hips, dared me to open it. "For you, my little duchess." I unwrapped it to reveal a large, greasy hunk of blood-tinged fat.

"What am I to do with this?" I asked.

"Beef tallow," said Moodie, "a gift from Betty Fye." And when I wrinkled my nose, he laughed. "For making candles and soap, my dear. Think of the money we'll save." He winked at Bel. Damn his enthusiasm.

JANUARY 10, 1833

Following a brief period of mild weather that taunted us as cruelly as a mirage in the desert with the unlikelihood of spring, the brutal cold has returned. The ground is frozen solid and covered in snow, making travel over the previously impassable roads possible. Moodie decided to take advantage of the favourable conditions and make the journey to Douro Township to visit Sam and the Traills. I begged him to allow me to go too, as I could hardly contemplate remaining here alone with the trees and the snow and the cold, cold wind, but my condition and the difficulty of such a journey—at least two days by sled and on foot—made it impossible.

He and James left yesterday in the bright, brittle sunshine. The sleigh, borrowed from Albert and Betty Fye, is as exuberant a contraption as can be imagined. Painted bright red and drawn by two horses outfitted in shiny black harness decorated with a myriad of little brass bells, the jaunty conveyance jangled gaily down the road as Katie and I waved the men on their way. Long after it had disappeared from sight, we could hear its cheerful clamour gradually fading into the forest.

The brief elation I felt then disappeared with the failing light of day. For most of the night, I could hear the wolves howling, a sound as mournful and foreboding as loneliness itself. At first, the wailing was just a rumour, but soon the beasts seemed to be moving closer and closer. I stayed up until our last candle sputtered into oblivion, listening until the eerie chorus stopped and all I could hear was the sound of the giant pines creaking in the wind. After stoking the fire, I crawled into bed, but I did not sleep.

JANUARY 15, 1833

This morning, I left Kate in the care of Bel and struggled through the snowdrifts to call on the Harrises. My excuse: to prevail upon them to lend me a wax candle until I can bring myself to attempt making my own. But truly, I was yearning for human society of any kind. It meant setting aside my pride, as I have railed eloquently and publicly against the colonial propensity for "borrowing" from one's neigh-bours, a tendency that in practice is more like theft, since almost nothing that has left my house has ever been returned.

The candle was handed over by the much-improved, monosyllabic Phoebe in return for a canister of rum. On every other occasion we have met, though I try to speak to her in a friendly way, the girl has kept her eyes cast down, refusing to acknowledge my existence. This time, how-ever, as she passed me a pair of hand-dipped rush lights, she tilted her head and raised her eyes to mine, appraising me with almost brazen curiosity. I asked her how she was feeling and she nodded shyly. We were alone, standing on the front veranda of what should be my house. The sounds of domestic squalor tumbled through an open window.

"Phoebe," I said, an idea beginning to percolate, "have you ever been to school?" Of course, I knew the answer. She lowered her eyes again and shook her head.

"Can you read?" She looked at me as if I had asked her if she could fly.

"Pa can," she said. "A little. But he has no use for it."

"Would you like to?"

"I dunno." Then she actually smiled. "Maybe."

"All right, then. I will give you lessons. We can begin tomorrow afternoon. Come by after your chores are done."

We'll see if she shows up. In any case, I now have my candles and I won't have to spend another evening with the firelight casting ghosts on the walls but never giving off enough light to work or read by. I try not to reveal my terror of the dark for fear of frightening Katie. I have even attempted a few childish songs at bedtime, but the quaver in my voice is more unsettling than the silence. Bel, more resigned than afraid, curls up on her pallet as soon as the sun goes down and remains there for the night, occasionally whimpering in her sleep. As hard as I try, I cannot banish from my fevered mind a story Moodie related, as though for our entertainment, of a creature living in the forest, half man, half beast, known as Windiga. The Indians say it is driven by an insatiable appetite for human flesh, and that its malevolent spirit awakens on cold winter nights and wanders the woods in search of sleeping victims. I lie awake for hours, listening with a thumping heart, certain that every sigh of the wind and moaning tree limb signals a death too terrible to contemplate. I know it is superstition, but with only the night noises and the ominous silence behind them as reassurance, I nurse an unshakable conviction that Moodie will return to discover nothing but our savaged, half-eaten remains and the snow vivid with our dying blood.

In the clear light of day, I resolve to conquer my fears, to rise above these base surroundings and the unending cold by throwing myself wholeheartedly into my work. I have two poems under way. The first is a paean to sleigh bells, the sound of which as Moodie drove away allowed me a brief respite from my depression. It is a music I strain to hear once more, for it will herald the return of my beloved.

'Tis merry to hear, at evening time,
By the blazing hearth the sleigh-bells chime;
To know the bounding steeds bring near
The loved one to our bosoms dear.

The other, I fear, is a less salutary composition that expresses some of my disenchantment with this Canada:

The swampy margin of thy inland seas,
The eternal forest girdling either shore,
Its belt of dark pines sighing in the breeze,
And rugged fields, with rude huts dotted o'er,
Show cultivation unimproved by art,
That sheds a barren chillness on the heart.

Now that I have my candle, I intend to compose a letter this very evening to a certain Dr. Bartlett, editor of *The Albion*, a New York literary journal of eminent repute, entreating him to publish my work.

And then there is the education of Phoebe Harris. May it also bear fruit.

JANUARY 18, 1833

My dearest Moodie has returned from the wilds of Douro Township, brimming with good spirits and welcome news of my cherished sister and the little brother I have not laid eyes upon for nearly eight years.

Kate and Mr. Traill are "thriving" he declared with his usual enthusiasm, providing, like most men I have ever known, scant detail as to their actual state. I questioned him more closely and learned that my sister is to bear her first child this summer. To think we will be facing the travails of birth at close to the same time and yet will be kept apart by a few miles of impassable wilderness. Forty miles! That is all that lies between me and the consoling companionship of my childhood soulmate. To Moodie's dismay, my tears flowed unchecked as memories of those distant halcyon days flooded my imagination.

I could not stop.

"Susie, Susie, please. I cannot bear this." He placed his strong arms around me and I laid my head on his shoulder. Perhaps it was the strain of the long days and nights he has been away, perhaps the quickening of life inside me, but I made no effort to calm myself and turned on my husband, raging through my anguish.

"I feel about this dreadful country as a condemned prisoner must feel about his cell. My only hope of escape lies in the oblivion of death. And then to be separated so cruelly from the one person who could support me in all of this."

He lifted my chin with his thumb and forefinger, and I saw the concern in his blue eyes.

"You have me, Susanna. I am here. Always. I would give my life for you. You have everything to live for. Stop it, please."

Now, as he lies sleeping, I am calmer but still filled with fear for the future. How can he be so buoyant? By what quirk or trick of nature does John Moodie see only light and possibilities where I am cast down by every twist in the road? He, like sweet Catharine, meets every hardship, every trial with bottomless reserves of optimism and cheer. If only I were blessed with such sanguinity. Still, there are times when I fear their positive dispositions blind them to a host of negative realities. At least my dark side allows me to gird myself against the inevitable hardship that lies ahead.

It sounds as if my sister is passing her first winter in the New World in relative comfort. She and Mr. Traill have moved again and are now living in a "sturdy and generous" log cabin closer to Sam and his family, while their own is under construction. The letter Katie sent back with Moodie describes in rapturous detail her blossoming friendships with two new neighbours, the Shairps and the Caddys, particularly Emilia Shairp, a young Englishwoman "of gentle manner and adventurous spirit."

"I am learning," Kate wrote, "that with a little practical diligence, it is possible to make a home in the lonely woods an abode of peace and comfort."

Sometimes I think my sister has landed on another continent from the one I currently inhabit. How is it she finds herself surrounded by genteel, educated women, also skilled in the arts of jam and bread making, while I am reduced to begging for candle stubs from sullen, backward harpies? Why should Kate be favoured again? My childish heart protests the unfairness of it.

She doesn't mention her husband, whom Moodie, who never utters a discouraging word, described as "a little subdued." When I pressed once again for details, he ventured: "The harsh weather has not improved Traill's disposition. I believe he would be much better if he engaged in physical activity. But he prefers to sit by the fire with a well-worn volume of Voltaire on his lap as he stares into the flames." Come spring, Mr. Traill will have as much physical activity as he can tolerate when he and Kate move to their new home, sixty-five uncleared acres on Lake Katchewanooka, near the mouth of the Otonabee.

Moodie saw nothing in his travels north but beauty and

possibilities. For days, he has been enthusing about his brief sojourn in the backwoods.

"They possess," he said, describing monumental forests punctuated by archipelagos of shining lakes, "a grandeur that aroused in me an indescribable awe for the powers of nature."

"Yes," I ventured, "powerful enough to break the backs and hearts of strong men." But he pretended not to hear me.

"In the presence of such grandeur," he continued, addressing himself exclusively to his little daughter now, "all human endeavour seems small and irrelevant."

He then informed me that with Sam's help, he has set about securing title to his own property on the shores of Lake Katchewanooka.

"Who knows. Perhaps one day we will move there," he said, adding that Sam has reminded him that his military land grant will expire if it isn't claimed within two years. "Anyway," he said, bouncing Katie on his knee, "I'm sure we have nothing to lose."

And now I cannot stop thinking about Kate and Sam and the gentle society they have cultivated (it is not just the soil that needs tending—what of the soul?), while I languish, freezing to death, in a cowshed.

Still no sign of my errant pupil. I have already devised a few simple exercises for her, and I am surprised at how much I relish the prospect of bringing a little light and refinement to the poor ignorant girl. Perhaps if I can be of some use to our rough neighbours, I will find their society more palatable.

JANUARY 20, 1833

My foolish and short-lived vocation as a teacher has been thoroughly crushed. Old Joe Harris arrived on my doorstep this morning in a half-drunken state. It took me a few moments to understand what he was on about as he attempted to spew his vitriol through teeth clenched firmly about his ever-present pipe. He finally removed it after I invited him in and tempted him with a cup of rum. As I suspected, his ire concerned his daughter Phoebe. Apparently, he thinks I am "puttin' ideas in a poor girl's head." After accepting the refreshment, he exhorted me to mind my own business and stay away from his family if I know what's good for me.

"You and your fine fella act like we are the dirt under your feet," he railed, stabbing the smoke-dimmed air with the aforementioned pipe in one hand, though he was careful not to spill a drop of the drink he held in the other. "Your book larning and fine manners is of no earthly use here. If you spent less time mooning over 'the finery of autumn'"—there was a sneer in his voice as he said this (apparently he had seen my poem in the newspaper and taken the time to read it)—"and more time gettin' your hands dirty, you wouldn't be livin' worse 'n the livestock you and the mister have to borrow money to feed." He looked around the shed in disgust.

I was apoplectic. How dare he? This rancid little squatter standing there, drinking my rum, still living in my house. I grabbed a broom and raised it over my head. "Get out, you sack of vermin, before I beat you to death." And I would have too, if he had not fled like the coward he is. When Moodie came in an hour later, I was still shaking. I told him what had happened and he laughed. "That old rascal," he said, as though I had just related an amusing anecdote. But it is not funny. How would Old Joe know of our debts? I can almost hear the whispering that is going on behind our backs.

FEBRUARY 2, 1833

James disappeared two days ago without a word, leaving poor Moodie with sole responsibility for chopping and splitting the firewood, as well as the care and feeding of the animals. Our delinquent servant had a riding horse, a yoke of oxen, three cows and a family of pigs under his care. I knew he was unhappy and have long feared this would happen, so it came as no surprise. But that has not lessened our desperation, considering the unlikelihood of finding a replacement this time of the year, a season the locals are already calling "the iron winter."

And then there we were, making the best of yet another interminable night in the wilderness—Moodie on his flute, Bel attempting to execute a miserable jig in the confined space, me defiling a pair of torn britches with a recalcitrant needle and fingers stiff with cold—when a violent knocking nearly stopped our hearts. Moodie opened the door, and the apparition standing before us set Bel to screaming as though she had seen the anti-Christ. Tall, so gaunt you could see the ribs through its thin shirt, with a head of black hair falling in thick, unruly mats that nearly obscured its dark and hungry sunken eyes. The creature, its flesh the colour of ash, its feet wrapped in rags, stood there shaking as though possessed by the devil himself. I immediately thought of the Windiga and cried out to warn my husband to shut the door against this embodiment of evil. Before I could pull myself from my chair, the flesh-eating creature collapsed like a suit of empty clothes across our threshold. And as Bel and I cowered in the corner, pleading with him not to, Moodie dragged the unconscious body across the room and propped it up against the woodbox.

"For heaven's sake, girl," he said, rubbing the intruder's thin arms and pulling a quilt over its purple feet. "Pull yourself together. Can't you see the poor fellow is freezing? Bel, please, some hot milk. A bowl of soup."

I could see now that the body draped against the logs was more man than beast—indeed little more than a boy, and a gravely weakened one at that. Bel, however, was unmoved and, refusing to lift a hand, hung back, muttering angrily in the shadows. This was not the time to deal with her insubordination, so I got up myself to warm the milk and the remains of supper for our still groggy but now sentient guest. With a wan smile of gratitude but not a word, the boy quickly demolished the soup and half a loaf of yesterday's bread with it.

"Who are you, young man, and what is your business?" Moodie asked after the food was gone.

"John Monaghan, sir, from Haldimand Township," he replied. "I've been walking these past two days with naught to eat and neither shoe for my feet nor hat to my head. I beg you, let me spend the night, for if ye turn me out, I shall surely perish in the snow."

This pathetic plea was delivered in an Irish brogue as thick as boiled cabbage, the sound of which elicited a cry of outrage from Bel, who came forward, her terror apparently forgotten, her gentle blue eyes now dark with fury, to denounce our guest.

"Filthy papist swine," she thundered. "He'll only rob and murder us in our sleep. I'll not stay under the same roof with the likes o' that 'un."

"You will do as you're told," said Moodie in his sternest voice, though I could see that underneath he was as bewildered as I at our usually obedient servant's intransigence. "Isobel. Now! Make up a bed for Mr. Monaghan. You can leave if you like, but you'll not have a say in whom we receive in our home."

Like Bel, I hold little respect for the Irish, but if our first day with John Monaghan is any indication, we are both mistaken: this Celtic boy is a credit to his race. He tells us his previous master beat him brutally (the still-bloody lacerations on his back and shoulders being ample proof of his mistreatment) for neglecting to unyoke a team of oxen. And so he fled, fearing the man and his sons would surely murder him one day.

This morning, John Monaghan and I bundled Katie into her sled and tramped across the misty fields beyond the big house to the vast stand of sugar maples, where our neighbours from around the township have come to make maple syrup at a communal gathering known as a "sugaring off." Although I have been sweetening my tea these past four months with this oddly flavoured condiment, until now I had little idea of its provenance. The day was wet and mild, a symphony of black and white, snow, trees, snow, trees, and a fog so pervasive it obliterated the horizon, making the sky above scarcely distinguishable from the wet ground under our feet. Red-winged blackbirds called from the marsh. *Ka-creee. Ka-creee.* A chorus of peepers filled the soft air with their song. As we approached, we could hear the voices of men and women, the children's laughter; we could smell the smoke from the roaring fire, a bright ember in the distance. And before long, we could make out their ghostly forms gliding wraith-like through the foggy woods, gathering buckets of sap from where they hung on the mighty trees: the Canadian maples, whose stout trunks rise as straight and clean as ships' masts until their branches, like the arms of angels, reach upwards to the heavens.

The sap, which flows this time of year beneath the bark and is collected by way of wooden dowels hammered into the tree, tastes like barely sweetened barley water. Gallons and gallons are poured into a vast kettle and boiled constantly over a wood fire for days until the liquid gradually condenses into a thick, smoky syrup whose flavour can only be described as "maple" for it tastes like nothing else on earth.

"Hullo, you there, missus. Bring us the babe. She's in store for a treat." It was Old Joe Harris, who seemed to have entirely forgotten our last encounter, calling to me as he stirred a large wooden paddle round and round in a steaming vat of boiling sap. As we watched, he instructed one of his daughters to ladle some of the thick, hot liquid onto a patch of untrammelled snow. The syrup immediately congealed, and grasping one end of the golden puddle, the girl handed the other to me.

"Pull," she commanded. "And turn, like this." I followed her lead, and in an instant, we were swinging a thick, twisted rope of taffy, which we laid on a nearby log. Quick as an otter, John Monaghan appeared with a hatchet and chopped the maple rope into chunks, which he then distributed to the waiting children. Before long, Katie was a sticky, happy mess, her hair and face and clothing clotted with maple taffy. And for the first time in many months, I found myself laughing—not just laughing, but joining the others in a collective merriment I had thought I would never be part of again. At that moment, we all, the Harrises, old Betty Fye, even that conniving swindler Clark, seemed like fellow travellers, part of a harmonious whole. And there was music—Moodie on his flute, accompanied by a juice harp and a home-made guitar—and generous bowls of venison stew and bread and butter, food that now winter's end is firmly in sight could be shared without compunction. It makes me hope we are being accepted at last.

"Spring, ma'am," said John Monaghan as we sat on a log and watched.

"What?" I said.

"Spring," he repeated. "Back home, the daffodils will be in bloom."

I looked around me at the snow and fog, the roaring fire and the clouds my warm breath was making in the cold, damp air.

"Spring," I said. "Yes."

JUNE 7, 1833 (MELSETTER, HAMILTON TOWNSHIP)

I am writing these words whilst sitting at a real desk in the bright, spacious parlour of our Melsetter home. At last. Old Joe and his brood vacated the big house a week ago, and a sorrier parade you have never seen: eight children (including a still feeble-looking Phoebe) Mrs. Joe and her new babe, as well as a trio of half-starved dogs. They carried their belongings in two pushcarts and on their backs as they headed north in search of lodgings, an abandoned barn, perhaps, or a farm tenancy somewhere. Mr. Clark finally threatened to call in the bailiff and have them forcibly evicted. If only I had known last fall this was an option, but I suspect Clark kept it to himself in order to milk us for the rent on the cowshed for as long as he could. I also suspect my constant complaining persuaded Moodie to put greater pressure on his so-called business partner.

In spite of everything, I felt a twinge of remorse as I watched them leave. The feeling did not last long. John Monaghan discovered that Old Joe, in a spirit of revenge, had girded all our best apple trees. And the state of the house was almost beyond description, the filthiest mess I have ever seen, worse even than our lowly cowshed: walls black with soot, windows opaque with fly dirt; dog feces everywhere; old soup bones, dirty rags and broken glass; and a chimney that has been leaking water, making large puddles on the kitchen floor. Then there was the noxious odour that permeated the whole house, a miasma that brought tears to our eyes. We searched everywhere for the source of the smell, until John Monaghan located the Harrises' foul housewarming gift in the back of a high cupboard above the mantel: it was the rotting carcass of a skunk. The odour of death lingers still, though we have been burning salt and sulphur on tin plates, and Bel has arranged bouquets of pine and spruce boughs throughout. It took three days to scrub the house into a livable condition. And then on our first night, we found our beds so infested with fleas that we scarcely slept at all. As for the mice, Moodie has set traps, and so far, we have disposed of about two dozen of the intruders, which has certainly put a damper on their persistent society.

Nevertheless, what heaven is this compared with our former quarters? Now that it is clean, it is as though I have returned to the womb—a vast, light-filled womb with boarded walls and ceilings, snow-white fringed curtains fluttering gently over windows that allow a view of distant hills and a clear blue sky. The chairs and tables are arranged by the fire as though waiting for a happy family to arrive. A gaily striped carpet enlivens the plank floors, and in a touch that brings tears to my eyes, Moodie has hung the cherished drawing of Reydon Hall (given to me so long ago by dear Kate) beside the portrait of Mama, both stored all these months in the barn, along with other nearly forgotten treasures, emblems of the life we once lived. Here is the precious Coalport tea service Mama gave us as a wedding present, rescued from the flour bin and arranged now in the glass-fronted cabinet, a silver platter set on the rough beam of the mantel, antimacassars (antimacassars!) draped over the backs of the chairs. Here in this, our first true Canadian home, I will bring forth our second child, our Canadian babe, and I am filled with hope for a future that only weeks ago seemed as constrained and limited as that rough and dirty cowshed.

On the advice of Mr. Clark, we have let that unfortunate hovel to a young couple originally from Essex, Diana and George Owen, who have recently moved here from Hope Township, a few miles to the west. They dropped by this morning on their way to Cobourg and seem charming and articulate. They have recently sold their farm and need temporary lodgings until they can find a new property in the area. I am delighted to think there is to be such congenial company so nearby, and for me, perhaps, a new friend. Once this baby is born, I am determined to invite Mrs. Owen for tea. Moodie says Mr. Clark has arbitrated some kind of mutually beneficial arrangement with the Owens regarding the working of our farm, as Mr. Owen professes considerable knowledge of crops and the management of livestock. With his help and John Monaghan's muscle, my husband is certain we can expect a profitable harvest this year—enough, I hope, to start paying off our accumulating debts. It will also leave Moodie more time to pursue his real estate ventures with Mr. Clark.

I have received a letter from Agnes and with it another tidal wave of homesickness. It isn't just my longing for England, which is always with me like a phantom presence, it's that I crave good conversation and, above all, the society of like-minded women, my sisters, and the gentle friendships of my youth. My elder sister's letter is filled with boastful news of her publishing successes—a poem here, a story there—and the kind of literary gossip I once devoured with great relish but now regard with sickening envy. To think that yesterday, my greatest delight was a supper of biscuits I made myself and a trout Moodie caught in the creek.

It made me laugh through my tears to read Agnes's suggestion that Kate and I should become editors, start a penny magazine and publish local poets and authors on subjects from history to home-making. "If you could make but five pounds a week, it would be worthwhile trying . . ." As though Kate and I meet for luncheon every Tuesday, as though the miles between us are crowded with coaches and dotted with country taverns. As though my days are spent composing glorious odes to fallen kings, instead of plucking chicken feathers and combing the woods for wild greens.

JUNE 21, 1833

My waters broke in the late afternoon of June 8 as I was putting the finishing touches to a watercolour of two brilliant goldfinches perched upon a purple thistle. Moodie rode to fetch Betty Fye, whom I had already enlisted to assist me in my lying-in. The older woman has nine children of her own and has ushered dozens more into the world, and though her manner is brusque, it belies a gentleness she strives to conceal. An hour or so after her arrival, the usual agony ensued, lasting throughout the night and into mid-morning, the whole sordid spectacle witnessed this time by a reluctant Moodie, who (it gives me some satisfaction to know) now comprehends the full consequence of his conjugal overtures. Shortly before noon, I presented my husband with another baby girl. Though he had cherished a fervent hope for a son, he clasped little Agnes to his breast with extravagant delight, while I, in my stupor, could only gaze into the eyes of the squirming stranger and marvel that she had just moments earlier issued from my body. It was the most unsettling feeling of disconnection. I did not recognize her; she might just as well have dropped from the sky above into my arms.

Her first week was peaceful enough, but she has been crying ceaselessly for the past three days. I sleep in snatches when she does, but it is not enough and I cannot shake the fog that has enveloped me since her birth. This morning, as I was hanging out some clothes to dry, I was overcome by an unnameable sadness and my tears flowed unbidden until her cries called me back to myself.

Betty Fye tells me the worst of the mosquito plague is over for the summer (or nearly so), and if there is a little breeze, it is quite tolerable to be out of doors in the evening. The light at this time of day has none of the brittle harshness, the relentless reality of midday, instead taking on a melancholy softness that suits my temper. The auburn sky, sometimes streaked with the bloody entrails of the dying day, presides over a landscape of deep and mysterious shadows.

Diana Owen paid me a visit, bringing a tiny smock she sewed for the baby. Since she has thus far been unable to bear children of her own, she told me, her pretty heart-shaped face clotted with sadness, it brings her joy to be able to provide something for my little one. Her kindness touched me deeply, and it has been so long since I have had a friend that I invited her to stay, and we talked until Moodie came in from the fields. In my weakened state, I found myself confiding in her my fears and my dreams. I leaned against her and wept until I had no more tears, and afterwards, a kind of peace settled over me. Through it all, she said nothing, just held my hands and listened. I have asked her to come again and she has promised she will.

Yesterday, Moodie presented us with a dog, a black-and-white explosion of fur and happiness that, to Katie's delight, covered her face with wet pink kisses before stampeding around the kitchen with unrestrained energy. The animal's unfettered joy made me laugh despite myself. We have named him Hector.

AUGUST 20, 1833

Mrs. Owen has not returned. And with good reason. It had seemed like a sensible idea: Moodie and I are not used to hard physical labour, but we are in possession of some (limited) financial resources. Mr. Clark said why not let this strong young couple do the ploughing, planting, clearing and harvesting, while we provide the seeds and equipment? The idea being that we would then share with them the vast profits generated by our farm operation. Naturally, Clark would oversee the couple—for a fee, of course. But now we find they have cheated us. When Moodie consulted Mr. Owen about "our share," the man said the wheat harvest was poor and that he sold what there was and used the funds to repair the plough. The hay, our hay, he fed to his own cattle. We have been swindled. Mr. Clark has expressed dismay at this turn of events, but he stated quite clearly that the work was done, he had seen to that, and it was not his fault if Mr. and Mrs. Owen made off with the profits. Clark has put the couple out of the shed, but we have learned they continue to live in the area, perhaps working their charms on other unsuspecting fools.

Moodie was in a fury. "How are we to get through the winter without hay for the livestock, without wheat to sell? How?"

"Well," I began, as calmly as I could, "we'll just have to buy some more—"

"Susanna, Susanna, Susanna. You don't understand. We have nothing left. There is no money to buy hay or anything else. It is all gone. Spent." And with that, he smashed his hat onto his head and left the house.

Not only is our money gone, we are deeply in debt. Moodie has been borrowing money from Mr. Clark to buy tools, livestock, seed, even furniture—confident, I suppose, that with the first harvest, he would easily repay what he owes. And perhaps we might have, had we not been so heinously taken in.

Of course, Mr. Clark is only too happy to extend the loan until next year. "Take as long as you like," he told Moodie. Oh, how I imagine he would love to swoop in and repossess this farm for a second time should we default, the scheming buzzard.

They hate us here. The animosity is palpable: no one comes to call; we are now excluded from local gatherings (mean as they are); and should we encounter our neighbours, their subdued greetings are underscored with an air of sneering amusement. Much of the social rejection we are increasingly subject to is, I am certain, thanks to Mrs. Diana Owen. The woman I so foolishly took into my confidence is a tireless gossip and has spread lies about our financial affairs. She also publicly mocks my literary inclinations. In general, authors are held in the highest contempt in Canada. God knows I have done everything in my power not to give offence, avoiding all discussion of literary subjects so as to convince the rubes and philistines we live among that I am no more than a simple wife and mother. I have endeavoured to conceal my bluestockings beneath the suffocating robes of conventional womanhood. I can mend a shirt as well as any of them! And yet the ridicule continues.

OCTOBER 27, 1833

Heavy rains have divested the oaks and maples of their fall finery, and now there is nothing to look forward to except the certainty of coming winter. And, I fear, the possibility of ruin thanks to another of my husband's schemes.

Mr. Clark came by this morning while Moodie was in the wood-lot, cutting firewood. When I saw him ride up to the house, I considered taking to my bed and instructing Bel to say I was indisposed. But something in his posture as he dismounted, whistling tunelessly and tossing the reins around the post as though he was in a hurry and had important news to impart, made me receive him as graciously as I could, out of curiosity if nothing else.

After dispatching Bel to fetch Moodie, I offered my guest a cup of tea, which he accepted, but only after pulling a silver flask from his coat pocket and asking if I had any objection to his "enhancing" the pot. I was sorely tempted to remind him that, in these parts, English tea is a good deal harder to come by than whisky, and that it seemed a shame to dilute the delicacy of the former with the dubious virtues of the latter. But I held my tongue.

"So," he said, seating himself in the Windsor chair by the fire, leaning back and crossing his long legs at the ankles. "So," he repeated as I fussed over the kettle with my back to him. I could tell he was bursting with news but uncertain what, if anything, he should reveal to me. At last, he finished his sentence. "So your ship is finally sailing, no?"

"Indeed," I said, turning and smiling, though I had no idea what he meant. "You have more information?"

"Yes, yes," he said, rubbing his hands together, though not, I decided, in order to warm them. "Yes. The funds came through. Your husband is now part owner of the *Cobourg*, the finest steamship to ply the mighty waters of the Ontario." The smile that erupted on his disconcertingly chinless face stopped short of his narrow eyes, which regarded me with a boldness that bordered on indecent. "That's right. Twenty-five shares. The last available. Your husband just made it, but now your fortune is assured."

I'm sure Clark could hear the clinking as with shaking hands I passed the cup and saucer to him. "Milk?" I asked weakly.

Just then, Moodie returned with Hector, who burst in, tail wagging, until he caught sight of Clark, whereupon he stopped in his tracks and uttered a low growl. He is a better judge of character than his master.

The commotion of their arrival allowed me to compose myself, and as I did, my shock gave way to a low-burning anger.

"My dear," I chirped, "Mr. Clark has brought the good news that our fortune is assured."

It was Moodie's turn to blanch . . . like a peeled potato. He gave me a brief, furtive look, and then, recovering his perpetual good humour, he grasped Clark by the hand and began bobbing up and down like a minor courtier in a bad play. Furious but unable to express my anger, I left them to their mutual admiration fest and, taking up Addie in her basket and Katie by the hand, went out to the garden to help Bel, who was digging up the last of the carrots.

After Clark rode away, Moodie called to me from the porch. "Susie? A word. Please."

I stood up, a clutch of gnarled carrots in one hand, trowel in the other, and wiped my forehead with a muddied wrist, watching him as he rolled along the path toward me, chest out, arms away from his side, like a sea captain returned from a long voyage. Evidently, they had emptied Mr. Clark's flask in my absence. Hector galloped ahead of his master and, before I could stop him, stuck his head into the basket and gave Addie a wet kiss. She began to cry, a jerky, irritated mewling that made my breasts tingle. I picked her up and faced my husband, aware, though not for the first time, that standing on level ground, it was he who looked up to me. It should have been an advantage, but it wasn't.

"Susanna . . ." he began.

"I have to feed her," I said, whirling around and walking back toward the house. Whatever it was, I didn't want to hear it. Normally, this would have been Moodie's cue to repair to the woods or the barn, anywhere rather than witness this most menial yet necessary procedure. Instead, he followed and waited wordlessly until I had arranged myself by the fire.

"Yes?" I said, not even trying to keep the coldness out of my voice.

"It's not what you think."

"What is it, then?" I closed my eyes and leaned my head against the back of the chair, struggling to keep my temper. Addie lost her grip and slurped noisily. She began to cry.

"Settlers are pouring into Canada. The waterways have never been busier. Trade is growing every day. We are lucky to get in on this. Why, if it hadn't been for Clark's influence, we might have missed the . . ." Here, he gave a helpless shrug and grinned, his dread of me overcome by his own damnable enthusiasm. "Well, we might have missed the boat."

"But a steamboat?" I said. Even over the baby's cries, I could feel the pull of his excitement, like oats to a hungry mule. "How did you manage that? I thought we had no money."

"Ah, well." He drew a wooden chair up close and, straddling it, folded his arms on the upright back, leaned his chin on his wrists and smiled. "My pension. My military pension."

"What about it?" The oats vanished. Addie's screams ceased abruptly as though she knew what was coming.

"I sold it."

If I had been able to move, I swear I would have reached over and ripped his beard off.

"I know, I know," he said, raising both palms when he saw my face. "But hear me out. It was the only way. It brought almost nine hundred dollars, enough to buy an interest in the *Cobourg*. The *Cobourg*—don't you love the sound of it?" He giggled and touched my hand. "And enough left over to buy hay."

I pulled back as though his hand were a nettle. "Dear God, Moodie, what about the income? It's not much, I know that, but it's something at least. It's all we have. A pension for the rest of your life. And you sold it for a few shares in a boat?"

There are no words to describe my feelings. I sat there, bodice open, helpless as the babe in my arms, while he went on to dismiss my concerns, speaking to me as though I were a hysterical child and he the patient parent.

"I did it for your sake, Susanna. You and the girls."

He explained that with the unsettled political situation in Europe, giving up his military pension now means he cannot be called up for service at a moment's notice.

"Imagine, Susanna, if I had to leave you now, with winter coming on, to fight in some far-off war for King and country. You wouldn't want that, would you? Oh no, I have done the right thing. You'll see. In a few weeks' time, the dividends will come pouring in and we'll be as rich as thieves. Now, what's for supper?"

The farm is sold. To Mr. Clark, of course. And for less than we paid for it fourteen months ago, though my husband would not say how much, only that our debts will be settled and we will have capital to spare. We are going to join the Traills and Sam in Douro and try our hand at farming in the backwoods. Moodie returned from another visit there earlier this month, brimming with plans, and I admit that at first the idea of being reunited with dear Kate won me over completely. Our time here has been an unmitigated disaster, and it seems best to revive our original plan and head north. This morning, Moodie made arrangements for a livery service to transport our belongings once the roads are frozen and passable.

And yet, despite all our trials here, I feel a great sadness at the prospect of leaving. From where I sit by the front window, writing this, I can see our cattle grazing in the paddock beside the barn. Moodie's prized riding horse, a black gelding called Ebony, trots briskly through the orchard, tossing its head. Down near the stream is the cowshed we lived in all last winter, a bitter reminder of the low blows fate can deal if she has a mind to. And yet here am I, rocking in the warmth of my own house, a good house, our home. It seems a long journey from that miserable hovel to this genial parlour. And now I am going to give it up?

Why is it I can never make up my mind what I want or where I stand on anything? I am as changeable as the weather, like a goose separated from her flock, flapping through the thick, murky air, honking loudly, changing direction with the fluctuating currents, uncertain which way is up, which way is down. Doomed to indirection, I drift over a landscape of alternating promise and heartbreak, stretching before me, as unending and unfathomable as the dark forests. I don't know where I am anymore, only that I can feel the chill of coming winter in my bones.

PART FIVE

1834

THE BACKWOODS

It is two weeks since I was reunited with my dear sister and long-lost brother, and sitting here now in front of the Traills' wood stove while the winter winds buffet their modest log home, I already feel transformed in some unknowable way—no longer Susanna of the Suffolk heath and broads, but a changeling I am only barely coming to know.

The circumstance of my rebirth comes to me as if in a dream: Our journey north from Hamilton Township. The sledge poised on the crest of a fallen tree, the horses struggling to haul it down the other side, the driver calling out, urging them on, his whip cracking, and then slowly, slowly, the whole conveyance teetering and finally crashing onto its side, our worldly goods spilling out, pots and blankets, axes, barrels, tools, the paraphernalia of a settler's existence. And then the box of china—the blue-and-gold Coalport tea set Mama gave me—tumbling through the air, emblems from another life, smashing into a thousand pieces against the immoveable frozen shield. I fell down weeping, ridiculous with exhaustion and rigid with cold after an eleven-hour bone-shattering journey from Hamilton Township (our drivers having decided to push through and make the two-day trip to Douro in just one day).

Shards of porcelain glinting in the moonlight—remnants of my old life. To think I carried that tea set across the vast ocean and over mud roads and forest tracks, that I stored the cups and saucers with such tenderness at the bottom of the flour bin all through our first winter huddled together in a lowly cattle shed. On the worst days, when the wind coming through the walls was like knives, and the sour smell of tallow and woodsmoke turned my stomach, and I thought I would give my first-born for a cup of real coffee, in tears, I would take the box out, dust off the gold crest embossed on its mahogany surface and press the cool, civilized sheen of a cup or a saucer to my rough, wet cheeks and think of Reydon Hall, of the lilacs in bloom, of the carpet of rosemary spreading between the flagstones in the back garden, of Sarah playing Mozart on the pianoforte. Foolish, foolish woman.

On my hands and knees in the snow, I began frantically gathering up the bits of crockery, making little piles, fitting this splinter onto that fragment like pieces in an unsolvable puzzle. But everything was destroyed, all except the sugar bowl's delicate lid with its gold-leaf handle, which I slipped into my pocket, a grim reminder.

Moodie pulled me to my feet. "Praise God, no one is hurt and the horses have been spared. Leave the china, Susanna. It doesn't matter." He helped me back to the other sledge, where the babies slept on in blissful oblivion. And I knew he was right. None of it mattered. The past. England. The woman I used to be.

We were within sight of Sam's house when the carnage occurred. And the only thing that kept me from coming completely apart was the figure of my brother emerging from the shadows like a knight errant. I didn't realize who he was at first and watched, numb and emptied out, as this bearded, barrel-chested man clad in a great fur coat took charge of the situation, calming the horses and directing Moodie and the drivers in their so-far-fruitless efforts to right the overturned sledge. But when I heard his voice, resonant with the scenes of my childhood, though deeper now and suffused with self-assurance, I knew it was him, and the broken china was forgotten. I climbed down onto the moonlit snow and went to greet him, weak with joy at the sight of my own flesh and blood at last. But Sam, dear no-nonsense Sam, with a brusqueness that makes me gasp to think of it now, merely took me by the shoulders and ordered me back into the sledge.

"We're not there yet," he announced. "You'll be staying at Westove. Kate and Mr. Traill are expecting you."

"But Sam," I protested, as horrified that he had barely acknowledged me as I was that our ordeal was not yet over. "Sam, it's me, Susie."

He paused and flashed me a broad grin, aware perhaps that he should make more of our long-anticipated reunion. "Sister. You look well," he said. His smile faded imperceptibly. "Different. But good. Good." And then he was off, grabbing one of the horses by its bridle and heading into the trees. A man of action, not words. I had forgotten.

In the end, it was only ten minutes more until I was transported into the consoling circle of my dear sister's arms. I can barely recall it, but Moodie tells me I half swooned and had to be almost carried into the smoky comfort of Kate's little home, into the halo of her embrace.

After an orgy of greetings and tears, once our wet clothing had been removed and our stomachs filled with a sweet and spicy stew—"Venison," said my sister, "from my Indian friends, and juniper berries"—we lapsed into a formidable silence. Too much has happened. Too much to say. Her little son, James, awakened by the invasion of noisy visitors, sat on his father's lap and regarded us with solemn curiosity. Addie, almost the same age as her cousin, brazenly reflected his gaze from the safety of Moodie's arms. Kate, who has not seen her namesake since she was a tiny baby, turned her full attention on my shy two-year-old, coaxing her onto her lap with promises of songs and stories. Sam left the cabin, returning with an armful of wood for the blazing hearth. My little brother Sam. Who is this sturdy pioneer? What do you say after so long?

But Kate, my sister Kate, is hardly changed—thinner, and if anything prettier, but still Kate. And as I watched her putting out bowls and pouring hot coffee, laughing like the young girl she once was, her cheeks red from the warmth in the room, the incredible swirling warmth, then all the months and miles, all the oceans and rivers and lakes that have been between us, melted away. We were together again.

I pulled my sister's shawl closer. It smelled of chamomile and woodsmoke. While the men stood by the fire and talked of land prices and the weather, and Kate amused her niece, I looked around the cabin, at the walls hung with maps and hunting prints, at the green-and-white curtains covering the tiny windows, a rug woven in zigzags of colour covering the rough planks of the floor, tidy rows of jars and tins lining the pantry shelves, bouquets of dried weeds and flowers strung from the rafters, baskets decorated with dyed quills and coloured beads, a row of moccasins by the door, a quilt, both simple and intricate, draped over the back of a pine settee. I surveyed all this and considered Kate, so competent, so resilient, whereas I . . .

The room seemed to wobble and then fade, and then come into focus again. And for the next hour, Kate and Sam and I revelled in our memories, in the shared language of our childhood, finishing one another's sentences, speaking in a code that must have bewildered Moodie and Mr. Traill, who listened in amused silence and then finally took the children to their beds, leaving my sister, my brother and me to our talk and laughter until I thought I might pass out from happiness.

The next day, Moodie, Kate and I bundled the babies into a hand-drawn sleigh and walked a mile back along the tracks in the snow made by our own horses the night before, to visit Sam at his farm, called Homestead. It is, according to Moodie, the first home to be built in North Douro, just three years ago. Palatial by backwoods standards, my brother's log house stands on twenty-five cleared acres—the best land around here, Moodie says. As we tramped over the hard snow in the crisp sunshine, through thickets of cedar and birch under a labyrinth of oak trees, their bare branches clutching at the sky, and pines poking at the heavens, I was humbled by the monumental task that lies ahead. Kate boasted that with Sam's help, Mr. Traill has already cleared nearly five acres on their own farm, enough that they were able to plant a small crop of wheat before the snow came. As we walked through the clearing, I noticed it was dotted with piles of brush waiting to be burned next spring.

Mary Reid, my sister-in-law, is a flit of a thing, all busy-ness and bustle, as intent upon her household duties as a nesting sparrow. Not once during our visit did she sit down or cease her constant movement. With four little ones, plus Sam and his first wife Emma's son, Richard, the Strickland household is a carnival of activity, and I was reminded of the happy circus that once prevailed at Reydon Hall. Later, while Moodie and Sam went out to investigate our own sixty-six-acre holding a mile up the shore of the lake, past Westove, Kate showed me the root cellar she dug with her own hands, half-filled still with carrots, turnips and potatoes from her garden. I helped her prepare a simple soup from the vegetables and a bag of pork bones Mary had sent home with us. Now, after two weeks together, our new life is taking on a patina of everydayness. Can it really be this easy?

The crowded conditions—four adults and three little ones—make me long for better weather so that we can spend at least part of the day outdoors. But when I venture beyond the protection of these four walls, I am, as always, diminished by the incomprehensible forest that surrounds us on all sides. There is nowhere to look except straight ahead into the unending undergrowth or straight up at the distant sky.

Winter persists. And construction of our own cabin goes slowly. Moodie has hired three men, and Sam helps when he can with advice and muscle and tools. Kate and I nurse the children and wash and cook and mend. She takes real pleasure in tasks that I consider mere drudgery: kneading coarse flour into a lumpy dough, boiling lye for soap, the mindless labour of churning milk into butter, dipping rags in tallow, rendering pork fat, and gutting the rabbits and squirrels the men bring home. I admire her industry, but more than that, her ability to distract herself with tiny triumphs, whether it's a pan of muffins or labelling jars of dried herbs and arranging them in careful rows on the kitchen shelves. I admire her refusal to succumb to the mire of home-sickness that I can't seem to extricate myself from. This morning, as I watched her rolling out pastry on the flour-covered table, I had to tell her how much I respect and envy her perseverance.

"Oh, but I have so much to learn." She blushed, and wiping her forehead with the back of her forearm, she straightened to look at me. "We would not have survived without Sam's help, and the others—the Hagues, the Caddys, Emilia Shairp. You will meet them all. The Chippewa too. Chief and Mrs. Peter. They know the secrets of the forest. They are the spirit of this land. They have a great deal to teach us."

For a moment, I wondered if she might have a fever. The lilting mystical tone was new.

"I'm sure I will be a very poor student," I said. "Remember how Cook always said I could burn water if I put my mind to it?" I had a vision then of the kitchen at Reydon Hall. Cook's suet puddings, Sarah's brown bread, Tom with gooseberry jam smeared all over his face. I cried out loud at the thought of my littlest brother. "Tom, away at sea," I said. "We will never see any of them again, Kate. Sometimes I can't . . ."

She passed me a biscuit cutter and a tray. "Susanna, that life is behind us. Think of something else. The best defence is staying busy." Her expression was animated by determination, the task at hand. She paused to tuck a stray wisp of hair behind her ear. "I will never forget England. Of course not. But I will remember it with joy, not regret. We have new challenges. You must keep a steady heart."

At that moment, as I looked around her rough cabin, evidence of that steady heart was everywhere abundant. The children played at our feet. Hector watched us from his place by the hearth. I felt a sort of gladness then. My natural pessimism resists Kate's view of our situation, but it is impossible not to be affected by her good spirits.

"You must work at happiness, Susanna. Make room for it." She stopped and smiled at me. Kindly. "Now, shall I add some currants to this last batch? What do you say about that, James? Currants?" She stooped to pick up her little son and held him, covering his dirty face with kisses while he giggled and squirmed.

I am trying. And if I pay attention, sometimes I am struck by an unexpected and surprising joy at the simplest things—the sound of sap dripping into a bucket, the smell of freshly baked cornbread, the evening sun sinking into the shining lake—and always by the persistence of another life turning inside me. (I am certain this babe will be a boy.)

Bathed in Kate's goodness, my homesickness is changing from a dull, hopeless ache into an almost comforting nostalgia. Katie adores her aunt, who has fashioned for her charming little dolls out of scraps of wool and cloth. My sister listens long and patiently to my daughter's childish sermons, and acquiesces to baby Addie's insistent demands for attention with amused equanimity and a genuine interest that I cannot find within me.

News arrived yesterday from Agnes that Uncle Charles, our mother's brother, fell from his horse in July and never recovered from his injuries. He was dead within weeks. Mama is stricken but resigned to the loss. "He was the youngest, her favourite brother," Agnes wrote, "and the most successful of all the siblings. He had a penchant for risk-taking that served him well in the law but obviously proved his undoing in less cerebral pursuits. I have always believed that riding to hounds and whisky are not entirely compatible."

Uncle Charles died without heirs, his wife and only daughter succumbing scarcely a year ago to smallpox, which means my sisters and I are the beneficiaries of his modest estate. It seems unjust to benefit from another's misfortune, but this legacy is nevertheless the answer to our prayers. Seven hundred pounds!

When I told him, Moodie could not speak. He simply threw back his head and laughed out loud.

MAY 30, 1834

My sister's garden is nearly planted. Potatoes, peas, onions, and we shall have cabbages in the fall. Today, I helped her sow the "three sisters": corn, beans and squash. It is an Indian technique Kate has adopted along with her moccasins and medicinal herbs. I admit I am eager to see the outcome: the cornstalks supporting the bean vines, which in turn nourish the soil. The broad leaves of the squash shading the roots of all three from the summer sun. The sight of those mounds of earth, their implicit bounty, the streaks of sweat on my sister's forehead, the little ones playing in the dirt, the heaviness in my belly—all have aroused in me eager anticipation for what lies ahead that I have not felt in a long time.

I am sewing new shirts for Moodie from the bolt of flannel Agnes sent from home. I detest making shirts with their collars and cuffs and straight seams, but my husband's work clothes are already in tatters and it is only the end of May. Most of the ready-made wardrobe we brought from England is still packed away: tailored woollen suits and dresses, trimmed capes and jackets entirely unsuited to the hot Canadian summers. And too fine to be subjected to the work we do here. It is endless, this mending and making of clothes for my family. We wear our dresses and breeches and shirts until they are too tattered to be respectable, then take them apart to use as patterns for new ones. I am becoming very adept with a needle and can whip together a dress for myself or a child's pinafore in the time it takes to bake biscuits. (I am a better seamstress than cook.)

Despite this never-ending occupation, I try to keep up with my writing. Agnes, in her last letter, urged me to produce amusing tales of life in Canada, with the promise of certain publication in England. But when the daily work is done and I am sitting at this table, quill in hand, with nothing to distract me but the blue jays calling in the pines and the smell of burning cedar on the breeze, I am unable to squeeze a single syllable from my sluggish brain. The paper sits before me like a foreign land. Never in my life have I been at such a loss for words—me, for whom the pen has always been a lifeline to my imagination, through which images and ideas and colourful stories run like water over a precipice. But nothing will come. Perhaps I am too close to it. The humorous sketch that has been percolating in my mind, of Old Joe and the dead skunk in the cupboard and a house overrun with vermin, amusing and pathetic as it is, arouses in me only a familiar sadness, and disgust that all the hopes of my youth should come to that: a rotting carcass in a cupboard. Someday, I will be able to laugh about it, but I need more distance.

A word about Mr. Traill. The hard physical labour of homesteading has improved his previously sallow and frail physique. He looks almost rugged now. But his mental state does not seem to have responded with the same vigour. When he and Moodie return from their day's work, Traill sits in his chair and says nothing. He is never hungry and must be coaxed to come to the table for meals. My husband has given up trying to engage him in conversation. Even the ebullient Sam's tolerance is wearing thin.

"He's like an old man, Susie," my brother said to me yesterday as we watched Mr. Traill unhitching the oxen at the end of the day. "A beast of burden, without even the will to rebel. How does Kate endure it?" I told him I have tried to talk to her, but she insistently attributes her husband's despondency to the long winter, and expects his mood will soon lift. She cannot let go of her determination that all will be well. It's as if she thinks she can will not only her own happiness but everyone else's as well.

JUNE 1, 1834

Emilia Shairp. I met her yesterday for the first time when she stopped in at Westove on her way from Peterborough to her bush farm, where she will spend the summer. I confess I have felt some apprehension and a twinge of jealousy at the thought of meeting this person Kate says is like a sister to her. Like a sister.

Mrs. Shairp is fair-skinned and thin as a poplar, and her energy is like that of a reined-in colt. All this time, she has hovered in my imagination as a reincarnation of Anna Laura. But unlike our departed friend, she is neither quiet nor fragile.

A prickle of electricity filled the room as she entered, obscuring the fact that her features are unremarkable, even plain, but animated nevertheless by a liveliness that I wanted to reach out and touch. She was wearing a very smart tweed riding jacket that was out of place in our present context. But it set off her narrow waist nicely and complemented her light brown hair, which she had pulled back into a hasty coil from which stray wisps escaped, framing her face in a happy riot of curls. She fairly danced into the small parlour, her long arms reaching out to pull Kate into a laughing embrace.

"Oh, my heavens. I am so happy to see you." She straightened and, closing her eyes, drew in a long breath through flared nostrils.

"How I have missed this air, and the quiet. You have no idea what a pestilential pit Peterborough can be when the weather gets warm. The smells . . . ugh." She wrinkled her nose and then laughed. Laughter like wind chimes. "Oh yes, I am so glad to be back." She threw the parcel she was carrying on the table and, placing her hands on her hips, executed a half turn one way and then the other. "Do you like it? The cloth comes straight from Savile Row. Made by Peterborough's finest—all right, *only*—tailor."

She began pulling apart the brown paper parcel. "I know, I know. Ridiculous. Such fine cloth in the middle of nowhere. A riding habit to wear milking cows. Anyway, I don't care. A girl has to have her little indulgences. And look, I've brought five yards for you, Kate." She unrolled the bolt of textured wool and let it billow over the back of a chair. "A pair of trousers for Mr. Traill. A fine new suit for little James. There." She dropped the tweed and turned her breathless attention to where I was standing with Addie on my hip, both of us struck dumb by the force of her considerable personality.

"You must be Susanna," she said, and her eyes—such pale eyes—were quieter. "Welcome to the backwoods. Are these your angels?" Abruptly, she sat down on the floor, crossed her legs under her skirt like an Indian and reached a closed fist out to where little Katie was peering through the spindles of a kitchen chair. "I have something for you," whispered Mrs. Shairp. "But first you must tell me your name."

"Katie," my daughter whispered back. She let the pretty stranger drop a cluster of sweets into her tiny upturned palm.

"There you are. Candied violets." Mrs. Shairp stood up, wiping her hands on the front of her skirt. "My mother makes them. Reminds her of England, I suppose. Now, let's have some tea."

With the introductions over, my sister asked her friend if her husband (Lieutenant Alexander Shairp) had returned yet from his business in the United States.

Mrs. Shairp shrugged her thin shoulders and grew serious for a moment. "No, and I don't know when to expect him." Then she added lightly, "Perhaps he has gone for good."

"Emilia, really," said Kate.

"Oh, don't worry, darling. It's all right. He'll come back. He always does." She turned to me. "Your sister does not entirely approve of me, I'm afraid."

"Emilia, that is simply not true and you know it. It's just that I wonder how you manage on your own."

"Well, you needn't. I am perfectly able to tend a garden and chop wood myself. Now, Susanna, when will your house be finished? You must be eager to move in."

After she left, I asked Kate about Lieutenant Shairp and his absences, but she professed ignorance (my sister does not approve of gossip). Then, when I related what Moodie had already told me about Shairp's reputed fondness for whisky, Kate said, "Nonsense. Emilia would have said something."

"Maybe you should ask her. Maybe she needs a confidante."

"Susanna, it is none of our business. I urge you to stay out of it. You heard her. She can take care of herself."

Perhaps she can. In any case, I find myself drawn to this fine young woman's energy and good humour. Though she is nearly a decade younger, I hope we shall be great friends. I told Kate as much.

"I knew you'd love her, Susie," she said. "My two favourite people in the world. I am so pleased."

JUNE 2, 1834

I am feeling more hopeful every day. But still, the Canadian spring seems interminable: days of bright sunshine that set the brooks singing and the spirit soaring are followed by icy rain-storms and bitter winds, and even snowstorms in April, in a cycle of hope and despair that lasts for months. Then, without pre-amble, summer, with its torpor and insects, descends like an itchy blanket. The brutality of winter is forgotten instantly, and one longs absurdly for relief from the inescapable heat. Lacking the temperate influence of the great lake to the south, the climate here in Douro is colder in winter and hotter in summer than what we knew in Hamilton Township. The land is rockier and the veg-etation miserly by comparison—all except the colossal brooding pine trees, some more than one hundred feet tall with trunks five or six feet around.

Although every square inch of this land seems to be covered in forest and the giant pines glower down upon us from the edge of the clearing, there is no shade to be found in the vicinity of the Traills' stifling shelter, every single one of the surrounding trees having been cleared to make way, I have been assured, for some form of agriculture. This morning, seeking a little coolness, I strolled with Kate, Addie toddling along behind (she took her first steps a week ago and has been in perpetual motion ever since), through a plantation of stumps to reach the water's edge. Lake Katchewanooka, which means "lake of the waterfalls" in Chippewa, is long and narrow, about five miles from end to end and one mile across. Every week, another manmade clearing such as our own springs up along its verdant shores as settlers continue to arrive. The shoreline here is muddy and shallow, and we removed our shoes and stockings and waded among the weeds until the girls were covered in muck and the mosquitos finally drove us back to hot, dry land. In quiet times like these, I can't help but reflect that it is the shimmering lakes and pure streams, the eternal forests, at once beautiful and terrible, and all around them the formidable inhuman silences—in short, all the things we defile with our relentless will to survive and prosper—that I find most inspiring about Canada, and that move me to take up my pen in praise and wonder.

Moodie goes off each day to supervise the construction of our cabin or to trade, borrow or buy the necessary equipment and materials. He is becoming well known in Douro for his gregarious nature and willingness to make a deal. His capacity for the company of others seems inexhaustible, and he returns in the evenings covered in grime and itchy red welts but bursting with plans and schemes. Give this man a project, I have learned, and he is happier than a hog in a wallow. The same compulsion to busyness infects my sister Kate, who putters endlessly from dawn to dusk. As I write this, she is in the forest, gathering wild plants and flowers for a book she plans to write about Canadian flora. Yesterday, she took me down the lake to where the Chippewa have set up their summer camp. We took with us flour and eggs and a few yards of flannel to trade. Several young squaws ran out to greet us, smiling with obvious delight and a great deal of incomprehensible chatter. They were dressed in animal skins and red leggings, their long black hair hanging in mats to their shoulders. It is obvious that Kate has become a favourite with the band, and her own affection for these strange people is just as clear. She introduced me to her friend Mrs. Peter, the chief's wife, whose dark face is as creased as the bark of an ancient willow, and her daughter Ayita (it means "first to dance"), who has shown Kate all the best places to pick berries and harvest rice. Mrs. Peter has also taught her to identify many medicinal herbs. I admit I was wary of these people at first; their black eyes, their heavy, inscrutable features and their heathen ways frightened me, and I hung back while Kate met them like old friends. But knowing that Agnes and the others would be eager for details about these "noble savages," I soon overcame my hesitation. We exchanged our goods for a pair of decorative baskets and a deerskin headband embroidered with beads that Kate insisted I should have. I will never wear it in a million years, but I was very taken with a doll-sized miniature canoe Ayita had fashioned from birchbark. I think Sarah will treasure it, and it will give me comfort to picture it adorning the mantelpiece in the library at Reydon Hall. Now that I have survived our first encounter, I no longer fear that these strange natives might murder us in our sleep; they seem to be a friendly, ingenuous breed.

My sister, in the meantime, has embraced their ways with her whole heart, even forsaking her sturdy English shoes. She has taken to wearing deerskin boots decorated with brightly dyed porcupine quills and laced almost to her knees. She carries little James as the squaws do, on her back, swaddled onto a rigid frame called a papoose, an arrangement she maintains leaves her hands free to garden and bake and quilt and mend in an endless round of meaningful activity that leaves me exhausted just thinking about it.

Kate and I paid a visit to the Shairps this afternoon. Their farm is picturesquely situated on a point of land jutting into the lake. From the front veranda of the house, one can see as far as Young's Point, where Katchewanooka empties into Clear Lake. Lieutenant Shairp has returned from wherever he was, and the couple received us with a deliberate cordiality that made me think we had arrived in the middle of some kind of marital drama. Mrs. Shairp (Emilia) showed us into their parlour, which unlike my sister's is separated from the kitchen and servants' quarters by a full wall. The house reminds me very much of our Hamilton Township house, with its covered veranda, ample windows and enclosed stairway to the second-floor bedrooms.

The lieutenant is very handsome—tall, broad-shouldered and clean-shaven except for a brief and precise moustache. He does not look like any farmer I have ever met, and even dressed as he was in loose trousers and a canvas shirt, he had the unmistakable bearing of an officer. A look passed between them as we entered, then Emilia, her nervousness betrayed by the faintest flutter to her smile, introduced me to her husband. There was an edge of defiance in her voice, as though our appearing at that very moment was proof of some argument or difference between them.

Kate and I positioned ourselves on the settee while Emilia saw to preparing the tea. Lieutenant Shairp (like many former officers here, he has not reverted to a civilian form of address) stood by the Franklin stove, not speaking, lighting his pipe with uninhibited concentration. At last, he exhaled a plume of smoke into the air and regarded my sister and me with amusement.

"You have a lovely home, sir," I said to break the silence. He lowered his eyes and allowed a smile, almost insolent, to play on his lips.

"My wife must take all the credit, I'm afraid. I have no talent for interior decorating." He caught my eye in a way that seemed to hold a question, though what that might have been, I had rather not speculate. I have seen the look before, a boy's look, brazen with the belief it can have whatever it wants.

Kate, I could tell, was completely taken with his air of authority and his sly charm.

"Lieutenant, you are too modest, I'm sure," she said.

"Oh no," said Shairp. "I have had no say in any of it. Indeed, if not for the generosity of my wife's parents, we would surely be living in a teepee like savages." He smiled.

A stillness came over the room. Emilia returned with a tray.

"Isn't that right, my dear?" he asked.

Emilia said nothing, setting the tea things on a low table. Her cheeks were burning.

"Emilia?" His voice was low, threatening.

She looked up, serious, her eyes meeting her husband's above our heads. A warning in them.

"It's true, yes. We have been most fortunate . . ." Her voice trailed off and her lips tightened as though she knew what would come next.

To my astonishment, Shairp raised his arm and brought the flat of his hand hard against the wall, causing the pictures hanging there to rattle and threaten to fall. Without saying a word, he nodded curtly and left the house.

"Oh dear," said Kate. "I am so sorry. We have come at the wrong time." She stood, but Emilia motioned her to sit down.

"No, please. Don't go." Emilia was trying hard to cover her embarrassment. She began pouring the tea. "They are like children sometimes, don't you find?" she said, passing me a cup. Her voice was high. Her hands shaking.

"I apologize for my husband's bad manners. What he said is true. Without my parents' help, we could not have built this house, or cleared the land. Not on a naval pension. Everyone knows it." Emilia's sigh was rueful. "But pride is so unproductive, don't you think? Such a waste of energy. What are we against all of this?" She spread her arms as if to encompass the universe. "Surely, we need all the help we can get." She lifted her cup to her lips, then stopped mid-thought. "I understand how hard it must be for someone like him to accept financial assistance, to adjust to the life here too. I do. I came to Canada ten years ago, when I was a child. This is home to me. I hardly remember England. But my husband . . ." She exhaled audibly through her fine nostrils.

"How did you meet?" I asked.

"We are cousins. After the war, Mr. Shairp planned to leave Scotland to claim his free land here, but he was in need of a wife. A relative put us in touch. For months, we wrote to one another, and then a year ago, he arrived on my doorstep. He was so handsome. A hero. He fought under the Duke of Wellington at Salamanca. I fell in love instantly and we were married within a month."

Emilia sipped her tea.

"What a lovely story," Kate said.

"Yes, lovely," mused our hostess. "Except that we—this new country and I—have not met his expectations, I'm afraid. The wilderness does not suit him. I have disappointed him."

"Oh now, you must give him time," Kate clucked. "I'm sure he will come around. Once you have little ones, it will be different. Why, just look at what you've accomplished thus far. Your farm will thrive and you with it. I can tell."

Emilia's laughter was like church bells. "Thank you, Catharine. Your optimism is infectious; you almost make me believe you are right." She jumped out of her chair and threw her arms around each of us in turn. "What good friends we are going to be."

I had not said a word, but I returned Emilia's embrace with genuine affection, grateful to be included in the circle of my sister's friendship. I thought of how lonely I have been, of how much I have longed for the comfort of female companionship. Emilia's eyes met mine, and I thought again of Anna Laura, of her dying promise to return in some form. Right then, her spirit seemed very close.

The lightness did not last. On the walk back to Westove, Kate expressed surprise at Emilia's candour. "Is nothing sacred between a man and his wife?"

"Kate, how can you say such a thing? She deserves our sympathy."

"I think some things are better left unsaid, Susanna. You mustn't meddle."

"Surely it is not meddling to show tenderness toward a friend in need. We must support one another however we can."

"You have Mr. Moodie for support. Emilia has her lieutenant, and I"—she hesitated—"I have Mr. Traill."

The path narrowed as it curved away from the lake and into the trees. I fell back and let my sister take the lead.

"You like Mrs. Shairp, Susanna?" It came out as a question. She did not look back.

"Yes, I find her . . . I sense a spirit similar to my own."

"Do you? Sometimes, Susie, I wonder about your sensibilities."

My sister's sharpness baffled me. Could she really be jealous, afraid I would come between her and her friend? I don't know Emilia very well, but I must say I find her candour a refreshing change from Kate's mouldy certitudes.

The log cabin is nearly finished. Moodie says it will be ready for us in another week, as soon as the interior walls are built. Kate and I will walk over tomorrow to inspect the new roof and chimney.

I have just learned that Moodie has obtained title to 350 acres adjoining our original sixty-six-acre allotment. Kate told me this morning. Apparently, my husband has been bragging about it to anyone who will listen—anyone but his pregnant wife, of course. Kate could see the rage spreading over me like a rash in the tropics.

"Susanna," her voice was stiff with caution, "he is your husband . . ."

I knew he had been contemplating such an acquisition, but I assumed it was just talk. I should have known. Kate reached out and gripped my shoulder, but I shrugged her off and marched out the door, across the clearing and into the woods, on my way to confront him.

She caught up with me halfway there. "Susanna. Wait."

I slowed. "How could he, Kate? Do I have no say in our future? I cannot stand it."

"Trust him. It will be all right."

"You always say that. But it isn't. None of this is all right."

I stopped to catch my breath, leaned my ungainliness against the rough comfort of a cedar tree. I breathed deeply. Once. Twice. Three times.

"Let's go. He said he would show me the cabin."

As we came out of the shadows of the forest and entered the clearing, I saw Moodie standing on the roof of our new home, a ragged messiah addressing his followers. It was a blustery day; fitful gusts lifted the thin soil into twisted apparitions and dropped them abruptly. The trees swayed above us, and the wind whipped the words from Moodie's mouth. He did not see us standing there.

"King of the wilderness. That's what they'll call me," he said, spreading his arms wide and throwing his head back until I feared he might fall. "All of this, as far as you can see, it's mine now."

"Hear, hear," cried Sam, shouldering his axe and raising a

clenched fist. (Does my brother have a part to play in this folly?)

Mr. Traill, aware suddenly of our presence, turned and caught my eye. He shrugged.

Moodie laughed and hurled his hat into the air, and then, catching sight of Kate and me, he slipped to his knees, grabbed the edge of the eaves, swung to the ground and leaped the few yards to meet us. His face was creased with good spirits, but his grin disappeared like the sun passing behind a cloud when he saw my face. The men resumed their chopping and banging. Apparently, nothing can dampen a boisterous work party faster than the presence of a pregnant woman. I forced a smile.

"It looks . . . positively . . . palatial," I said. There it was, the raw log cabin, set in the naked clearing like a newly hatched chick. And though it pales in comparison with the comfortable home we left behind in Hamilton Township, it is, by backwoods standards, commodious enough. (I hate to make these kinds of comparisons, but I could not help noticing, it is somewhat larger than the Traills'.)

"Come, come, come," Moodie cried, taking Kate and me by the arms and pushing us through the front doorway into the dimness. When my eyes adjusted, I found myself standing in a small parlour with a brand-new Franklin stove at one end. A partial wall separates the sitting room from a rather spacious kitchen with a deep stone fireplace and hewn log mantel. The ceiling above is open, supported by crossbeams, and a ladder leads to a loft above the parlour. Beyond the kitchen are two small bedrooms. Through the single window at the back of the kitchen, I could just glimpse a silver sliver of the lake through the trees.

"Oh my, Susanna," said Kate. "How beautiful it is. Mr. Moodie, you have outdone yourself. This is, indeed, a manor fit for a king!"

My sister's allusion to my husband's previous outburst created a brief silence and brought a flash of colour to her cheeks.

"Well," she said a little too loudly, "we must find a sunny corner for your kitchen garden, Susanna. It's not too late to plant a few peas and some lettuce. And potatoes, lots of potatoes."

With that, she slipped out through the low doorway, leaving Moodie and me alone in our new home. He placed a tentative arm around my non-existent waist.

"So, my darling girl, what do you think?"

I looked around once more, at the dirt floors and the chinked walls. *We have endured far worse than this*, I reminded myself.

"It's going to be fine," I said.

Moodie's sigh of relief was so poignant that it was like water on the flame of my earlier anger, and I could not bring myself just then to raise the matter of our land holdings. I waited until we were alone, walking back to Westove along the now well-worn path through the woods. Moodie chattered away about the work yet to be done.

"I have hired three men this week to begin clearing. If we really apply ourselves, I estimate we will have about ten acres cleared by fall—enough to plant a good crop of wheat." It was obvious that he relished the idea of the work that lies ahead.

"How will you pay them?" I asked.

I tripped then on an exposed rock in what amounts to a sea of exposed rocks and would have fallen if not for the steadiness of my husband's arm. I am not a farmer, but I can see that even with the undergrowth removed, there is precious little soil on this land. A crow scolded us from the top of an oak tree. Tiny blackflies swarmed, alighting on my face, in my hair. I pulled the brim of my bonnet down.

"Piecework," Moodie replied. "Eleven or twelve dollars each for every acre of hardwood they chop, log and fence. Fourteen for pine and spruce. Luckily, the site we have chosen—"

"But where will the money come from?" I persisted, though I knew full well.

He cleared his throat and gave an impatient little snort. "Your Uncle Charles's legacy, Susanna. You know that. It will be money well spent. By next year's harvest, we are certain to be self-sufficient. We cannot reap what we do not sow."

I decided to ignore this simplistic homily.

"And did you dip into Uncle Charles's legacy to purchase the land you were speaking of back there?" I know what's mine is his, but my husband's failure to at least discuss the matter with me first is more than unjust; it is dishonest. I bit down firmly on my tongue lest it take control.

He hesitated. Emboldened. "I did. And to buy tools and seed as well."

"But Moodie, 350 acres of rocky swampland and dense forest?"

His sigh of exasperation sent waves of indignation through me; I reined in my anger.

"Susanna, trust me," Moodie said. "In a few years, I will sell the land for a fortune. Immigration is exploding. Soon, these woods will be crawling with settlers. Consider this an investment in our future."

"Like the *Cobourg*?" I said. His silence was as stony as the path under our feet. "Has there been any word from Mr. Clark?" I kept my tone light, like a June breeze.

"No," he said, clearly irritated. "And I do not expect any. It has been barely six months since the venture began. We must be patient."

Moodie stopped in his tracks and, brushing the flies from his hair, placed his hands on my shoulders and turned me to face him. A trickle of dried blood snaked down from behind his right ear to the collar of his shirt. "Darling girl, darling girl," he said, shaking his head and looking up into my face in a way meant to disarm me. "You must stop worrying. That is my job." He lowered one cracked and callused hand to my belly. "This, my darling girl, is yours. Now," he said, pushing me gently ahead of him, "let's occupy ourselves with happier thoughts. Tell me, truly, what do you think of the house? I have decided to call it Melsetter. Melsetter Two."

Kate says I must defer to my husband's judgment in matters of property and finance. She says she has absolute faith in Mr. Traill's ability to make sound decisions regarding the management of their affairs. "Everything will unfold as the good Lord intends it to."

Sometimes I want to strangle her. Does she really think that pickling spruce buds and collecting wildflower seeds will keep us from starvation? I am truly beginning to prefer Emilia's pragmatism regarding male infallibility to my sister's blind faith in everything men do. But sadly, now that I have found in Mrs. Shairp a kindred spirit, it has been taken away. We learned this morning that the lieutenant has abandoned his farm again. I sent word offering Emilia whatever assistance we can furnish, but she has returned to stay with her parents in Peterborough for the time being. Moodie speculated that Shairp has plans to return to naval service.

"And so the rigours of the wilderness have defeated another," I said to Kate. If that young couple with their ample resources cannot succeed here, I wonder what hope there is for us. My sister refused to engage, cutting short my gloomy musings by announcing her discovery yesterday of a new genus of fern as yet undocumented by mankind. I feigned enthusiasm, and then, to her obvious annoyance, continued my speculations. (I do find people so much more interesting than plants.)

Moodie is trying hard to make amends. As condescending as he is when I question his judgment as I did the other day, it is also obvious he is unsettled by my disapproval. I have been punishing him all week with my silences, still furious at his latest ill-considered investment. Today, he returned early from work on the log cabin. And although he clearly had something on his mind, I ignored his feeble attempts to get my attention. Finally, he asked me to accompany him on a walk.

"I have a surprise for you," he said. I gave him a look of weary indifference. "Please, Susanna . . ." he wheedled. "I mean it. Come with me."

Kate offered to watch the girls. "Go, go," she urged when I tried to plead a headache. And so, because anger takes more energy than I have these days, I relented.

Moodie, his excitement unleashed, took me by the hand, and I lumbered down the long slope to the lake. "Now," he said, "cover your eyes. Promise me you won't look until I whistle."

As he rustled about in the cattails, I shut my eyes and listened, slapping at the mosquitoes that landed on my face and hands. He seemed to be dragging something through the weeds. I could hear splashing, a creaking sound and the banging of wood on wood. Then silence, and finally a long, low whistle. I opened my eyes and there, a few yards from where I was standing, I beheld an Indian boat, a canoe, sleek and curved like a sleigh runner on the water. It was about twelve feet long with a cedar frame and covered entirely with birchbark, a real-life replica of the tiny version I had sent home. Moodie, in his bare feet, his breeches rolled above his knees, stood in the water, holding the bow.

"Come," he said, holding out his hand. "Get in. I'll take you for a paddle." His expression was that of a small boy after he'd shinnied up the tallest tree. I climbed into the bow. Moodie handed me a paddle and, getting into the stern, manoeuvred the craft away from the shore. At first, I could only clutch the sides in terror as he paddled slowly into open water. Even the slightest movement seemed to send the canoe rolling from side to side in the most alarming manner. I dared not even turn to look behind me, certain that if I did, we should both end up drowning.

"Relax, Susie. Relax. The stiffer you are, the worse it is. I won't let us tip. That's better. Now take your paddle. One hand on the butt, the other down lower, above the blade. Good. Good. Now dip it in slowly and pull back. Again. Easy, easy. Yes, that's it. Like stirring soup. Good. Good."

And then we were gliding over the velveteen water in perfect rhythm, causing barely a ripple on the dark glass of the lake. And the faster we went, the more stable the canoe seemed. It was truly glorious. For a while, I could almost forget the heaviness, the awkwardness of my earth-bound self. For a brief time, as we slid through the water with amazing grace and in utter silence, skirting the rocky shoreline in the blue-black shadows of the mighty spruce, I became the swan I never, ever imagined I could be. We had not laughed as we did on this day for a very long time. Ever the Orkney lad, Moodie intends to erect a sail and affix a keel to our canoe. What a sight that will be. Whatever else he is, my husband, he is a boon companion, and his affection for me is as deep as the waters of Lake Katchewanooka.

No matter what chameleon tricks this, my adopted land, has in store, I will always cherish the peace and beauty I felt today. And soon enough, I know, poems will flow from my heart to my pen. When we are settled in our own little house. When this new baby is born. But not now. It is all too close and words desert me. The powerful feelings of the present are, as the great Wordsworth observed, better recollected in tranquility.

It seems, these days, I have little but time on my hands. Mary, our new girl, is proving diligent and good-humoured, and after the morning chores are completed (eggs gathered, children fed and dressed, baking set out to cool and laundry done), the long, lovely afternoons spread out before us in unblemished, cloudless perfection. Moodie too, now that our log cabin is finished and we have moved in, has fewer chores to occupy him, the brute labour of clearing the trees and stumps being left to John Monaghan and the three hired Irish. I abandoned my objections to paying to have the work done when I saw how arduous a task confronts us here. It seems insurmountable and has altered forever my attitude toward the trees of the forest. No longer the monuments to God's grandeur I once thought them, they now present themselves as intractable obstacles to our very survival. A single giant white pine takes three men as many days to fell, and then the stump must be extracted, a task requiring an even greater investment in blood and sweat.

Each week, the forest recedes a few yards farther, and swaths of merciless sunlight glare down on the small opening we have made here, an island in an ocean of green. The once mighty trunks of oak and maple and elm lay helter-skelter in criss-crossed confusion, waiting to be sawn into logs and stacked—and hopefully sold. Unruly piles of tangled brush litter the open ground, some burning in desultory conflagrations that thicken the still air with smoke. Armies of ragged stumps stand like twisted, blackened sentries. In the past week or so, the long, cool spring has turned dry and hot. And as I watch the men chopping and burning and excavating from dawn until darkness, I cannot help but make mental calculations as to how much longer our money can last.

The cattle and remaining livestock (we have only the few chickens and oxen we brought with us) will be driven up from Hamilton

Township next week, which will add to Moodie's responsibilities. Until then, he supervises the clearing or rides with Mr. Traill to visit my brother Sam at his thriving farm. His success is the ideal to which we all aspire. Not yet thirty, Sam and Mary are expecting their sixth child this fall.

"I take very seriously my avowed intention of bringing settlers to this vast, generous land," my brother, the former land agent for the Canada Company, likes to boast, "even if I have to produce most of them myself."

Sam is clearly suited to this life and takes as much joy in building fences as my own husband takes in dancing and playing the flute, or Thomas Traill in reading Voltaire. He is the beating heart of the small community we have found here. Just last week, my brother organized a barn building for Mr. and Mrs. Crawford, newly arrived from Dorsetshire. Strong as the oxen he so ably manages and a decade younger than his brothers-in-law, Sam is their colonial mentor, and I do not know how we would manage here without his common sense, good humour and encouragement.

On sleepy afternoons such as this, with the children napping and Mary putting out the wash, a complacency comes over me, and I am almost lulled into believing that generous days such as these are all that lie ahead. The simple fact of being mistress of my own house has instilled in me an attachment to this place I would not have believed possible mere weeks ago. But I'm afraid it has been months since I have written anything more than a few letters home, extolling with an enthusiasm I do not always feel "the august grandeur of the vast forest" and "the magic spell it has cast upon our spirits." Sometimes I think it is Kate's optimism and almost aggressive cheerfulness that has cast a "magic spell" upon my usual realism. Or maybe she is right and if I believe hard enough that all will be well, I can make it so.

In the meantime, my pen is as arid as July. Unless you count this, the meagre product of today's indolence:

Come, launch the light canoe;
The breeze is fresh and strong;
The summer skies are blue,
And 'tis joy to float along.

Under the careful tutelage of the young squaw Ayita, I have become surprisingly adept at manoeuvring our little boat solo in the shallow waters along the shore. And now, before the babes wake up and Moodie returns, before the mosquitoes assail us on the late-afternoon breezes, I will indulge myself with a paddle in my beautiful canoe on our imperturbable Lake Katchewanooka, which truly does possess a thousand wonders in my eyes.

JULY 8, 1834

Emilia Shairp has returned. And when she entered our dark cabin this morning, she brought the light in with her. She has cut her hair short into a careless mop blown here and there as though she has been out in the wind all day without a hat. She seemed fragile (but then to me, in my advanced condition, everyone looks small). She was wearing yellow calico, a loose shift tied at the waist with a homespun apron. Her bonnet had fallen off and hung from her neck on a blue ribbon. In her arms, she carried a loaf of currant cake, still warm and wrapped in a checkered cloth. She placed the bread on the table almost shyly and clasped her hands in front of her, waiting to be acknowledged. I was washing, bent over the laundry tub, my hair pulled up in a torn cap, my sleeves rolled to my elbows. I stood and beheld her, a bar of soap in one hand, suds everywhere. Before I could speak, she came around the table to embrace me.

"You look a fright," she said. "I'm so sorry. I should have sent word or waited for an invitation. I wanted to see you." A certain sadness, like the pulse of a baby bird, trembled beneath her smile. She could see I felt awkward, dishevelled.

"It's all right," I said, drying my hands with the soaking wet apron that clung to my immense belly. "I'm glad you're here. I've missed you. Let me make some tea? No, of course not. It's much too hot. Here, have a chair. Sit down, please."

"Susanna, can we go somewhere—down to the lake, just for a moment? I know you're busy, but . . ."

"It's all right. It's only laundry. It will keep." I scooped up little Addie, a filthy bundle digging holes in the dirt floor with a tin spoon, and called to Katie. "Come, girls, we're going fishing. Maybe we can catch a big pike for Papa's supper."

Emilia took Kate's small hand in hers and we walked through the tall, wet grasses to the big fishing rock. It took me a few moments to set Katie up with her rod and bait. There, in the shade of a giant willow, I turned to Emilia Shairp sitting in the dappled sunshine with her skirt hiked above her knees.

"Now," I said, leaning my bulk against the rough tree trunk, holding Addie on what remained of my lap, "tell me, what is it?"

"He's back," she said. "The good lieutenant has returned." She pressed her lips together and said no more.

I could not read her expression, which remained neutral, though her lower lip quivered a little. And although we had never spoken of it before, I could tell by the way her eyes held mine that she knew I knew. About the drinking. Everyone did. But the community had neither applauded nor lamented Lieutenant Shairp's abrupt departure

242

a month ago. A drunkard, they said—a handsome, charming rascal. Is one better off with or without such a husband? I do not know.

Addie, who had squirmed off my lap and the rock and was sitting waist-deep in the shallow muck, began to cry, reaching up her fat arms to be rescued. I passed her a small tree branch and her tears ceased abruptly. She began splashing and singing to herself.

"How sweet," said Emilia. Without a word, she removed her shoes and stockings and slid into the water to sit with Addie, careless of the fact that her skirt and apron were completely drenched. "Oh my, that's so much better. Isn't it, baby girl?" she said, and the two of them began splashing lightly in unison.

"Is this good news or bad?" I asked as I rebaited Katie's hook.

"I'm not sure," Emilia said. "At first, I was overjoyed. All the ugly scenes forgotten. He simply rode up to the house two days ago and swept me into his arms like a returning hero. Irresistible. Now?" She shook her head. "I resent it, I guess: that all the choices are his to make. I love him. Or at least the idea of him. But it is difficult sometimes."

I was silent. Emilia stood and began wringing out her skirt. Wet curls clung to her forehead. She sighed. "Of course, he has promised to stop." She met my eyes. "You know. The bottle. And so. Good news or bad?" She shrugged and, reaching up, stripped a handful of leaves from a willow branch hanging about her head, crushing them in her fist and dropping them lightly into the water.

"Mama, Mama, a fish. Mama. Look."

We turned our attention briefly to Katie and her predacity. But her line was merely caught on a dead head. Bored, she went ashore to pick flowers. Addie, tired of playing in the mud, allowed Emilia to pull her out of the water. She stuck her thumb in her mouth and curled up in my friend's lap.

"Everyone knows," Emilia said, stroking the baby's forehead as she drifted into sleep. "About his drinking, I mean—though they dare not speak of it to me. As though it is my shame that my husband loves the bottle more than good sense." She looked at me with bright, weary eyes. "I am tired of the awkward silences wherever I go. 'Poor Emilia Shairp.' I am tired of pretending everything's all right. When it's not."

I was touched by her candour. "Are you safe with him?" I asked.

She nodded. "He is quick to anger when the whisky takes over, but he has never harmed me. I don't think he would. I am not afraid of him. It's his unhappiness I can't bear. But no matter what I say, it's the wrong thing. I must learn to hold my tongue. It is a curse sometimes being a spirited woman in a world that values daintiness and submission in the fairer sex." She laughed as she said this, reaching over to place a hand on my belly. "Enough about me. How soon?" she asked.

I groaned and shifted uncomfortably. "Not soon enough. Six weeks at least."

"You must be excited?" It came out as a question, and rather than answer, I rolled my eyes. We both laughed.

I took up Katie's fishing rod and cast the line into the smooth water. There was little chance of catching anything in this heat, but a fresh fish for supper might assuage some of the guilt I was feeling for taking the afternoon off.

"You know," I said, "I have never told anyone." I hesitated. "Well, other than Catharine. But at times, I feel such rage." I swallowed, surprised at the hot tears in my eyes. "Such . . . rage. Moodie is a good man, but he has no head for business and I fear his endless schemes will soon ruin us. But there is nothing. You know? There is nothing I can do. I love him. But sometimes . . ."

"And what does your sister say?" Emilia asked.

"She says I must pray for patience. That God will guide Moodie. That he is my husband and he will do the right thing." Katie returned with a handful of limp buttercups, her face red and happy. I sat her between my legs and placed the fishing rod in her hands again. "But I don't believe he will. I know he hasn't in the past. And now"—I spread my arms—"his schemes have brought us here. To this. And like you, what can I do about it?"

"Mama!" Katie shrieked, and sure enough, a lazy pike sleeping away the hot afternoon in the cool mud close to shore had taken the bait. And with much ado, we pulled it in and dispatched the slippery creature with a rock. Mary would take care of the rest. Walking back to the cabin, our long shadows stretched up the slope ahead of us like advance guards. Emilia carried the still-sleeping Addie and we held Katie's hands, swinging her between us. My friend broke the silence.

"Your sister is a saint, Susanna, but I could never talk to her the way I am talking to you. Sometimes saintliness is not enough. Sometimes you have to fight back. Just a little. The trick is knowing when and how much."

I understood exactly what Emilia meant, and I felt a reassuring solidarity with her that made the weight of all this a little easier to bear. If only I possessed the wisdom to know how much to accept without giving in and what to rebel against if we are to survive.

Poor Addie. Diarrhea again. She seems oblivious, but I am beginning to worry. It started this morning—the result, no doubt, of all the lake water she ingested on our fishing expedition. I pray the well is not contaminated. If she doesn't improve in a day or two, I'll see what Kate has in her medicine chest. Moodie too is complaining of cramps and light-headedness. I hope it is only the heat.

JULY 10, 1834

I have sent some of my old poems to Mr. Chatterton at the *Cobourg Star* and others to *The Albion* in New York in hopes that seeing my work in print again may spur me on to greater literary endeavours. My motivation comes not from a sudden burst of inspiration, but from garden-variety sibling rivalry. While I have been languishing in my prenatal torpor, and penning this self-regarding diary with its useless reflections on my lugubrious moods and endless complaints, the ever-industrious Catharine has been keeping detailed journals of her Canadian experiences, as well as her extensive botanical observations and the medicinal plant lore she has gleaned from her Indian friends. Using these and drafts of her many letters home, she has cobbled together a text she calls *Letters from the Wife of an Emigrant Officer.* I have not read any of this masterpiece of domesticity; indeed, I had no idea my sister was even working on it until yesterday, when she burst into my kitchen, the pages of a letter fluttering in her outstretched hand like butterflies in a windstorm.

"Susanna, oh Susanna, I have the most wonderful news." She stopped and executed a clumsy pirouette, banging into the sacks of flour hanging from the rafters, causing them to envelop her in a sifting of fine powder. Fairy dust for a domestic goddess, I suppose.

"I am to be published. Look. Yes, a book. Published. Truly."

She was so out of breath that rather than go on, she handed me the letter. It was from Agnes, and as I took in its contents, I felt as though I had been stabbed. Yes, Agnes has taken Kate's letters and housewifely musings and shown them to one Charles Knight, publisher for the Society for the Diffusion of Useful Knowledge (surely not!), and he, apparently desperate for new material to include in a series called "The Library of Entertaining Knowledge," has offered my sister £110 for a completed manuscript, which he plans to issue as a book-length manual for prospective pioneer women.

How base and selfish I am. Instead of revelling in Kate's surely well-deserved good fortune, here I am nursing my resentment like a sore limb. The worst of it is, it's not so much Kate's success that I mind (though I do, I do); what really burns is the fact that Agnes and Eliza have taken on the not insignificant task of deciphering Kate's often-illegible script and organizing her tempest of notes and letters into some kind of coherent whole. I know only too well they would never extend the same support to me.

And so these meagre poems for now. God knows I am collecting enough stories about roughing it in the bush to yield a dozen manuscripts. I must continue with my notes and this journal too. If my sister can manage it, so must I. After expressing cursory congratulations at her news, I told her of Emilia's visit and our fishing expedition, how much the girls love her, how close we have become and so on. Kate took it all in without comment. I was trying to make her jealous. Now I'm sorry if I hurt her, but there is a smugness in her manner that irritates me profoundly.

I admit I am frightened by the powerful effect that Kate's news has had on me. Why do I feel so threatened? Her success does not come at my expense, I know that, and yet in my battle to become a writer, she has emerged as the enemy. I will not be eclipsed by what I know to be an inferior talent. There, I have said it. I will show them all.

I was so distracted by all of this that, of course, I forgot to ask Kate's advice about Addie's ailment. Under the circumstances, I couldn't bear the thought of going to her for help, so when Moodie returned (he is feeling better today), Emilia, who was visiting, and I tramped down to the cedar swamp to find Mrs. Peter. It was nearly nine o'clock when we set out, but a saucer of moonlight painted the evening sky as bright as day, and faint stars winked above us as we ran together down the shadowy slope, whispering and laughing as we went, along the path by the dark, shimmering lake as free and easy as children.

And for a few glorious moments, all my worries fled and I was filled with great joy simply to be alive. Mrs. Peter invited us into her wigwam and spread out a buffalo skin for us to sit on. Outside, a group of little boys dressed in red shirts and nothing else played with a small puppy on the trampled earth. There were no men in sight, and Ayita explained in broken English that they were away in the forest, hunting deer. All at once, Mrs. Peter put a finger to her lips to quiet us, and cupping her ear with one hand, she whispered, "Whist, whist." We stopped and listened, but there was no sound except the little boys scuffling in the dirt.

"A deer," said Ayita. "Listen." Apparently, the old squaw had heard twigs cracking in the distance as the animal wandered through the forest. All at once, she whistled to an old hound and, grabbing her rifle, ran off into the bush. A few moments later, we heard a shot, and Ayita left to help her mother haul home her prize. We waited perhaps twenty minutes until the pair returned, dragging a mortally wounded doe, which the other women immediately set upon, brandishing knives, while the children used sticks to keep the dogs away.

Before we left, I addressed myself to the smiling squaw. My attempt to describe diarrhea using sign language and sound effects defies description here, but when Mrs. Peter finally understood what I wanted, our mutual amusement needed no translation. She sent us home with a small packet of herbs that I think come from a plant known as jack-in-the-pulpit. After two doses of the bitter tea, Addie is already improving.

As much as I find the Indians here an unkempt, uncivilized lot, their natural talents—an uncompromising honesty and senses as acute as the animals they hunt—continue to command my utmost wonder and respect.

My sister and I have quarrelled. Silly, really. Ostensibly about a bake kettle they borrowed from us a month ago. Mr. Traill returned it yesterday. After he left, Moodie turned the pot over and saw that the cast iron was split across the bottom as though it had been left on the fire too long.

"Damn that man," he said. "Look at this. It will mean a special trip to Peterborough, if it can even be fixed. As if I didn't have enough to do. I have a mind to take it back to them. Let Traill deal with it."

Not wanting a confrontation, I urged him to let it go for now, saying I would speak to Kate myself. And so this afternoon, I walked to Westove, leaving the little girls with Mary, and with Moodie, who had come in from the fields early. The heat was formidable, exhausting. Even Hector declined to accompany me. Nevertheless, Kate was in her garden, thinning carrots with a kitchen fork.

"How can you work when it's like this?" I said, fanning myself with a handful of leaves.

She straightened and regarded me for a moment, then offered me a ladle of water from the bucket by her side.

"What about you, walking all this way in your condition?"

It was true. I sat heavily on a stump and drank.

"I've come about the bake kettle."

"What about it?"

"It's cracked."

"I know. We couldn't use it."

"What?"

"It leaked. So we returned it to you. Without using it."

There was something about her attitude, an evasiveness, an impatience that I had not seen before.

"That's impossible," I said.

"I'm telling you, Susanna, that kettle was cracked when it came here."

Something flared, and I shouldn't have, but I brought the subject around to the thing that had been simmering inside me for days.

"You know, Kate, just because Agnes is writing a book for you doesn't make you better than everyone else."

"I beg your pardon." She pointed the fork at me. Her hand was shaking. "I know what this is, Susanna. You're jealous and you're behaving like a petulant child. If you would cease your continual whining and complaining, and spend less time gossiping with Emilia and more time working, you might accomplish something other than producing a new baby every year or so."

I was aghast. Kate accusing *me* of being jealous? Though I am, of course. It's true. I immediately felt ashamed that it had come to this.

Just then, the door to their cabin opened and Traill emerged. He walked stiffly, like an old man. I could see the coming of winter in his face. He came over to Kate and placed a protective arm around her shoulders. To my astonishment, she began to weep.

"That's enough, Susanna. I think you should go now."

I ignored him. "Katie, what's the matter?"

But she only shook her head and buried her face in his chest.

"Please go," said Traill. "If you insist, I will have the kettle repaired, but your sister is right: it was already broken."

There was nothing for me to do but leave. All this over a pot? Something is dreadfully wrong.

Moodie went to bed early without any supper, complaining of a headache and chills.

JULY 17, 1834

My husband has not left our cabin since the ague struck him like a battering ram three days ago. How well I remember poor Tom Wales's suffering, and to see Moodie, who has not been sick a day in all the time I have known him, ailing this way fills me with dread. He is alternately delirious with fever, sweat pouring off him in rivulets, and then overcome with shaking so violent that his teeth chatter until I fear they will break. At times, he does not know me. Small sips of water are all he will take when these fits abate and allow him brief periods of sleep.

How long he will be laid up I cannot tell. One of the Irish labourers, a young lad named Paddy, told me this morning, when I took the men water on their break, that during the summer of 1832, while he was employed building locks on the Rideau, operations ceased during the entire month of July, so many men were afflicted. He said the fever is caused by the "bad air" in and around areas of swampland. And indeed, I have often noticed a noxious odour rising when the muck is disturbed in the marshy regions adjacent to our land. Paddy said he had seen many a good man die from the ague, and he prayed such a fate would not befall Mr. Moodie.

"Sure and he's a gentleman and yet can do the work o' two," he said. "We'll not be getting near as much done, 'thout his help." And with that, he shouldered his axe and went back to work.

I cannot help but notice that their progress has slowed considerably since Moodie became ill. John Monaghan has taken charge, but the other men do not pay him the same heed as their master. I pray that Moodie recovers, and soon, or I'm afraid we will never realize our goal of clearing ten acres before winter. And the construction on the barn is halted, as well as a shelter for the oxen and chickens. There are fences to be built, cows to be milked, pigs to be butchered. Yesterday, I endeavoured to help John Monaghan with tethering the cattle that had arrived that morning from Hamilton Township, but my fear of the beasts was so great, I could not bring myself to approach them. Our beleaguered servant finally ordered me back to the cabin lest they sense my terror and trample me for sport.

Little more than a month until my time. Please, God, spare my dear husband. I beg you.

JULY 19, 1834

The fever has passed and Moodie felt well enough this morning to set out for Toronto. He has asked Mr. Traill to accompany him—an olive branch, I suppose, after the contretemps over the bake kettle, which Moodie has apparently forgotten, though nothing has been settled. Both men appeared pale but happy as they rode off. Moodie's mission has something to do with securing official title to our increasingly vast land holdings. I think my brother-in-law went along more for a change of scenery than any official business. Rather than increase his acreage, Mr. Traill is talking of selling his farm altogether and finding some kind of civil sinecure, perhaps in Toronto or Cobourg, a life more suited to his aesthetic temperament.

While my sister Kate goes about merrily finding heaven in every wildflower and joy in all manner of adversity, her dour husband makes no secret of his hatred of this place and his regret at ever leaving England. The daily toil is anathema to him, and after long days spent clearing brush, he is too tired to read, the only occupation that he truly enjoys. He complains constantly now and makes no secret of the fact that their funds (like our own) will soon be depleted. In his opinion, the land here is unsuitable for growing much more than hard wheat and a few potatoes. What Kate makes of such negativity, I can't imagine. Moodie, who of course is gripped by a completely different outlook, can barely tolerate his brother-in-law's company, so I was surprised when he informed me of Traill's intention to accompany him to Toronto. I stood in the doorway and watched as he saddled Ebony. Hector whined persistently from inside the shed, where I had locked him so he couldn't follow his master. The breeze was rising and the gelding, eager to be off, pawed the dry ground with a forefoot. Moodie had donned his best boots and waistcoat for the journey.

"Thank you, Moodie," I said.

He placed a foot in the stirrup and in one smooth movement was astride the horse. Despite his recent illness, or perhaps because of it, he looked almost boyish, eager for adventure as always. A quizzical look came over his features.

"For what?" he asked.

"For taking Traill with you. Things have been so tense between us."

"Well. Perhaps the diversion will dilute the bile that seems to be his main source of sustenance," Moodie said. "But I swear, if he begins again with his infernal, incessant whining about the drought and the drop in wheat prices and, oh, I don't know"—here, he slapped his own thigh, causing Ebony to skitter sideways and execute a polite little buck of impatience—"I swear I shall spook his horse and leave him by the side of the road." Then he smiled and tipped his hat, and the sight of him like that, my good-hearted Moodie, made me thankful for his ebullience in the face of all that confronts us. How my sister can bear the sucking sound of energy leaving the very room her husband enters is beyond me.

Kate and I hardly speak, but when we do, it is as though her tears the other day never happened. I cannot forget the things she said, however. In anger, yes, but still . . . In what I hope is a gesture of reconciliation, she has invited me and some of the local ladies to Westove for tea this afternoon. Emilia and I will walk over together with the children. Her reconciliation with Lieutenant Shairp seems to be complete, and to my great happiness, she says they intend to reside permanently at their log cabin. She tells me her husband is like a new man since his return. I hope so.

Kate has also invited our sister-in-law, Mary Reid, and another neighbour, Mary Hague, whom I have not met. She is the daughter of a former neighbour of ours in Hamilton Township, now a lumber baron in Peterborough. Mary and her husband, James, live four miles south on the Otonabee River in considerable comfort. And of course, Mrs. Hannah Caddy, wife of Colonel John Caddy, will be there. Mrs. Caddy is a decade older than my sister and I, and frankly, I would never seek out her company on my own, as I consider her a common old fusspot who talks incessantly without saying much of anything. But then, Kate's standards have always been far more catholic than my own. I wish I didn't have to attend. I welcome the social contact, I suppose, but I dread the prospect of having to endure the mindless domestic patter of other women, as though jam-making and straight seams will save the world. And then there is the awkwardness between my sister and me.

In the beginning, it was all harmony and happy talk. Kate had gone to considerable trouble (and expense), laying out her best china (oh, my lost Coalport!) and an impressive array of cakes and nutmeats, dried fruit and preserves. She even unearthed from her dwindling store of treasures brought over from England a few hard candies for the children. It was Addie's first experience of the sweet bite of peppermint, and she howled in shock and then nearly choked on the offending candy, which I quickly replaced with one of the plain biscuits I had brought with me. I was soon relieved of the little harridan's incessant demands by Mrs. Caddy's eldest daughter, a sturdy girl of about twelve, who took the younger children—my two and little James, as well as two of her own siblings—out to play a rudimentary game of Scotch hobby in the dust. Mrs. Caddy's two older boys shinnied up and down the limbed trunk of a giant spruce. The possibility that they might fall and injure or kill themselves did not seem to cross her mind, as the mother of five (who appears to be expecting another, though it is difficult to tell as she is naturally stout) ignored her offspring other than to bark the occasional order, preferring instead to regale us with detailed accounts of how to remove the grit from bread flour before baking and the best uses of whey. While Mrs. Caddy held forth, we worked on the sewing each of us had brought—"idle hands," as they say—in my case, a new pair of sorely needed trousers for my husband. Emilia, who says she is hopeless with a needle, helped Kate set the table for our tea, then produced a book of sonnets, which she read aloud while we worked. For once, the heat had lifted; the day was cool and verdant under low clouds imminent with rain that didn't come. And for a short while, I felt safe and enclosed in the small, pleasing room.

When Mary Hague arrived, the mood changed from one of cosy diligence to alert attendance. Of French–Irish heritage, Mrs. Hague has an inherent dignity and warmth not eroded by the decade she has already lived in these woods, or by her unfortunate inability to have children of her own, which may account for her obvious delight in the sound of ours, who could be heard right then chanting rhymes in unison outside the open door. Emilia suspended her reading, and we all admired a basket Kate had assembled, a rainbow of dyed rushes decorated with quills and filled with an array of botanical speci-mens—tiny animal skulls, bear claws, eagle feathers, arrowheads and fossilized rocks. The children pounced delightedly on this amazing display while my sister outlined the provenance of each one.

Not to be outdone, Mrs. Caddy resumed her litany of domestic trivia. Kate was very attentive to all that the older woman had to say, even stopping to take notes at times. Material for another book, I'm sure. She also offered some of her own domestic truisms as well as an amusing anecdote about discovering a patch of wild garlic at the edge of her clearing after the milk from her cows became unpalatable. To all appearances, she was in her element: my sister, surrounded by others, busy as a bee, jumping up to pour more tea or slice the cake, the perfect hostess. And yet there was something brittle about her good cheer, a whiff of despondence beneath the bustle. Kate paid particular attention to Emilia's comfort, insisting she sit by the open window, where it was cooler, even bending down to whisper some secret thing in her ear, which made them both laugh. All this for my benefit, I am certain. Mrs. Caddy rattled on, now in a distinctly confidential tone.

"Why, the colonel says the roads are nearly impassable from Gores Landing to Cobourg. They've had rain on the south shore of Rice Lake and it's washed away the bridge over Gage's Creek. His horses almost foundered trying to cross last week. I do wish they'd send some of that rain our way, though. The fallow here is like tinder—one spark and *whoosh*. Our corn is barely knee-high and it's already the middle of July, and the wheat . . . well, the colonel says there'll be none to sell this year . . ."

She put down the cotton dress she was piecing together and began fanning herself ostentatiously, taking two deep breaths before beginning again. "They're saying, you know, that we can expect dire shortages this fall and winter. Tea, rice, sugar. So I hope you ladies are stocking up. It's because of the tariffs, the colonel says, though I'm sure I have no idea what that means. I only know I do cherish my cup of tea."

"Now, Mrs. Caddy," said Kate, passing around a plate of walnuts and dried apples, "let's not borrow trouble. I'm sure the good merchants of London and Toronto would do anything rather than deprive gentlewomen such as ourselves of the sustaining pleasure of a cup of tea just for the sake of a few tariffs."

Emilia and I exchanged glances. I rolled my eyes, then went back to my work.

Mrs. Caddy continued. "And did you know that new reports show that immigration has nearly dropped off completely? The rush of the past two years seems to be over, and Cobourg has become a ghost town. They say it's the fear of cholera here, and the rumour that there's free land for the taking in America. Everybody's going to Texas now, that's what the colonel says. I think the word is getting out that the joys of pioneer life have been somewhat exaggerated."

We all laughed at this observation, but in some ways, it sounded like the laughter of the doomed. Who now, I wondered silently, will buy the uncleared land that is our investment in the future? Who will seek passage on the mighty *Cobourg*? The room was silent for a while until Kate, sitting by Emilia, turned to the younger woman and cheerfully asked her if she had any idea how the Lloyds were getting on.

"Your husband and Mr. Lloyd are good friends, I know. They say Captain Lloyd has been away on business. I imagine it must be lonely for his wife. Have you had any news?"

Sometimes I think my sister has potatoes for brains. Either that or she was deliberately provoking Emilia. Captain Lloyd and his wife, Louisa, and their six (or is it seven?) children live over in Dummer Township. It is a well-known fact that the captain, though outwardly respectable, is an abusive drunkard who mistreats his servants and neglects his family. Kate was present last month at the logging bee Sam organized to help us with our clearing. She witnessed the captain in full bore as he whipped his oxen viciously and would have turned the leather upon his manservant had not my brother intervened. Surely Kate is aware that before Lieutenant Shairp's rehabilitation, he and Captain Lloyd were frequently seen drinking together. And though none of us (except my credulous—or cruel?—sister) would ever speak of it in Emilia's presence,

Captain Lloyd is widely thought to be the cause of the younger man's bad behaviour (now thankfully at an end, I assume).

Emilia blushed and frowned. Why would Kate, her friend, bring this up now, and in company? She shook her head and gave me a beseeching look. Kate continued to stare at her in innocent expectation. If I had been sitting next to my sister, I would have given her a sharp kick in the shins. Instead, I was trying frantically to think of a way to change the subject when the ever-well-informed Hannah Caddy delivered Emilia from the necessity of responding to my sister's cross-examination.

"No one knows, Mrs. Traill, if or when Mr. Lloyd will return from his 'business' trip," she said, laying her sewing on her lap. "The colonel told me just yesterday that he has it on good authority the rogue has gone to the United States, abandoning his wife and children. And that is all we know."

At the word "rogue," Kate exclaimed softly, "Oh my!" (*She knows perfectly well his reputation*, I thought.) Still, this latest development was news to us all.

"But what will become of Louisa and the children? How many? Is it six or seven?" I asked.

"One is tempted to believe they will be better off without the likes of Captain Lloyd," said Mrs. Caddy. "The oldest boy is grown enough to manage the farm. Still, it will be a long winter, sure enough."

Mrs. Hague added the welcome news that Mrs. Lloyd has the aid of a strong and loyal servant. "Jenny Buchanan may be illiterate and rough in manner, but she has been with the Lloyds for many years. Those children are as dear to her as if they were her own. And I am told the girl has endured much in her efforts to protect the family during her master's frequent tirades."

"Well," said Kate, "I had no idea. To think there is such ignominy in the world. I'm sure we should all be most grateful to have married the good and virtuous men the Lord has seen fit to bless us with. I think whisky is the devil's own elixir."

This proved to be too much for Emilia, who gathered up her sonnets and, bidding us a terse good afternoon, fled out the door and into the woods. I would have gone after her, but my bulk and the gauntlet of chairs and tables between me and the exit prevented me. In any case, the party was over. Mrs. Caddy summoned her brood, and she and Mrs. Hague took their leave without comment. Mary Reid slipped away as quietly as she had come, the earlier conviviality of our gathering having burst like a soap bubble. While I began clearing the table, Kate brought my girls and little James inside.

"I do believe dear Emilia was not herself," she began.

I was incredulous. "Not herself. I should think not. How could you be so insensitive?"

"I'm sure I have no idea what you're talking about."

"You're perfectly aware of Lieutenant Shairp's drunkenness, and of Emilia's trials, of her struggle to keep her household intact . . ."

"Don't be silly. Of course I've heard the talk, but I consider it nonsense. I do not believe it. I have always found Mr. Shairp to be a perfect gentleman. Quick to anger, yes, but Emilia has never said a word about him drinking. Not one word." She plucked a feather from her basket of trinkets and pressed it into her palm. "In any case, it's none of our business."

And then it all came tumbling out. "Of course it is. Whose business is it if not ours?" I said. "Unpleasantness does not simply disappear if you ignore it. What is wrong with you? You with your head bobbing above the dark clouds like a red rubber ball. You with your endless panaceas, your penchant for silver linings. Your effusions of goodwill and onwards and upwards . . ." I bent down to pick up

Addie, who was pulling at my apron, her "Muhmuhmuh" about to escalate into something more urgent.

"She wants a drink, Mama. I think she's thirsty," advised her big sister.

"Do you seriously not understand the trouble we are in here?" I went on. "Are the trees so straight and tall that you cannot see they constitute a forest? A dark, inimical forest that literally and figuratively will soon prove our undoing?"

Addie was crying now. I peeled her off my hip and put her on the hard dirt floor. Katie, ever the peacemaker, produced a half-empty cup of tea and offered her little sister a sip. I was not finished.

"Look," I said, pointing to the empty chair by the fire, the chair usually occupied by Thomas Traill. "Look at your own husband. Good and virtuous? Oh yes, indeed. A good man, but a man broken in spirit, dragging himself day after day into the wretched undergrowth. Do you really imagine his efforts, all our efforts, will produce an Eden on earth?"

My sister, aghast at first by my outburst, had rearranged her pretty features into an expression of patient forbearance. "Susanna, I really think you must calm yourself. In your condition—"

"Catharine, our money is nearly gone. Spent by your *good* man, and mine, oh yes, by my good and virtuous husband, squandered on worthless steamboat stocks and pointless brutish field work and acres and acres of swampland and bush that no one will ever buy. We have been had. Can't you see that? As miserable as he is, at least Mr. Traill knows it, at least he is not such a fool as his doe-eyed, 'it will all work out if we just persevere' little wife!"

And then she slapped me across the face.

The blow was like cold water on a flame. I stepped back, holding my cheek, the fire gone out of me. I could see by Kate's expression that she too grasped the ugliness of what we have become.

"Susanna . . ." There were tears in her eyes.

"What is wrong with us? Why are we fighting this way?"

And then she told me. "I lost the baby. The day you came about the bake kettle, that morning . . ."

"Baby? You mean you were . . . I would never have . . . You didn't tell me."

"I'm sorry. How were you to know? It was very early. These things happen. I thought it would be nothing." Her face crumpled. She was trying hard to smile anyway. She shook her head as if to clear away the sadness. "I can't seem to . . ." She gulped for air. "When"—her eyes were wide and liquid—"when will it stop?"

There was nothing to be done. Nothing more to say. We held each other for a while. Kate wiped away her tears with her best apron, and I helped clear the table before taking the girls and setting out for home. Little more than a month until I give birth. Will it break my sister's heart?

JULY 21, 1834

We are alive. Today, a day like any other, our little log home sits on the edge of a blackened clearing like a lighthouse watching over a smouldering sea. Meagre sentries of smoke trickle upwards like the devil's own will-o'-the-wisps. Greasy puddles, like miniature tar pits, pock the exhausted earth all around. The air is acrid with the smell of wet ashes, and every breath paints our nostrils and lungs with sour brushstrokes. But we are alive.

It is enough to make one believe in miracles.

Yesterday: An airless afternoon. A yellow-and-grey sky that pressed down upon us with the same promise of rain that has tantalized this arid wilderness all summer. A smothering heat, oppressive and deadening, sucking the life out of everything, making my head throb and my limbs and belly as heavy as lead. I took to my bed to rest. Katie and Addie lay sleeping on the parlour floor, their hot little bodies like sponges soaking up what relief they could from the cool earth. I didn't smell the smoke and quite likely would have slept through my own death by asphyxiation if one of the labourers had not shattered the stillness, kicking in the front door and throwing himself under the table, where he crouched, his arms folded over his head while he emitted a staccato of high-pitched whimpers. As soon as I opened them, my eyes began to sting, and the boy's garbled warning was unnecessary. I could see for myself, as I ripped open the door, that a holocaust of flames was rising up all around us, a wall of fire, as though the earth had split open and hell had soared up from its depths. The noise was like the thunder of a train, a furious roar punctuated by sharp cracking sounds. And the heat turned the air into a livid living thing. I could see no break in the onslaught. The swamp below us was a glowing tangle spewing thick black smoke into the sky. The fallow lining the three sides of the clearing spat long licks of flame, and sporadic explosions leapt to the treetops, fuelled by a fierce wind that had arisen as we slept. And though the heat was immense, somehow my babies continued to sleep through the inferno.

I grabbed a quilt from my bed and ran outside, thinking I would soak it with water from the cattle trough and throw it over the little girls, as futile as that sounds, only to find the trough as dry as a bone and the cows nowhere in sight. The well has been dry since a week, and there was not a drop of water in the cabin. And now the blessed lake was cut off completely by a lurid panorama of flame. I retreated back inside to avoid the arrows of fire landing all around me. I knew it was only a matter of time before one of them ignited the cedar roof and burned us all alive, but right then, the little house was like an ark in the storm. Mary and I kneeled on the floor, encircling the children with our bodies, praying fiercely to an Almighty whom I was certain had abandoned us once and for all. The wind climbed in a billowing crescendo of flame and the skies grew as dark as night from smoke, yes, but also from the coiled ferocity of the storm, unnoticed in our terror, which we had been praying for so anxiously these many weeks. And with a tremendous crash of thunder, the heavens parted over Satan's dominion and poured forth a deluge that continued for the rest of the day and into the night. We are alive.

Now, surveying the aftermath of the terrible conflagration that left this house and all of us in it miraculously unharmed, I cannot help but think that the good Lord would not have intervened only to let us perish from starvation and disease in the long winter to come. Emilia and her husband, seeing the smoke, ran all the way here through the pouring rain and, expecting to find nothing but charred skeletons, broke down and wept with relief. Not a word from Kate.

JULY 23, 1834

My husband's joy at returning from Toronto to find his family alive and well amid the charred and blackened detritus of our near immolation has made me realize how grateful I am. Life, even life in this godforsaken backwater, is infinitely better than the alternative. It has taken a near disaster to convince me of this, and I take it as a message from God that I must persevere in the face of whatever the future holds.

Moodie held us all to his breast until I thought we might suffocate in his embrace. And there, within the circle of his arms, I was reminded of the strength of his love, and I was overcome with shame at my recent remonstrances.

The cholera is rampant in Toronto. Thank the Lord that Moodie and Mr. Traill were spared.

"A good profit could be made providing planks to build coffins," my husband joked when I chastised him for putting himself in harm's way. "Och, dear girl, we were never in danger. It's a disease of the lower classes, as anyone can tell. The squalor is what brings it on. And even when aid is at hand, the poor wretches still won't lift a finger to save themselves." He went on to describe public officials patrolling the city streets, passing out lime and whitewash, and ordering householders to disinfect their houses and privies and cellars in an effort to stop the spread of the disease. "But it serves little purpose," he said. "They pile their dead in shanties and set them on fire, then move elsewhere, taking the sickness with them. They say a thousand people are dead this summer already and no end in sight."

Moodie was more interested in the roiling political goings-on. "That odious little wretch Mackenzie has been elected mayor of Toronto. What we're in for now, God only knows."

The antics of the Scottish firebrand William Lyon Mackenzie have been keeping us entertained since we arrived in Canada, but I have never seen him in action. His scurrilous newspaper *The Colonial Advocate* has served us well as kindle for the parlour stove, the only proper use for the vehicle of such virulent attacks on the Lieutenant-Governor and his executive council. We have learned, however, to keep our establishment sympathies to ourselves. Our illiterate Yankee and Irish neighbours are most enamoured of "Little Mac's" tirades, which have been known to dangerously inflame the settlers' republican rancour and their utter rejection of all the traditions we hold dear. The lower classes harbour an innate antagonism toward stability and the rule of law. Not wanting to be burned in our beds by some unruly mob, we keep our own counsel.

Moodie, who seems wholly invigorated by his journey to Toronto, lit his pipe and continued, while Katie straddled his knee and gazed at her father with adoring eyes.

"Yes, indeed," he said, "it appears the Reformers have a stranglehold on the city. And if Mackenzie prevails, he could regain his seat in the House despite the Tories' best efforts to have him expelled. His ragged and rowdy constituents seem to have no end of affection for the little baboon."

For the first time in many weeks, I felt we were a family again. My husband's recovery from the ague seems complete, and this short respite from his backwoods labours has lightened his mood. Even the recent conflagration can be counted a blessing in disguise, since it has expedited our clearing efforts, and the ash left behind will help to nourish the thin soil.

He was silent on the subject that most interested me, however. "And the shares, Moodie? The *Cobourg* shares. What of them?" Part of his business in Toronto was to meet with the principals and attempt to sell his part-ownership, at a loss if necessary.

"Ah," he said, taking Katie's little hands and placing them over his eyes in a game of peek-a-boo. "There are no takers at present. But," he said, giving her his sweetest smile, "I was able to use them to secure a loan that will buy us a new plough. The old one will not last until fall."

AUGUST 12, 1834

Moodie is down with the ague again. He seemed better when he awoke this morning, the fever broken, and he announced his complete recovery, dressed and joined the other men in the clearing. Two hours later, he returned, shaking and sweating, to his bed. Addie too was listless and clammy this morning, refusing to touch her porridge and whining even more strenuously than usual.

By afternoon, she was sleeping sweetly, and so I left them both in the care of Mary and walked to Westove. I had not seen my sister in weeks, not even in the aftermath of the fire. Her prolonged silence was uncharacteristic and, I admit, more than a little hurtful. If not for the daunting prospect of a walk in the woods in my condition in this heat, I would have gone to her long ago. But today, blessed with a light breeze blowing off the lake, I felt lighter in both body and spirit, and oddly restless. (This can only mean one thing.)

I found Kate behind the cabin, at the edge of the clearing, picking raspberries. Baby James, walking since I last saw him, staggered across the uneven ground to meet me. I could hear the *thwack, thwack* of axes coming from the bush but saw no sign of Mr. Traill. My sister was polite but reserved, and we exchanged stiff pleasantries until finally I asked her if anything was the matter.

"You really don't know, do you?"

"Know what?"

"Mr. Traill has been appointed justice of the peace for Douro."

"Why, Kate, I had no idea. That's wonderful." Which of course it was. How often had my sister and I entertained fantasies of our husbands procuring some kind of government sinecure that would alleviate our almost complete dependence on subsistence agriculture? My happiness at the news was genuine, though, if I am truthful, accompanied by a small stab of envy.

"Moodie will be delighted. As soon as he is well enough, we must—"

"Mr. Moodie knows of the appointment. He hasn't told you? Well, I'm not surprised. You did not know, then, that one of the purposes of his recent visit to Toronto was to petition the Solicitor-General for the position of land registrar. When Mr. Hagerman informed him the position was already filled and offered him justice of the peace instead, your husband declined the lesser offer, saying it was beneath him to be performing marriages and collecting fines in the wilderness."

"But I don't understand. How, then, did Mr. Traill get the job?"

"He returned to Mr. Hagerman's office the following day and offered his services. And when your husband learned of this, he had a mysterious change of heart and accused Mr. Traill of usurping his jurisdiction. Those were his very words: 'usurping my jurisdiction.' Whereupon, Mr. Moodie once again presented himself to the Solicitor-General with the intention of reclaiming the position for himself and ousting Mr. Traill. To his credit, Mr. Hagerman refused to even see him."

I was stunned. Moodie had said nothing. More than that, I was humiliated that my sister should know of my ignorance of the whole affair.

"They have quarrelled dreadfully," she continued, "and Mr. Traill has asked that I respect his wishes and break off relations with you."

"Kate, you can't be serious."

"I think," she said a little more gently, "we must give this time to blow over. I'm sorry, Susanna."

I am loath to admit it, but her account of the matter is consistent with my husband's character. He is nothing if not ambitious, and it would explain his utter silence on the matter. Did he imagine I would not find out? Nevertheless, I found myself wanting to defend Moodie to Kate, though not being in full possession of the facts, I didn't dare.

"Very well," was all I said. "Have it your way."

I am more hurt than resentful. But why do Kate's meagre successes feel like acid on my own thin skin? The more we need one another, the more we are like curs haggling over scraps of meat. Our misfortunes have acted as a wedge, not the common ground we once shared. I am losing her and I don't know how to stop it.

Addie is ill with the same fever that continues to afflict Moodie and, according to John Monaghan, has brought down Mr. Traill as well. My poor little child, burning up and weak from vomiting, lies listless and pale in her cradle. Moodie has abandoned all thought of returning to work; it is all he can do to lift a cup to his parched lips, and so I have not raised the matter of my last conversation with Kate.

Emilia came by with a blueberry pie, which will serve as supper for Katie and me. It is too hot to light the stove. My friend stayed and helped me carry buckets of water up from the lake, the well being dangerously low again. Tomorrow, she goes to Peterborough to care for her mother, who has fallen ill. It is difficult to know if Lieutenant Shairp is in any way the cause of this latest visit to her parents, but I could not bring myself to ask.

"I promise to return before the week is out," she said, and pressed my hand to her cheek. "Oh, Susanna. I am so afraid for you. How will you manage?" Then she feigned a cheerfulness neither of us was feeling: "I would not miss the arrival of little Dunbar for anything. Tell him to wait until I get back."

Another of Sam's logging bees is set for next week, this time at the Caddys'. I'm certain I will be unable to attend. A relief. I sometimes think the drunkenness that prevails at these events is inversely proportionate to the work that gets done.

Our girl, Mary, is leaving. Her father has recently come out from Ireland and, with more wisdom than is generally exercised by his fellow countrymen, has purchased cleared acreage in Cavan Township. He now runs a thriving dairy operation, and his daughter is needed on the farm. Certainly, I cannot blame her for going. A far better life awaits her there than here in the bush, where, truth be told, in our present circumstances, I do not know how I could even continue to pay her.

Her departure could not have come at a more desperate time, and I am ashamed to admit I begged her not to go. I feel certain my labours will begin any day now, and then how will I care for little Addie, whose fever continues to rage? Moodie manages to leave his bed for a few tortured hours each day, but he will be of no help to me, as he is sorely needed in the one field we have cleared to sow our wheat. We have hired a man and his oxen team to finish the drag, and the work must be completed this week.

John Monaghan has been stricken too. Indeed, all the men in the shanty are down with it, and work in the clearings for miles around has all but ceased. How little Katie and I have been spared, I do not know—only that, at barely two and a half, the child is too young to care for herself when my time comes.

I have had no word from Westove, though Kate knows my time is near and must have heard of Mary's departure. Her silence is a revelation.

AUGUST 19, 1834

I have managed to procure a nurse to attend me in my confinement, a Mrs. Pine, wife of the local farrier, and then only on payment of shocking wages. A few spasms this morning, more like cramps than true labour. By noon, they had subsided. When I told my husband, he barely responded, only asked if he should fetch Mrs. Pine. "Not yet," I said.

So many are taken sick in these parts that there is scarcely anyone left to care for the ill. Mrs. Caddy, my brother Sam, and three of his little ones are all down with fever, and Moodie drags himself from his bed to the clearing like a ghost, listless and vacant. My sister? Well, I have ceased to hope.

I pray constantly for our dear little Addie. Her fever has broken, but still she is as weak as a minnow, her breath like the whisper of the sea on a still day, her skin the colour of sand. If she recovers, it is in no small part thanks to her older sister's tender and constant care. Today, Katie carried a bucket of water herself from the lake and sits bathing Addie's hot little body by the hour. As I watch them, I am filled with anguish for the times that little virago's iron will tried me so sorely that I fled this cabin lest I do her harm. What I wouldn't give now for a flash of those angry brown eyes.

AUGUST 26, 1834

On the night of August 20, after ten hours of agony, I gave birth to our first son, John Alexander Dunbar. Once again, I thought I might die, but more than that, I feared little Addie would perish without ever meeting her new brother. All through the ordeal, she lay pale as marble at the foot of my bed, scarcely breathing, while Katie tried bravely to console us both. Mrs. Pine, though not exactly a minister-ing angel, proved a competent midwife. (The baby is healthier than any of us.) But I'm sure she had more than she bargained for, since Moodie was too sick to assist in any way. No sooner had she wrapped little Dunbar and placed him at my breast than she too commenced shaking and vomiting. By the time her husband arrived to carry her home, she was burning up with fever.

Lieutenant Shairp, hearing of my dire situation, sent his maid-servant over for a few hours yesterday to tend to the children so that

I might have some rest. The girl returns today. (I shall never think ill of the man again.) Moodie is often delirious with fever, and during his brief periods of lucidity, too weak to do anything. I have thus been obliged to leave my bed sooner than is prudent, or we should all perish from neglect.

This morning, one of the labourers came by to inquire after Mr. Moodie. Recognizing our distress immediately, he placed a cup of cold water by his master's bedside and, without encouragement, made tea for me and a bit of toast for the girls. His name is Jacob and he claims to be a passable cook. Then he offered to milk the cows and churn a bit of butter. "There'll be little to do til this affliction passes and the men are fit to work, ma'am. Might as well keep out of trouble."

Sometimes I cannot decide if we are more blessed than cursed. Addie is markedly improved today, and the heat, at last, has lifted. Fall is in the air.

To think, a son.

NOVEMBER 11, 1834

A new girl, Elizabeth (Lizzie), has joined our household, but only because her own family (nine siblings) cannot feed her over the winter. She is just twelve and unsuited to many domestic duties; I am obliged to do most of the cooking myself, but she has a good heart and loves the babies. It is astonishing (and more than a little pathetic) to realize how much satisfaction can be derived from pulling a perfectly turned loaf from the oven.

A parcel today from Agnes. Silk stockings. I held them up to the shaft of tired sunlight coming through the window and wept. "Worn only once at court," she wrote. She couldn't know that I spent the afternoon sorting through my trousseau, selecting items I might be able to sell. I plan to keep for my own use only those garments that a farmer's wife must have or are too threadbare to interest anyone. There is just one article that I have not the heart to part with. In a moment of nostalgia, I unpacked my wedding gown. There, in the rough dimness of our bedroom, I undressed and pulled the delicate thing, all lace and innocence, over my shoulders. It hung on me like a shroud, and shivering under the weight of it, I carefully refolded the memory and put it away.

Moodie sold Ebony this week. I know it breaks his heart to part with his beautiful gelding, but I could not wring an ounce of sympathy from the rag that is my heart. Not when we have barely enough flour to last until Christmas. And no money to pay the miller. Our debts are mounting with every passing week. At least Moodie has conceded that our prospects for self-sufficiency this year are dim, although he still asserts there is every chance next year's harvest will make up for the past summer's drought and we will be on our feet again. I know he is trying to boost my spirits, but it is having the opposite effect.

I spoke to Sam about our situation, and he conceded that in his opinion, neither of his brothers-in-law is suited to this life. As much as I know this to be true, it was still hard to hear. "Your husband, Susie, would make a better salesman than a farmer. Why, I believe he could sell salt water to a ship's captain, but uncleared bush when the price of wheat is less than the cost of producing it?" He shrugged. "Even Moodie is not up to that."

"But you encouraged him," I protested. "You persuaded him all that land would be a good investment."

He raised his palms, a gesture of defence. "The markets everywhere are in decline, Susanna. No one could have foreseen it. No one can escape it. It is not all Moodie's fault. Two short years ago, it seemed the flood of new settlers would never cease. Now where are the roads and canals we were promised? Times are changing."

I asked him why, despite all this, he has done so well. He put a strong arm around my shoulders and squeezed. "My debts are paid, Susanna. I am already established. I can ride this out."

But I know it is more than that. Sam came here as a boy. This land made him resilient. It defines him and he is of it. Moodie and I left so much behind in England, more than we have found here. This land has been our undoing.

I tried then, standing with Sam in my stripped-for-winter garden, to describe to him my own perpetual uneasiness, the sense of dislocation I cannot shake. I told him of my fear of the dark, of the wild animals lurking there. At night, if I venture outdoors, I can feel their eyes, as hard and bright as amber glinting among the trees, waiting to claim me. And Sam, pragmatic and literal as he is, was at first bewildered by my stuttering attempt to articulate the strangeness, the blindness I feel here, but at last he seemed to understand.

"After time, Susie, you get used to them; they become you and even help to show you the way. You think too much. Stop fighting and just let them in."

Moodie and I talk all the time of leaving the bush. My husband's latest obsession is Texas, after he read an advertisement in *The Albion* encouraging emigration there. Since we have no money, he intends to respond with a proposal to write a book for the Texas Land Company in exchange for our passage and land on which to settle. I am so exhausted by his schemes that I cannot respond. At times, I think, *Anywhere but here.* But Texas! Snakes and bison and bloodthirsty Indians.

No, somehow we must sell this farm and settle closer to Toronto or Kingston. But who besides us would want this collection of rude huts and fallen trees? We are only here ourselves because the land was free. And even if we did sell, without his military pension or any other source of income, how would we live? There was a time when the idea of leaving my sister again would have been untenable, but I cannot forget her negligence of me when Addie seemed close to death and my labour began and I had no one to turn to. Her allegiance is to her husband at all costs, to a man broken in body and spirit.

Out of necessity, Kate and I have resumed a cordial relationship. The bitterness between our husbands persists but without much vehemence. As in our own household, the ague has robbed the Traills of much of their vitality. (Not that my brother-in-law could ever be described as "vital.") Indeed, I was shocked at his appearance on my last visit. His eyes when he looked up as I entered were shadowy caverns in his long, sallow face. He nodded, though with little interest, then resumed poking at the fire with a blackened stick. Kate bubbled on as usual, but she seemed wan and distracted nonetheless. They have both lost weight. It occurs to me that she is like a babbling brook and he a stagnant pond. What a strange marriage. I wish that Kate and I were better able to console one another. But the older I get, the more I realize that there are fundamental differences in the way we view the world, and it is a chasm we will never likely bridge.

Our feud may be over, but things have changed between us.

PART SIX

1835–1838

REBELLION

---◆---

MAY 27, 1835 (MELSETTER II)

It has been nearly a year, and at the sight of her, the hole in my heart closed over like a cauterized wound. I could not help it; I dropped my hoe and ran to where Lieutenant Shairp was helping Emilia dismount. I threw myself at her like a wild thing. She squealed with delight, and without a word, I buried my face in her neck so she would not see my tears. Her husband watched us with a benevolent smile, as though we were little children roughhousing. But she caught his eye, and I could feel her reining herself in, dampening down the big balloon of her personality.

"I said I would be back to welcome little Dunbar," she said, "and here I am, nearly a year late. Let me see him." We held hands and walked around to the shaded side of the cabin, where my little son slept in a basket under the eaves. Emilia bent down to admire him and, straightening, told me that she had missed me, missed the sheltering trees and the shining lake.

They are happy now. I could see that. And what a handsome couple they make, so young, so much promise. After a winter of separation and negotiation, Emilia and her lieutenant have come to some kind of reconciliation. I am happy for them. And for myself, overjoyed to have her back. I have been lonely, I know it now. Too busy, too hungry, too tired to acknowledge the emptiness that is always there.

Of course, I have Kate and Hannah Caddy and the others, but all this last winter, we have not been the comfort to one another we used to be. It has been too difficult. We are all of us worn out, and that is not something to share. Somehow, sharing only makes it harder.

Good as they are, my sister, my neighbours, they are not Emilia Shairp. She has returned, bringing summer with her. And if I am not mistaken, the promise of her first child.

JULY 11, 1835

So long has my existence been restricted to this small cabin surrounded by the eternal forests, so thoroughly have I been subsumed by the unending toil and incessant demands of my children, that I am numb in body and in spirit. All the long winter past and through the interminable spring, Moodie and I have been like strangers, condemned to these close quarters yet unable to confront the resentments that have been fermenting between us like sour wine. Since Dunbar's birth, I have rebuffed my husband's advances, not just because I fear the burden of another child will break something in me, but also because whatever ember of desire for him remained is now as cold as stone. And though I miss what used to burn between us, the bridge I would have to cross to meet him again has fallen into such disrepair that I cannot bring myself to set foot upon it.

Last night, it was he who took the first step. As we lay in bed, me with my back to him, waiting for sleep to release me, he placed a hand on my shoulder and, feeling me stiffen, pulled back as he always does.

"Susanna," he whispered, "look at me. Please." I turned to face him, though the darkness was so total, I could see nothing, only feel his breath, sweetish and warm, on my face. He reached for my two hands and drew them to his lips. "No," he said, feeling me flinch. "It's all right." And then in a whisper charged with boyish excitement, he said, "I have an idea. You know how we have often talked of making an expedition to Stony Lake?"

I nodded in the darkness.

"Let's go. Next week. The planting is finished and I can spare the time. We can take the girls with us as far as Young's Point and leave them with the miller and his daughters while we paddle on through Clear Lake to Stony. We'll leave Dunnie with Lizzie and John Monaghan."

I pulled back at this.

"Shhh," he said. "Just for the day. He will be fine."

It was a peace offering, an attempt to bridge troubled waters. And though I am reluctant to leave my little one, Moodie is right: he is nearly weaned and will survive without me for a day. I nodded my assent, and then I let him gather me into his arms and hold me like a baby until I fell asleep.

JULY 17, 1835

Stony Lake's magnificent and mystical beauty is the stuff of legend in these parts, but few white settlers have ever laid eyes on its mighty waters and verdant shores. To the Chippewa, it is a place of magical significance, and they have long spread tales of the wild beasts and poisonous snakes that lurk amid its islands and steep cliffs, in an effort, says my brother Sam, to discourage the likes of us from defiling a wild and tranquil spot with our insatiable need to slash and burn all of God's handiwork. I admit that when I look out my doorway at the desolation of this clearing—the charred stumps like angry dwarves invading this once sylvan place, the roughly ploughed furrows where moss and wildflowers used to flourish—I can understand how the Indians must view our drive toward "civilization."

We left before dawn, launching the canoe under a starry sky, accompanied only by the ghostly call of a loon fishing for its breakfast. With

Kate and Addie sitting quietly in the bottom of the craft, trailing their fingers over the side, we paddled out into open water, moving silently toward the first light. At last, the sun blazed through the dark forest, and Moodie raised a sail to catch a fresh morning breeze that sent us skimming over the water until we reached the head of Lake Katchewanooka. Here, nearer the shore, the wind dropped, and so we paddled on past rocky islands thick with low tangles of blueberry bushes. I made a mental note to return with Emilia and the girls in a week or so, when they would be at their peak. Moodie pointed out a grove of giant red cedar on the northern side of the lake, an impenetrable thicket of green and black said to be thousands of years old. The shoreline was a profusion of tiger lilies and cardinal flowers, and in the clear, pebbly shallows under the canoe, we could make out a bounty of black bass suspended like flightless birds in the transparent waters. How I would have liked to stop and throw a line into the lake, but there was no time to linger, our plan being to reach Young's Point before noon and rest there in the heat of the day before continuing on to Stony Lake.

After negotiating a set of gentle rapids, we paddled up the river until we reached the opening to Clear Lake, a deep, rocky channel with twelve- to fifteen-foot limestone walls supporting the roots of giant oak trees whose leafy green branches reaching out to one another across the chasm created a natural and awe-inspiring tunnel. At the end of the nearly mile-long channel, the waters tumbled and foamed over a thirty-foot drop down to the lake below. Fifty yards from the brink of these falls, fighting the current lest we be swept away, we drew our canoe up on the rocks and secured it to a tree, and Moodie helped us onto the shore. We had travelled a distance of about three miles from our Melsetter home.

"At your service, milady," he said, bowing deeply from the waist before taking my hand and leading me and the children up a flight of stone stairs cut into the rocky path that climbed to the mill. The miller, Mr. Young, a Catholic who emigrated to Canada from the south of Ireland, lost his wife several years ago. But he seemed well looked after by his two daughters, Betty and Norah, and his sons, Matt and Pat. We had sent word ahead, and the Youngs were eagerly awaiting our arrival. After the usual introductions, the eldest son, Matt, offered to show us around the property while the others got on with preparations for the midday meal. We toured the mill itself, idle now due to the rain-delayed harvest, and then Matt led us to the edge of a rocky promontory overlooking the shining waters of Clear Lake. Out of an inborn dislike of high places, I stayed back from the precipice. The panorama of sky and water was magnificent, but at that moment, I was more taken with the figure of my husband standing before me on that rock, his face turned up to the cloudless sky. And I realized that I had not looked at him with clear eyes for a very long time, this stocky, bearded, slightly balding other, and yet the object of my eternal love. How close we have been and yet how far apart.

The Young family home is a large rustic lodge flanked by several rough-looking outbuildings and set high on the rocky ridge. There, in a high-ceilinged great room overlooking the lake, the most amazing feast of bush dainties I have yet encountered in the New World awaited us. Spread upon a white linen cloth (a relic of a gentler time and place) that covered a large table rudely fashioned from rough boards supported by carpenter stools was an array of meats: venison, pork, chickens, ducks and various fishes. There was new butter and fresh cheese, molasses, preserves of all kinds, pickled cucumbers and wild onions, boiled peas and potatoes from the garden, as well as all manner of pies: pumpkin, raspberry, cherry and currant.

It never ceases to amaze me how alternately generous and withholding is this Canada, pouring such bounty upon us during this season of growth that we risk gorging ourselves to death. And then, like a fickle mistress, doling out such meagre, grudging favours all winter long as would have us starve.

During our meal, the whisky flowed copiously, which naturally elicited an anthology of outlandish storytelling, mostly having to do with wild animals—of a deer captured by hand, of outsmarting hungry wolves in winter. His emotions loosened by the generous libations, Mr. Young expressed his great love for his adopted country, standing to make a lengthy toast, hand on heart, to "this great and bountiful Canada." His maudlin, though heartfelt, outpouring aroused in me a frisson of pride that took me by surprise. I half expected him to burst into song, and if he had, I fear I might have joined in, but he sat suddenly and began lamenting how difficult it is to procure suitable wives in the wilderness for his two sons (the girls, Norah and Betty, both being wed and proud mothers of several little ones, who were running about the room half-clothed like little savages, while our own girls watched in wonder).

"Look here at young Matt," the old man said, waving a duck leg in his son's direction. "Has God ever fashioned a more handsome gift to womankind?" Matt, seated on my left, blushed deeply and gave Moodie and me a sheepish, sidelong look.

"Consider yourself blessed, Mr. Moodie," the old man continued (as though I were a prize hen), "to be in possession of such a fine woman as the missus there. And I'd wager she's good for more than paddling a canoe." He executed an elaborate wink and reached for another biscuit.

I marvelled again as I sat listening to Mr. Young's inebriated woodland tales, and as our little ones assisted a trio of urchins in grinding black currants into the floorboards, at the set of circumstances that brought us to this place. At how different my life would have been had I never set foot on the sturdy little ship that brought us here. What, I wondered, was my sister Agnes doing at that moment? Toasting the King in some Regency drawing room? Putting the finishing touches to her latest royal biography? And what, I wondered, if she could be here now, would she make of all this? Perhaps it was the whisky affecting me, but I could not shake a feeling of disconnection, as though I were outside myself, watching a dream.

It was after two o'clock by the time we rose from the table, and Moodie, most eager to resume our journey and never one to linger over meals, thanked the Youngs and took me by the arm. He was about to ask if one of our hosts would help portage our canoe when Mr. Young, still somewhat lubricated, insisted that he, his daughter Betty and his two sons would lead us on a guided tour of Stony Lake. I thought I detected a flicker of disappointment in my husband's eyes. I do believe he had envisioned for us a romantic tryst of some kind. (Once again, his capacity for hubris was showing itself. Adventures in a canoe being a Canadian aptitude I doubt I am ready to tackle as yet. Still, I was touched and amused by the idea.) Daughter Norah kindly offered to remain behind with Kate and Addie, who, smeared in currant juice, had by then fallen asleep on the hard floor.

The Youngs had purchased two brand-new birchbark canoes the day before, and Miss Betty, with me in the middle and Matt in the stern, climbed into one. The other held Mr. Young, Moodie and Pat. In grand style, we paddled in silence through Clear Lake, so named for the brilliance of its waters, for about a mile, until we came to the far shore, a monumental wall of rock rising perpendicular to the water's surface 150 feet or more, its ancient and impervious surface broken only by narrow ledges running across it every fifty feet or so. These terraces, Matt explained, are favourite haunts of black and brown bears, which apparently enjoy nothing more than lounging about high above the water, on the lookout for unwitting morsels such as ourselves. (As luck would have it, old Bruin and his friends were not about that day.)

We proceeded skirting the shore closely enough that I could smell and then see a patch of pale pink wild roses flanking a small natural beach that formed an opening in the underbrush. Matt slid the canoe onto the sand and, holding back some low cedar branches so that I might pass, led me along a narrow path to a clearing that was dominated by an outcropping of limestone perhaps a hundred feet long and half again as wide. Deep crevasses scored the length and breadth of the rock.

"Shhh," said Matt, stopping at the edge. "Listen." I did so, and over the rush of wind in the pines, I could hear something else— from below the outcropping came a chaotic, almost musical, cadence. It was the sound of water running, underground streams reverberating in unseen rocky caverns.

"The Indians say it is the voices of the spirits calling out from the underworld," said Matt. It was like nothing I had heard before, and my forehead prickled with the strangeness of it. Matt led me closer to the rock. In the sunlight coming through the trees, the inanimate expanse of it seemed to pulsate with millions of infinitesimal jewels. My companion knelt in a carpet of pine needles, and taking a stick, he tapped the limestone in front of him. "Look closely," he said. "What do you see?"

I knelt down beside him. There, faintly but unmistakably, was the shallow etching of what looked like a rabbit carved into the surface of the rock. Matt moved the stick. "And here." I could just make out the rudimentary outlines of a turtle, like a child's drawing. And then as we clambered over the smooth stone on our hands and knees, we found hundreds of carvings, of snakes and birds and other half-human creatures, some tiny, some nearly life-size.

"What," I asked in a whisper as I traced the images with my fingers, "is this place?"

"No one knows how long it has been here," said Matt, "perhaps a thousand years. The Indians call it 'the rocks that teach'— *Kinomagewapkong*, in their language. It has great spiritual significance for them, and even those who have long since converted to Christianity still come here to pray and leave gifts for their gods." He pointed to a smouldering heap of dried leaves encircled with bits of shell and feathers. "Tobacco, sage, cedar. The smoke carries messages to the spirits."

His words sent a shiver through me such as I have not felt since I was a girl of eighteen. Ridiculous. The heathen practices of a child-like primitive people. But I was strangely moved by the aura of the place, and I have resolved to ask Mrs. Peter what she knows of it. *Kinomagewapkong.* I asked Matt to repeat it. *Kino-ma-ge-wap-kong.*

Then, off to the side of the clearing, I beheld something that stitched together for me the chasm between this world and my own and caused me to blink back tears: a tuft of blue harebell cascading from the rocks in delicate profusion. A vision came to me immediately of the carpet of these unpretentious blooms that decorated the rockery at Reydon Hall throughout all the summers of my childhood. A longing for that time of happiness and innocence overwhelmed my senses, but it seemed like a sign, and I vowed then and there to embrace this savage land, its fierce beauty and brooding secrets.

"Bells of Scotland," said Moodie, who had come up unseen behind us. Seeing my tears, he looked questioningly at Matt. We showed him the rock carvings, but the spell had been broken, and their earlier significance seemed to slip away with the waning light of the afternoon. My husband put his arm around my shoulders and guided me back to where the canoes were beached at the water's edge.

When finally we rounded the last peninsula, the full glory of Stony

Lake burst upon us, its spreading waters studded with islands too numerous to count, some towering green peaks, some low undulations of pink rock, and others ghostly groves of the white birch that the Indians prize for their canoes. The stillness was profound, broken only by the loons calling and, in the distance, the shrill cry of a bald eagle. We sat in our boats, listening to the silence, and I was awed by the majesty of the scene and humbled by my own insignificance. Even Moodie, whose habit it is to disrupt such moments as these with some form of jocularity, remained reverential and still. Behind us, the sun was setting and its light cast rivers of gold across the still waters. I would have loved to go on, to explore this mysterious place, but Matt, remarking on the lengthening shadows, broke our reverie, and turning the canoes, we began paddling back from where we had come.

JULY 28, 1835

Today, on the morning after a summer storm of such devastating fury that I thought God must be re-enacting the original deluge, the skies are grey and calm. At my side, my innocent daughters play with their dolls; my precious son chortles sweetly in his cradle. The dog sprawls across the cool hearth, snoring, unaware. A light rain falls, plucking at the puddles—pockmarked mirrors spreading out across the clearing, swamping our careful rows of wheat, my deliberate hills of potatoes.

It is hard to believe that yesterday, a Satanic storm swept down upon us, raging across the lake and through the forest. At first, we felt only a deathly calm as the evening skies turned from blue to a bruised purple and a menacing yellow light hung heavily over the clearing and the forests to the east. Then came the thunder, low and continuous at first, rumbling vibrations we could feel in our bones, accompanied by sheets of platinum that set the horizon alight. When the first calamitous explosion shook the cabin, Hector crawled, whimpering, under the bed. Then jagged spears of lightning split open the sky, and the wind rose, bringing with it thick, heavy rain, falling in a pounding staccato that I feared would demolish us all. Terrified, I pulled the children from their beds and, holding Dunnie close, ordered them—as well as the girl Lizzie and a stunned Moodie—to sit with me in a circle on the parlour floor and hold hands until the full force of the storm had abated.

All night long, the wind and rain continued. At last, I fell asleep in my own bed, clinging to Moodie in the hot, airless room. Sometime in the hours before dawn, we came together. With dream-like urgency, I awoke into the centre of a passion that spent itself quickly and violently, almost unawares. I was not myself. This morning, my bosom rises and falls steadily, evenly with each breath. Unhurried. No one would ever guess. This is the peaceful, oblivious aftermath, the disarming lull that follows upon the upheaval.

It sounds crazy, but the storm undid something in me. Broke through like flood waters breaching a dam. I can feel myself being carried away by the current, helpless before the tide and yet still afloat.

AUGUST 3, 1835

For weeks, it has been wet and cool. An English summer. If only we were growing roses instead of wheat.

But today at last, the clouds parted and Emilia and I took advantage of the sunshine and paddled out to the place the Indians call Blueberry Rock. In no time at all, we had picked four pails of the tiny fruits and eaten half again as many. We will have jam to last the winter. We spread out part of our harvest on a piece of canvas to dry in the sun. The heat at midday was impressive, so we sat in the meagre shade of low-hanging cedar boughs. Before long, Emilia had stripped down to her petticoat and camisole and waded into the shallow water. She pulled the white cotton up between her legs and tucked the hem into her waist, fashioning a pair of billowy panta-loons that clung to her long legs like a second skin. The bulge of her impending child was visible and she took no pains to hide it. (I think of the way I have draped and covered my own body in an effort to disguise the fact of procreation, the thing that is surely a woman's greatest triumph. Where does such shame come from?) When she was chest-deep, she called out to me to join her. But, embarrassed at the state of my mended and discoloured underclothes, I held up my skirt and ventured in only as far as my ankles. Emilia splashed me lightly and, laughing, fell back into the lake, her arms outstretched, her short hair spreading out around her face like a halo.

And then I didn't care. Modesty, like coils of birchbark, fell away and, half naked, I too was soon in the water with her. Glorious, weightless, suspended in this wild place. How is it that all this time, living on the shore of this bright lake, I have never once just let myself float, never once relinquished control to the clear, cool water? It was a kind of baptism. Like being born again into a life I never expected. Afterwards, we clambered out onto the rocks and stood shivering until the sun warmed us, and we dressed again. As we pushed the canoe into the lake to head for home, I thought I glimpsed, in the shallows where the water lapped the rocks, a small snake, black and lithe and shining, as it slid away into the rushes.

August 22, 1835

Moodie continues to fantasize about Texas. The rain has barely ceased these past four weeks. The wheat is drowning in mud and the corn is not even waist-high. Lizzie has returned to her family and John Monaghan has left us too, heading out for the western territo-ries and the prospect of a better life. With sixteen acres cleared and planted, we had anticipated a handsome sale of wheat if the weather co-operated, more than enough to cover the fifty pounds spent on labour and seed. Now we will be obliged to harvest the meagre crop our sodden land will yield this year ourselves, without the help of servants or hired labour. Thank God (if he can be held responsible for anything) that the summer fever has not struck with last year's ferocity and we are still strong and able to work.

Necessity is an uncompromising master. With Moodie's assistance and my own determination, I have nearly conquered my fear of the cows. There is no one else to milk them. My mastery of hoe and axe would astonish, or should I say appall, my gentle and cosseted English sisters. They may have soft hands and good manners, but I know how to roast dandelion roots and grind them into a reasonable facsimile of coffee. Unlike Kate and me, my fair siblings have never learned to appreciate the benefits of steeped sage leaves instead of tea, nor have they had to come to terms with a diet consisting almost entirely of coarse bread, milk and potatoes. Oh, what I wouldn't give for a joint of English lamb!

Sometimes I am as proud of these small victories as I am of my poems. Sometimes I can feel this place entering me, as penetrating as shafts of sunlight in a blue-black forest. And for hours, even days at a time, I forget who I am. Can it be I have never really known?

OCTOBER 10, 1835

Yesterday Sam stayed for supper—which he provided: a plump hen from Mary's flock of prized Dominickers—and regaled us with tales of Mackenzie's rally in Peterborough last weekend. Hundreds turned out to hear the Scottish firebrand, who is travelling across the province to deliver his traitorous message to the increasingly intemperate Irish and Yankee riff-raff.

My brother claims he attended out of curiosity. "I wanted to see for myself what havoc the rascal is raising with the less prudent among us," said Sam when Moodie questioned him. My brother cautioned us once again to keep our political leanings to ourselves. "The little rapscallion is not above inciting violence in the interests of promoting his radical propaganda," he said. "More than a few heads, and windows, were broken in the brawl that erupted after that hothead's little speech. Tempers are running high."

Moodie could barely contain his excitement. "Just let the bastards get out of hand," he fumed. "We'll give them a trouncing they'll never forget."

After my brother left, Moodie's temper continued. "Oh, how I miss a soldier's life, Susanna: the company of men, the action." I did not say the many things I might have at that moment. Maybe now he has an inkling of what it is to feel like an imposter in your own life. I left him to his thoughts and went to bed.

We received word today that Moodie's *Ten Years in South Africa* is at last going to press, published by Richard Bentley in London. A cheque for fifty pounds accompanied the letter. Our benefactor will never know how opportune these funds are. Molasses for a Christmas pudding, and real coffee!

My own publishing successes, though meagre, have lifted my spirits a little. I have received word from Mr. Sumner Lincoln Fairfield, accomplished poet and editor of the *North American Magazine*. He has published two of the sketches I sent him last summer and has asked for more, and for some of my poems. It makes me blush to record this here, but in his editorial, Mr. Fairfield alludes to "the former Susanna Strickland" as having "a genius as lofty as her heart is pure."

No matter how difficult it is, I will find time to write.

Another baby is on the way. I am exhausted at the thought of it. But Moodie is overjoyed and hoping for another son, a brother for Dunnie. Kate, too, is expecting a little companion for young James. I only hope that a healthy baby will rekindle the light in her eyes that has dimmed since the loss of her last. And Mrs. Caddy reports that the Shairps are in Peterborough, where they will remain until Emilia's baby is born and the weather improves. I pray we all come through our labours safely.

JANUARY 10, 1836

Ten of six and there is still light. Through the open front door (to clear the smoke from the cooking fire), I can see the sun sinking behind shredded clouds that linger above the lake, streaking the ice rose and blue. In a quarter of an hour, it will be necessary to light the lamp or I must put my pen away. I had hoped to have the children asleep by now so I might spend an hour or two with my poems, but only Dunnie has finally settled. Moodie is in Cobourg, negotiating with the army of creditors who are like hounds baying at a sliver of the moon. The girls are under the table at my feet—Katie berating her doll for not finishing its supper, Addie trying to climb onto my lap, her entreaties rising in my ears like hot blood.

This morning, as they watched me shaping dough into loaves, standing on their chairs, scribbling with their fingers in the loose flour on the table, Katie pushed a ball of dough at me. "Make a pig," she said, laughing. Addie squealed and clapped her hands. "Pig, pig," she chanted. And for a moment, something in me shrank from their happy insistence. As though they were trying to claim me, to stake me out, to make me theirs, or some part of me I might never recover. The moment passed. But here I am again, trying, trying not to separate, like cream rising to the top. It is no use.

Six of our best hogs have wandered onto the ice and drowned. Moodie is certain they were deliberately driven to their death by an Irish ruffian who has been squatting in the workers' shed by the cedar swamp. The animals were to furnish us with meat for the winter.

James Caddy has brought word that Emilia is safely delivered of a son, Henry Alexander, at her parents' home in Peterborough.

The Chippewa band has returned and pitched their wigwams down by the dry cedar swamp near the sugar bush. Their presence is an indication that the sap will soon be running, a sure sign of long-awaited spring. Chief and Mrs. Peter paid us a visit yesterday, tramping across the frozen lake with snowshoes fashioned from strips of deer hide woven onto curved cedar frames. Chief led the way while his good squaw followed, pulling a "toboggan" laden with baskets and other goods. My husband invited the Indians to join us at the table for an impromptu meal of potatoes, salt pork and coffee, something we would never have done had our servant girl still been with us, as it surely would have caused a rebellion.

The gentle savage, a short, swarthy man with a prominent brow and heavy features, was much taken with a ceremonial Japanese sword belonging to my husband, as well as a survey map of local lakes and rivers that hangs on our parlour wall. He offered the decorative basket his wife was carrying in exchange, and when we demurred, he said in halting, stentorious English: "I give many furs, also blanket." He pointed to the colourful woven shawl covering Mrs. Peter's thick, tangled hair. When I explained that we did not wish to part with either the sword or the map, Chief produced a large haunch of meat from one of his baskets. "Venison," he said, dangling it before us. This item Moodie and I sorely coveted, as it has been many weeks since fresh meat has graced our plates.

I picked up a small silver spoon, the only thing of value I had to offer, and held it out to Mrs. Peter, who smiled politely but shook her head. I shrugged, and as my vision of Sunday's roast began to dissolve, she approached me, lifted the hem of my skirt and pointed to my quilted petticoat. Clasping her hands as though in prayer, she spoke a few quick and urgent words to her husband and then to me.

I know I will dearly miss the warmth of that petticoat, but the immediate appeal to my deprived appetites was more than I could resist.

Moodie has begun work on a book about emigration to Upper Canada in hopes it will elicit as much interest from London publishers as did his *Ten Years in South Africa*. An advance such as that my sister received for her book would be most welcome just now, as the small payments I receive from Mr. Fairfield do not even cover the cost of pen and paper.

Shocking news from home: Sarah has eloped with Mr. Robert Childs, dissenter, phrenologist, peculiar little troll. Beauty and the beast. Mama's hopes for a good match for her most eligible daughter are dashed. "She has taken to her bed again," Agnes wrote.

MARCH 8, 1836

My brother Sam is pessimistic about the future. After a family supper of pea soup and bacon at Homestead last night, while Mary, Kate and I cleared the plates and served a pudding of dried fruit and suet, the men discussed the dire situation facing bush farmers as land prices, according to Sam, continue to plummet.

"The economic boom that brought us all to Canada has ended," he said, blaming the slump on the crop failures of the last two years, the availability of free land in the United States, and our own government's failure to encourage emigration and improve transportation. "I am as loyal to the King's representatives as the next man, but Toronto is a long way from the lakes and rivers of Douro. We need to make ourselves heard."

"Like our friend Mackenzie?" my husband asked.

"Of course not," said Sam. "He's a madman and would sell us out to the Americans in the blink of an eye, but . . ." He paused to draw on his pipe, and the room went silent as we waited for him to finish his thought. "The seeds of such extremism are nurtured in the soils of discontent. The government should take heed before the contagion spreads and rebellion breaks out."

Had they cared to ask my opinion, I would have agreed with Sam. The government in Toronto has shown little regard for the needs of settlers such as ourselves, but we can hardly throw our lot in with the likes of Mackenzie.

Thomas Traill remained silent. In fact, he seemed about to fall asleep. His eyelids drooped, his face a blank. Moodie paced the room, stopping to jab a forefinger at Sam.

"You've been spending too much time among the Irish rabble, Brother. To my mind, Bond Head and his Anglican compact are the best hope for advancing our fortunes, and I, for one, pledge my allegiance to the Lieutenant-Governor and his distinguished appointees in Toronto." He raised his glass of whisky and pulled out his flute.

I suspect my husband's Loyalist bluster is a way of bolstering his own sagging convictions—and mine. He is doing his best to keep all our spirits afloat. But does he really believe that the Lieutenant-Governor and his minions give settlers like us a second thought? As I listened to Moodie play his rousing little tune and watched the others raise their glasses in salute, the doubts Sam had raised drifted away with the fading light, and we were once again united in support of King and country. Despite my reservations, I joined in. The traitor they call "Little Mac" and his followers are monsters and enemies of all we hold dear.

Moodie butchered the children's pet pig yesterday. Spot, as it was called, was adopted by Katie last summer when it was just a shoat, the runt of the litter. She nursed the little weakling for weeks, and the playful animal soon became part of our household, a source of endless merriment, particularly in its friendship with Hector. The two became inseparable and, when they weren't chasing one another all over the clearing, were likely to be found curled up together by the fire, sleeping on one of Moodie's old coats. Kate and Addie are bereft; little Dunnie is too young to understand, and yet his tears fell as copiously as the girls'. However, their grief was not so great as to come between them and the ribs we enjoyed for supper. Loyal to the end, only Hector refused to gnaw on the bones of his old friend.

Agnes has written to say that Kate's long-awaited *Backwoods of Canada* is garnering glowing reviews in England. My elder sibling will also intervene on her little sister's behalf in order to sort out copyright. Kate's efforts to wring further royalties out of Charles Knight have so far proved fruitless. The book is to go into a second printing next year, and she has yet to receive a cent beyond the original advance, or hold a copy in her hand.

A brother for Dunnie. We have named the new baby Donald. Although she is due to deliver soon herself, Kate assisted me in my labour, which was blessedly short, only three hours from beginning to end, though the pains were hard and close together. The boy is hale and hearty, a blessing since we have little in the way of amenities to ensure his continued survival. My condition has prevented me from working alongside Moodie in the fields these last weeks, and so the wheat and potatoes are not in the ground. The cows have not calved yet, so no milk for the children. If not for Kate's help and Mrs. Caddy's contributions of bread and eggs, and the bass and muskie Moodie pulls from the lake on good days, we should be forced to go hungry. This morning, I left my bed and managed to plant a few rows of carrots and peas. Tomorrow, corn and squash.

I can tell that Moodie is worried I may slip into the bog of sadness that sometimes attends the births of my children. He takes great pains to remind me of our relative good fortune. "All over the township, settlers are starving," he says, "or taking refuge in the solace a whisky bottle offers." The idea that I should be cheered in some way by the misfortunes of others only makes me sad. This morning, he took his newborn son into his arms and cupped the baby's small head with a rough hand. "He has your chin, Susie. He will prevail."

JUNE 30, 1836

A daughter for the Traills, Katherine Agnes (another Kate). Mr. Traill's old friend Dr. Hutchison from the Highlands rode out from Peterborough to attend the birth. Kate says he administered laudanum to ease her pain, and that Hutchison would not accept payment from them. When I consider that I have brought forth each of my babies in paroxysms of agony barely blunted by doses of whisky with the certainty I would surely die before it was over, I fervently wish we had such a friend. Mother and babe are doing well.

Mackenzie and his rabble-rousers have been thoroughly trounced in the recent elections in Toronto. The Family Compact controls the legislature and with it this country's inviolable connection to the English Crown. The threat of American republicanism is over.

Hard work and hunger are an anaesthetic. The losses and longings, resentments and regrets that once colonized my mind have fled like milkweed silk in a breeze. This place is overtaking me, as hard as I try to outrun it. I haven't the energy to dwell on the past or contemplate the future. Our lives are an accumulation of days. Every act is essential. The petty quarrels of the past are inconceivable now. Cracked kettles, girlish jealousies, imagined slights, infatuations, daydreams, desire. In the early morning, if I can, I slip down to the lake, and looking into that rippled mirror, at the bottomless sky, the unending forests all around, I can see in my own watery image the distortion of all that I was. I am disappearing. This land is erasing me, and beginning to remake me in ways I never anticipated.

And so I cling to the moment. The weight of a fat bass at the end of a fishing line; three carefully wrapped silver coins falling out of a letter from home; a perfectly plucked grouse; potato plants in bloom; the sound of children laughing; a strong back, dexterous fingers; my sister's maple cakes; Moodie, Moodie, Moodie, for all his foolishness—these are the things that make my days.

NOVEMBER 12, 1836

Mrs. Peter appeared at our door early this morning in a state of desperation. She managed to convey, in a torrent of her own language peppered with English words and frantic gestures, that an accident or illness of some kind had occurred at her people's campsite down the lake. Why she came for me and not my sister Kate, I do not know, but she was clearly imploring me to accompany and assist her in whatever way I could. Leaving Moodie with the children, I followed her back along the shore of the lake until we could hear Indian voices coming from one of the cluster of low houses of animal skins stretched over wooden frames. At first, it sounded like a tuneless chant, but as I approached the wigwam, I noted with satisfaction that the Indian women, who have only recently converted to Christianity, were singing "Rock of Ages" in broken English.

Mrs. Peter hurried me to the entrance of her hut, chattering urgently as she did so. I bent down to enter and was assaulted by the putrid odour of rotting flesh mixed with pine needles and smoke. In the dimness, I could make out the shadowy outline of a young man lying on the ground, covered in deerskin robes. Fighting the urge to retch, I knelt and examined the motionless form of what I realized was one of the squaw's sons, a boy of no more than twelve. The heat from the cooking fire was intense and his brow glistened with sweat. He did not appear to be breathing, but when I placed a hand on his chest, he stirred slightly and moaned. Kneeling beside me, Mrs. Peter, who was weeping loudly, raised the hide covering her son's right leg, causing him to cry out in pain and lurch to one side. I almost fainted at the sight of the grotesquely swollen and discoloured limb. Just above the knee, a suppurating wound girdled his thigh, and even in the shadows, I could make out the lurid green-and-purple lips of torn flesh. His sister Ayita knelt on the other side of his body, rocking back and forth without making a sound. Beside her, an old man wearing an elaborate headdress of skins and antlers was chanting softly and swinging a polished stone at the end of a rawhide string over the boy's injured leg. In front of him on a woven rug was a clay pot containing a salve smelling strongly of pine resin, which I assumed had been administered to the wound.

"White man medicine? Please," said Mrs. Peter, kneeling beside me. She placed her palms together in an attitude of prayer and bowed her head. "White man God," she mumbled into her chest. She wanted a doctor, a pastor, anything to save her boy. But even I, who know little of medicine and too much of religion, could see it was too late for either. I stood and crouched and, taking her arm, scuttled out of the ghastly shelter. Outside, the morning air was like a gulp of clear spring water.

"I'm sorry," I said. "It's too late. I am not a doctor. I cannot help your son."

Mrs. Peter understood. I had been her last hope, and a faint one at that. She sank to the ground, and as she did, a wail of agony rose from inside the wigwam and was picked up by the women and children gathered outside until the sound reverberated across the water and through the forest.

There was nothing I could offer in the way of comfort, and so I left them to their sorrow and walked home alone. After all Mrs. Peter had done for me and my family, I was abject at the thought I might have been able to help that youth, who is said to have fallen from a tree and broken his leg about two weeks ago. The bone broke through the flesh and soon became infected, causing him great pain. I thought of the times she had come to my aid, the gifts of food and medicine for my children. But I could only watch helplessly as her son died. At least his misery is over. When I described the scene to Moodie, he consoled me, saying that such an injury would have finished any of us, and there was nothing that white man's medicine or God could have done.

MAY 1, 1837

Our new girl, Jenny, arrived yesterday. Though to call her a girl is misleading, as she is at least twenty years my senior. Illiterate and uncouth, she is nevertheless a welcome addition to our household as she claims to be able to do the work of two men. She has offered her labour in return for food and lodging, and seems more than satisfied with the arrangement, one that is a far better situation than her last. Jenny comes to us from the house of Captain and Louisa Lloyd, where she served as a loyal servant for ten years. But she has been homeless a fortnight since the captain, in one of his drunken rages, beat her severely with the iron ramrod of his gun and has refused to allow her to return. Mrs. Lloyd and the children are now at the mercy of his unpredictable outbursts.

Despite her rough ways, Jenny manages the children with a gentle but firm hand. I have been without help since Lizzie left, and the household has lapsed into a state of benign anarchy. Some days, I would gladly trade them all for a flock of chickens. Even little Donald, only a year old, is turning into an unruly tyrant. This morning when his sister Katie prevented him from stealing Hector's bone, my determined baby went rigid with anger, and with his little fists clenched, his teeth gritted, he growled at the dog until it crept away in surrender.

Moodie is in the fields from dawn until dusk. The children hardly see him, as he falls into bed almost immediately after supper. It seems all we talk about, when we talk at all, are debts and crops and unpaid wages, and broken tools and droughts and deluges. It has aged him, this life of endless toil. His hair and beard are streaked with grey. His faded eyes look at me from nests of deep lines. His forehead is etched with worry and his stoop is that of an old man. But he seldom complains, and his natural ebullience seems to rise to the surface even under the weight of our debts and our precipitous slide into poverty. Sometimes I think that the only things that bind us are the invisible chains of mutual hardship. So little joy. So much sweat and tears.

Once again, he is writing letters to the Lieutenant-Governor in Toronto, petitioning him for employment of some kind, anything that might provide a stipend to help lighten our financial burdens. He and Mr. Traill have forgotten their disagreement, a moot point since my brother-in-law's appointment as JP was not renewed last year. Thomas Traill talks only of selling and leaving this place.

The Shairps will be taking up summer residence at their cabin in a few days. I cannot believe it is nearly eight months since I last saw my friend.

My monthly visitor is two weeks late. I left the children with Jenny and walked over to Westove this morning to ask Kate for help. I know she will not approve; her third child is imminent, an event she anticipates with unequivocal joy despite her circumstances. I admire her fortitude, but with four children under six, I don't know how I will manage another so soon.

After hearing me out, my sister sighed and pulled a small brown paper packet from one of the carefully labelled slots in her herb cupboard. "Blue Cohosh" it said. My face must have collapsed with relief as she handed it to me. Her children played quietly on the rug in front of the stove: four-year-old James and little Katherine Agnes, who is the same age as my Donald. Watching them, I felt terrible, but it did not stop me from stuffing the envelope into my pocket.

"It's not what you think, Susanna. That I cannot bring about. But if your menses are delayed, this will bring them on. Not too much, or you may do yourself harm. Make a tea from two cups of boiled water and one spoonful of the powder. Take a small amount two to four times a day until they begin."

I thanked her with tears in my eyes.

"Children are blessings from God," she said, leaning heavily on the door frame as she watched me leave.

A second son and third child for Kate and Mr. Traill. Thomas Henry (Harry) made his appearance this morning just as the sun was rising. As usual, my sister was attended by Dr. Hutchison, who arrived in the middle of the night, in time to deliver the infant. Kate accomplishes childbirth with the same ease and competence she brings to all her domestic activities: a few hours of concentrated effort and then the finished product, perfectly formed. She does not believe she needs the doctor's help, but Mr. Traill, who is as squeamish as he is somnolent, insists.

What a dynasty we Stricklands are establishing in the New World: my four, Kate's three, and Sam the proud father of five!

And yet.

Emilia arrived today to find me out behind the cabin, vomiting into a patch of milkweed. The bleeding started this morning but had tapered off by then.

"Dear God, Susanna, are you all right?" She had her son, Henry, with her, a solemn little boy of eighteen months. He has his mother's long neck and square face, and from his father, a shock of dark hair and huge long-lashed black eyes that gaze out of his child's face with adult knowingness. I wiped my face with my skirt and leaned against a fence post.

"It's nothing. A little nausea."

Emilia smiled. "Number five?" My friend has embraced motherhood with the same energy and delight as my sister. I could never tell her the truth.

"I dearly hope not," I said, pushing the hair out of my eyes and reaching for her hand to steady myself. As I did, my stomach clenched again. I bent double and groaned.

"Susanna . . ."

"It's all right. I just need to rest. And some water. I'll be fine."

She shifted Henry to one hip, putting her other arm around my waist, and together we limped around to where Kate and Addie were helping Jenny hang out the laundry. Dunnie and Donald, playing in the dirt, didn't look up. Hector raised his head and wagged his tail, then stretched out in the sun. I am barely visible to my own family. Even so, and despite my misery, the scene struck me as an island of civility in the oceanic void that surrounds us. Yes, we have accomplished something, but how much longer can we keep it together?

As Emilia settled me into my bed, her son stared at me with the unedited frankness of infancy, a look that made me shiver and turn my face to the wall.

SEPTEMBER 17, 1837

The air crackled with anticipation. Everyone—adults, children, even the dogs—seemed charged with energy, surrounding the horse and cart as we pulled into the broad clearing at Young's Point, cheering and tossing hats and bonnets in the air.

"Mac, Mac, Mac," they chanted, crowding our wagon until I feared the rowdier boys might be trampled, then dashing off when they saw their hero was not among our party. Moodie eased our way through the carnival, stopping on the far side of the mill, where Mr. Young stood watching the event unfold: women spreading blankets in the sun, unpacking their baskets of food; babies wailing; men clustered under the river willows, tipping back bottles of ale, their rough laughter rising and falling. The miller grabbed Bones's bridle.

"A fine day, a fine day," he bellowed as Moodie and Mr. Traill jumped down to tether the cart and horse we share between our two families now. Sam and his brood pulled up beside us in a bright red farm wagon drawn by a pair of Belgians.

"You may not agree with him," Mr. Young said, "but the spectacle is not to be missed." He surveyed the crowd. "His worship had better show up soon or this bunch might storm the ramparts. Have you ever seen such a party? It's like this wherever he goes."

"Matt—" he turned and called to his son, who appeared in the doorway of the big house with a young woman on his arm—"it's Sam

Strickland and his family. Give us a hand here with these horses, the ladies, little ones."

As if on cue, the crowd erupted in cheers punctuated by a smattering of catcalls, even a few boos. Evidently, there were others who, like us, came primarily out of curiosity to see the rabble-rouser at work. We were outnumbered, however, by legions of enthusiastic supporters jostling to get close to Mackenzie as he was escorted by a contingent of burly youths toward a hay wagon set at the top of a knoll in the clearing. The young men picked him up and bore him on their shoulders the last few yards, depositing their hero on the makeshift dais like precious cargo. Mackenzie brushed at a few shreds of straw clinging to his trousers, then straightened and faced the multitude. He stood there smiling, silent, letting his eyes travel over the assembly for what seemed an eternity. He was short and barrel-chested with thick red hair and a beard that bristled around his ears and under his chin, giving him an ape-like appearance. His arms were long, his legs short and bowed, his features unremarkable—thin lips, a straight nose—except for his eyes, which burned with intensity even before he uttered a word. He placed his hands on his hips and spread his legs apart in an attitude of defiance, then raised his arms in the air.

"Canadians!" he roared. The crowd exploded. Mackenzie waited for the din to subside and continued, his voice soft now. "Canadians. You and you and even you," he said, pointing to a little girl sitting on her father's shoulders. "All of you are citizens of this great land. And all of you. All. Of. You. All of you deserve a share in its riches. All of you deserve to prosper and grow. You came here seeking a better life, and now that life is being denied you, denied by people who consider themselves your betters, who are doing all they can to further their own interests at the expense OF YOURS."

More cheers and pitchforks raised in salute. From off to the side, someone yelled, "Kill the bastards."

Mackenzie raised his hands again, palms downward, gesturing for calmness. He waited for the murmurs to die down. "They call themselves the Family Compact, a self-styled aristocracy. But they are no better than you or I. Indeed, they are much worse. Corrupt and greedy, the Boultons, the Jarvises, the Powells, and of course their leader, Sir Francis Bond Head, that puffed-up tyrant who perches on his mahogany throne and dispenses favours and positions to his cronies while they swallow his bribes like sweet morsels of OUR FLESH." Little Mac pummelled the air with his fist, his voice shrill and angry, as he went on to enumerate the many sins of Queen Victoria's representative in Toronto. He had the crowd in the palm of his hands; they actually seemed to sway to the rhythm of his ravings, which alternated between jarring and mesmerizing. Moodie held my hand tightly. I could tell he was rapt and disgusted at the same time.

"The time has come," Mackenzie howled. "The time has come for change. They say we are on the verge of a revolution. I say it is ALREADY HERE!"

Later, at Sam and Mary's, over chicken stew and brown bread, my brother expressed his fears for the future. "A dangerous man, that Mackenzie. He is playing with fire. The people are restless and hungry . . ."

"And angry, I would say," added Moodie. "The revolution of which he speaks may not be so far off."

Mr. Traill spoke for the first time. "Surely it will not come to that. Bond Head and his friends may be motivated by self-interest, but they are not the French court. And Mackenzie is no Robespierre, nor we starving peasants. Cooler heads will prevail, I am certain."

It's true, my brother Sam's warm hearth and generous table on this fine September night belie the very idea of unrest. And yet, as I sense the shiver of another winter in every rustling leaf, the prospect of starvation is not the distant cousin it once was. Later, as we walked back to Melsetter, a harvest moon, huge and yellow in the eastern sky, cast peculiar patterns on the forest floor. I asked Moodie what he thought of Mackenzie's exhortations against the government in Toronto.

"Will they ever do anything to help us?"

"Believe me, Susanna, our best hope lies in the continuance of order and good government. We must do everything we can to stop that little baboon and his band of thugs." He stopped to pull Katie's sleeping arms tighter around his neck. Addie trotted along beside us. An owl hooted somewhere over our heads. I imagine he is right, but his words seemed as slippery as the shadows underfoot.

NOVEMBER 23, 1837

I am certain Moodie has broken his leg. He insists it is nothing, a little gash and a bad bruise, that he will be fine by tomorrow. But when he tries to put even the slightest weight on it, he cries out in pain, and all day long, his only means of getting around has been on one leg with my assistance. Although he won't admit it, he is in great discomfort and has finally fallen asleep thanks to a generous dose of rum. If he is not better in the morning, I will see if Kate has some laudanum put by.

He was ploughing the upper ten acres when the blade hit a large boulder and recoiled against his shin. It was all he could do to crawl home, leaving the oxen tethered to a bush, where I found them later. Mercifully, the gash is not deep, and I pray the bone is merely cracked, not broken in two, and that with time and rest, it will be as good as new. How we will finish the fall planting, I do not know.

I was just finishing Katie's reading and arithmetic lessons yesterday morning when young James Caddy brought word that Mackenzie and an army of rebels had marched on the legislature in Toronto. Breathless and agitated, the boy had been running up and down Douro Township, brandishing a proclamation from the Lieutenant-Governor calling upon all loyal militia in Upper Canada to shoulder arms and help quell the insurgency. Thomas Traill and my brother Sam have already left for Peterborough and will go on to Port Hope, where they will await further orders. Thank heavens, they have persuaded Moodie not to accompany them, as his leg is still very weak. But he has been thrashing about like a caged lion since the other men left, declaring that, injured or not, he must rise up and defend this country in the name of the new Queen.

"Toronto is burning," he thunders from his couch as he whittles a crutch from a length of green ash. "They say Bond Head has been taken hostage or worse. Indians are slaughtering women and children. The Yankees are preparing to invade. It will take every man and musket to stop them. I must go. It's my duty."

"But, Papa, what if you are killed? What will become of us?" Little Katie sitting quietly in the rocker with baby Donald on her lap gave voice to my thoughts exactly. I abhor the traitor Mackenzie, but I love my family more.

He is gone. Throwing a pack over his shoulder, armed with nothing more than his old gun, he hobbled away from us before dawn on a hand-hewn crutch, with only a bowl of porridge to sustain him. Is it possible that the last of my words ever to fall upon my husband's ears will be the shrill, hysterical ravings—"I hate you! I hate you! I do not care if you ever return!"—hurled into the frigid morning darkness as he disappeared from sight? Is this how he will think of me as he lies bleeding to death on the battlefield?

The fool! He means to walk the eleven miles to Peterborough. With a broken leg. He says he will borrow a horse from Emilia's father and ride alone to Toronto to intercept Mr. Traill and Sam.

As soon as he left, the snow began falling in thick and indifferent gusts, obliterating his footsteps. I knew I could not go through this alone; there is no firewood, no water, not enough flour to last until Christmas. What if the rebels come this far? And so I bundled the little boys onto the toboggan and, with Katie and Addie and loyal Hector, trudged along the slippery path to my sister's house. She is as distraught as I am. We will remain here until our men return.

DECEMBER 9, 1837

The first blizzard of the season has trapped us, frantic with worry, within these four walls. The children, sensing our distress, are subdued and uncomplaining. To pass the time, I am writing a new poem. I call it "An Address to the Freemen of Canada," a call to arms to Canadians to rise up in defence of freedom and our never-to-be-forgotten homeland.

By all the blood for Britain shed
On many a glorious battle field,
To the free wind her standard spread,
Nor to these base insurgents yield.
With loyal bosoms beating high,
In your good cause securely trust;
"God and Victoria!" be your cry,
And crush the traitors to the dust.

And so on.

Kate has pronounced it "stirring" and is certain I will have no trouble placing it somewhere.

Reading the verses over once more, I cannot help but observe that words once committed to paper take on a life of their own. I am not certain I actually feel such patriotic fervour; sometimes it is as though the act of writing imbues these sentiments with a power of their own, and that an invisible hand, one I have little control over, guides my pen. Of course, my loyalty to the Crown and her Canadian envoys goes without question. Still, it has occurred to me that although we are inextricably connected by breeding and education to the governing Toronto oligarchy and the distinguished families they represent, we are as excluded from their world by virtue of our poverty as are the Irish paupers and Scottish labourers who are our unavoidable neighbours. Would it be treasonous of me to suggest that our political masters might do more to encourage emigration and to improve roads and shipping in the backwoods? Sometimes, I can feel Little Mac's anger as though it were my own.

But outweighing such partisan considerations is the unthinkable possibility my husband may not survive the insurrection. That and the fear we will all be murdered in our sleep by some crazed rebel.

Kate tries to quell my anxieties. "God will watch over them. You must have faith, Susanna."

I do, I do have faith—faith that we are all doomed. The worse things get, the more resilient she seems . . . and the more I love her. At least these tense times have thrown us back into one another's arms, though now our mutual enemy is more sinister than a bossy older sister.

DECEMBER 11, 1837

Mr. Traill and Sam have returned from Port Hope without seeing action (to our great relief and their reported dismay). There is no word from Moodie, who, good as his promise, proceeded directly from Peterborough to Toronto, where he would have joined forces against the "Great Rebellion" had it not petered out before he arrived. It seems the cowardly Mackenzie and his ragged band of farmers and field hands armed with clubs and pitchforks turned tail and ran as soon as they faced the muskets of our brave militia. The little traitor has fled across the border, and there is a price on his head.

My sister and I are relieved beyond measure at the news. We hitched Bones to the Traills' sledge, and Kate drove me and the children back to Melsetter through the snow-bound forest. We laughed and sang as we haven't for many months, and I recited my fiery poem while the babies clapped their hands and stomped their little feet. I think there is nothing like a common cause to lift the most leaden spirits. Kate and I pledged that no matter what it takes, we shall make this the best Christmas ever. We have invited Emilia and her little son, as Lieutenant Shairp is in Toronto and will not return until the new year.

DECEMBER 14, 1837

Moodie has been made a captain in the Queen's Own Regiment! He is to report for duty in Toronto right after Christmas. Despite its swift suppression, the recent rebellion has raised fears of further unrest. And so my knight in shining armour has returned home triumphant, though his stay will be brief. On hearing his news, the miller agreed to extend our credit, and my returning hero brought with him a supply of flour and tea.

"You see, Susanna, my haste has paid off," he boasted. "Men with military training are in great demand right now. I put myself in the path of opportunity and it found me."

He will have a salary of fifteen dollars a month. I wept openly at the news, and I did not ask how he will manage with a leg that is still very weak. He is not strong enough to chop wood or haul water up from the lake, but he does manage to limp about the cabin playing rousing marches on his flute for the children's entertainment.

Moodie has obtained a team of oxen from James Fowlis, but only by signing another note, which will come due in six months. How we will honour it, even with his militia pay, I do not know, but the animals are sorely needed if we are to sow any crops next spring.

DECEMBER 27, 1837

Our Christmas celebrations were bittersweet. On the one hand, there was the promise of better times ahead; on the other, the knowledge Moodie would be leaving the next day to take up his duties with the Queen's Own, and now the prospect of my getting through the winter alone.

My sister managed to pull together, under the circumstances, the most extraordinary feast. Kate festooned her little house with ropes of cedar bound up with strings of bright red cranberries. Her table fairly groaned under the weight of three roast ducks (a gift from Sam) and all manner of preserved vegetables. There were maple candies for the children and, to Moodie's delight, treacle beer, a treat Kate has been secretly brewing these past weeks as a surprise. Moodie declared it delicious after toasting the Queen and the new year.

Mr. Traill tried to rise to the occasion, but it was clear the black dog was upon him. He sat in his usual chair by the fire and observed the gaiety with dull eyes. In addition to his understandable disappointment at not receiving a military commission, he was nursing a sprained ankle he'd sustained falling from his horse. While Kate, Emilia and I bundled up the children to go tobogganing, our two lame husbands could be heard discussing the futility of trying to farm this unforgiving land of rocks and swamp. At least they agree on something. Shairp is still in

Toronto, and when I asked Emilia about his return, she admitted she did not know when he would be back. It was impossible for me to talk to her alone, but I have a feeling the Shairps' truce may be at an end.

Later, after we had returned home pulling the children through the woods on their new toboggan, Moodie was unusually ruminative and, perhaps for the first time, entirely candid about our situation. He told me he has realized for a long time that he is completely unsuited to farming in the bush but has been unable to admit it to me or to himself. He said he has been determined not to entertain the possibility of defeat, fearing that if he did, what strength he has left would desert him entirely. For a long time, he has felt he had no choice but to put his doubts aside and carry on.

"We will find a way out of here, Susanna. I promise. I am going away, and I know that is hard. But it is the beginning, a step on the road to a new life. I know it."

An ember of something like hope stirred inside me. I let it flicker for an instant and then doused it before it burned too brightly.

As we may not be together again for a very long time, I relaxed my usual strictures last night and allowed my husband more than a few liberties, for which he was inordinately grateful. It has become something of a joke between us that he is forced to plead for conjugal benefits that, he argues, surely should be his by right. I am glad he has a sense of humour. And I pray I do not come to regret our little celebration.

Now that he is gone, I fear the silence that lies behind all the noisy exertions of our days will swallow me entirely. To drown it out and keep a piece of him close, I sing to the children and hum to myself as I go about my work. *"Oh where and oh where does your Highland laddie dwell . . ."*

Emilia has enlisted my help on a mission of mercy. Louisa Lloyd and her family are in severely straitened circumstances. It seems Captain Lloyd abandoned the family again four months ago, this time taking the eldest boy with him. Mrs. Lloyd has been forced to sell their last cow. She and her second son, a boy of eleven or twelve, can barely cut enough wood for fuel, let alone manage the farm. For months now, they have subsisted on a few bad potatoes. Emilia said that a group of generous ladies in Peterborough had directed her to pay Mrs. Lloyd a visit to confirm the extent of her misery. My friend asked me to go with her to Dummer Township, taking what we can spare to bring some relief to the deserted mother and her six little ones.

Standing here in this dim cabin with its smoke-blackened walls, with my children clamouring for her attention, their clothing as ragged as any London street urchin's, I waited for Emilia to absorb the pathos of my own situation. She looked radiant, prettily turned out in a fine woollen cape and matching hat, apple-cheeked from her snowshoe along the lake with two-year-old Harry strapped to her back. Motherhood becomes her.

I have not a penny to my name or clothing warm enough for a journey such as she proposes. It is nine miles through the bush on a narrow, ill-used trail. Nevertheless, perhaps foolishly, I have agreed to go. Short of food as we often are, we are not yet starving. And Jenny, who nurtures a deep attachment to Mrs. Lloyd, her former mistress, pleads with me to do what I can.

My friend and her son spent the night, and Emilia and I lay awake for hours, whispering in the darkness like schoolgirls, planning our expedition of mercy in great detail. Serious as our business is, I was reminded of the nights of my girlhood, of Reydon Hall and my sisters, our childish pursuits, our harmless ghosts and imaginary friends. Oh, how our present troubles carry within them the sad echoes of past joys.

Before we fell asleep, Emilia told me that following the failed rebellion in December, Mr. Shairp left Toronto for Texas to investigate the opportunities there that we have been hearing so much about. "He will be away a long time—all winter, at least." She paused. "I think he would rather be anywhere but here." Then in the darkness, I could almost feel her gathering herself together, her hurt turning to defiance. "Anyway, I don't care if he ever returns. I am more fortunate than Mrs. Lloyd. I have my parents. And you." I took her hand and pressed it. Despite her bravado, I think she loves her lieutenant very much.

Today, we asked Mr. Traill for his assistance. As I hoped, my brother-in-law has risen to the occasion. A light came on in his eyes that I have not seen in ages as we told him of our plans. I believe that the travails of others often serve to wrench us from the swamp of our own despair. Contemplating Mrs. Lloyd's condition, I am thankful for what resources I still possess, and my resolve to carry on has been strengthened. Mr. Traill immediately offered to bring his farm sleigh tomorrow morning and drive Emilia and me through the beaver meadow to the edge of the great swamp, which will shorten our journey by at least half. After that, we must continue on foot, cutting through very wild country until we reach Dummer Township.

Jenny, who will remain here with the children, has spent all afternoon baking bread and wrapping a large piece of boiled venison. Emilia has brought with her a smoked ham and several buffalo robes. Mr. Traill is contributing more bread and bacon, and at my sister Kate's insistence, precious tea and sugar.

Neither of us has ever met Mrs. Lloyd. Emilia tells me she is said to have a warm and gentle disposition, but she is a proud woman. I wonder how she will respond to our gifts, well-intentioned but charity nonetheless. When I imagine myself in a similar situation, I cannot decide whether gratitude or shame would be the stronger emotion.

JANUARY 28, 1838

I am so exhausted from our journey that I have scarcely left my bed since late Wednesday night, when what I believe must be the longest day I have ever endured finally ended. Emilia has slept continuously for the past thirty-six hours. I have persuaded her to stay with us until her strength returns. What an ordeal. Now, as I begin to recover, I feel a weary satisfaction knowing that we have brought relief to others less fortunate than ourselves. But an ominous shadow lingers too, for while I have not reached the depths of deprivation I witnessed in the house of Louisa Lloyd, in my heart I know that there but for the grace of God . . .

What we encountered that day chilled me even more than the raw wind and my freezing hands and feet. Just before we arrived at her doorstep after our long trek, Mr. Traill and James (having decided to leave the cutter with Colonel Caddy and accompany us all the way) waited down the road at a neighbour's, not wanting to alarm Mrs. Lloyd with a posse of saviours. Emilia and I knocked on the door of the respectable-looking log house. A thin stream of smoke rose from the chimney, and though the property seemed in good enough repair, there was a disquieting sense of abandon to the dilapidated outbuildings and sheds. A young boy of about twelve finally responded to our increasingly insistent summons, stepping out onto the snow-covered porch in his bare feet and closing the door behind him.

"We have walked here all the way from Douro to see your mama," Emilia explained, "and we would very much like to speak to her."

The boy politely said that he would see if his mother would receive us and re-entered the house, leaving us out in the cold. So many minutes passed that we were about to leave our bundle of food on the doorstep and join Mr. Traill and James across the road, when the door reopened and the boy ushered us into a living space not much different from my own modest home. Mrs. Lloyd was seated on a rude bench by the fire, wearing a delicate muslin dress that she must have hurriedly donned—the only respectable thing she had left, I imagine, but entirely unsuitable to the setting or the climate. She presented a picture of forced composure. Her hands were folded in her lap, her hair pinned back in an untidy bun, her chin raised and tilted slightly in polite inquiry as to our purpose. Here, amid the inevitable squalor, Louisa Lloyd's beauty and attitude reminded me in an instant of my own mother and her determination to keep up appearances at all costs.

Standing behind her with his hand on his mother's shoulder was the boy who had let us in. Seated on a stool at her side was a girl not much younger, wrapped in a worn blanket and cradling in her arms a baby swaddled in rags. Another little girl wearing rough burlap knelt on the floor at Mrs. Lloyd's feet, looking up at us with luminous dark eyes. The little tableau was like a sad parody of a Gainsborough. In the corner, on a rough bedstead, two little boys huddled beneath an old quilt pulled up to their chins. A pot of water bubbled over the desultory fire, and on the table were six peeled potatoes. A small black dog eyed them possessively.

No member of this heart-rending scene uttered a sound as I placed the sack of provisions on the table, but their collective gaze followed my movements with a patient intensity that was as eloquent as any cry of hunger. At last, Mrs. Lloyd spoke.

"I don't believe we are acquainted?" she said, her tone wary but respectful.

Emilia, who had been standing behind me, stepped forward. "Mrs. Lloyd, we have not met, but like you, we are officers' wives and mothers too. We have walked all the way from Douro to bring you this, this . . ." She indicated the sack of food, which lay there now, radiating salvation.

I jumped in. "It is only a little bacon and a few supplies to tide you over. We are hardly strangers, Mrs. Lloyd. Your girl Jenny has served my family this past year. She baked the bread with her own hands and sends it as a gift for Eloise—little Elly, she called her."

At this, the doe-eyed girl at Mrs. Lloyd's feet uttered an exclamation and covered her mouth with her small hands. "Mama," she said, looking up. "It's from Jenny?"

A hardness came over Mrs. Lloyd's features. But her tone was almost jaunty. "You are very kind, but we have enough. We will manage, I'm sure. My son and I . . ." As she spoke, the baby began to cry—not cry really, but mew like a kitten. The older girl pulled it closer, and as she did, I could see the bare flesh stretched tightly over the infant's tiny ribs.

"Mama," said little Elly, getting to her feet and facing her mother, "please. It's from Jenny."

A faint whimpering came from under the ragged bedclothes, and at the sound, the pride in Louisa Lloyd's face melted like a painting left out in the rain. Without a word, I began unpacking the food.

Slowly, their sad story unwound. They were, indeed, on the verge of starvation, having sold their last cow several weeks ago for six dollars and a bushel of potatoes, the last of which were slated for lunch that day. As for the cash, it was in the form of notes drawn on the Farmer's Bank—an institution long gone from this world—and utterly worthless.

Mrs. Lloyd maintained her composure and offered us a cup of tea and something to eat before she would allow her children to help themselves. Before we could accept, Mr. Traill and James appeared, urging us to go as it was nearly two o'clock and we had the long trip back to Douro ahead of us.

In a single day, we walked more than twenty miles to Dummer

and back in the bitter cold, through tangled, dense swampland, fording icy streams, climbing snowy ridges and trudging along endless rough tracks with no nourishment except the bowl of porridge that sent us on our way. Many times as we made our way home at the end of our mission, and as the miserly winter light faded with the afternoon, I wondered how I would find the strength to take another step. Exhausted in body but exalted in spirit, I was reminded of Rosalind in the Forest of Arden. "Oh Jupiter, how weary are my legs!" And yet, plod on we did until we recrossed the great swamp and reached the beaver meadow. There, at the edge of the bush, to our considerable relief, we found Colonel Caddy waiting with the sleigh for the four of us. Mr. Traill and James Caddy rode up front with the colonel while Emilia and I nestled into the straw and buffalo robes on the bottom of our conveyance and slept the remaining four miles home, where a warm fire and a meal of fried venison and hot fish awaited.

It was a humbling experience. I will never forget Louisa Lloyd's dignity and gratitude, but also the look of hunger in her eyes at the sight of that cured ham. Civility and savagery were inextricably mixed in her person at that moment, and I was reminded that there is an element of both in all of us. I only pray that the contest between them in my own breast is never settled in favour of the latter.

FEBRUARY 2, 1838

Brutally cold. This morning, we awoke to find everything frozen solid. The water in the cooking kettles had turned to blocks of ice, and yet I dared not add too much wood to the stove for fear the pipes would overheat and set the roof on fire. Damn Moodie. He knew those pipes would not see us through another winter. The children whimpered like a litter of forlorn pups as I struggled to dress them, and then they huddled by the meagre heat of the stove, gnawing on frozen crusts of bread while I waited for yesterday's coffee, still solid in the pot, to thaw for my breakfast.

When Jenny came in from feeding the animals, her cheeks and the tips of her fingers were bloodless, the colour of milky tea. She does not complain, and I think her gruff forbearance is the only thing that prevents me from giving in. It is difficult to describe this cold to anyone who has not experienced it. The temperature at dawn was fifteen degrees below zero, and although it had risen somewhat by noon, a stiff wind makes it feel much colder. Exposed skin becomes numb in a matter of minutes. I cannot send Kate and Addie out to play, as they have no adequate shoes, and so we are cooped up in here, where the temperature is only a few degrees warmer, but at least we are out of the wind. Outside, the sun shines brilliantly through a veil of ice crystals that hangs like frozen mist in the air, air so crisp it seems it could shatter. The snow underfoot screeches with every step, and the tree branches creak and complain in the wind. Nothing else moves. No birds or other living creatures. And yet, venture out we must. Today, Jenny and I will somehow take the swede saw to a fallen beech at the edge of the clearing if we are to have firewood to get us through another month.

Moodie has written to say that my poem "An Address to the Freemen of Canada" has been published in a new Toronto journal, *The Palladium of British America*. The editor, Charles Fothergill, has asked for more. In his editorial, he calls me "Daughter of a Genius— and Wife of the Brave!" I am grateful for such extravagant praise, but humbled though I am, I wonder why my talents, such as they are, should be attributed to others, both of them men.

And I have just received a letter from a John Lovell, editor of the *Montreal Transcript*, requesting permission to reprint the poem. Even better, he is starting a magazine called the *Literary Garland* and has asked me to be a regular contributor of both prose and poems, for which he promises prompt and generous payment! I have sent him four more.

Moodie is to leave Toronto within a week for Niagara, where his regiment will be positioned in order to repel invasions from the rebels, who are said to be skulking south of the border. Apparently, the traitor Mackenzie has persuaded a small contingent of Yankees to join his crusade to "free" Canada.

And so my dearest one moves even farther away from me. How I miss his happy face, his encouraging words. How I loathe this interminable winter.

As I feared, my usual visitor is late.

February 17, 1838

This child, this demon that somehow emerged from my womb, shall surely be the death of me. Or I of her. Sometimes I think Addie will drive me mad with her incessant demands and her terrible temper. Even when she is happy, she sings and whirls about with an energy that will not be subdued. But when her intentions are thwarted or her desires denied, she erupts into uncontrollable fits of hysteria. Today, I snapped. She refused her supper, a squirrel pie I had laboured over for hours. Fresh meat, after weeks of nauseating monotony, of nothing but roasted potatoes and salted fish. Fresh meat thanks to Jenny's skill with a slingshot. But no, the littlest duchess pushed her plate onto the floor and demanded toast and jam. And when I ordered her to her room, she threw herself to the ground, screaming and kicking like a deranged dervish. The boys left the table and began fighting over a wooden rifle until Dunbar struck Donnie over the head and he started howling. A raw wind rattled the windows, blowing snow through the holes in the walls that appear as quickly as we can patch them. Something inside me let go. I pulled Addie to her feet and slapped her hard, but it was like pouring oil on a fire. She threw herself against me, then against the table, and then the only thing that seemed to matter was how to make it stop. I started shaking her. I could feel myself being drawn into the maelstrom, into the swirling chaos of my daughter's fury. Katie too began to cry, pleading with her sister.

"Addie, Addie," she begged. "Stop, please stop. Mama, don't. Mama?" But it was like a voice coming to me from far away, from a place I had already left.

If Jenny had not come back from the barn at that moment, I fear I might have done real harm to my own child.

She is sleeping now. Jenny held the sobbing little demon in an iron embrace until her rage subsided, and then soothed her with warm milk, and yes, toast and jam. If I have learned anything from this, it is that in a battle with a four-year-old, unless you kill her first, she will always win. I am ashamed. If only their father were here with his flute and his playful distractions.

Without him, it is as though a light has been extinguished in our home, and in its place are only shadows and dark joyless corners. Emilia has returned to Peterborough for the rest of the winter. My sister Kate, with an exhausting mile of snow-bound forest separating us, seems as far away as spring.

FEBRUARY 28, 1838

In a burst of energy, I have hammered divots into a dozen maple trees for my first attempt at sugaring off. The days have been mild and sunny, the nights below freezing—perfect conditions for the sap to run. Thus far, we have collected enough to fill the large kettle Jenny has hung over a tripod in the clearing. The girls are kept busy gathering firewood to keep the cauldron boiling day and night. The promise of sweet maple treats spurs them on.

Maybe it is the spring-like conditions, or maybe the beginnings of another life stirring inside me, but I am blooming with eagerness to begin the work of sowing and growing that only a few months ago, I viewed as chores dreamed up by Satan himself to torment me. The nausea and fatigue that usually accompany my condition are absent this time. And perversely, I find myself welcoming this birth as a harbinger of better things to come.

With the recent thaw, Mr. Traill visits every other day or so to see that we are all right. I'm sure my sister sends him—anything to give herself a break from the oppressiveness of his despondency, and in hopes the walk over here may raise his spirits. My brother-in-law is wretched indeed, and talks only of his wish to leave the bush. He would sell his farm in an instant, but land values have plummeted even further since the rebellion, and he speculates it is worth far less than the money he has already put into it. In this we are all similarly affected.

Kate, too, is expecting another baby this summer, her fourth. And Harry only eight months old. Traill's mental lethargy prevents him from most heavy labour, and because, like us, they can no longer afford to pay wages, the lion's share of the field work falls to my sister and whatever help Sam can provide. She confided in me that she does not see how Mr. Traill can endure another winter in the bush, but it is obvious she too is worn to the bone.

"A Loyal Song" has appeared in the *Literary Garland*. Mr. Lovell wrote to say it is the ninth reprint (!) of a poem that, dare I say it, has captured the nationalist pulse of the era. Twenty pounds it has brought me already, and Lovell has also accepted "Otonabee," my poetic tribute to the mighty river that flows south from Lake Katchewanooka. I have instructed Mr. Traill on his next trip to Peterborough to pay the miller what we owe him, and there will be enough left over to purchase tea and sugar.

Sam has brought me the wonderful news that my fungus paintings are much admired by the regimental wives living in Peterborough. These are creations of my own imagination. All winter, I have been painting birds and butterflies on the surface of the large growths that can be found attached to the trunks of the beech and maple trees. My brother has sold a few and now informs me a certain wealthy officer's wife has ordered two dozen to send home to friends and family in England. At one shilling each, the paintings will enable me to buy shoes for the children.

A letter today from Moodie, who complains of the bad food and the prolonged ennui of military life: "Our only exercise is a leisurely stroll each morning to 'patrol' the shores of Lake Erie on the lookout for marauding rebels and Yankees, of which there has been no sign in all the time we have been here."

Morale is very low, he wrote, a sure product of giving a group of restless young men little to do and not enough to eat. Rumours proliferate.

"They say Mackenzie and his rabble have headed west, determined to find new frontiers wherein to sow the seeds of their discontent. And so we wait and fulminate, growing more discontented ourselves with every day that passes."

He relayed the news that Westminster has recalled the Lieutenant-Governor. Bond Head is being held responsible for fostering the unrest that led to the recent rebellion.

"The men here say Head and the Tories stole the election of 1836 by using bribery and intimidation," Moodie wrote. "They say there were Orangemen running up and down the streets, crying, 'Five pounds for a Reformer,' and if any man blocked their way, he was knocked down." My husband has come to see Head as an "incompetent scoundrel," who did nothing during his tenure to encourage immigration to Canada, or to improve the lot of settlers such as ourselves.

I have written, teasing him about his newfound political views. "I do believe you will be calling yourself a Reformer before long."

We can only hope the new man, Sir George Arthur, will prove a better governor.

After a fortnight of boiling, we have six gallons of the sweetest syrup, twelve pounds of fine, soft sugar, and six gallons of excellent vinegar.

MAY 23, 1838

The spring planting is nearly done. Jenny Buchanan's energy is like a blast of warm air blowing us into action. Every morning, she arises in the dark, a sturdy Venus in homespun, and after feeding the livestock, stoking the fire and fetching water for cooking and washing, she rouses us to our porridge (now adorned with heavenly syrup). After breakfast, it's out to the fields. Jenny hitches the oxen and ploughs the thin soil, while I follow, dropping seed potatoes into the carefully tilled furrows. Kate and the little boys make piles of the rocks that spring from the dirt in the plough's wake like fish rising from the sea. Oh, that stone soup could nourish us through the winter, so plentiful are these fruits of the grudging earth. And while we work, Addie slays imaginary dragons with a tree branch or sits sulking under a bush.

Every evening, after the little ones are asleep, I do my best to produce crops of the literary kind in the hopes the effort may bring me a few extra dollars. I wish I had more energy left over to attend to Katie's lessons. She and Addie, and the boys too, will eventually need to go to school if they are to prosper. But how? And where? In low moments, I can't help but wonder of what benefit education will be to the lives they are likely to lead. And I confess that sometimes the sight of neatly hoed rows of corn at the end of the day arouses in me more satisfaction than a perfectly wrought line of verse.

How strange it is that since we have been apart these many months, I feel more united with my dear husband than ever before. Could it be that absence does indeed make the heart grow fonder, or is it that finally he and I are united in a single purpose, and that is to find a way out of this hopeless wilderness, this unending poverty? I only know that my desire, my need for him grows stronger with every passing week. At night, alone in my bed, I weep for want of him, as though a part of me is missing and I will not be whole again until it is returned. To think that all through these difficult years, I have chafed in the harness of matrimony, like a carriage horse condemned to pull a plough. To think that in my discontent, I have been blind to his goodness, to the light that his enduring love shines on me. And now I see we are like a team of oxen, yoked forever to one another, pulling in the same direction, one foot in front of the other, one step at a time. We will survive, and we will do it together.

JULY 2, 1838

I have learned in a letter from my editor Mr. Fothergill that the new Lieutenant-Governor, Sir George Arthur himself, has admired my poems, remarking that the "national enthusiasm" therein "is an elixir certain to hearten and encourage the loyalist spirit throughout the colony." Mr. Fothergill relates that Sir George has spoken to him highly of "the Strickland sisters and their literary accomplishments" and said that he follows my career with great interest.

I am almost embarrassed to acknowledge the effect this trickle of praise has had upon me. If I had been a wounded soldier dying of thirst and someone had handed me a cup of clear, cold water, I could not have been more grateful. How pitiful that a few words of encouragement should be as nourishing to the spirit as the most lavish feast is to the body. The idea, too, that my voice has reached beyond this prison of trees and rocks and is being heard in the wider world affirms my existence as something more than a beast of burden.

It would be foolish not to take advantage of such notoriety as I have achieved, and so I have written to the Lieutenant-Governor, asking for his help. I told him about everything, all the setbacks, the hardships—the crop failures, the fevers, the worthless steamboat shares, the Yankee hucksters and recalcitrant servants. I begged him to find Moodie a civil position, saying that a gentleman of my husband's stature is demeaned by the brutishness of this farming enterprise. I said that the patriotic poems he so admires were composed by me in a rough log cabin by the light of rags dipped in tallow, with sleeping babies in my lap.

"My children have no shoes, our clothes are in tatters, all winter long we subsist on pork fat and potatoes. If you admire my writing as much as you say, if you feel that my verses, brought forth in the midst of suffering and deprivation, have in any way contributed to order and the Loyalist cause, then I beg you to help us."

I feel no shame in this. Desperation drives me to it.

My dearest one is coming home; he will be here to welcome our fifth child after all. His regiment has been disbanded, the danger of rebellion apparently over. The children are mad with excitement.

As joyful as I am at the thought of Moodie's return, I wonder how we will survive without his militia pay. The thought of another winter with no income other than what little my scribblings will yield is impossible to contemplate. I pray for a good harvest, knowing even that will not be enough.

A fourth child for Kate: a little girl called Anne Fotheringhame after Mr. Traill's first wife, who died ten years ago on this very day.

While Moodie and Jenny manage the other children, I swoon over our four-day-old son, John Strickland Moodie, drinking him in, his downy forehead and blistered lips, his blue-veined eyelids, the labyrinth of his ears, his little fingers spreading on my breast, the unspeakably soft soles of his feet. I can scarcely explain it, but I feel in my heart that this child is destined for an extraordinary life. Last night, I dreamed he had grown into a handsome young man with dark hair and deep blue eyes. Through a cloudy window, I watched him as he strode down a twisted path away from me toward the lake. He was wearing a red tunic with gold buttons, and he said nothing, just smiled and waved. I called to him to come back, but my cries were carried away like feathers in the wind, floating upward and turning into white gulls that balanced above him in the gusty air. When I tried to run after him, my legs, leaden and inert, refused to take me, and all I could do was watch mutely as he stepped out onto the surface of the water and disappeared over the horizon.

I had just finished tightening the lid on the last jar of pickled beets when Moodie came up behind me and, placing his hands on my shoulders, began massaging the tightness that lives there like a coiled snake.

"Well, Mother, will your work never be done? Can you not spare even a few hours for your poor neglected spouse?"

I wriggled out of his embrace, irritated at first by his playfulness when there is so much to be done—always, always more to do: carrots to dig, cows to milk, bread to bake, children to feed, clothes to mend, wood to chop. Sometimes I find myself moving through my days like an augur through a tree trunk: grim, purposeful, unfeeling, with only a dull anger fuelling the grinding effort.

And then I gave in to it; I let his thumbs knead the knotted flesh down the sides of my neck, at the top of my spine. My knees felt weak. Before I could protest, he slipped the loop of my apron over my head, took my hand and led me outside into the soft October sunshine. The day buzzed with a warmth made melancholy by the certainty of winter. A blue jay wheedled from a spruce tree. The lake shimmered in the determined sunlight.

"Indian summer. We must make the most of it," Moodie said, pulling me toward the water. "All summer long, while I brooded over the passive, grey Erie, it was this, our little lake, that stirred my heart. Let's go for a sail. It's been such a long time."

And so, leaving the babies with Jenny, we raised the canvas on our canoe and launched into the afternoon. A steady breeze blew us across water that rippled like the belly of a whale. Moodie sat in the stern, manning the makeshift tiller and handling the mainsheet, while I knelt in the bow and, bracing myself on the gunnels, leaned into the breeze. I'm sure I presented a rough-and-ragged figurehead, more crone than mermaid. We made a steady broad reach up the length of the lake to where it narrows toward Young's Point, and pulling our boat onto the rocks, we clambered a hundred feet or so over the sun-warmed stones to the cranberry bog Mrs. Peter showed Kate last year. In less than twenty minutes, we had a small bucketful.

"Now if we only had a turkey to go with them," I said, a gentle jab at my husband's thus far futile attempts to bring down one of the birds. Though wild turkeys are plentiful this time of the year, fat from gorging on the leavings of wheat and oats scattered in the clearings, the ungainly creatures have an uncanny ability to fly into the tallest treetops at the merest sign they are being hunted.

"I, for one, am dreaming of your succulent squirrel pie," said Moodie as we sat in the sun, warming our reddened feet and ankles on the limestone shelf. "Indeed," he said, "I spied a pair of likely candidates scurrying up the hemlock by the woodshed just this morning."

We were silent then for a while. How long had it been since we had time like this away from the children, since we were free, if only briefly, from the urgency of daily life? And yet there was nothing I wanted to say. To dwell on the past only brings on nostalgia and recriminations. To contemplate the future is to peer down a long tunnel in search of a light, and a dim one at that.

And then my husband, unable to still the writhings of his overactive mind, began relating his latest scheme, one that I foolishly thought he had forgotten. He has offered to write a book for the Texas Land Company in exchange for passage and property there. I took a deep breath.

"What kind of book?"

"Oh, you know, Susie, a book about Texas: the scenery, the climate, the opportunities there for men of action who want to prosper in America. And for every settler my book draws, of course I would receive a commission. Money I could use to buy more land to sell to other settlers."

"But you've never been to Texas. You've no idea what it's like."

Moodie ignored this, waving my words away like so many midges suspended in the air. He sat up and wrapped his arms around his knees.

"I didn't tell you because I thought nothing might come of it, but I responded to that advertisement that appears every year in *The Albion*, you remember." He got to his feet. "I made an offer to Dr. Beales of the Texas Land Company: a book for land. And he has replied, Susie. With enthusiasm. I have asked for a salary . . ."

He reached out to take my hands, to pull me to my feet, but I turned away and covered my ears.

"For God's sake," he said. "I don't understand you. You know what this means? We can leave this place. Start over somewhere warm, where the soil is fertile and our children will—"

I stood up and waded into the water beside the canoe. The cold only fuelled my anger.

"Do not," I said, "do not talk to me of starting over. I will not move to Texas. A book, passage, commissions, a salary? I do not believe you."

We paddled home in silence, and Moodie has not raised the matter since, but he spent this evening poring over the maps and pamphlets the speculator Beales has sent.

NOVEMBER 10, 1838

Texas is forgotten. A letter bearing the Lieutenant-Governor's coat of arms and signed by His Excellency's secretary came from Toronto today, announcing my husband's appointment as paymaster for the militia units protecting the north shore of Lake Ontario. He will be based in Belleville! (I have said nothing to Moodie about my letter to George Arthur; a man's pride is sacrosanct, after all. Let him strut and preen and take credit for what I pray amounts at last to a reversal of our fortunes.)

It is a temporary posting, but we have great hopes it will be extended, and surely one such posting can only lead to another. The salary is £325, which is beyond anything I could have dreamed of and gives us some hope of paying off our debts. My prayers have been answered.

We have discussed whether the children and I should go with him and have decided it would be best for us to stay here until Moodie is settled and the future more certain. Another winter alone with Jenny and the children. I have done it before; I can do it again.

Flushed with pride at his sudden elevation in status, Moodie was magnanimous with his praise this evening, confident that I will manage without him.

"I do believe that for a member of the fairer sex, your agricultural skills are quite impressive, my dear," he said, raising a celebratory glass of rum in salute. "Even better than my own, I dare say." He chuckled. "Though that would not be saying much for a professional soldier such as I. Farming is simply not in my blood."

I accepted the compliment, such as it was, without comment. But the implication rankles: that my husband considers himself above all this, but that it is good enough for me. Does he think of me as little more than a common drudge? I am not a farmer either; I am a writer, and though I would not dream of telling him, Moodie's new career is a direct result of my literary efforts.

He is to report for duty December 1. So soon.

DECEMBER 25, 1838

Now, as I contemplate the possibility of leaving this place, a vein of sadness runs through me. (Sheer perversity, I know.) But this evening, this Christmas night, as Jenny and I rode home from Westove along the narrow road through the ghostly woods—the three little boys sleeping, Kate and Addie flushed with exhaustion and full stomachs, old Bones straining at his traces, eager to be home—on this night of Christ's birth, our old sledge might as well have been the finest horse-drawn sleigh and we, ladies and gentlemen returning from the ball. A million stars danced about a gibbous moon, and the night was so still, it seemed to be holding its breath. For once I was not afraid.

Without Moodie, our feast was bittersweet. A goose stuffed with wild rice. A pudding made from currants and dried apples. And while the children—nine of them now, including the babies, Johnny and Annie—spent hours sliding down a bank of snow until their faces shone with brisk joy, Kate and I indulged in memories of Christmases past, sweet thoughts of Reydon Hall. The bitter possibility we will never return was seasoned by the firm belief that we were, at that moment, as alive in our mother's and sisters' thoughts as they in ours. And I truly felt, as I used to as a girl, their presence in the very fact of their absence.

Mr. Traill's despondency worsens, especially in the wake of my own husband's good fortune. They have only Traill's half pension since his term as justice of the peace ended. Feeling sorry for my brother-in-law, I sat with him for a while and tried to engage him in the book talk he loves so well. But my cheerful observations about Milton's views on republicanism were met with a faded smile. I offered to read to him from a mouse-nibbled copy of *The Winter's Tale*, but he waved me away and resumed his contemplation of the fire. My sister watched, twisting her apron strings into desperate corkscrews, as I tried to coax her husband from his sorrowful fugue. Finally, she sighed and went back to her work.

Moodie wrote that he is settling into his new position in Belleville, a community that he says has much, including a moderate climate and a strong Loyalist presence, to recommend it. He is determined to sort out the rather chaotic regimental accounts in hopes his efforts will bring him notice and a permanent position of some kind. And in typical fashion, he is touting the advantages of purchasing a two-hundred-acre farm on the shores of the Ontario, though he knows that barely a week goes by that I do not have some creditor or other demanding payment. And not a penny of his salary has materialized—delayed, Moodie says, by circumstances beyond his control.

"I am certain, my dearest," he goes on, "the economy will soon recover and our shares in the *Cobourg* will finally pay off."

I am more certain than ever that my dearest husband has lost his senses. And yet I cannot help but be optimistic. As I sit here writing, and nursing this babe, this tiny citizen of the New World, I am warmed by the conviction that all will be well.

PART
SEVEN

1839

DARK
DAYS

---- ◆ ----

JANUARY 19, 1839 (MELSETTER II)

So much for conviction. Two days after Christmas, my left breast began to ache, a persistent throb at first, but within hours, an obstinate and ongoing agony. Jenny tried to apply a mustard poultice, but I could not tolerate even the slightest touch. Every movement was excruciating, and nursing Johnny a torture I had no choice but to endure. I know I should not have let it continue for so long. Perhaps it was the pride I take in my strong constitution. While everyone else is brought down with an assortment of fevers and ailments and injuries, I have managed to remain strong and healthy. I thought I was somehow blessed, invincible, and that time and rest would do their work, as they always have. But this was different. For more than ten days, I suffered the most unspeakable agony, unable to move or be moved without screaming in pain. I was like a snake writhing and groaning, feverish and raving, almost wishing for easeful death to deliver me. Finally, I could bear it no longer, and uncertain I would live until morning, I sent Jenny to find Mr. Traill, who made the three-hour walk to Peterborough in the darkness and bitter cold to fetch Dr. Hutchison, the man who delivered all four of my sister's children. It is the first time a doctor has crossed our threshold since we came to Canada.

At first, in my delirium, I mistook Hutchison for my husband. His cool hand on my forehead, his soft Scottish burr, so like Moodie's, might as well have been the attentions of an angel. Then he instructed Jenny and Mr. Traill to restrain me, pinning me to my bed as though I were a pig about to be slaughtered. And when I beheld the thin steel blade glinting in the candlelight, I thought I was under siege by the devil himself. Without a word, he applied the knife, and with a sharp, decisive slash, like a trout breaking the surface of a lake, he lanced the flesh of my angry, swollen breast. I cried out, but in truth, I felt nothing. No pain at least, only a blessed sensation of release as the poison poured from my body. Dimly, as though from deep under water, I was aware of Mr. Traill letting go of my right arm and shoulder, and of the sound of retching as he moved away from the bed. It must have been a fearful spectacle, for Jenny told me later that more than a pint of noxious effluent drained immediately from the abscessed area.

For the first time in days, I was able to move my arm, and realizing that I would live, I was immediately overcome with gratitude to this man who had travelled through the cold, dark night to deliver me from the jaws of death.

"You are not out of danger yet, Mrs. Moodie," the doctor said as he bandaged the affected area. "This dressing must be changed daily and compresses of hot water applied every four hours." He looked down at the children gathered, shivering, at the foot of my bed. "How old is the infant?" he asked as Johnny's mewling gave way to a full-blown wail and Jenny placed him at my breast.

"Three months," I said.

"Normally, I would insist you find a wet nurse to take over the feedings," he said, letting his gaze travel over and around the darkened interior of my home. As he looked about, even in my weakened condition I was compelled to see the place through his eyes, and I was filled with shame. The smoke-blackened walls, the rags and newspapers bunched into the gaps between the logs, the film of soot

336

that covered everything, the hard dirt floors, the stovepipes so brittle we dare not keep a fire going at night. I was both thankful and humiliated that in the meagre light thrown by the wretched coal-oil lamp, all we had to ward off the darkness, Dr. Hutchison could not see the condition of the furniture and books, eaten by mice and mildew. Though he must have noticed the children's scanty, torn nightclothes, their tangled hair and pale faces.

"But I can see," he said, "that finding such a nurse out here in the bush might be . . ." And then he stopped. He slammed his medical case shut and struggled into his coat. "For the love of God, Mrs. Moodie, get out of this place."

The following day, I had barely left my sickbed when Donald and baby Johnny came down with the scarlet fever that is sweeping through the township. Thankfully, the other children were spared, but my two youngest languished for nearly a week, both covered in an angry red rash and wracked by coughing fits and burning fever. Jenny and I did what we could to relieve their suffering, applying mustard plasters, warm baths and liberal doses of castor oil. Traill went again to fetch the doctor, but this time Hutchison refused to come because of the weather. "He said there is nothing he can do," my brother-in-law reported. "The illness must run its course. Keep the little ones warm, and pray."

When she heard of our illnesses, Mrs. Caddy walked here in a terrible snowstorm. She wanted to stay to nurse me and the children. I would not consent to it. But I accepted her gift of fresh beef broth gratefully. Emilia came up from Peterborough on New Year's Day, after hearing from Dr. H how ill the children and I were. She stayed a week, and I could not have managed without her. The charity of my kind neighbours is causing me much distress. How shall I ever repay them?

There was nothing left but prayer. All day and night, I held my babies to my breast, rocking and singing and begging God not to claim their precious souls. The fever has taken the lives of children through-out the district. Mr. Traill says my sister is too ill herself to come to my aid, or I know she surely would have. He refused to enter our cabin for fear he might carry the affliction home to his own little ones.

Moodie wrote that he misses me "as the stars miss the moon." It is the first letter I have had since Christmas. He says his appointment in Belleville is for six months only. The news has dashed my hopes for moving the children and our goods before the sleighing is over. This illness has tamped down my spirit. I do not know how I can continue here. Nevertheless, the good Lord has heard my prayers. We did not die. We are weakened in body and in spirit. But alive. And in my darkest moments, I wonder: To what end? So that a mer-ciful God can strike us down once more? These thoughts infect my mind and poison my imagination.

Today, on my way out to the woodpile, I discovered a brace of partridge hanging from the porch rail. A gift from Mrs. Peter. Looped around the neck of the largest bird was a webbed circle made from deer hide, decorated with green and purple beads and four iridescent feathers.

"A dream catcher," said Jenny. "Hang it above your bed and it will keep the nightmares away."

I am touched by their kindness. A dream catcher. But in this waking nightmare, I am too tired to dream.

FEBRUARY 10, 1839

I had just sat down to give Katie and Addie their lessons when Hector began barking at two men riding into the clearing on a pair of mules. Through the window, I could see them, dressed in ragged deerskin tunics and raccoon hats. The taller one dismounted, walked to the house and began banging a belligerent tattoo on the door. Their general appearance was one of dissolution and menace. But as I observed them, I realized, to my astonishment, that the taller one was no other than the land jobber Charles Clark. I immediately sent Jenny and the children into the back bedroom and then peered out through a crack in the door. Without opening it, I demanded to know their business. Hearing my voice, the shorter man pulled a piece of paper from his saddlebag and, dismounting, took his place beside Clark.

"Official business. From the sheriff's office of Hamilton Township," Clark bellowed, and began banging again with his open hand. "Open up or we'll break it down. Mrs. Moodie, I know you're in there. Open up."

"Who are you? What do you want?" I called again through the rough planks. By the look of him, it seems the past few years have not been kind to our old nemesis. He was unshaven and dirty, and he did not look like official anything. I was only too aware of how vulnerable we were, two women and a cabin full of babies, our only protection an old musket and an aging dog. Nevertheless, I opened the door about a foot and positioned myself in the gap.

"My husband has gone to the post office," I said, still not acknowledging him. "He will return this afternoon. Please save your business until then."

Clark ignored this and gave his partner an elbow in the ribs. In a parody of civic rectitude, the short man began reading from the paper in his hand. "Aw right, then," he said, clearing his throat. "Youse be informed that the government herein demands payment of sixty dollars immediately to one Charles Clark of Hamilton Township or face the consequences."

This was too much. We owe money all over Douro and in Peterborough, but we long ago settled our affairs with Mr. Clark. I opened the door and stepped out, closing it behind me.

"That debt is paid," I said. "We do not owe you a thing, Mr. Clark. In fact, if there is any kind of divine justice, it is you who are beholden to us. The good Lord knows you have already made untold profits at our expense."

Clark placed his hands on his hips and spread his legs. His laugh oozed insolence.

"Ah, but you are mistaken, Mrs. Moodie. I have it right here. A note signed by your husband nearly four years ago. I have come to claim what is rightfully mine." He waved a scrap of paper at me, then removed his cap and bowed ostentatiously.

"Impossible," I said, though a needle of doubt pricked my conscience. How much do I really know of my husband's affairs? "Now, I warn you, leave before he returns and shows you the way himself."

Clark looked around the dismal clearing. "Them cattle," he said, pointing at the two heifers and Daisy, our milk cow. "They yours?"

"Yes," I said, "but I told you: we do not owe you anything."

He stroked his matted beard and gave me a look of pure condescension. Turning, he took his partner's shoulder and pushed him roughly in the direction of the cattle shed. "Go on, Orville, round 'em up."

Orville ambled off and Clark faced me again. He sighed heavily and took a step closer. "Me and my partner is awful thirsty, Mrs. Moodie. We'd be most grateful for a bit of whisky and a brief rest." He grinned and then let his eyes travel slowly down along the length of my body. I stood still, not breathing. "Mighty lonely out here for a woman, I imagine," he said as his gaze retraced its path up again and met my eyes with unveiled contempt. I stepped back until I was up against the rough logs of the cabin. Clark moved toward me and, placing the flat of his hand on the wall beside my head, leaned his face in until I thought the stink of his breath, putrid as a rotten animal carcass, would make me faint. I tried to slide away, but with

340

his other hand, he gripped my throat and pushed my head back cruelly. "Like I said, ma'am. Orville and I were hoping for a little hospitality after riding all this way."

Inside the cabin, Hector raised a frantic alarm, barking and at intervals hurling himself against the closed door. But Clark ignored the noise. I silently prayed Jenny would stay inside. Then my assailant loosened his grip on my neck and let his hand slide down over my collarbone, stopping at my left breast; with a sadistic grimace, he twisted it so hard that I cried out in pain. A moment later, the door flew open and Jenny stepped out, shouldering Moodie's musket, which she pointed directly at the intruder's head.

"Git," she barked. "Now. Or I'll blow a hole right through you." At the same time, Hector catapulted into the yard, knocking the man called Orville face-first into the snow.

Clark put his hands in the air and backed away slowly, grabbing his mule by the bridle to stop it from bolting into the woods. "Whoa, Mrs. Moodie. Like I said, I just want what's mine."

His partner lay on the ground, whimpering, while Hector, a snarling bundle of fur and teeth, hovered over him.

"And I told you, that debt is paid," I repeated, indignation trumping my fear, though I knew the gun Jenny brandished was not loaded. "Now get off my property."

"Do as you're told," growled Jenny, taking another step in their direction.

"Well then, I guess we'll be off. We don't want no trouble," Clark said, tipping his cap in Jenny's direction before slowly remounting his mule and addressing me. "You tell your husband he owes me and I aim to collect." His sidekick mounted up, and without looking back, the two rode off in the direction from which they had come.

Jenny led me, shaking, back inside. The little ones gathered around me and I held them close one by one.

"Mama," said Katie (she is seven years old and understands more than I give her credit for). "We heard you scream. We thought he kilt you. Mama?"

"No. Not this time," I said. "It's all right."

Though it's not. I dare not consider what might have happened. How can I protect my children with nothing but an empty musket and an old dog? When Moodie's debts erupt like mushrooms in the darkness, poisonous and invisible? If my husband has kept this from me, what else?

FEBRUARY 12, 1839

I feel another toothache coming on, its faint throb a familiar echo of the exquisite agony that will surely follow.

In search of at least temporary relief, I strapped snowshoes over the moccasins I have fashioned from old cloths and went to the Traills'. The day was bright and still, with a lightness in the air, something benign—birdsong, I realized, chickadees stupid with happiness. Things seem easy between Kate and me these days. While I warmed my feet by her fire, I told her about Clark's visit, but not wanting to burden her, I turned the incident into a light-hearted anecdote starring Jenny and the dog and a pair of bumbling rascals. We talked of everyday matters: firewood, the weather, baby teeth, roasting chicory, mending socks. She praised my skill at drawing and lamented her own clumsiness.

"If only I had applied myself more fully to Eliza's lessons when we were little," she said. "I try to make accurate sketches of my specimens, but I will never equal your skill."

Yes, I thought, *while I was submitting to the rigours of Eliza's exercises, you were tramping over field and meadow with Papa. Serves you right.* (How is it that reaching adulthood has so little effect on the atavism of a shared childhood? Sometimes the most striking thing about getting older is not how much we change, but how little.) I held my tongue and offered instead to make a few drawings for her.

She showed me her collection of moths, a dozen or so, labelled and neatly pinned in rows on a pine board. If the leaden presence of her husband, slumped at his post by the hearth, weighed on her in any way, she did not show it. I have learned that the key to getting along with my sister Catharine is to rake the soil lightly, to avoid the cultivation of troubling ideas, to be cheerful at all times. When we are together, I relinquish any impulse to dig deeper, to look beneath the surface. And I never complain. I think it is only by keeping her eyes relentlessly focused on the tiny things, by taking the moments of each day one by one like flower petals or moth wings, that she survives. I think her impulse to classify and label, to collect and list is a way of exerting control in a place where we have very little. And I do understand. As bewildering as I find her inability (or refusal?) to acknowledge the tragic absurdity of our situation, it is a relief some-times to allow myself to float along encased in the shiny bubble of her optimism. But the realization that we are not, after all, two sides of the same coin, but rather different currencies altogether, saddens me and makes me feel more alone than ever.

She does not look well. The last baby, little Annie, is sickly and as difficult as my Addie was, and I can see by the dark circles around Kate's eyes that exhaustion stalks her like a hungry fox. Give in to it and the black clouds of sickness will descend without mercy. We are both hanging on, but barely.

She gave me a precious vial of oil of cloves for my tooth. Then, over coffee (roasted chicory) and hard biscuits, we shared the latest news from home. The first two volumes of Agnes and Eliza's *Lives of the Queens* are to be published soon. Her work on the books has catapulted Agnes, at least, into the upper reaches of high society. (Although she does at least half the writing and research, Eliza is not named as author. My retiring sister regards any kind of notoriety as vulgar.)

"Since I last wrote you, I have been down to Windsor," Agnes wrote, "and had a long morning in the Royal Library. Yesterday, I drank tea with Lady Bedingfield . . ." And so on.

Reading these words aloud in the menial comfort of a wilderness cabin as the snow began to fall in the waning afternoon, even Kate could not help but reflect on the strange and unpredictable twists of fate that find us in this place.

Mr. Traill escorted me home, and we indulged in a lengthy lament on our situation, regretting we had ever left England, cursing the Canadian climate and expressing many more sentiments neither of us dares raise in the presence of our defiantly optimistic spouses. And yet how far away my old life seems, that "sceptred isle" obscuring into the passing years. I had not thought it possible. Before leaving to head back to Westove, Mr. Traill told me he believes that the sale of his farm, something he has been desperate to achieve for some time, may be imminent. And then what?

FEBRUARY 20, 1839

I have not slept in three nights, the torture of my aching tooth wracking me until I finally sent Jenny to fetch Sam, who brought Dr. Hutchison's instruments and extracted the offending molar. He was very skilled, and I suffered minimally thanks to the whisky, but his manner was brusque. I think my brother is losing patience with us, is weary of the litany of troubles that afflict us and the Traills, tired of constantly having to come to his sisters' aid. Our continuing incompetence must be like a foreign language to him, incomprehensible. He loves us, yes, but there is a trickle of contempt running through his generosity. A few weeks ago, when little Dunbar fell headlong into the wood stove, cracking his skull so severely that I could not staunch the blood pouring from his poor scalp, I sent Katie for Sam. By the time he arrived, the danger was over, and my brother bore the inconvenience with good humour but little sympathy. Looking around the cabin at the bloodied aftermath, he said, "I know you are longing for red meat, Susanna, but must you keep this place like a slaughterhouse?"

Today, once the tooth was out and with the haze of whisky still upon me, I asked Sam to investigate the claim that we owe money to Mr. Clark of Hamilton Township, and he said he would. Will this quicksand of debt never end? I feel sure the note is paid, but a tickle of doubt remains. This on top of everything else.

MARCH 15, 1839

Emilia is here again. Since last Saturday, I have been wracked with fever and a cough that threatens to turn me inside out. The sound in my chest with each breath is like the drag of waves on a pebbled strand. I have been drifting in and out of sleep, unable to rouse myself to the simplest tasks. Yesterday, I awoke to find my dearest friend bathing my forehead with a damp cloth and saying my name softly. It was as though an angel had landed. As soon as I was able to sit up and sip the broth she spooned into my mouth, I asked for pen and paper. A feverish energy possessed me, and I was convinced that because I had not written a word since before Christmas, Mr. Lovell would think I had perished. Emilia reports that she was unable to restrain me and that I rambled on incoherently about a sketch I was writing about last summer's logging bee and the drunken melee that followed, about our neighbour Malachi Croak, an inebriated sot who plays the bagpipes and flirts unmercifully with the ladies. My friend indulged me until my momentum was spent, then led me back to my bed.

The weather worsens: cutting winds and drifting snow. I have had no word from Moodie since January, and in my anguish, I imagine he is ill or even that he has deserted us altogether. Please, my dearest husband, a letter, or I will surely die of your neglect.

MARCH 17, 1839

I seem unable to rouse myself. Grey, grey, grey. Emilia and Jenny stand over me, phantom-like, and whisper while I feign sleep that comes only fitfully, a merciful salve to my abraded spirit. Worse, the baby has fallen ill again, his little body shuddering with every cough, his skin clammy and pale. And me too weak to even hold him.

What a damp and crowded prison this cabin has become with three women and six children (my own plus Emilia's Henry). The snow has ceased. Instead, a cold rain falls in steady viscous sheets that cling to the trees and buildings like liquid pewter. At night, my sleep is punctuated by the monotonous intermittent *plunk, plunk, plunk* of water dripping into the buckets and pots set out to catch the leaks. Our roof is little better than a sieve. To make room for Emilia and her little one, I share my bed with baby Johnny and whichever of my children's turn it is to sleep with Mama. At first, there was a good deal of conflict over this issue, until Jenny devised a method of "taking turns." I am too tired to understand how it works, but last night, I was awakened by a sharp kick to the small of my back, followed by a cry of outrage from Addie, who then let fly with both feet in the direction of Dunnie. The melee that ensued woke the entire household. I am ashamed to say that instead of pulling the covers over my face as I should have done, I joined the fray. By the time Emilia and the other children appeared, Johnny had slipped to the floor, squalling pitifully, and I was on hands and knees like a she-lion protecting her cub, hurling murderous threats at the other two, who cowered in terror at the monster their mother has become.

If only the rain would cease.

Thank God, Johnny has rallied. My fever, too, has broken, and my chest feels almost clear. But I am so weak, I can barely push my quill over the paper Jenny has left by my bedside. I overheard them this morning.

"The writing usually gets her up and doing," Jenny said to Emilia in the low tones that have become background music to my idleness. "She'll be wanting to write the master, I'm sure."

But I don't. I cannot bring myself to commit my self-pity, my resentments, to paper; it will only deepen my distress. His letters have resumed, filled with lively news about regimental this and regimental that, with expressions of affection for me, for the little ones. Chatty missives full of plans for the grand appointments he anticipates, the lakeside farms with their spreading orchards and splendid stables, the stone houses, the gentle, welcoming future I no longer believe in. I cannot bridge it: the distance between his vision and mine. I feel limp, hollowed out. This old bed, these patched walls, this dismal rabbit warren sinking under an apathy born of hunger and hopelessness. This is my world. The children do not enter my room. Not since Addie was born have I been so low, and this time, I do not know that I will be able to pull myself out of it.

"Nervous agitation," I heard Emilia tell them. "Your mother must rest." But I cannot quell my turbulent heart.

The Traills came to say goodbye. It is done. Mr. Traill has sold Westove to the new minister, Reverend Wolseley, for two hundred dollars.

"He wanted to turn it down," my sister told me, speaking as though "he" were not standing right beside her. "But I told him he must accept. I know it's a paltry sum after all we have put into the place, not just money but the labour. My gardens . . ."

Mr. Traill said nothing. He leaned on his walking stick and let his vacant eyes travel up and over the ceiling as though searching for something loftier there. Kate placed a maternal hand on her husband's arm and continued.

"We had no choice. He cannot endure another winter here. We have resigned ourselves to the fact that our farming venture has failed and we must seek other means of providing for ourselves. We are moving to Ashburnham, where Mr. Traill can enjoy the company of educated gentlemen such as himself." Traill nodded and pinched the bridge of his nose, still not speaking.

"And what will you do?" I asked Kate.

"I would like to start a school for the local children. Heaven knows one is needed. We have found modest lodging in the village, and once we are settled, I am sure Mr. Traill will be able to secure a government job. I have high hopes."

I can hardly bear it. My sister is to be delivered from this place while I languish here, too ill to even wish her well, my only thoughts for myself. She would leave me now? Like this? I could barely speak.

"But when?" The words came out thick and bitter.

"Soon," she said. "Tomorrow. We have come to say goodbye, Susanna. Reverend Wolseley is eager to make alterations to the cabin before the spring planting season." And then, taking it all in, the reality of it, me bedridden, my shoulders drawn up under a ragged shawl, the outline of my body like a corpse through the rough covers, she softened a little. "It is only eleven miles, Susie. When you are well and the roads are dry"—she hesitated—"and Mr. Moodie has returned, you will all come to visit. The children . . ." She looked over at the clutch of solemn faces crowding the entrance to my room. Kate, Addie, Dunbar, Donald, little Johnny asleep in Jenny's arms. "You will all come to tea, and we will have strawberries and cream," she continued in a strained falsetto. "And James and our Kate, and little Harry and Annie, will be so happy to see you. We will make dolls and chase pirates . . ."

Addie, who has travelled the well-trodden path to her Aunt Kate's house more than any of us in her short life, broke ranks and ran to bury her face in my sister's skirts. She is closer to her aunt than she is to me, I thought, allowing a brief shaft of bitterness to mar our goodbyes. Kate, leaving me now. If I had not been so forlorn, I would have laughed out loud. We have been getting on so well these past few months.

While Kate consoled Addie, Mr. Traill leaned down and placed one of his callused, elegant hands on mine. "You are a brave and capable woman, my dear. I have written your husband to tell him so, that you are a treasure of which he can be very proud."

Ah, then the tears flowed in earnest. After they left, while Jenny and Katie did their best to stifle Addie's heartbroken wails, Emilia sat on the side of my bed and held me til I slept. I am doubly lonely now.

MARCH 23, 1839

One last visit from Mr. Traill early this morning to leave us the wood stove from Westove. A blessing, as our own is in such pitiful condition.

Jenny picked over the root cellar today and removed sixty bushels of frost-rotten potatoes. We shall not have enough for seed.

Moodie, Moodie: this weary longing after you makes my life pass away like a dream.

Mary Hague came calling today. Embarrassed that one of the finer ladies of Douro should see me in my haggard condition, I arose and tried to make myself as presentable as possible under the circumstances. I could not, at first, understand what this respectable and prosperous young woman was doing in my ghastly living room, but over a rudimentary tea of chamomile and dried apples, Mrs. Hague's intentions soon revealed themselves. Throughout our somewhat stiff conversation, she lavished a noticeable amount of attention on Addie, who, unlike my other children, has no fear of strangers. Indeed, her precocity in the presence of adults, particularly women, is a tendency I have tried without success to curb.

Addie began by surreptitiously fingering the hem of Mrs. Hague's overskirt and looking up at our guest, trying without words to divert her attention from the teacup she was holding on her lap. Mrs. Hague smiled and stroked Addie's tangled curls. "You must be Agnes," she said. "I hear you are an accomplished dancer."

"Oh, yes," bubbled the little girl. "And I can curtsey too. Papa taught me."

"Addie, I'm sure Mrs. Hague . . ."

"No, please," said our guest gently, leaning forward in her chair. "I should love to see you curtsey, Addie." The child held her little apron out with her thumb and forefingers and, crossing one leg over the other, executed a deep bow. Mrs. Hague clapped her hands and laughed, which prompted Addie to pirouette around the room, a precocious little princess, landing, finally, face forward, giggling, in her mentor's lap. I suppose if I had not been so ill, I might have shared in the general hilarity that my daughter's impromptu display elicited, but the minor spectacle only filled me with irritated fatigue.

Then Emilia poured me a second cup of tea and, placing a cool hand on my fevered brow, asked me in the gentlest of voices: "Susanna, how would you feel about Agnes going to stay with Mary for a little while?"

I am ashamed to say that the tears that fell from my eyes on hearing this were of relief, though Emilia and Mary Hague both assumed them to be a sign of my resistance to the idea. They began pleading in low, earnest voices: "You have been so ill . . ." "With Mr. Moodie away, how can you expect . . ." "It will only be for a short while . . ." ". . . time to get your strength back."

I silenced them with a mute nod, and placing a hand on Addie's cheek by way of farewell, I got up and returned to my bed. What sort of mother am I?

APRIL 4, 1839

Emilia has gone back to her parents' in Peterborough. I turned my face from her as she leaned down to kiss me goodbye. She cannot stay forever; I know that, but in this fog I inhabit, her departure has left me unmoored, an empty canoe turning in the current. We have talked, she and I, of our bond, of love and marriage, of duty, of friendship. We have sat together night after night in the unending cold and laughed until the squalor and the darkness receded just a little. Her lightness, and her clarity, have kept me sane.

How I detest the self-pitying hag I have become. I often think of my old friend Mrs. Shelley's declaration that a woman's necessary vocation is the nurturance and preservation of marriage and family, that we cannot help but give ourselves up to those demands. But my children are drifting away, rousing nothing more in my maternal breast than an uneasy guilt. My husband is living the life of an unencumbered soldier. He has yet to send any money and our debts continue to mount. Anger is all I feel. Vocation, choice? Indeed.

When I try to picture his face, I cannot.

Yesterday, after a gap of two weeks, a letter and a parcel arrived. Today is our wedding anniversary. Eight years ago on this day, in the tiny chapel at St. Pancras, we began this adventure.

A woollen shawl in softest heather. Shoes for me and the children—those who remain, at least. Hannah Caddy came yesterday and took four-year-old Dunbar away with her.

"Just for a few weeks," she said in her gruff, busybody way. "Until you're feeling more yourself."

"Poor thing," I heard her whisper to Jenny before she led my boy into the woods. I did not lift a finger to stop them.

Jenny tells me Addie has taken to her new life like a dancer to the stage. "She struts around in her new shoes and dresses like a proper princess, ma'am. And Missus Hague is giving her lessons. Reading and writing. A quick little whippet she is, I'm told."

Mary Hague does not know the damage she does.

A fine woollen shawl. Six dollars. He had to tell me that. Six dollars that might have gone to pay the servant. To buy real coffee. *It is only six dollars*, I tell myself, *so little while our debts are so large.* And the shoes—I did not have the heart to tell him they are too small.

"You guessed the size of my foot exactly" is what I wrote.

Sometimes at night when I cannot sleep, I rise and light a candle and sit down and compose long, anguished missives to this man I married. I tell him of my extinguished hopes, my brittle heart, my swelling fears. I write about the hunger I used to feel, the need to write, the longing for something, something more than this. Where did it go? And then when I have emptied myself onto this scrap of paper, I take the criss-crossed tangle of scribbles between a thumb and forefinger and hold it over the flickering flame until it darkens and curls and falls into an ashy heap.

One night, I dreamed that Moodie came home at last, and when I threw my arms about him in joyous welcome, he pushed me away, saying he had taken a vow of celibacy. My shock was so great, I was startled from my sleep, and lying there in the dark, I began to laugh like a Salem witch. I rose immediately and wrote him a brief, chiding letter, saying that if dreams come true, then surely all my troubles will be over now.

I seem to be cursed with a double vision, doomed to see both the tragedy and the comedy of our situation at the same time. It's like being in two places at once. At least it spares me the dead end of a single perspective. And besides, I take a sustaining satisfaction, a bitter delight, in the perversity of fate, as though God were playing a cruel joke. And I am in on it.

I have sold the musket to Colonel Caddy for eight pounds. I do not think Mr. Clark will return. Sam reports that the scoundrel has been passing himself off as a bailiff in order to collect imaginary debts throughout the territory. There is a price on his head.

MAY 15, 1839

Another season looms and I do not know where I will find the strength to begin the hard work of ploughing and planting. My cough is gone at last, and Johnny, thank heaven, is thriving again, but I am plagued with a terrible weakness, like heavy chains dragging me down in body and spirit. Old Jenny, too, is bothered by feet so swollen, she says every step she takes is like the agony of Christ.

Moodie has written to say his militia duties will likely keep him a few weeks longer. His temporary position as paymaster is officially terminated at the end of this month, but he is determined not to depart without completing an audit, leaving the militia's records in exemplary order. Only then will he be paid in full and have confidence that his superior, Baron de Rottenburg, will exert his influence on our behalf with Sir George Arthur.

In the meantime, Jenny has made an arrangement to lend our oxen to a new neighbour, Mr. Smith, to put in his crops. In return, he has promised to plant for us about eight acres of peas, corn and oats.

MAY 18, 1839

To be rejected by one's own child is surely worse than losing her altogether. Mary Hague visited today with Addie. They stopped first at Ashburnham to see the Traills, and by all accounts, my daughter flew into Kate's arms like an arrow shot from Cupid's bow. Afterwards, Sam ferried them the rest of the way here by ox cart. But when they arrived, Addie refused to climb down to where I was waiting with open arms. Instead, she buried her face in Mary Hague's bosom while her benefactor smiled sheepishly at me.

"Addie," she chided, "say hello to your mother. Remember what we've learned about good manners." She peeled the girl away from her and helped her out of the wagon.

"Good afternoon, ma'am," Addie said in a small voice, her eyes fixed on the beaded reticule she held in front of her.

"Our lessons this week have been on the subject of etiquette," said Mrs. Hague. She nudged my daughter lightly with the handle of her parasol. "There now, Addie, give your mother a kiss."

I shaded my eyes with both hands, not to keep out the sun but to hide my tears. "Never mind." I placed a hand on the top of her head and pushed her gently toward three of her siblings, who were sitting in a ragged knot on the doorstep of the cabin, suddenly shy in the presence of the sister they hardly recognized. Katie was the first to speak, reaching out a timid hand to touch Addie's shining brown ringlets, which bobbed like tulips in a summer breeze.

"Are they real?" she asked, looking first at her sister and then at me.

"Of course they are," said Addie, her eyes flashing. "Aunt Mary does my hair up in rags every night before I go to bed." She paused and smoothed the front of her dress. "I have my own room, you know. And there's a small dog called Pug."

"I would like to speak to my daughter alone," I said to Mrs. Hague. She was standing by the carriage with the sun behind her in silhouette, and I could not make out her expression.

I took Addie's hand and she followed me quite willingly past the stumps and the rows of green oats pushing up through the dark soil, until we reached the edge of the forest. The air was soft and mild and filled with birdsong. I looked down at her.

"I've missed you, Addie."

She squinted up at me. "Aunt Mary says I am too much for you. But I think I am not enough."

"Why, Addie? What makes you say that?"

"Whenever I get mad, you say, 'That's enough, Addie!' But it's not. Because there's more. It's not enough."

"Do you want more? Do you want to live with Mrs. Hague?"

She nodded slowly—unsure, I think. I pray.

"Will you give me a kiss?" I asked, and quickly she pressed her face against my belly, then ran back to the waiting cart.

Perhaps I should just let her go to what is a far better future than anything I can offer here.

MAY 22, 1839

Dunnie comes home tomorrow. We will have a feast.

Mrs. Peter has brought us some wild ducks and dried cranberries.

What a delight they will be to our weary potato-deadened palates. And the birds will be the first meat we have tasted in a fortnight. She would take nothing in return, insisting she was happy to share what the good earth has provided so bounteously. (I paraphrase, of course.) She was able to communicate to Jenny, who understands some of their language, her gratitude for the time two years ago when I tried, without success, to help her poor dying son.

The rain is unceasing, the ground too wet to even think about planting potatoes. I busy myself with fulfilling more orders for the hand-painted fungus that Moodie says is in great demand by Belleville's ladies. And I have sent off two more poems to Mr. Lovell at the *Literary Garland*.

Oh, to hold my dear little boy again.

With Emilia gone and Moodie's tenure in Belleville dragging on interminably, I have allowed the last vestiges of civility to desert me. Last evening, as I sat down alone with the children to a supper of bread and lard and mushroom soup with wild leeks, while Jenny retreated as usual with her bowl to a low stool by the hearth, the utter ludicrousness of such an arrangement hit me like the butt end of an overseer's whip. Just who, I suddenly thought, is the superior individual here? Me, with my pretensions, or old Jenny, with her patience, diligence and loyalty? If not for her practical abilities, we should all have starved by now. It is only thanks to her management and fortitude that I was sitting there, able to lift a spoon to my lips. Who is master and who servant? Here, a world away from the polite drawing rooms of my youth, of what use are such distinctions? I called out to her, bidding her to come and sit across from me. I expected the old woman to demur, but no, in her plain country way, she only nodded briefly, then rose and sat at the table. The children were silent, as though understanding the fragility of the moment.

"Ma'am," said Jenny without looking up, her spoon suspended in the air between the bowl and her mouth, "I think tomorrow I will call on Mr. Smith. Them oxen has been gone more 'n a week now. It'll soon be too late to plant anything."

Here in the backwoods, we are almost equals.

JUNE 1, 1839

Meanwhile, Moodie's tenure continues with no end in sight. Instead of complaining, he sends long letters on the subject of the Durham Report. It seems that after a lengthy investigation into the causes of the rebellions here and in Montreal, Lord Durham has, among other things, recommended that Upper and Lower Canada be merged into one colony headed by a governor sent out from England.

"But here is the exciting part," Moodie wrote. "Durham sees the governor as merely a figurehead and has urged that the legislative assembly be elected by the people! He has called Bond Head and his band 'a petty, corrupt, insolent Tory clique' and has urged Sir George Arthur to take steps to encourage immigration to Canada. Do you know what that would mean, Susanna? More settlers will require more land, and then surely our investments will finally pay off. In every way, our hopes lie with George Arthur and the Reformers."

Oh yes, I know . . . and then *we will be rich beyond our wildest dreams.* Our silent argument continues irrespective of the miles that separate us. I can almost hear him whispering in my ear the magic words I have heard so many times. But I am sick of words. I want him here so that I might have a husband to help plant the wheat and corn we need to sustain us—no, more than anything I want to leave this place. Our life here is worse than hopeless. I want to be myself again.

I wrote it all down. And this letter I have sent. I told him that another winter such as the last will bury me alive, that I am paralyzed by his long absences, that his recurring silences are sowing noxious seeds in a mind that is fertile ground for weedy resentment. I do not know what to do about the farm, and I am so dispirited that I have ceased to care. I have no money to hire labour to cut the grain even if by some miracle there is a decent crop. And as my body and my will collapse, my mind, like an open wound, festers from disuse, itches with the need to write. "I am not meant for this life, Moodie, any more than you are. Oh heaven, keep me from being left in these miserable circumstances another year. I am so tired of living alone; this must be the last winter of exile and widowhood or my heart will surely break."

May 23, 1839

The pair of animals Jenny led home yesterday through the clearing bore little resemblance to the healthy creatures we so trustingly delivered to our neighbour three weeks ago. Gaunt and lame from overwork, dull-eyed with hunger, their thin hide covered in sores from ill-fitting harness, they are in no condition to undertake the hard work of planting our own fields.

Jenny was twisted with anger. Nothing gets under her tough skin like the mistreatment of helpless animals.

"I told Smith's son, 'No wonder ye have no livestock o' yourn, if ye run 'em into the ground like this.' But he only laughed and said his father would be back in a few days if I had complaints. 'Them animals was sick when they came,' he said. But they wasn't," she fumed. "They were fine and strong."

In any case, young Smith made no mention of his father's promise to help with our planting. The oxen will need to rest for at least a week, and by then, it will be almost too late. And without a harvest, we will surely starve come winter.

JULY 3, 1839

Nearly six weeks since I have heard from Moodie. My ultimatum goes unanswered. Has he forgotten us? At night, alone in my bed, his absence is a dark void. I whisper into it, "Is this what you want? Has it all come to this?" But there is only silence.

JULY 9, 1839

I was hanging out the wash and a small movement on the lake caught my eye. A canoe carrying a single figure rounded the point, heading toward our beach. Even before it landed, I recognized Emilia and ran down to the water to meet her. She was flushed and breathless from her paddle—into the wind at that time of the morning—but also from the news she brought.

I helped her pull the canoe through the cattails onto the shore. Two strong women, our skirts soaked to our thighs, our forearms bare and muscular. We stowed the paddles and sat in the long grass, pulling petals off daisies with methodical concentration. She told me everything. Lieutenant Shairp is going for good, back to England to seek a naval position. After being absent for two winters, he returned last month intending to claim his wife and return to his homeland to start a new life.

Emilia was subdued, resigned. Her usually mobile features sphinx-like. "He asked me to go with him and I refused." She drew in a long, audible breath. "I believe he is a good man," she said. "But I could not make him happy. Alexander Shairp is a soldier, as fearless as they come, but here in the bush, he was like a warhorse harnessed to a stone boat." Her bright eyes, with their pale lashes, held mine. "He tried. I tried." She looked out over the water. "But he was never cut out to be a farmer." She laughed. "Farmer—it means something else in Canada. He expected respectable Sussex hayfields; he got this."

I was stunned. "But what about the militia here? Could he not find a commission? Moodie would help, I'm certain . . ."

"Mr. Shairp commanding a bunch of ragtag mercenaries in the colonies? Alexander the Great? No. He has his pride and it seems that nothing here quite meets his lofty standards."

"But little Henry . . ." I dug a thumbnail into the daisy's soft yellow centre. I wanted to tell her how glad I was she was staying, but it didn't seem the right response. "What will you do, then?"

She fell slowly onto her back and, rolling over, jumped quickly to her feet, pulling me with her. "You, Susanna, you are my true friend. My sister. And I have come today to ask you something. No. Don't say a word until I have finished. I have a plan."

She looked over my shoulder at the familiar setting: the crooked little cabin, the stumps, the bony cattle picking through the weeds.

"You cannot go on living like this. It is killing you, killing your children. It is destroying your family. And John, where is he? Will he ever return? And even if he does, what then?"

I pulled away from her, shaking my head. "No, Emilia. Please don't say that."

"Susanna, listen to me. Louisa Lloyd—you must have heard? Thanks to the benevolence of certain Peterborough citizens, she has moved there. She has been furnished with a large house and a small income. Her children want for nothing. Her trials are over. She is safe. You"—she held my arms and shook me as though I were a recalcitrant child—"you and I brought this about."

Of course I knew about Louisa Lloyd. How many times as I laid out another meagre supper for my own children had I not considered her fate? And in my twisted heart, have I not marvelled at the cruel joke that I, her benefactor, am surely facing starvation unless by some miracle we are delivered from these woods before winter?

Oh, Emilia, I wanted to say, *I lie awake every night and curse God for his perversity. Did you know that my own husband petitioned the officers in his militia and raised forty dollars to aid Mrs. Lloyd in her distress? Forty dollars. While his own family dined on salt pork and turnips. While his own children had no shoes. Oh, Emilia, resentment grows in me like a cancer.* But I said nothing.

Two thumbprints like ripe red cherries stood out on her unlined cheeks. "I am selling the farm and moving to Peterborough, Susanna. To live with Mrs. Lloyd. We plan to start a school. Come with me. The house is fine. There is plenty of space; you and the children would have three rooms to yourselves." She took both my hands in hers. "We will get Addie back."

I pulled away.

"I will help you. My mother and father will too. Surely your need is as great as Mrs. Lloyd's. So many children, debts, an absent husband . . ." When I flinched, she smiled sadly. "Papa has such regard for your stories and poems, Susanna. You are a writer. He will be your patron."

The lump in my throat was like a fist. I swallowed tears and tried to stem the visions flooding my mind: a tree-lined street, a quiet room, a desk, real paper, pens and ink, schools . . . and absurdly, cotton sheets, tea and cakes. Time and rest. Addie.

And then the desire to write, a desire gone dormant all these many months, all at once was like a giant roused from a long sleep. I could not answer her. I bowed down and leaned my head on her shoulder. Emilia. We stood like that for a long time, until Katie came for us.

"Mama, Aunt Em. Raspberries. Dunnie and I have picked a whole bucket. Jenny says we shall have them for tea. With biscuits. Hurry. Come."

Oh, how the view from here has changed since yesterday. My first reaction was no, but Emilia made me promise not to answer, to take my time and think about it. And now I can think of little else. Am I seriously considering such a possibility? Giving up on my husband? On all of this? I must decide soon. And so I turn her offer over and over in my mind, twirling it like a bright penny spinning endlessly in the sunshine. No, it is not possible. Yes, it is. As long as the coin continues around and around, I can hold on to the fantasy. And as I go about my work, my load is lightened by a blur of possibilities. In the mornings, I let myself luxuriate in the prospect of the new life my friend has laid before me. And my fantasies are bathed in white light, draped in lace and linen, all solace and sunshine. By noon, the glare begins to blind me, a flare fuelled, I know, by outrage, by my anger at Moodie, reducing him to a small dot on the horizon. I can almost forget him as he has forgotten me. Can I? I know that sooner or later, the coin must come to rest . . . on one side or the other.

When James Caddy delivered the letter, placed it in my hands, the question in his eyes mirrored my own apprehension. I took it from him without comment and walked to the lake. The pages shivered in the heat. Relief mingled with shame. I had almost given up, almost abandoned the idea of marriage for a different dream. But here it was: a letter. Even unopened, its implicit reassurance obliterated my doubts like a scythe flashing through undergrowth. And I almost wept then. But still, a thread of uncertainty held me back, and I sought to prolong the fragile possibility of my deliverance—what if, even now? I lifted my skirt and stepped onto the sun-warmed surface of the fishing rock, then leaning against the big willow, I opened it and read, and the anvil lifted at last.

My husband has written to say he has received a letter from Sir George Arthur's secretary, promising that "a permanent office" will be offered to him at the "first possible opportunity."

"You see, my darling girl, all will be well," he wrote. "Oh, how I wish I were there to dance you round the clearing. How brave and patient you have been. My hard work has paid off. We are to be free at last."

He will return home as soon as he can wrap up his duties and arrange for a horse, by September at the latest.

"I can hardly bear to be parted from you and the babies a moment longer, my dearest." And in a postscript: "You should know that the Lieutenant-Governor wants me to understand that this promise is not only on my account, but also from *the esteem and respect he entertains for you, Mrs. Moodie.* You and your most eloquent pen. I am so proud. Bravo."

I am ashamed to admit that for a moment, my joy at the prospect of our reunion was displaced by the warm rush of knowing my work is being read and appreciated in such high places by such august persons. As I write this, hours later, I am still giddy with the idea.

Rejection can be as difficult to deliver as it is to receive. She risked so much in extending to me the gift of a shared life, the risk that I might do just as I have done: taken her offering and handed it back to her, unopened, like a thing unborn.

For a little while, I had allowed myself to imagine us together in a stone house, the children, my writing, a life of friendship, carefree, understanding. Gentleness everywhere, two minds in sympathy with one another. I considered it, and the possibility gave me some comfort for a time.

A look of tenderness came over her face when I told her Moodie had written. That's all I said, just: "He has written. He is coming home." And she nodded. She knew.

Every day, my constitution improves, and slowly I feel my old vigour returning. My imagination, too, is imbued with a renewed energy, and I apply myself to my writing so diligently that Jenny reproves me for my efforts, saying I will surely wear myself out.

Mr. Traill paid me a visit two days ago, the first since their leaving in March. As usual, he made no effort to varnish the splintered truth of their situation.

"I would not worry you unduly," he said, his long face the colour of mud, his eyes dark and bruised, "but your sister is still not well. She has never fully recovered from Annie's birth and has been nearly bedridden since our move. The baby, too, is sickly and weak. I do not know if it will survive." He sighed mightily, like a bellows losing air, after delivering this sobering report. Then he continued: "I think my presence, too, is a dark cloud, but surely despondency is the only sane reaction to all this." He raised his lugubrious face and held out both palms in a feeble salute to futility.

We were standing in the kitchen garden amid tidy rows of spinach and carrot fronds. Ruddy-cheeked pea blossoms peeked out from pale green vines. Dunnie and Donald were taking turns as circus performers, balancing one foot in front of the other along the rail fence. Katie filled her watering can at the well. The sun shone. In this brief moment of domesticity, Mr. Traill's distemper hung like the odour of something dying. Oppressiveness enveloped him like a threadbare cloak.

"Oh well," I managed with false heartiness, wishing he would leave. "I'm sure this fine weather will soon have you both on the mend."

Now that Traill has gone, though, my concern for Kate is growing.

SEPTEMBER 4, 1839

Language is a blunt instrument when it comes to human expression. The words we have for sadness or love or fear cannot convey the nuances of these emotions, and so we try to express their myriad complexities by comparing them to something else. But metaphor is a feeble stand-in for truth; it merely skirts the edges of meaning, evoking a sense of what is, but never allowing us to name the thing itself.

Seeing Moodie again after so long set up a confusion in me that I cannot explain. How do I feel about this man whom I have promised to honour and obey? Whose children I have borne? With whom I have shared everything?

The sight of him riding up to the door a week ago, his short legs straddling the broad back of the sturdy chestnut cob he had borrowed from Baron de Rottenburg, made me want to laugh and cry together. The children ran to meet him at the edge of the clearing, and he pulled all three, Kate, Dunnie and Donald, up in front and behind him, the accommodating horse making no complaint about the additional passengers. They trotted toward Johnny and me, a squirming mass of shrieking delight. I laughed at the touching spectacle of a family reunited, and tears of pent-up anxiety flowed then like poison from an infected breast.

Moodie brought with him the best possible news: he is to be sheriff of the newly formed Victoria District, taking up his post this fall. We are to move to Belleville as soon as he has found suitable lodgings and we can sell this godforsaken farm.

Strange, now that it has finally happened, I am more wistful than elated. It is what I have dreamed of for so long. And yet, and yet . . . something in me is broken. I cannot find complete joy, not even in this, only a lightness in my chest like the emptiness that follows a long crying jag.

Moodie seems oblivious to my reserve and dances and plays his flute like the benevolent pied piper he is, enveloping us all in a cloud of unconcern, concocting grandiose schemes for our future as civilized gentle folk, raising the spectre of riches and the certainty of unalloyed happiness forever and ever amen. I do not contradict him; there is no point. Marriage demands much in the way of self-suppression and tolerance. I am learning. His worst qualities are also his best. It is mostly a matter of perspective.

The only blemish on the happy complexion of our reunion was the absence of Addie. The morning after he got back, Moodie rode to the Hagues' to claim his estranged daughter, who on her return greeted her poor relatives with all the condescension and contempt of a little duchess. I have missed my noisy harridan terribly these last months, but absence creates a kind of forgetting. I was soon reminded what a stubborn and wilful wee thing she is. Moodie adores her.

"I will not let her go. She reminds me too much of you, Susanna." I scoffed at this, but I know there is more than a little truth in it. Addie is like me. Too much. Not enough. Is that why we clash so terribly? Do I inflict a hatred of myself upon her? I only know how glad I am to have her back.

The alteration in our fortunes has changed my husband. The pall of failure that has clung to him these last few years, a cloud I was barely aware of until it lifted like mist in sunlight, is gone. He stands straighter, is quieter, less irritable and defensive. In the darkness, his ardour is undiminished, but his advances have acquired a forthrightness that was not there before. He comes to me now almost defiantly. In the light of day, his affection is full of good-natured teasing, friendly condescension, manly superiority. Our marriage is a conspiracy of all we have shared. We are as loving as stablemates, grateful for the warm bedding and the nosebag full of oats.

But last night, lying together in the darkness, we were equals. "It hasn't been all bad, Susie. Remember that." I nodded. And then he whispered into the night, "'Our hut is small, and rude our cheer, / But love has spread a banquet here . . .' You wrote those lines."

He could not see the astonishment on my face.

"Yes," I said, "my poem 'The Sleigh-Bells.'" Moodie quoting my poetry?

"There will be more. Much more," he said. It was an acknowledgement. He was saying he has heard me, that he sees me as I am.

This morning, I watched him ride away again, back to Belleville. His absence is nothing now that I know it is nearly over. In three months, as soon as the snow comes and the frozen roads can bear the load, we will slide out of these woods like sleepers slowly waking from a dream.

OCTOBER 11, 1839

It must be the time of year, the gold-and-bronze haze, the cool rippling air, the hush of autumn. They fill me with an invigorating sadness. I go about my daily routine with a lighter step, seeing everything—this clearing, the cabin, our shining lake—in a new way, already bathed in the forgiving glow of nostalgia. I will never forget these years of hunger and drudgery, of cold and despair. I will not forget them, but perversely, I will clothe all the misery and wasted anguish, every crust of coarse bread and scrawny chicken, in a fine, soft mantle of wistfulness. Already, I anticipate the way it will all blur into the misty realms of good times past. But I must harden myself; I must not be seduced by the ameliorating effects of time. I must remember it as it really was.

The harvest has been indifferent. It does not matter. The farm is sold—to Reverend Wolseley. It is as though an iron yoke has been lifted from my shoulders. I do not have to care. There is corn enough and wheat to last until the snow falls. We will eat the seed potatoes and the chickens. I have sold the plough, the hoes, the axes, the livestock to the reverend. We are starting over: a new place, a new life. A life I can scarcely contemplate.

When I imagine myself in the society of town people, the picture will not coagulate. In my mind's eye, there are my new neighbours, turned out in frock coats and gowns, in polished boots and lace caps, smooth-cheeked, bright-eyed, hands soft and composed, voices measured and polite. But I am not among them. I am crouched on the staircase with Kate, watching the festivities, clad in a thin night-gown, shivering. It has been eight years since I danced, since I tasted champagne, since I sparkled in the diamond light of clever banter. I am old now, and I have forgotten how to be among people such as I used to be. I have seen another kind of life, and it has changed me in ways I will not fully comprehend until I behold myself in the mirror of their civilized eyes. I do not relish the idea.

Today, I took my little Johnny (walking already, though he is less than a year old; a sweet, happy soldier, he is the finest of all my children with his blond curls and ready smile) and walked down past the cedar swamp to where the Chippewa have been camped all summer. I brought a few old pots, a child's sled, one of my hand-painted fungi, a broken mirror. Mrs. Peter accepted these paltry cast-offs with gratitude. Standing stiffly, my shoulders hunched inside the entrance to the low-ceilinged wigwam, I explained as best I could that we would be leaving soon, moving away to the place of many houses by the big water. A murmur radiated like a rising breeze through the gathering of women and children sitting in the shadows. Mrs. Peter stepped closer and pulled me into a tight embrace. She smelled of animal fat and mint. It was the first time an Indian had ever touched me, and I did not flinch as I surely would have when I first came to the backwoods. I felt as sad then as I have ever felt at leaving friends. A small entourage rose and escorted us back to the clearing, and we shed many tears before they finally turned and silently made their way back along the narrow path to the lake's edge.

OCTOBER 17, 1839

I have just returned from visiting my sister at Ashburnham. Whatever happens now, at least Kate and I have made our peace. I think finally we have learned to understand one another without judgment.

The Traills are renting a modest frame house in the village, and although it is small, they and the four children seem comfortable enough. It has a mature orchard and Kate has planted a large garden, which she says yielded enough carrots, potatoes and turnips to see them through the winter. They have about thirty chickens.

Sam dropped me off on his way to Peterborough, saying he would return the following day. He even managed to coax a reluctant Mr. Traill into accompanying him on his errands, leaving Kate and me alone for the last visit we may have for a long while. It is the first time since becoming a mother that I have been away from all my children for more than a few hours—and Johnny barely a year old. The sensation of being without them was odd at first, like venturing outdoors wearing only a petticoat. I kept hearing their voices on the wind, feeling the tug of their little hands on my skirts. But as the hours passed, I grew accustomed to an old lightness of being that I had completely forgotten since becoming a mother.

My sister's two youngest were quite ill with a recurring fever that Kate says they can't seem to shake, and James (six years old already) has a persistent eye infection, so a lot of our time together was spent nursing the babies. I didn't like to say anything because she is so proud, but I wonder if any of them is getting enough to eat. They have only Mr. Traill's half pension, which, as I well know, is not enough to live on. The village school she started in September in her front room was suspended after only a few weeks because Kate was too ill to teach. Ever cheerful, she says she has managed to earn a few dollars for her services as a midwife, successfully delivering her first baby last week. She also anticipates a lively trade in selling herbal remedies for every physical complaint known to womankind. She is working on another book, for which she has high hopes. And then there's the egg money.

But it is obvious that Traill has no prospects, that his despair is slowly sinking them all, and that Kate herself is weak from the relentless chores and sleepless nights caring for her children's constant illnesses. A whiff of destitution hangs over the household. And, she told me with somewhat forced enthusiasm, she is pregnant again. There was some part of me that wanted to admonish my sister for finding herself in such circumstances, as though I myself have never been in dire straits. But then, after we had settled the children briefly and I made her a cup of the tea I had brought with me, Kate let fall the scrim of optimism that persistently blurs the facts of her life.

"I feel as though I have failed, Susanna. I thought if I worked hard and believed, I could overcome anything, that I could coax wheat from the stony soil, that I could put light back into my husband's eyes. But I could not." There was resignation in her voice, and I thought this might be a good thing, that by acknowledging her limitations she might begin to find a way around them.

"Acceptance is not necessarily defeat," I said.

"Is that what you have done, Susie? Accepted defeat?" "Oh, Katie, I don't think I ever expected to win."

She smiled. "You were always like that. Certain everything was hopeless."

"But it's not, is it?"

"I was just going to allow that you might be right." She smiled at the irony in that.

From the other room, a child began to whimper. Kate took a deep breath and started to rise from her chair. Had it come to this, our roles reversed: me full of hope for the future, Kate cast down? I wanted to say something to cheer her up. Me.

"I have tried so hard to love this country," I said. "I felt I should. But you really do. And slowly, your vision is becoming mine.

"To you," I continued, "everything is a garden. But to me . . ." I struggled to find an apt analogy. "It's mostly bush."

"Can't it be both?"

"A bush garden?"

At this, my sister sat back in her chair, and we laughed together, laughed hard enough that for a moment or two we drowned out the baby's cries. She pulled herself to her feet. "Promise me one thing, Susanna. Promise me you will write about all this one day. The truth. Beyond wildflowers and bread recipes. It needs to be told."

The next day, while Sam quieted a team of horses eager to be on their way, my sister and I embraced briskly. Her composure had reasserted itself—a skiff of ice on a still pond, brittle, beautiful. For once, I found this reassuring.

"Just think," she said, "a sheriff's wife. "You will prosper. I know it."

"You are home to me," I said, and we held each other tight.

But as the wagon jolted north over the corduroy road that runs beside the rushing Otonabee, through swamps and forests linking the clearings to one another like uneven beads on a necklace, I realized that this too is home. Though I have fought hard against it, this landscape, this Canada, is part of me now. I accept it. And that is a kind of victory.

DECEMBER 12, 1839

The boys scan the raw grey skies, looking eagerly for signs of the snow that will cover the roads and smooth the path to our new life. They miss their father. His letters are full of grandiose tales of fine carriages and white horses, of shops filled with sweet buns and toys, of plank walks and milk that comes in bottles, of steepled churches and stone houses. These last, my children cannot comprehend.

"Houses made of stone? Won't they be cold as ice?" asked Katie. When I told her that in Belleville, the inside walls of the houses are as smooth as a tabletop and covered with beautiful flowered paper or painted in soft colours, her brown eyes widened; she shook her head and placed a tiny hand on the abrasive logs that are the only walls she has ever known.

The job of sheriff is proving to be a snake pit, but one my husband relishes. "The battle lines are immutable," he wrote. "Reformer or Tory. Nothing in between. Choose your pistol and fight to the death. But I will not take sides no matter how they tighten the noose. A sheriff must be as neutral as he can be. Dear God, it won't be easy." And then: "If we have another son, we will call him George Arthur. What do you think?"

I fill my days sewing proper school clothes for the children from the bolts of cloth Moodie has sent. And I wait.

Today, Sam and I loaded everything but the beds onto two sleighs. The frozen roads, bare and rutted, are still impassable except on foot or horseback. When the weather turns, my brother and James Caddy will drive the children and me and old Jenny to meet Moodie. Sam was quiet as we worked. But after he had tightened the last rope holding the contents of my life in place, he looked up at the brooding late-afternoon sky and shivered. "Not long now," he said. He was about to mount his horse, then he stopped and grinned. "I nearly forgot." He came back and put his arms around me, kissing the top of my head. "I'm proud of you, Susanna. You almost did it," he said, swinging into the saddle.

"Did what?"

"Learned to see in the dark," he said.

It was my turn to shiver. Those amber eyes. A little longer and these woods, they might have become me. But not now. I am already gone.

And as I watched him ride away, it began to snow.

AFTERWORD

*R*oughing *It in the Bush*, Susanna Moodie's account of her life in the backwoods, was published in London in 1852, twelve years after she and her family moved to the town of Belleville on the shores of Lake Ontario. The book was an immediate success and brought her fame (if not fortune) during her lifetime, on both sides of the ocean.

While life in town was easier than farming in the wilderness, the Moodies' troubles were far from over. A sixth child, George Arthur, died within weeks of his birth in the summer of 1840. The following winter, the house they were renting burned to the ground. Although, happily, another son, Robert, was born in 1843, tragically just one year later, Susanna's favourite of all her children, six-year-old Johnny, drowned in the Moira River.

For the next twenty years, the Moodies' lives were caught up in the partisanship, political infighting and social machinations that characterized Upper Canada at the time. And the couple was chronically in debt.

John Moodie retired as sheriff of Victoria County in 1863. He died six years later, aged seventy-three, leaving Susanna bereft emotionally and with no means of support. She spent the remaining years of her life moving between her son Robert's home in Seaforth,

Ontario, and her daughter Catherine's in Toronto. She never returned to her native England. In 1885, Susanna Moodie, her mind ravaged by dementia, slid into a coma and died. She was eighty-two. Her beloved sister Catharine was by her side.

FACT AND FICTION

As nearly as possible, this fiction is consistent with what we already know about Susanna Moodie's life, both from her letters and novels, particularly her most famous work, *Roughing It in the Bush*, and from the extensive research of historians Michael Peterman, Elizabeth Hopkins and others. I am inexpressibly grateful to Charlotte Gray for her wonderful 1999 biography of Susanna and her sister Catharine Parr Traill, *Sisters in the Wilderness*. That book is the essential inspiration for this one.

However, in the interests of fashioning her life into a compelling narrative, I have taken some liberties. There is no evidence, first of all, that Susanna kept a diary. As well, her encounter with Mary Shelley is completely fictional, but also, I believe, entirely plausible, since they were close to the same age and living in London around the same time.

In the interests of economy, certain individuals who played a role in Susanna's life do not appear (James Bird and Emma Bird, George Seaton, for instance). Others are composites: Thomas Harral is a composite of several publishers and editors who mentored the Strickland sisters, and Chief and Mrs. Peter stand in for the many Chippewa who helped the Moodies survive. Their daughter Ayita is a fictional character. I have included just six of the steady parade of servants and hired hands who came through the Moodie household over the years, but there were many more. And in the soul of Hector the dog reside the loyal hearts of many other canine friends.

Susanna wrote two slave narratives, those of Ashton Warner and Mary Prince. Only the latter is mentioned here. There were two terrible cabin fires that the Moodies survived; I have written about only one. And I have filled the many gaps in what we know of her life with imagined incidents too numerous to mention here.

While it goes without question that John Moodie was the love of Susanna's life, I have characterized the couple's years in the wilderness as the test they surely would have been to any marriage. I have also cast Susanna's relationship with Emilia Shairp as embodying the type of close friendship that I imagine would have arisen in such difficult circumstances. And I have portrayed Susanna's connection to her beloved sister Kate as fraught with the inevitable tensions that I know from experience can arise between sisters. The same applies to her feelings about her second child, Agnes.

The references to "amber" eyes in the entries of November 11, 1834, and the final entry, December 31, 1839, I borrowed from Margaret Atwood's poem "Departure from the Bush" in *The Journals of Susanna Moodie*. And I cannot take credit (nor can she) for Susanna's observation in the entry of September 4, 1839, that "marriage demands much in the way of self-suppression and tolerance"; that honour goes to the great George Eliot.

This book is a work of the imagination, an attempt on my part to "get inside" Susanna Moodie's head, and as such, it reflects many of my own prejudices, as well as my experiences as a daughter, mother, wife and sister. For that, I apologize.

---◆---

ACKNOWLEDGEMENTS

In the 1980s, I lived for a time with my two young daughters in a rented farmhouse in the countryside north of Port Hope. Across the road, there was a historical plaque nailed to a fence post, its bronze letters proclaiming the site of Susanna and John Dunbar Moodie's first Canadian home. One summer afternoon, the girls and I climbed that fence, wandered across a rolling hayfield, and there beside a dry stream bed and a copse of young poplars, we could see a pile of rocks said to be the remains of the cattle shed where Susanna and John Moodie and their baby girl Kate spent their first Canadian winter, the "iron winter" of 1832.

As historical sites go, it isn't much, but we used our imagination, and in the library of the rented farmhouse, we found a tattered copy of *Roughing It in the Bush*, Susanna's account of her seven years in the wilderness. History came alive that summer for two little girls, aged eight and eleven, as we read about Susanna's tragic, yet somehow absurd, travails. And her determined spirit seemed to reside with us in that old house set in the lee of a drumlin that Susanna herself may have climbed to gaze out over Lake Ontario and beyond at all she had so foolishly left behind. We were captivated by her story, marvelling at the nearly incomprehensible hardships she endured. What was it really like to bear and raise five children in a remote log cabin? To live on little more than potatoes all winter? To have no money to buy shoes for her children? To write stories and poems with an infant on her lap, by the light of a rag dipped in tallow, for the few dollars they might bring?

Mrs. Moodie has also haunted the imaginations of such Canadian luminaries as Margaret Atwood, Carol Shields, Robertson Davies, Charles Pachter and many others, in particular Charlotte Gray, whose 1999 biography, *Sisters in the Wilderness,* lifted Susanna and her sister Catharine Parr Traill from the mists of CanLit obscurity. I would like to thank them all and to apologize for having the temerity to add my voice to what surely amounts to a chorus of angels.

This book would never have happened without the support of my wonderful agent, Jackie Kaiser, whose faith in me over the years has been like a lifeline to a drowning person (I'm not kidding). As well as providing her encouragement and her brilliant negotiating skills, Jackie read two early drafts of this novel and provided invaluable editorial advice.

I owe everything (well, not everything, but a lot) to my editors: Helen Reeves, for helping me see the forest for the trees early on, and Jennifer Lambert at HarperCollins Canada, for her sensitivity to my work and her unfailing instincts. I cannot tell you what a privilege it has been to have had the benefits of your guidance.

My debt to Charlotte Gray is immense, for her generosity in reading an early draft, and for her encouragement. Trent University's Michael Peterman, Canada's premier Susanna Moodie scholar, was an early reader too. His vast knowledge saved me from more than a few embarrassing errors. I would also like to thank Hugh Brewster for reading the manuscript in its very early days, and for the benefits of his insight.

Thank you to my lovely and talented daughters, Leah McLaren

and Meghan McLaren, for keeping Susanna Moodie alive all these years, and for teaching me about motherhood. I apologize for being such a slow learner.

And to my one and only Basil, without whom there would be no book. Not only did he create the space I needed in my life to write it, he was the one who for years kept saying, "You have to write the Susanna Moodie book," until I finally did. I love you. Here it is.

A NOTE ON THE TYPE IN WHICH THIS BOOK IS SET

This book was set in Electra, a Linotype typeface designed in 1935 by William Addison Dwiggins. A man of many talents, he was an illustrator, calligrapher, writer and the first professional designer to dedicate his skill solely to books.

Electra is a typeface created for legibility but also for its ability to convey the warmth of human ideas, which makes it popular for setting poetry and lends an intimate, epistolary feel to this book. The namesake of this typeface is a heroine from Greek mythology, a woman of integrity capable of righting the wrongs of those closest to her, even at great cost to her person.